T0144265

Romance to the Rescue

Romance to the Rescue
Denis Mackail

MINT EDITIONS

Romance to the Rescue was first published in 1921.

This edition published by Mint Editions 2021.

ISBN 9781513283036 | E-ISBN 9781513288055

Published by Mint Editions®

MINT
EDITIONS

minteditionbooks.com

Publishing Director: Jennifer Newens
Design & Production: Rachel Lopez Metzger
Project Manager: Micaela Clark
Typesetting: Westchester Publishing Services

Contents

(All the characters in this story are entirely imaginary)

I

Mrs. Cartwright's Great Charm

I

A London square. Not one of the historical squares of Mayfair, nor yet containing a sufficient percentage of professional brass plates to be identified at once as north of Oxford Street, but a good enough square for all that. Quiet and withdrawn from omnibus routes. The houses are small but neat. Where they are plaster-fronted, the paint is of recent date; where they are brick-fronted, the pointing has clearly not been neglected. For there is enough external variation in this square to give that suggestive, though often misleading clue to the character of its inhabitants, which to the speculative mind forms one of the chief attractions of a walk through the more comfortable portions of London.

Number 15, for instance, has built itself out a little bow window on the ground floor, Number 9 has attached to itself a diminutive glass porch, Number 24 has grown an extra top story. Number 18 moves with, if not in advance of the times; its dining-room curtains suggest the Ballet, and the vivid colour of its front door cannot be pleasing to Number 17, which clings to the traditions of the nineteenth century, has a bead blind in its fanlight and the only non-electric bell left in the square. Other trifling eccentricities and methods of self-expression may be noted in the remaining houses; scarcely one but has its own idea of knocker or steps or window-box.

At Number 35, however, you pause. Complete absence of individuality here fixes your attention as surely as the presence of Royalty in a photographic group. There have been no accretions to the façade of Number 35 during the hundred-odd years of its life. On this Sunday afternoon in December the street lamp reveals the same reserved, discreet, and gentleman-like exterior that it has shone on ever since its erection. There is a glow of light from the edges of the windows on the first floor, and at this there has been gazing for the last five minutes from a position by the square railings one of the principal characters in the story.

Do you scent romance here already? The resemblance to Act II, Scene 2 of "Romeo and Juliet," it must be admitted, exists; but with more than all the difference between London in December and Verona in summertime. For it is now a Sunday afternoon, and no commentator has yet suggested that the balcony scene was intended to take place at such a time as this. The aroma of romance will, however, always cling to the episode of the man gazing upwards at the lighted window. This is not Shakespeare's fault; he merely used an axiomatic truth to strengthen a stage situation, and sentiment has responded to this scene since the invention of the first window.

Romeo's modern representative is called David Lawrence. He cannot, by the look of him, be more than nineteen, and it seems quite possible that he may be less. He is wearing a dark overcoat and a silk hat, and carries a neatly rolled umbrella. He would like to put the umbrella up and shield the silk hat as far as possible from the rain, which is everywhere condensing in sooty trickles. And, if it comes to that, he would like to cross the road and ring the bell at Number 35, which, having been invited by the occupier to call on any Sunday, he has every right to do. But inaction and indecision hold him in their grip. To tell the truth it is the lighted window which has atrophied his faculties in this regrettable manner. Of course, when he had been introduced to her nearly two months ago, Mrs. Cartwright had undoubtedly said, "You must come and see me any Sunday that you are in London," and at the time she had certainly appeared to mean what she said. Moreover, in applying for a night's leave from Oxford on the ostensible grounds of seeing his father off to Switzerland, he had certainly had in his mind all the time the possibility of making this call. But now that he was apparently on the verge of bringing it off, it would have given him greater courage, in presenting himself at the front door, if there had been more uncertainty as to his hostess being at home. He ought never to have crossed the road for the purpose of looking up at her windows. It would have been far better to have made a dash straight up the three steps and have rung the bell there and then. If she had been in, well and good. But if not, there would have been certain advantages in leaving his card and escaping at once. It would have shown, for instance, whether she really did want to see him, for it would have given her the opportunity of narrowing down her original invitation to a more definite point. It might have shown, also, whether she really did remember him at all.

He shuddered slightly at the thought of the alternative possibility, and for the thousandth time ran over in his mind the circumstances attendant on his first meeting with Mrs. Cartwright.

It was so strange that the actual introduction should have been made by his father. The always shy and reserved Dr. Lawrence, both these characteristics accentuated since his wife's death, had been making one of his periodical attempts to get to know his only son. It is difficult to say whether, as a rule, parent or offspring disliked these attempts more. David had come to recognise the premonitory symptoms with horrible certainty, and knew every time that, until the climax was passed, there must be days of forced emotions, regretted confidences, and nervous strain. He wondered sometimes whether his father looked forward to the inevitable ending with any less longing than he did himself.

At any rate the climax of this particular *rapprochement* was to take the form of dinner and a theatre before David's first departure for Oxford. Auguries of failure were by no means wanting. In his wish to please his son, Dr. Lawrence had taken seats for a musical play, not realising either that David had been to it by himself the week before, or that no entertainment of this description could possibly survive the destructive criticism of his own expression. The two had met by appointment in the hall of the restaurant, and David had instantly become aware that he was to incur public disgrace through the shape of his father's collar; while the doctor's upper lip had simultaneously lengthened at the sight of his son's hair. When would he learn not to smother it in grease like that? Silently they handed their hats and coats to a flunkey (his knee-breeches and powdered hair warrant this antique expression) and silently they moved towards the entrance to the dining-room, and then, just as despair was settling on both, the interruption had come.

A woman rose from a wicker armchair and held out her hand.

"Hullo, Martin!" she said.

"Helen!"

The doctor stopped and took the outstretched hand. Shuffling uneasily in the background, David became aware of a strange phenomenon. Over the top of that disastrous collar his father's neck had assumed an unusual tinge. If this was to be taken as indicating a similar discoloration in front, he must be actually blushing.

"Why, I thought—"

"Oh, no," the woman broke in. "I've been back in London for some time. After all, why shouldn't I?"

The arrival of a fresh group of diners made Dr. Lawrence move to one side, and the woman looked at David.

"And is this your son?" she asked.

Thinking it over afterwards, David realised that the pleasure he felt at this moment could largely be accounted for by the fact that she had not said, "Is this your boy?"

His father turned towards him. "I want to introduce you to Mrs. Cartwright," he said.

He seemed to signal some kind of enquiry as he spoke her name, and she in turn gave a confirmatory movement with her head.

Further handshaking.

David thought he had never realised before what the epithet "bright" could mean when applied to the human eyes. At the same instant his manly prejudice against the use of scent disappeared once and for all.

Somehow or other he was in the background again.

"He's very like," said Mrs. Cartwright.

By the softening of his expression you might judge that Dr. Lawrence felt no incompleteness in this sentence.

"And you'll come and see me now, won't you?" Mrs. Cartwright went on, and for the first time in his life David heard his father tell a lie.

"I'm afraid I am just going abroad," said the doctor. "I'm taking a working holiday at Davos."

Now David knew, and his father knew he knew, that the Davos plan was not due for another six weeks at the earliest.

Mrs. Cartwright, bouncing gently off this refusal, turned again to David.

"Well, you must come and see me, then," she said, "any Sunday that you are in London. Ah, I see my host," she broke off. "I must go. Good-bye."

She shook no hands this time, but moved quickly away. And then, with her back to the Lawrences, but still apparently addressing one of them, she added, "Don't forget."

Father and son continued their interrupted journey towards their table and took their seats in silence. A waiter came up with a menu. The doctor nodded comprehensively at its contents, and the service began. Reeling though he still was at the moment from the effects of his first meeting with that amazingly attractive woman, David yet noted his father's action with interest and surprise. At previous dinners of this description, economy and professional knowledge of possible results had always caused the doctor to reduce by about forty percent any programme submitted to him. A still stranger event was to follow. Dr. Lawrence summoned the wine waiter, and a whispered conference took place. Nothing new so far, it must be admitted, except that the conference was a little longer than usual and the deference of the waiter perhaps a little more marked. But after that. . . !

From this point the evening never looked back. In addition to the unprecedented champagne, the doctor pressed unparalleled brandy and an epoch-making cigar on his guest. At the conclusion of dinner, although the theatre was known to be about two hundred yards away, a taxi was ordered and totally unnecessary tips flung at further flunkeys. During all this part of the evening the doctor, in violent contrast to his usual taciturnity, had poured forth a flood of reminiscence of his early life. Singularly uninteresting they seemed to his son, stimulated though he was by Mrs. Cartwright and the champagne, these stories of "old Johnny Boulter," of "the old Gardenia," and of somebody whose name his father had forgotten, but who was identified as "old Toothpick." So incredible did it appear that his parent should ever have moved in the world which he was trying to describe that David felt no shock at the unexpectedness of these revelations. Like the history which he had been taught at school, he accepted them as something incapable of proof and therefore impossible to deny. At the same time his father's strange behaviour, together with the stimuli noted above, had made him feel a real approach towards the something of himself which he suddenly recognised as existing on the other side of the table. These slender threads of sympathy survived transportation to the theatre, as did the doctor's supply of reminiscences. The entertainment sparkled with all the wit which can be given by a good dinner beforehand. David felt, if possible, even greater appreciation of the efforts of all concerned than at his first visit, and the summit of the evening's success was reached when his father joined in a song which the principal comedian had expressly invited the ladies of the audience to sing. The comedian's comments will not bear transcription to these pages, but at the time they appeared the very acme of humorous impromptu both to the Lawrences and to the rest of the audience.

And yet after this a reaction set in. True, the father did not, as the son feared he might, suggest a return by Underground. But he was quite silent again in the cab, and his well-known nervous cough, which had been in abeyance all the evening, broke out again in the hall.

Nevertheless it was in the hall that David asked the question which he had been wanting but hesitating to put for the last three and a half hours. Mrs. Cartwright had not reappeared in the restaurant so far as he was concerned, for his seat was placed facing towards a corner of the room, and he had looked for her in vain on his way out. And yet he had never really been thinking of anything else from the moment that he had first seen her. His procrastination in asking his question was not due to the usual cause, reluctance to risk a snub from his father, but to some inexplicable physical phenomenon which had put an obstruction in his throat whenever he had tried to say her name.

But now his last chance was going. Quickly, before the remnants of his father's good humour should have vanished, he must find out more about her.

"Father," he said. "Who was that Mrs. Cartwright this evening?"

His father was already halfway up the first flight of stairs, but he stopped and turned round. For a moment David thought he would not answer, and then he said:

"She married Leo Cartwright. I used to know her."

He swung round and continued his ascent. Then at the turn of the flight he stopped again. This time his voice sank almost to a murmur, as he gently released his words over the banisters.

"I think I should leave her alone, if I were you," he said, and, as he spoke, turned off the hall light from the two-ways switch on the landing. The effect was to close the conversation finally.

The next morning Dr. Lawrence was invisible in his consulting-room, and did not emerge even when the newly fledged undergraduate drove off to Paddington.

II

THOUGH HE WOULD HAVE SHOWN dangerous resentment if any one had dared to suggest it, it was not a bad thing for David that in the absence of a mother he should have carried in his mind during his first term the idealised image of Helen Cartwright. I do not pretend that this image protected him from any of the risks which he certainly did not run. But this ridiculous and intensely purified passion did help him to a kind of balance and sense of proportion which saved him from swallowing Oxford in the indigestible gobbets which were bolted by most of his contemporaries. His affair (the poor idiot already thought of it as such) gave him a calm superiority to the youthful enthusiasms of his fellow students for the female members of visiting theatrical companies, which they found singularly irritating. About the second week of his residence he discovered a photograph of his heroine in an illustrated

DENIS MACKAIL

paper. "Snapped in the Park" was the only editorial comment, but there could be no doubt of her identity. A few days later this appeared in a frame on his mantelpiece, and he would balance himself on the fender before it with an ask-me-who-that-is-if-you-dare expression on his countenance, which in any society less genuinely tolerant of poses would have led to physical disturbance.

On one occasion the calm was indeed shattered. A gathering of freshers who had taken unto themselves the modest title of "The Elect," had met one evening for the purpose of hearing Mr. T. H. J. Gryffyn read his paper on Modern Drama. For the better appreciation of its subtleties the Elect had provided themselves with considerable quantities of coffee, bottled beer, bananas, dates, cigarettes, plum cake, and Turkish delight. In a thickening atmosphere Mr. T. H. J. Gryffyn had droned through his paper. Detailed description of it is quite unnecessary to the progress of this story, but it may be noted in passing that its tendency was to judge everything by a kind of inverted commercialism. Nothing that paid could be good, and nothing that was good ever paid. The doctrine is agreeably simple and appeared to find favour with the audience. At the conclusion of the paper there was a weighty silence, broken at length by a short speech of thanks to Mr. Gryffyn by the President and the announcement that the subject was now open for discussion.

You know the kind of discussion that followed better than I can describe it. Recent history mercifully reduced to a minimum the use of the word *spielhaus*, but the eccentricities of every country except Germany were gloated over in savage comparison with the mediocrity of the United Kingdom. Mr. M'Alister seized the opportunity of repeating once more his description of the Sicilian marionettes. A Rhodes scholar weighed in with praise of Greenwich Village. More than once the presidential bell (or wineglass) had to be used.

So far David had remained among the listeners. But now Mr. Budleigh challenged attention by the revolutionary statement that in his opinion the modern drama in this country was all right as long as one could see performances like that of Leo Cartwright in "Pale People." The audacity of this tribute to a popular favourite in a popular success staggered Mr. Gryffyn and his followers, but there was a murmur of agreement from the quieter part of the members.

"Yes," continued Mr. Budleigh, encouraged by this support, "and, what is more, it takes real intelligence to act like Cartwright. You mayn't agree with me, but I say that Cartwright is a better influence on the stage today than any of these Frenchmen or Poles. And he's had to put up with just as much discouragement too. Why, even his wife left him because he wanted—preferred, mind you—to play outside London when he started, because he knew he could improve himself by it."

A quite uncontrollable force took hold of David, causing him to tremble all over. A sound, hardly to be recognised as his own voice, burst from him.

"That's absolutely untrue," he said.

There was an utter silence, broken only by the splintering of the presidential bell as it crashed to the ground. The rules and regulations of the Elect provided for no such breach of decorum as the giving of the direct lie by one member to another.

David stumbled out of the hot room and down the stone stairs, and, as he went, the Elect all began talking at once in a nervous effort to efface the memory of this scene. The President picked up a new bell and struck it with a spoon.

"I call on Mr. Gryffyn to reply," he said. Mr. T. H. J. Gryffyn rose to his feet and began speaking. The crisis was over. In the background Mr. Budleigh was comforting himself by murmurs of "I didn't imagine he knew him. Surely a man can say what he thinks," and so on. Strange to say, the feeling of the meeting was on the whole favourable to the absent member. For this David might be partly grateful to certain doubtful actions of Mr. Budleigh at the beginning of the term, by which he had incurred the suspicion of presuming on the possession of a brother in his fourth year. At any rate the incident was never mentioned again.

In the quad, David, to his horror and surprise, found himself actually struggling to keep back tears. "Beasts! Cads!" he gulped, with very little justice, as he made his way to his rooms.

He lay awake most of the night going over again in his mind the scene of this ridiculous outburst. If you imagine from his behaviour that he had the very slightest idea whether this accusation against Mrs. Cartwright was based on any shred of fact, you are wrong. With the exception of his father's use of the past tense in connection with her marriage, this was absolutely the first intimation he had received that the actor and his wife were not an ideally happy couple. But if it were so, he was glad. His devotion seemed the more noble, his service should be the more acceptable. In this romantic mood he at length fell asleep.

And in something approaching the same mood and with the strangely comforting thought that his father was beyond Paris, he now settled his tie for the five hundredth time, left his post by the square railings, crossed the road, and rang the bell of Number 35.

III

WE NOW REACH MRS. CARTWRIGHT'S DRAWING-ROOM and have our first opportunity of seeing Mrs. Cartwright herself. She certainly is a very beautiful woman still, although cynics like the reader and myself will manage to avoid any outward sign of surprise on being told that she will never see forty-five again, and is in fact now engaged in seeing forty-six. David's tribute to her eyes will receive confirmation from us, albeit with the mental reservation that her drawing-room is certainly very carefully lighted. Well, and why not? If a beautiful woman may not arrange the lights in her own drawing-room, what may she do? And Mrs. Cartwright has had plenty of time since her return from the south of France to discover and arrange a London setting which shall be in every way worthy of her. For it was quite at the beginning of the war that she transferred the Villa Mercédès, where she had lived for nearly eighteen years, to the Croix Rouge and returned to take up life again in London.

The superstitious author of the lines,

> "Change the name and not the letter,
> Change for the worse and not the better,"

must be credited with some slight justification for the apparent tautology in his brief poem, whatever the actual facts as to his statement may be. So many marriages turn out not to be changes of any description at all. In Helen Chandler's case, however, the bard would have found a good deal to support his view. Her friends, at any rate, would have told you that her marriage had been a change for the worse from the very outset, and certainly its early and sudden end would point to some justification for their remarks.

She had been left an orphan while still at school, and the solicitors charged with the administration of her father's very considerable estate had arranged for her to spend her holidays and subsequently to live with some relations of the senior partner, to whom the rich Miss Chandler's contribution was more than welcome. It enabled them, in fact, to move from West Kensington to Real Kensington, and there seemed every reason for great and continued efforts to be made to keep this jewel in their midst. Unfortunately, however, the girl was not only extremely pretty, but possessed also of a quite exceptional store of high spirits. Do what they could, the poor relations could not keep young men from the house. They came in droves, and among them came a young medical student named Martin Lawrence. Martin was as badly hit as the rest of them, and for a time became quite a special source of alarm to the Stanley-Smiths. The climax arrived, as they thought, on the evening when young Lawrence drove Helen home in a hansom at half-past nine. With bated breath Mr. and Mrs. Stanley-Smith discussed dreadful possibilities behind the drawing-room curtains. They knew, and Helen knew, that they dared not blame her openly, for she was of age and could take herself and her money off tomorrow, if she chose.

The young man and the young woman stood talking together on the pavement for some time, and the Stanley-Smiths breathed a sigh of relief when they saw Lawrence's face in the lamplight, just before he drove away alone. Their deductions were correct. He had proposed in the hansom and he had been refused, but, as an unusual and aggravating addition to this ceremony, Helen had pointed out to him who it was that he really ought to marry. At the time, it must be admitted that he received this advice with undisguised distaste, but it was characteristic of Helen's insight that two years later he should have married the very girl that she had selected. Helen was always so much better at seeing what other people ought to do than what she ought to do herself, though to do her justice she seldom told them.

So the Stanley-Smiths smiled a smile of thankfulness and prepared to resume their watch and ward, while continuing to curse the fate which had caused their only son still to be but eleven years old. These maledictions were, of course, singularly unjustified, as it was precisely this fact which had made their selection by the senior partner possible.

And then if, after all, a week later Helen hadn't come home to lunch and calmly told them that she had married Leo Cartwright!

Before the storm which immediately broke over her she bent gracefully, but did no more than bend. Smiling sweetly at charges of ingratitude, insanity, and immorality, she packed a gladstone bag and asked for a cab. Mr. Stanley-Smith, acting up to his hyphen at the last moment, carried this bag down the steps, though he still muttered horrible words beneath his breath. Helen held out her hand through the window of the cab.

DENIS MACKAIL

"I'm sorry you should take it like this," she said; "but please don't think I'm ungrateful for all you've done for me. Won't you shake hands?"

Mr. Stanley-Smith put out his hand; the cab started with a jerk; and he found himself clutching a bundle of banknotes.

"To help you to forget me," Helen called out of the window, as the four-wheeler clattered away.

Intolerable that young girls should be allowed to insult men old enough to be their father like this! Ruined by her money! That was it. Ruined by her money.

Mr. Stanley-Smith turned to look at the house which he must now leave, and saw that Mrs. Stanley-Smith was no longer at the window. His hand moved quickly towards the inside pocket of his coat.

It was ten months after this that Mrs. Cartwright called on the senior partner.

"I want a separation," she said, and proceeded without a pause to describe, in language which left little or nothing to the imagination, the grounds on which she considered that her request should be met. To the senior partner's suggestion of further consideration she was deaf.

He left his desk and stood with his back to the fireplace. His confidential clerk could have told you that this was a serious sign.

"You know," said the senior partner, "that, if you give us time, you probably have grounds for a divorce here?"

"Oh, yes; thanks very much," replied his client. "But you see I'm not at all sure that I deserve that; and I'm quite sure that Leo doesn't."

"Legal processes rarely result from what one deserves," said the senior partner. This was his notion of humour; but as he didn't smile, Mrs. Cartwright didn't laugh. Otherwise, of course, you could rely on her.

"I don't want you to think I'm trying to punish other women," she said. "I think I'm really trying to protect them. They won't know the worst as long as they can't marry him."

"But you—yourself?"

"It's just as well that there should be something to stop me making such a fool of myself again," she said.

This was a new philosophy to the senior partner and he was unwise enough to argue the point. When he had quite finished, Mrs. Cartwright said:

"I'm sorry to appear unconventional, but I'm afraid I've made up my mind. Besides, I want to travel; and if I'm going about alone, separation is respectable, but divorce isn't."

Echo du temps passé.

"There's another thing," Mrs. Cartwright went on. "I want to make Leo an allowance. Not to stop him working, but just pocket money. I'm afraid I've rather taught him to be extravagant while we were married."

In this she was wrong, and the senior partner was as certain as he could be that she was wrong, but he had already learnt not to argue.

"We can arrange that," he said.

"But it's to be paid on condition that he doesn't come to London during the next five years," said Mrs. Cartwright. "I want to be certain that I shan't see him when I'm here. And what's more," she added, "I think it will do his acting good."

"We will endeavour to arrange that also," said the senior partner. "Perhaps you can tell me the name of your husband's solicitors."

"Tracy and Paull see to his contracts always," said Mrs. Cartwright, and the senior partner made a note on a slip of paper.

"Then that's all at present, I think," added Mrs. Cartwright in the tone one uses at the village stores.

The senior partner, however, was not going to play the part of the courteous shop assistant.

"I should like to offer you my most sincere condolences," he said, "on the very unfortunate way that your marriage has turned out. It is a matter of very great disappointment to me personally, as well as in my capacity as trustee for your father's estate, that this should have happened. As a lawyer, I have learnt the uselessness of crying over spilt milk, but—"

The look in his client's face stopped him.

"I hope the future may hold very many happy years for you in spite of this mistake," he concluded.

"You're very kind to me," said Mrs. Cartwright and, stepping forward, she kissed the senior partner on the left whisker. "Good-bye."

After this business interview she went back to her hotel, and lay on the bed with the room darkened, crying and crying and crying.

The next day she started, with a newly acquired maid, on her travels. But the original plan of seeing the world broke down almost at once. The Messageries boat was delayed at Marseilles. There would be ten days to wait. Mrs. Cartwright and her maid began pottering about the Riviera, and on the sixth day she saw the Villa Mercédès. The unexpected pathos of a broken shutter and a fountain choked with leaves caught hold of her. "This house needs taking care of," she said.

And for the next eighteen years it received the love and care which, but for Leo Cartwright, might have been wasted on some man.

IV

Mrs. Cartwright was not alone in her drawing-room on this Sunday afternoon. She had a caller, in the shape of John Ormroyd. His friends and admirers say that Ormroyd's best work will still be written, but he was already a quite reasonably successful novelist with a growing public in England and America. At this time he was not much over thirty, and a bachelor. John Ormroyd cultivates a stern exterior. If he has a joint in his armour, it is perhaps to be found in his weakness for that photograph of himself smoking a pipe, which, although at this time five or six years old, still appeared at given intervals on the literary page of the weekly illustrated papers. Something in the way in which he grips the pipe in his mouth adds an appearance of strength to his jaw, and, although there is nothing wanting in this feature when pipeless, there is no doubt that this photograph gives him considerable comfort. Lest any one should think that I am unfair to John Ormroyd, I hasten to add that he is a D.S.O. and a very good fellow.

Half an hour ago Ormroyd's expression was marred by a look of discontentment. So many of Mrs. Cartwright's friends arrive at her little house with this expression, for there is undoubtedly something about her which makes everyone bring his troubles to her, and she has come to regard her Sunday evening headache following on her Sunday afternoon outpouring of sympathy, as quite a permanent institution. For there is nothing half-hearted about this sympathy. No matter how petty the disappointments or tragedies which you bring to Mrs. Cartwright on her afternoons at home, she will spend the last ounce of her strength in seeing that you do not leave her until the weight has been lifted. Women of forty-six who envy the brightness of her eyes might do worse than follow Mrs. Cartwright's example, if they are able.

John Ormroyd's trouble is a familiar one. Like all successful novelists he believes that he can write a play. And like most successful novelists he has begun by dramatising one of his own books. "Odd Man Out" was published as a novel six years ago, but it has a "strong" plot, and the third Act brought tears to Mrs. Cartwright's eyes when the author first read it to her. This does not mean that it would necessarily have the same effect on the eyes of the British Public, but it was an encouraging sign none the less.

Twelve months ago Ormroyd submitted his typescript to the management of the Thespian Theatre. He did this direct in a fit of pique, because the agent to whom he had originally shown it had had the audacity to ask for a deposit to cover preliminary expenses. A month later he was sent a beautiful lithographed letter, with a decorated heading of masks and tassels, informing him that the management of the Thespian Theatre had received his drama and that it was under consideration. As he had taken the precaution of registering his original package, this intimation added very little to his knowledge, and he continued to possess his soul in patience.

Six weeks after this he got a telegram which read:

Can offer you fifty pounds four months option on your play odd man out possible production autumn wire acceptance and will forward agreement Thespigram.

The innocent John was in the seventh heaven of delight, and wrote to a man whom he knew asking him if he would put him up for the Garrick Club. He also telegraphed to the management of the Thespian, "Accept subject agreement satisfactory," and began wondering whether he should make a speech on the first night or merely bow from his Box. Of course, fifty pounds was a mere trifle—only ten times what he had made over his first novel; but the words "autumn production" carried a fine flavour, worth more (at the moment) than paltry gold.

However, after their telegraphic outburst, the management sank back into a state of coma, and it was not until three weeks later, after many letters, notes, and thwarted attempts at interviews, that John received his copy of the agreement.

The arrival of this document gave him a foretaste of the separate and special torments which are reserved for dramatic authors. For, although it bound him hand and foot as to any attempts to dispose of "Odd Man Out" elsewhere, no mention was made in it of production in the autumn or any other season, and the closest inspection failed to reveal any reference in it to the fifty pounds. As an offset against these omissions there was inserted a clause giving the management of the Thespian Theatre the sole power to dispose of the cinema rights on the author's behalf during the continuance of the option.

In any other walk of life you might have expected John at this stage to seek a personal interview with the management in the hopes of clearing up the several very doubtful points about this agreement. But his experience of the theatrical world, brief as it had been, had already taught him the uselessness of attempting this, and that the only method of communication recognised by the management was the telegram. He accordingly telegraphed as follows:

Agreement received but no mention author's fee is autumn production still expected would prefer retain cinema rights.

To which the Thespian replied:

Payment naturally understood cheque follows production dependent on usual arrangements Thespigram.

This last was a very clever example of the Thespian's telegraphic style. For in the first place it retired gracefully from an attempt at what is generally known as a "try-on"; in the second place it made the quite unjustifiable assumption that John's telegram had been a conditional acceptance; in the third place its second clause, while meaning nothing at all, was nicely calculated to retain the author in the toils; and finally it omitted all reference to the vexed question of the cinema rights.

The effect was as intended. For three days John put supposedly supposititious cases to all his friends and received a great quantity of contradictory advice. On the fourth day the cheque suddenly arrived. Exhausted by his friends' advice, and calling to mind the gross injustice of his first agreement with his publishers, on which he had, however, found it quite easy to make subsequent improvements, he signed the document and posted it off.

There followed four months of complete silence on the part of the Thespian, at the end of which they despatched another telegram.

Do you agree extension option on your play odd man out further period six months on original terms hoping arrange production after christmas Thespigram.

John tore his hair, but the magic word "production" was too much for him. He telegraphed back an acceptance.

Now if you suppose, as I am afraid John foolishly did, that he was going to get another fifty pounds for this, then you had better have a second look at the last telegram. Its ambiguity is as clear as mud, but there was a bitter exchange of telegrams before he finally accepted his fate, which, needless to say, did not result in the transfer of any further sum of money from the Thespian coffers to the author's pocket.

In the autumn John Ormroyd's thwarted ambition received some consolation from the success of his new novel "The Sky Is Falling," and he set feverishly to work on an original drama for submission, unasked, to another management.

And now, on this Sunday in December, a double blow had fallen, dealt by statements in two contiguous columns of his Sunday newspaper. For in the first column, under the heading "Stage Doings," there was a semi-official pronunciamento foreshadowing future arrangements at the Thespian. The success of "Pale People," it remarked, was such that no plans for any new production had yet been made; but if and when the drawing power of this delightful comedy should be exhausted, the management had in contemplation the presentation of a translation of the very successful Norwegian work "The Pastor of Aarvaag," the representation of which by the Scandinavian Players had been such a memorable triumph for the Sunday Club last summer.

Scarcely had John staggered under this shock, when his eye was caught by the name of his beloved "Odd Man Out" in the adjacent column. He rushed up to the top, took in the caption "The World of the Screen," and tore back again only to read the following:

The Barnes-Battersby Company are engaged in the screening of a version of Mr. John Ormroyd's successful novel "Odd Man Out," for which Miss Angel Hobbs has been engaged to play the leading part. A number of beautiful scenes have been taken on the Cornish coast where the story is laid, and it is rumoured that a record sum has been paid for the rights of this great popular thriller.

Cut off from the telegraph service by the piety of the Government, John's thoughts turned almost instantly to Mrs. Cartwright. Subconsciously he realised that nowhere else could he tell the story of his wrongs either with such certainty of receiving the right kind of sympathy or with such complete freedom from the necessity of pretending that he had come to talk about anything else. He immediately got through to her house on the telephone. Could Mrs. Cartwright lunch with Mr. Ormroyd today? Mrs. Cartwright, said the maid, was very sorry, but

DENIS MACKAIL

she had some friends lunching with her. She would, however, be in all the afternoon, if Mr. Ormroyd cared to call. At this point a crackling took place in the receiver of John's telephone, signifying that Mrs. Cartwright had switched the call through to her own room.

"Hullo! is that you, John?" she said. "Did you want me as a chaperon or as a friend today?"

"A friend," said John. "It's about my confounded play."

"Come to tea," said Mrs. Cartwright's voice. "I'm not expecting anybody and I want to hear all about it."

So John arranged to go there for tea, and somehow or other the thought of this engagement enabled him to get through the day without bursting a blood-vessel, though whenever he remembered the words "popular thriller," he was in great danger of doing so.

And yet, when you come to think of it, it was a rather remarkable fact that John should be taking his troubles to this particular house. That he did so was but another proof, if one were wanted, that you do not often come across women like Mrs. Cartwright.

For you may have noticed that, in speaking of the Thespian Theatre, I have so far avoided personalities and have limited myself to the one impersonal phrase "the management." My reason for doing this is because John Ormroyd adopted exactly the same phraseology in describing his difficulties to Mrs. Cartwright, and John Ormroyd's reason for doing this was that the management of the Thespian consisted to all intents and purposes of one person, and that one person was (as you are of course aware) Mr. Leo Cartwright.

But for his experience as a novelist, John might well have found difficulty in producing enough synonyms to save himself from the actual utterance of this name; especially when you consider that it was against this one individual that all his feeling was really directed. Nevertheless, through more than an hour of passion and invective the ingenious author continued to observe his self-imposed restriction, and this notwithstanding the fact that from the very first Mrs. Cartwright had spoken of Leo as Leo and as nothing else.

The period had now arrived when John, having repeated the story of his wrongs with every conceivable detail and variation of wording, was content to browse on sandwiches, while his hostess poured words of consolation into his ears. To tell the truth, he was at this stage really enjoying himself very much, and, but for occasional pangs brought about by a mental comparison between the photograph with the pipe and his recent entire abandonment of self-control, would have been absolutely and completely happy.

Mrs. Cartwright's consolation was taking, as it always did, a number of exceedingly ingenious forms, and the prospect of a record Sunday evening headache was rapidly becoming more certain. She had from the first dismissed the possibility of *mala fides* on the part of her husband. "Leo has his faults," she said, "but he is never mean. You must remember, John, that he is probably very much in the hands of his business manager, and that the business manager must always feel a great deal of responsibility to Leo's Backers." She did not over-elaborate this line of defence, however, but went on to subtler and less relevant methods of sympathy. A reference to the comparative failure of Stevenson and Kipling as dramatists made it easy for her to pass on to admiration for the success of "The Sky Is Falling." It was then a simple matter to begin praising John's one outstanding failure, "She Loves Me Not," which with the perversity of all authors he persisted in regarding as his best work. Even here, however, Mrs. Cartwright did not make the mistake of overdoing her praise. Just as you begin (or should begin) scratching your cat under the chin, before the pleasure of having her back stroked has had a chance to pall, so Mrs. Cartwright, by an inspired *non-sequitur*, switched suddenly over to the question of John's marriage.

It may be said at once that this was an entirely theoretical subject; but as handled by Mrs. Cartwright it was none the less interesting for that. You would never have guessed, as she drew a flattering picture of John's ideal and of the happiness which was waiting for him round some hidden corner of the future, that her own experience of marriage had been anything but idyllic. Truly there are few pleasanter things than this form of flattery, when offered by a beautiful woman who you know cannot and does not wish to marry you herself. If John could have purred at this point, he would certainly have done so.

In the hall below, the front door had just opened to admit David Lawrence.

"Is Mrs. Cartwright at home?" he asked.

"Yes, sir," said the neat-looking maid.

She assisted with the removal of his overcoat, and then paused at the foot of the stairs.

"What name, sir?"

"Mr. David Lawrence," said David, preparing to follow her up the staircase.

But the maid didn't move.

"There's a letter for you, I think, sir," she said.

"A letter?" repeated David, taken aback. An absurd thought that his father had chosen this method of reiterating his original warning flashed through his mind.

The maid was examining a number of unopened letters and circulars which lay on a cassone; but a minute later she turned round again, looking a little pink.

"I beg your pardon, sir," she said. "I'm afraid I made a mistake."

David agitated his vocal chords so as to produce a suitable sound, and the interrupted procession to the first floor was resumed.

In the drawing-room Mrs. Cartwright's experienced ear had caught the sound of the front-door bell.

"There's some one coming," she said. "I hear the bell. Now, John, before we're interrupted, listen to me. You've got to remember that hundreds and thousands of the best plays ever written have been hung up like this, very often for years, before they got put on. And hundreds and thousands of authors have had to put up with much worse things than getting an option from Leo. I quite agree that they have behaved disgracefully over the cinema business, but you go and have another look at your agreement and see if you don't get something out of it yet. Besides, you ought to know better than to believe all that you read in a Sunday newspaper about record payments. So cheer up, John, and think of all the other poor writers in their garrets. Why, if it comes to that, do you know that I once wrote a play myself?"

It is perhaps the greatest tribute that has yet been paid to Mrs. Cartwright's charm, that a look of real interest should have appeared in the rival playwright's eyes at this intelligence.

"No, did you really?" he said. "I wish you'd tell me about it."

But at this moment the drawing-room door was opened and the neat-looking maid appeared.

"Mr. Lawrence," she said, and David made his entrance.

Mrs. Cartwright gave an odd little gasp and half rose from her seat. Infinitely brief expressions of bewilderment and recognition flitted across her face, and then she held out her hand.

"Why, of course," she said. "How nice of you to remember to come and see me. John, I don't think you've met Mr. Lawrence, have you? This is Mr. Ormroyd."

"Didn't you write 'She Loves Me Not'?" said David, shaking hands.

John's original impulse to resent this interruption, and his silent exclamation of the word "Puppy," were instantly forgotten. David's unconscious exhibition of tact had triumphed.

"Yes, I did," said John. "But I didn't know any one had read it."

"I thought it was topping," said David, smiling. And John smiled because of his pleasure at this genuine praise. And Mrs. Cartwright smiled, because her old and her new friends were smiling. David thought she looked even more wonderful than his remembrance of her.

"You'll have some tea, won't you?" said Mrs. Cartwright. David, seeing only remnants on the table, was just going to decline, but his hostess had not waited for an answer. "Ring the bell, John," she said.

While fresh supplies were being brought, she entertained her callers with an exaggerated account of the importance of Martin Lawrence in the medical profession, appealing to David from time to time for confirmation of her more outrageous statements, but never really giving him the opportunity of saying anything. David, in spite of the rugged honesty of his nineteen years, found this vicarious flattery singularly pleasant. Somehow or other it enabled him to feel that he was meeting the celebrated John Ormroyd more as an equal and less as an undergraduate still in his first term. And this was exactly what Mrs. Cartwright intended. For her, all her guests were equal; and if any of them failed to realise this, she took the quickest, though the most tactful means of bringing this equality to their notice. Not that John Ormroyd possessed so much as an ounce of the kind of conceit which would have tempted him to show off in front of this boy, even though the boy had just paid an unsolicited testimonial to "She Loves Me Not."

Very soon afterwards, however, John rose to his feet and said that he was afraid that he must be getting on.

"Well, mind you let me know exactly what happens," said Mrs. Cartwright, accompanying him to the door. "And mind you remember all I've told you."

As if any one could possibly forget! thought David. And all the time he kept saying to himself "I'm actually in her house. We're actually going to be alone together. Isn't she wonderful?"

Mrs. Cartwright sat back again in her armchair.

"Now, then," she said.

("Now then," thought David.)

"Where have you been all this time?" continued Mrs. Cartwright. She could not, as David could, tell you the exact number of days since

their first meeting, but she knew it was considerably more than a month. This conversational opening does not, perhaps, exhibit Mrs. Cartwright at her best, but to tell the truth she was finding David's unblinking gaze of admiration just the least little bit embarrassing.

"I've been at Oxford," he said, and, though the gaze was not for an instant removed, the name of the town restored Mrs. Cartwright's conversational equilibrium. She knew the next move now. It was the same for Cambridge, Sandhurst, Dartmouth, and a number of other towns beloved of tailors and tobacconists, and she proceeded to ask the most fascinatingly idiotic questions on the subject of University life.

If the same questions had been put by his aunt (as, indeed, had happened during a visit from this lady a fortnight ago), David would have given surly and obscure replies and expressed unnatural ignorance when driven into a corner. This does not mean that he was normally in the least inclined to surliness, but all the world knows that people are divided into those who can ask you about what you do and those who can't. The former class is very small, but there is no doubt that Mrs. Cartwright occupies a leading position in it.

However, she suddenly broke off in the middle of her search for knowledge, or rather directed it to a fresh subject.

"There's something you've not told me yet," she said. "Considering that I knew your father a long time before you were born, I'm not going to know you now as 'Mr. Lawrence.' You're not called 'Martin' too, are you?"

"No," said David. "I'm called 'David.'"

"David?" repeated Mrs. Cartwright, with really quite unnecessary astonishment.

"Yes. Why, do you know somebody else with the same name?"

It was not like Mrs. Cartwright to show confusion or indecision, but at this moment she certainly showed both.

"Yes. No. I mean, not exactly," she said; and with this answer David had to be content.

Intelligent readers will connect her strange reply with the Mystery of the Letter, already recorded some pages back. But they need have no fear that this is going to turn into a detective story, for the solution will be provided at the very first available opportunity.

Meanwhile it must be recorded how David stayed on and on and on in Mrs. Cartwright's drawing-room; how Mrs. Cartwright, partly through inherent kindliness and partly through sentiment which carried her back to a certain hansom cab in the nineties, exerted herself indefatigably

to entertain her guest; how the headache induced by her séance with John Ormroyd was succeeded by a quite different headache brought on by her efforts with David; and how David, in spite of a horrible consciousness that his interminable call could not really be adding to the good impression which he so longed to make on his hostess, remained rooted to his seat for over two hours, during the whole of which time he never once removed his eyes from Mrs. Cartwright's face.

In final desperation, after she had exhausted the possibilities of the most unmistakeable hints, after she had called her guest's attention to the beauty of the clock on the mantelpiece and asked him by what train he was going back to Oxford, Mrs. Cartwright was forced into the open with a downright lie.

"I'm very sorry to have to turn you out, David," she said, "but I'm afraid I must go and dress now, because I'm dining out." She stood up, and David was compelled to uproot himself. The absurd look of misery in his face softened her heart, though it could not cure her head.

"Ring me up again, when you're back in London," she said, "and we might go to a matinée. Now would you like a taxi?"

"No, thank you," said David. "I think I'll walk."

They both moved towards the door.

And then it was that David gave utterance to the strange remark, the recollection of which made him for days afterwards hot and wretched, whenever it came as an unwelcome and preposterous intruder into his thoughts and dreams about this wonderful woman.

"I say," he said, rather huskily; "if there's ever anything I can do for you, I wish you'd let me know."

Mrs. Cartwright was not faced with the problem of finding a suitable answer to this offer, for her guest did not pause, but gripped her hand, turned, and stumbled down the stairs. She waited until she heard the latch of the front door click, and then called over the banisters.

"Hilda," she said.

"Yes, madam?"

"I'm going to bed now. I'm feeling very tired. Will you ask Rose to put two hot bottles in my room? And if you'll just send me up a little sole, I won't have anything else."

"Very good, madam."

So Mrs. Cartwright went upstairs and lay in the dark with an eau-de-cologne compress over her bright eyes, and the kitchen feasted on the remainder of the dining-room dinner.

DENIS MACKAIL

Meanwhile David proceeded slowly on foot to Harley Street, with the intention of changing his clothes and catching the late train to Oxford. Not even a succession of collisions with other pedestrians could recall him to this world from the dream in which he moved. His victims fell back in baffled fury, as, completely unconscious of their existence, he strode through the drizzle and fog, murmuring imaginary conversations and planning impossible deeds.

And David also went without his dinner. It did not even occur to him that he had omitted this childish ceremony until he was back in college, and then his nineteen years reminded him with insistent pangs. He consumed half a stale chocolate cake which he found in his cupboard, and, flinging off his clothes, fell into a dreamless sleep.

II

Presenting Leo Cartwright

I

In the city of New York the number of theatres, and consequently the size of the population, are constantly increasing, and simultaneously with this growth the whole of the theatrical district is continually being driven in pursuit of the fashionable quarter by the expansion of the business area at the lower end of the island. Eventually, it is to be imagined, the theatres will be driven off the isle of Manhattan altogether and will be sprinkled in myriads around Yonkers, while by that time no self-respecting millionaire will dream of having his town house farther south than Tarrytown. Meanwhile this continual movement, this constant birth and death of playhouses, makes it possible for any star who survives three seasons on Broadway to have a theater named after him or herself, outside which the stellar cognomen, however unbeautiful it may be, will twinkle cheerfully every evening until the rising tide of business shall sweep the whole edifice away.

In London, on the other hand, not only has theatreland been centred round the same district for several hundred years, thus preserving a continuity of nomenclature, but quite apart from this there appears to be (with very few exceptions) a definite prejudice in the older city against the use of a living actor's name for the title of any temple of his art. You will remember that a hundred years had passed before even Garrick was honoured in this way, and delicacy forbids me to point out how quickly the original name of the present Globe Theatre was changed.

Thus it was that when, fifteen or sixteen years before the date of this story, a collection of city men, bookmakers, idlers, tradesmen, and dagoes determined to adventure varying portions of their spare capital in the erection and maintenance of a special shrine for the genius of Leo Cartwright, there was but little hesitation in rejecting the suggestion of the intended occupant that it should be named after himself, though it was not before considerable discussion that a basis of agreement was found in the word "Thespian."

You will probably remember the Press puffs which enlivened what used to be known as the silly season during the building of the Thespian Theatre, or, if you have forgotten them, it will do just as well if you remember the descriptions of any other similar erection, for they showed no marked variation from the normal. In them you would read how in Mr. Cartwright's new theatre every member of the audience would obtain a clear and uninterrupted view of the stage; how the whole building was constructed of doubly reënforced asbesto-line-ferro-concrete, thus rendering it completely fireproof; how in spite of this it could be emptied in three minutes; how the gallery seats would be bookable (this, of course, was altered before the opening night); how the bars would be directly under the management (so was this); how an entirely novel scheme of double-reflecting, ultra-compensating lighting was being installed; and, finally, how the aim of the new management would at all times be to provide the public with a frequent change of the very highest examples of the works of modern dramatists, relying on this for support more than on the despicable practice of the long run.

You may also remember how, notwithstanding the above, the Thespian Theatre at length opened with a revival of "The School for Scandal," the enormous success of the first representation being only slightly marred by the protests of those members of the audience who found themselves unable to see the stage, and how Mr. Cartwright managed to establish a new record for this masterpiece by continuing to play to crowded houses for three hundred and thirty-three nights, and then only terminated the run because he was under contract to produce an entirely new dramatic version of "Jane Eyre," in which he doubled the parts of Rochester and St. John.

Those had been the great days of the actor-manager, when rival members of the craft had rushed in crowds and sold their souls to money-lenders in order to establish themselves in the West End; had engaged in incredible struggles with fate, each other, bankruptcy, and their own incompetence in order to maintain their positions; had gone down gurgling in a compulsory American tour, only to rise still breasting the waves in another London theatre. Their actions appeared to be governed by the movement of some mysterious cycle. Thus at a given moment they would all announce that they were on the point of appearing as Coriolanus; a little later they would all engage a leading lady who couldn't speak English; at one instant they would all be suddenly discovered in

Marienbad or Monte Carlo, at another they would all bob up in the witness-box at a *cause célèbre*.

And yet, in spite of this strange unanimity, they had one by one dropped from the bough. Hermes Blount was now domiciled permanently in Long Island, Lucius Wilkinson had died in a fit at the Green Room Club, Mortimer Marlowe had retaliated by having a fit at the Cavour, but had unfortunately failed to die, and still ingered on as an imbecile ghost. Braybrooke Silver had come off best with a knighthood, which he still aired every morning in Bond Street and exercised every afternoon at his club in St. James's Square; while St. John Crawford and Eric Goldstone still trod the boards, though miserably shorn of their former glory. For Crawford was being worked to death by a syndicate, who fined him whenever he took a holiday and even hired him out to concert halls on Sundays, while poor Goldstone toured the smaller twice-nightly variety houses, doing the quarrel scene from "Julius Caesar" in a morning coat.

But somehow or other, through all these changes and disappearances of his former rivals, and in spite of the growing success of the actress-manageress and the syndicate, Leo Cartwright had continued to fly his standard at the Thespian, and, while always keeping them in their places, to earn for his Backers every year a steady average forty percent. For whatever his detractors might say as to his private life or his artistic conscience, it must be admitted that Cartwright had for these fifteen years filled the Thespian with his own personality, and when an actor can do that with his theatre, he can be pretty sure of filling it also with a real, live, paying audience.

II

IN THE VAST AND COMPLEX organisation constituting the management and staff of the Thespian, there has from the beginning always been one post to which has been given the title of Personal Manager. The duties expected of the holder of this office were originally so vague, and have in the course of time become so varied, that it is very difficult to attempt to describe them. Personal Managers have been many, and the reason for their removal has always been that they have either exceeded or failed to perform their mysterious duties; but as they are almost all now well established in the theatrical world, it may be assumed that the experience gained under the Thespian banner has proved useful to them in their careers. The few who have failed to pass on to better-paid jobs have been heard, in the confidential atmosphere of the Bodega, to employ the phrase "boot-licker" or some impolite synonym in connection with their former employment; but why should we listen to disappointed men? So far as it is possible to be precise, the work of these officials seemed to consist in an attendance at the theatre of not less than eighteen hours a day, and the assumption from about seven o'clock onwards of a dress coat with bone buttons and a silk hat with a curly brim. Should a Personage be present in a Box, the dress coat and silk hat will appear in the last interval and conduct him through the iron door to Mr. Cartwright's suite of rooms; should an author require kicking downstairs, the Personal Manager will oblige.

These Grand Viziers, as they may be called, have been largely, but by no means exclusively, recruited from the ranks of the two tribes which were not lost, and they preserve unbroken the tradition of invariably addressing Mr. Cartwright as "Chief."

As to the origin of the Vizier in office at the time of this story, I am uncertain. His name was certainly Albert Gordon, and I can swear that he was not Scotch; but further than this I am, on the information at my disposal, hardly prepared to go.

Although, as has been indicated, Mr. Gordon's duties were of a numerous and nebulous description, so that he was constantly coming into collision with the Business Manager or the Stage Manager or the Advertising Agent or the Treasurer or even the Musical Director, still, as the creation of his office had received the original approval of the Backers, the architect of the Thespian had been given instructions to provide a separate room for the Personal Manager. It is true that in no other building than a theatre would a gentleman in receipt of Mr. Gordon's or his predecessors' salary have tolerated for a single instant relegation to such an apartment; but the long line of Viziers had learnt the wisdom, nay the absolute necessity, of having some place on the premises to which they could retire and lie hidden, while the lightnings and thunders of the local Sultan were discharging themselves throughout the building. Mr. Gordon, certainly, had never complained of his quarters.

The P.M.'s room (as it was known) was indeed a very interesting specimen of theatrical architecture, and but one more example of the results following from the well-known difficulty of rectangulating the semi-circle. For observe that, while the auditorium of the Thespian conformed very nearly in shape to the latter geometrical figure, the shape of the site on which it was built was practically an exact square. When in conjunction with this it is remembered that the floors of the various tiers of seats had necessarily to be constructed on a series of slopes, while the architect had clung desperately to his guiding principle that any façades for which he was responsible must show a set of level and equidistant windows, it will be realised that a collection of strange and even unexpected rooms must result. This particular room, for instance, was approached by a little staircase of its own from the side of the dress-circle bar. It had five walls, all of different lengths and one of them curved; across the ceiling there ran, in a positively devilish lack of parallelism with any of the walls, a whitewashed steel girder; while the window, because it was really the upper part of a window on the stairs up to the gallery, extended from the level of the floor to a height of only thirty-six inches. A kind of wire fender in front of it prevented visitors from accidentally slipping into the street on the rare occasions when it was opened.

The walls were entirely covered with framed photographs and programmes, and the furniture consisted of a roll-top desk that wouldn't roll, a revolving armchair that wouldn't revolve, and a sofa that—but as a matter of fact the sofa was all right, and as evidence of this it may be stated that there was reclining on it at this present moment no less a person than the Chief himself.

Though the air is thick with the smoke of cigarettes, it is still possible to see what a fine-looking man Leo Cartwright is. There is just that slight accentuation of feature, that trifling exaggeration of contour which may be observed in successful barristers and American senators. But although he is now close on fifty-five, and his hair, though thick, is well powdered with grey, his figure is as good as it was thirty years ago. There is nothing about his dress on which the caricaturist could fasten, with the possible exception of the pearl and diamond tie-pin, which seems (although it isn't) just a little too good to be true. The offering of an admiring archduke, in the days when there were such things, it is the only piece of jewellery which Mr. Cartwright has ever been seen to wear.

If you examine his face in detail, expecting to discover there signs and traces of the reasons which made his wife leave him twenty-five years ago, you will not find very much to help you. His eyes are clear, with no adjacent pouches or rings, his nose is too large, but at the same time it is certainly not coarse; his mouth also, though set slightly crooked, is far from a bad mouth. His skin is only very little roughened by the constant application and removal of paint. No, from the evidence of his features, it is impossible to say that this is a man the course of whose life has ever been shaken by excess in any of the grosser connotations of the word.

Yet his whole expression, when his face is at rest, is desperately sad. If you didn't remember that forty percent, you would say, "This is the face of a man who has failed, who is haunted by the ghosts of it-might-have-been; the fire of his ambition is extinguished, and as he shivers over the ashes, he looks backward at disappointment, not forward towards hope."

III

THE ONLY OTHER OCCUPANT OF the P.M.'s room at this moment was the P.M. himself, who occupied a precarious seat on the corner of the roll-top desk. As far as it is possible to judge from his exterior, you would say that his manner indicates him to be on the defensive, and this is indeed the case. For it is a pretty sure sign that Mr. Cartwright is himself conducting offensive operations when he visits any of his lieutenants in their own rooms, instead of summoning them to the presence chamber.

Mr. Littlejohn, who has been Business Manager at the Thespian since the very beginning, could, if he chose, have told Mr. Gordon what the trouble was. But he has never regarded it as part of his duties to act as interpreter for any Personal Manager. For the symptoms which the Chief had now been showing for some weeks were recurrent ones, and were always liable to appear at any time after a Thespian success had been running for more than six months. The fact was, that after this period the Chief got deadly sick of the whole thing and longed for the stress and excitement of a new production. But he was much too wary to admit this himself, and would consequently take endless pains to fix the responsibility for terminating the run on one of his underlings. Many of the past Viziers had fallen into cunning traps laid for them in this way, and had subsequently been sacrificed to the infuriated Backers.

But Mr. Albert Gordon, though he had occupied his present post for less than a year, had learnt his Chief's ways better than the majority of his predecessors, and so far had taken very good care not to be drawn.

The discussion at the present moment was ostensibly based on the paragraph in the Sunday newspaper which had recently caused John Ormroyd such annoyance and disgust.

"I don't know which of you sent this thing to the Press," said the Chief from his sofa, "but whoever it was, ought to have known better than to put in that old gag about 'if and when.' In the first place you know perfectly well that business has been rotten for the last fortnight, and in the second place you ought to know that there's no better way of letting the public and all the other managers know it, than to use an old *cliché* like that. It's undignified."

"Business is always bad just before Christmas," replied Mr. Gordon warily.

"And this is the best way to make it worse," retorted Mr. Cartwright, flicking his ash on the carpet.

"Well, Chief, the announcement about the 'Pastor of Aarvaag' was made on your instructions. You surely wouldn't have it put in without letting them know that 'Pale People' is good for a long life still."

"Bah!" said the Chief testily, feeling himself foiled. He was silent for a moment, and then, elevating himself to a sitting position, launched a fresh attack.

"I'm not at all sure in any case that I want to do that damned Dutchman's play," he said provocatively.

Mr. Gordon correctly understood this description to apply to Dr. Bransen, the distinguished Norwegian author of the "Pastor."

"You gave him a contract," he said gently.

"You mean Littlejohn gave him a contract," replied Mr. Cartwright, with a childish disregard for the principles of legal obligation. "Littlejohn gives contracts to a great deal too many silly fools."

The Personal Manager knew as well as the Chief himself that all contracts were countersigned by the latter, but he was much too wise to mention this.

"That's where the money goes," continued Mr. Cartwright peevishly. "I've got Ormroyd coming to see me today and the Lord knows what I'm to say to him. If I let that play of his go, it's making a present of a winner to some other manager. But I can't put on everything at once."

He rose and began pacing the room.

"Now how would it be if we did that Swiss play" (thus he alluded to the unhappy 'Pastor') "for a series of matinées? Make it a real highbrow sort of affair. You know. No orchestra; that would save money. No footlights. Three bumps. Grey curtains. Amber arcs in the gallery. Special prices."

The great man's eyes began to gleam, as he sketched this outline. Unconsciously he raised his cigarette and simulated a pastoral blessing, while his wonderfully expressive face took on an ecclesiastical appearance which made you almost see the plate coming round.

DENIS MACKAIL

With a savage stab of reality Mr. Gordon pricked the bubble.

"The contract's for a regular run," he said.

The Chief sank, groaning, into the revolving chair and covered his face with his hands.

"It's too bad," he moaned. "It's too hard. Why can I never do what I want to? Why do I spend my life playing these piffling nincompoops like in this horrible 'Pale People,' when my whole soul cries out for something noble, something heroic? Why," he continued, with an unself-consciousness at once superb and pathetic, "why can't I show the public what I really am?"

Mr. Gordon opened his mouth to speak, appeared to think better of this idea, and then, once more changing his mind, uttered these memorable words:

"The public would never pay to see that."

He might have added that, pay what they might, the public would be asking to see something which it was well-nigh impossible for Mr. Cartwright to show them. But Mr. Gordon was not a philosopher. He had merely stated his business creed, which was that, when people came to the theatre, they came to buy illusion and not truth.

The Chief, however, decided to disregard this remark, and proceeded with his lamentation.

"And to make it worse," he said, "I've found the very play I've been waiting for all my life. A play with beauty, romance, delicacy, truth, pathos; and yet with humanity, red-blood, and strength." He rose to his feet again. "Why must I be tied and fettered by contracts? Why can't I pitch my caravan in the open market-place, and draw all England to see and hear the beauty of it?"

"Is it a pageant?" asked Mr. Gordon suspiciously.

"A Pageant of Life," replied the Chief, and sinking his voice to somewhere near his diaphragm, added, "and of Death."

Mr. Gordon applied his only test.

"Who is it by?" he enquired.

Mr. Cartwright shook his head wearily.

"The name," he said, having in truth forgotten it, "is of no importance. And yet one day the whole of London shall ring with it. If only," he muttered, "this cursed 'Pale People' will ever come to an end. But no, the fools won't keep away. The same old grind, the same old endless treadmill. I tell you, Gordon, something has got to be done."

Mr. Gordon was inclined to agree. Details of bookings were not and never had been confided to the Personal Manager, but he had detected no apparent falling off in the popularity of "Pale People." And yet here was his employer not only embroiled with two would-be authors of successors, but apparently just on the point of entangling himself with a third. It was all very well to get a good stock of plays about you, but this talk of production was the very dickens! If it led again, as it had before, to litigation, Mr. Gordon wouldn't give very much for the security of his own job. He knew too well in which section of the management the scapegoat would be found.

In this dangerous predicament his mind again turned to a subject which had for some days been exercising his thoughts. In his capacity as Grand Vizier he received many strange requests from persons wishing to interest the Chief in their private or public plans. Authors, actors, agents, bill-sticking contractors, and charity matinée fiends, one and all, came sooner or later to Mr. Gordon, hoping to secure through his good offices that which they mistrusted their ability to obtain by other means. And for services rendered in these cases Mr. Gordon, like other Viziers, was not above accepting this, that, or the other in return. If the Chief and Mr. Littlejohn were aware of this arrangement, they had never expressed any objection to it, and indeed, after all, Mr. Gordon never undertook to do more for his outside clients than "lay the suggestion before Mr. Cartwright" or "bring the matter personally before Mr Littlejohn." This much he was clearly entitled, if not employed, to do.

But apart from his duty to himself and his employer, the Personal Manager had also to consider his duty to a third, and at least equally important interest. It was to this interest, or rather to its most important representative, that he owed his present position. When Mr. Imray, the acknowledged leader of the Backers, had, seated in his office in London Wall Buildings, given him the letter of introduction which had secured him his present post, it was an understood matter—though no words passed between them—that Mr. Gordon should occupy that post with at least a watching brief for these gentlemen. And this he correctly interpreted to imply that, whatever his other duties might be, he must at all times do everything in his power to prolong to the utmost the runs of Mr. Cartwright's successes, and, when this could no longer be done, to frighten him away from producing anything except what Mr. Imray would describe as "gilt-edged" plays, and Mr. Cartwright as "winners."

Now the latest suggestion which Mr. Gordon had been asked to put before his Chief, and on the advantages of which he had been ruminating for the last few days, was one which he had realised from the first might prove very useful in dealing with a crisis such as the one with which he was now faced.

If he had not hitherto brought the matter to Mr. Cartwright's notice, it was partly because no such crisis had arisen, and partly because he was as yet still undecided what exact form of payment he would require from the client in question. But now the crisis was on him with a rush; the matter of payment must in this hour of danger be shelved, or rather he must simply rely on the gratitude which the Backers would, if there were any justice on earth, feel for his efforts.

For Mr. Gordon held in his possession a card which, if used now, should with any sort of luck switch his Chief's volatile attention over to a new activity that should take the place of the rehearsals and preparations for which his soul was sickening, and yet without endangering the life of "Pale People." On the contrary, it might even extend it.

If he should succeed in this, he would deserve more than well of the Backers, and he would take care that in such an event no bushel should be interposed between those gentlemen and his personal light. No one knew better than he that the position of Personal Manager at the Thespian Theatre was but a stepping-stone in his or anyone's career; but whether to higher or lower things must depend on the use he made of it, or, to be more accurate, on the use which Mr. Imray and the other Backers could be induced to believe that he was making of it.

Meanwhile time was pressing. The Chief was clearly summoning strength for another soliloquy, and Mr. Gordon must broach his scheme quickly, if he was to do so at all. He was only too well aware that the Chief's soliloquies were in the habit of forming a prelude to the Chief's effective exits, and that it would be impossible for him, as an audience of one, to recall his employer after the exit had been made. So he began hastily, and consequently a little clumsily.

"I'm very glad to have this opportunity of seeing you alone, Chief," was his opening.

"Eh?" broke in Mr. Cartwright with a nervous glance.

Mr. Gordon realised instantly the resemblance which his introductory phrase bore to that commonly used by those seeking an advance in salary, and added hurriedly: "Not on my own account."

"Ah," murmured Mr. Cartwright.

"I had a long talk a few days ago with Brisk," pursued Mr. Gordon.

"Be careful, Gordon," said the Chief, sitting suddenly upright in his chair. "Be very careful what you say to Brisk."

"Oh, that's all right," replied the P.M. "We weren't talking about the Thespian; at least not in the way you mean."

The Chief's firmly marked eyebrows shot three-quarters of an inch up his forehead, thus registering Surprise and Enquiry.

But at this point it is essential that explanation as to Mr. Brisk's identity and character should be inserted. We must, therefore, with many apologies, hold Mr. Cartwright's eyebrows in suspense during a brief intermission.

Mr. Alexander Brisk is the senior partner in the Theatre Ticket Agency of Brisk and John, the most preëminent firm of speculators on the market, and as such his importance in the world of the stage can hardly be adequately appreciated by the ordinary layman.

At every first night in every West End theatre, two of the best seats in the house are reserved for Mr. Brisk. One of these he occupies himself, and the other is generally occupied by his hat and overcoat. Now you begin to realise his power and influence, for what ordinary mortal would be allowed to treat an invitation to such a theatre as, for instance, the Thespian in this manner? On the rare occasions when the second seat contains an occupant, that occupant may be identified not as Mr. John, but as Mrs. Brisk. For Mr. John, though a magnificent business man, is also a pillar of nonconformity. Consequently although he attends to every other part of the firm's affairs with indefatigable skill and industry, he has never been inside a theatre in his life.

During the intervals of the first representation of a new play, the members of the management and of the cast rush in turn to the spy-hole in the curtain. They do this not to see their friends, not even to study the appearance of the dramatic critics, but in the hope of ascertaining from Mr. Brisk's manner or expression some clue as to his opinion of the entertainment in question. In this hope they are invariably disappointed. For behind his rimless spectacles Mr. Brisk's globular face remains completely and absolutely unmoved by the wildest farce, the most sparkling comedy, the blackest tragedy, or the most nauseating revue.

At the end of the performance there takes place, generally in a room placed at their disposal by the management, a meeting of the representatives of the various ticket agencies. And here, while the critics are dashing about in cabs, looking up their classical dictionaries and otherwise preparing, as they imagine, to mould public opinion, the real fate of the play is settled.

DENIS MACKAIL

At these meetings Mr. Brisk, by an unwritten law, always acts as Chairman. Though the other members of the fraternity make a pretence of offering their observations on the evening's entertainment, no decision is really reached until Mr. Brisk has spoken, and it may be added that what Mr. Brisk says, goes. His summing up is extremely brief, but equally definite. If he says "Rotten," then the Business Manager, who all the time is waiting outside the door, may as well go straight away and put the fortnight's notice up on the Call Board. For in that event no desperate expedient of sandwich men, newspaper competitions, or denunciations by bishops can save the play. If Mr. Brisk says "It will do," then the management may prepare themselves for a reasonable run, but, if they are wise, they will be looking about for a successor. If, however, as must happen occasionally, Mr. Brisk says "A winner," then the Business Manager will have champagne for supper, the leading lady will order another car, the humbler members of the company will breathe again, and the author will buy a new hat. For when Mr. Brisk's criticism takes this last form, it means that the management will be able to dispose of seats to the value of anything up to twenty thousand pounds in one fell swoop.

And yet Mr. Brisk has not really formed or altered public opinion by his utterance, any more than the critics will succeed in doing so in the morning papers by theirs. He merely happens to possess a judgment, corresponding to that of the highly skilled wine-taster, which has so far been infallible; and on this judgment and his reputation as its possessor the firm continues to flourish like a green bay tree; so that every year they are able to open new branches and take more space in programmes and newspapers for the publication of their one immutable advertisement.

You probably remember this slogan. It runs as follows:

> *Buy your seats from Brisk and John,*
> *The best place to get them from.*

Neither Mr. Brisk nor his partner has yet discovered that the above couplet does not rhyme and can only with some violence be made to scan. But why should they trouble about this, when the irritating effect which it has on the educated ear makes it as unforgettable as its constant repetition does to the rest of humanity?

I return hastily to Mr. Cartwright's eyebrows; but not, I hope, before you have been made to realise why it was that he told Mr. Gordon to be so very careful and why he should be so much surprised on learning that his lieutenant's conversation with the great man had not concerned the Thespian.

"It came as a bit of a shock to me too, when I first heard of it," said Mr. Gordon.

"Learnt of what?" asked the Chief. "Don't be so abstruse."

"Perhaps you knew it all the time?" continued Mr. Gordon maddeningly.

"Come, come, Gordon," said the Chief. "Is Brisk leading a double life, or what is it?"

"Well, he is in a way," replied Mr. Gordon. "Anyhow, he's the Chairman of the Local Traditional Association."

(You will remember that this was the period at which the political interests of this country were beginning, after the disruptive convulsions brought on by the war, to settle down again into two main divisions, known to their respective adherents as the Traditional and the Representative parties.)

"I fail to see," said the Chief, closing his eyes, "how that affects me, or why you should think it likely to interest me."

To emphasise his statement he rose again to his feet and moved towards the door.

"Wait a minute, Chief," said Mr. Gordon, "There's more to come."

The managerial eyebrows made a second, but much slighter ascent.

"You know that Sir George Braham has been very ill?" continued Mr. Gordon.

"I don't," replied the Chief. "And what's more, I don't know who Sir George Braham is. Really, Gordon, I wish you'd hurry up and get to the point, that is, supposing that there is one."

"Braham's the Member for Covent Garden," said the Grand Vizier, "and this is the point. Brisk tells me that there's very little chance of his getting better; in fact so little that his Association met last week to agree on a new nomination. Now this is the point. The Association didn't come to an agreement on any of the names submitted, but they did agree that they wanted a local man this time. Brisk didn't make the suggestion at the time, because he wanted to sound you first, but, if you consent, he will put forward your name at their next meeting, and I don't mind telling you that with Brisk behind it the chances of its adoption would be about a hundred to one."

Mr. Gordon paused for a moment, but the Chief neither moved nor spoke, so he dashed on again.

"There is a great deal in your favour, if you come to consider it. In the first place, nobody knows what your political opinions are, so you start with a perfectly clean slate. That's an enormous advantage. Then you've lived and worked in the Division for the best part of twenty years, you're a leading representative of its chief industry (that is, if we leave out the hotels, where they're all foreigners), and besides that, every one remembers how you were the first to close your theatre during the electricians' strike."

"I had to close it anyhow," said the Chief. "The play was a thorough frost."

"I know, I know," said Mr. Gordon; "but it helped the electricians to win all the same, and it would be worth any amount of Representative votes to you, if the thing came to an election. But Brisk says it can't. Why, there's only been one contest in the Division in the last sixty years. It's as good a cinch as the City of London, once you're adopted."

Again, Mr. Gordon paused expectantly, and again the Chief remained silent. But this time he was not unmoved, either physically or emotionally. For as the Personal Manager resumed his seat on the corner of the desk, he was treated to a truly amazing example of Leo Cartwright's powers as a pantomimist. For the moment quite unaware of his audience, the Chief had assumed an expression considerably more legislative than that of any professional politician. He might, in fact, almost have posed for a composite photograph of the Cabinet. And with this expression as the basis of his representation, he began, silently, to address an invisible assembly.

Even Mr. Gordon, hardened little ruffian and hanger-on that he was, was overwhelmed by the artistry of the performance. First of all, apparently, it was a big election meeting. The candidate's reception had been by no means unanimously cordial, but he was dealing with questions and interruptions with such frankness, such good temper, and withal such conviction, that gradually not only were the doubters converted, but the enthusiasm of his declared supporters boiled over into a tremendous demonstration of confidence and applause. But the candidate raised his hand to his throat. They must excuse him. The strain of his great labours in the service of his party and the Empire had put a heavy burden on his voice, but he could not rise to put the resolution of confidence in the grand old Traditional Party without referring to the noble work of their late member, Sir George Braham, who had literally died in harness while fighting the battles of this important and enlightened constituency. Tremendous cheering took place at this point; strong men wept and women were carried out in handfuls. Amidst a roaring accompaniment of "He's a jolly good fellow," the overtaxed candidate resumed his seat.

But not quite. He was on his feet again immediately, and this time it was clear that the scene had changed. The legislative countenance was now thrown into strong relief as he attempted to shield his eyes from the glare of the arc lights which lit up the balcony of the Town Hall. A confused but overpowering roar came from the street below, from where the clamorous populace had just seen the result hoisted on a banner by the Mayor. The candidate, or rather the new Member, as he now was, raised his hand for silence. Instantly a hush fell over the multitude, so deep that you could have heard a pin drop. Then followed the second speech. A speech of triumph and thanksgiving, but also of magnanimity towards the defeated opponent. The voters must remember that it had been a hard fight on both sides, but thank God! it had been a clean fight, a straight fight and an English fight. (Colossal cheering.) He took this declaration of his fellow-countrymen's opinion as the most encouraging sign for the future of their great Empire that there had been since Magna Carta. (More frantic cheers for Magna Carta.) But (and here he extended the right hand of friendship to the defeated candidate) they would remember that throughout this great contest his cry had ever been, not "Let the best man win!" but "Let the best cause win!"

At this point it was clear that the excited mob had carried the Town Hall by force. The new Member was borne shoulder high down the marble staircase and lifted into his car. His supporters were harnessing themselves to this triumphal vehicle, preparatory to drawing their chosen hero round the constituency, when the scene again suddenly changed.

It was now the heart of the Empire, the historic chamber in which the liberties of Englishmen and the security of the dependencies had for centuries been fought for and guarded inviolate. A representative gathering (among whom, as far as one could judge from Mr. Cartwright's expression, might be noted Gladstone, the two Pitts, Disraeli, Canning, Cobden, Burke, and the members of the present Government) had assembled to see the new Member take his seat. But for a groan of terror from the Opposition benches, there was a deathly silence as he advanced to the table and took the oath. And as he passed, still amidst silence, to the corner seat which had somehow been reserved for him, it was difficult to say whether modesty, responsibility, or efficiency were more clearly depicted on his brow.

It was the second reading of the Finance Bill and feeling was running high in every part of the House. Time and again Honourable and even Right Honourable Members were called to order for their heated and unmannerly interjections. Suddenly there was a hush. Whispers began flitting about the green benches. "The Member for Covent Garden has caught the Speaker's eye."

The maiden speech began quietly, even inaudibly. There were a few cries of "Speak up!" from the back benches. But as he warmed to his subject, the new Member's manner and delivery improved. The House settled itself to listen in rapt silence. Honourable Members began crowding in from the lobbies and smoke-room, so that presently they were standing in clusters by the doors. Meanwhile the pitiless exposure of the Opposition's duplicity and treachery in opposing the second reading went forward to the accompaniment of increasing murmurs of approval. The speech was notable not only for the cogency and clarity of the argument, not only for a knowledge of Parliamentary procedure and precedent which astonished all present, but for a delicate though pungent vein of humour which found the weak points in the enemy's armour and pierced them with shafts of satire and ridicule. The Leader of the Opposition squirmed in his seat, while the sweat poured down his face. Bursts of applause began to interrupt the maiden speech, growing in volume and enthusiasm as it proceeded, until finally, after a passionate peroration, with one last simple and dignified gesture indicating appreciation tempered with humility,—the same gesture, in point of fact, with which Mr. Cartwright was wont to retire between the tableau curtains before the lights in the auditorium of his theatre were raised,—the new Member resumed his seat. It might be understood that in the subsequent division, which only took place after the House had stormed and cheered for nearly a quarter of an hour, the Government majority reached the unparalleled figure of seven hundred and two.

Although the performance which I have just attempted to describe had represented a period not less than six weeks in length,—that is, including the intervals between the different scenes,—it had actually only occupied between two and three minutes of non-theatrical time. For the Chief, however, it had been a real experience from beginning to end, and as the green parliamentary bench on which he had just flung himself turned back into the revolving chair which, to Mr. Gordon's eyes, it had all the time remained, he let his lids drop with an appearance of complete exhaustion, while his breath could be heard coming and going in hard-drawn gusts. Truly it would seem that there must be certain disadvantages in being a very great actor.

So long did the Chief remain in this trance that Mr. Gordon at length felt compelled to attempt to rouse him from it.

"Well, how does the idea strike you, Chief?" he asked.

Mr. Cartwright wearily opened his eyes.

"I suppose I could learn up the political part of it all?" he said.

"Oh, easily, easily," replied the P.M. "There's nothing in it really."

"Wouldn't it clash with the theatre?" continued the Chief.

"Of course you couldn't be at the House in the evenings," said Mr. Gordon. "Nor on Wednesday afternoons. But it should be quite easy to put in as much time there as any one would expect of you. Quite easy."

"Is there a salary?" pursued Mr. Cartwright.

"Eight a week," said Mr. Gordon, translating into theatrical language. Noting the Chief's look of surprised contempt, he hastily added: "They all get the same, you know. And they're talking of raising it."

Mr. Cartwright appeared mollified at this intelligence, and sank again into a reverie. He wished to present to his Vizier the appearance of a man deeply exercised over the pros and cons of the problem, but as a matter of fact, from the moment that he had first, as it were, tried himself in this new part, his mind had been made up. If the Association could be induced to adopt him, they should have him. He saw at once, as Mr. Gordon had hoped he would see, the wonderful possibilities of a life consisting entirely of rehearsals, rhetoric, and publicity. For thus, in his ignorance and innocence, did the life of a Member of Parliament appear to him, and thus, to do him justice, had it appeared to Mr. Gordon. Also thus, to tell the truth, had Mr. Brisk hoped that it would appear to both Mr. Gordon and Mr. Cartwright, when there had flashed into his brain this solution of the deadlock into which the rival ambitions of its members had driven his Association.

For the time being, at any rate, Mr. Gordon's tactics had succeeded. The Chief had completely forgotten that he had orginally gone up into his Personal Manager's room in order to induce him to suggest that "Pale People" was nearing the end of its popularity. For the moment he did not care if "Pale People" went on running until all was blue; for he would be studying a new part, stepping into a new and more brilliant kind of limelight, preparing to play to a larger and more critical audience and, granted that he succeeded, winning fresh laurels for himself and his beloved theatre.

He roused himself from his contemplative catalepsy, and addressed his Vizier.

"What does Brisk expect me to do about it?" he asked. "Is he going to write to me, or what is the next stage?"

The Vizier assumed that these enquiries meant that the bait had been taken, and, concealing with difficulty his relief and satisfaction, replied:

"I think the best thing would be if you were to drop a line to Brisk, and ask him to come and see you."

"Ha!" said the Chief. "Very well. Very well. I will do that."

"And if you like, I'll give you some stuff to read about the Traditional programme," continued Mr. Gordon.

"Programme? What programme?" enquired the Chief, for whom the word had only one meaning.

"I mean their political aims and that sort of thing," explained Mr. Gordon easily, and for his easiness was instantly rebuffed.

"Thank you, Gordon," said Mr. Cartwright; "but I think I am quite able to appreciate the political tendencies of the day, without any outside assistance. However," he added graciously, "I am glad that you mentioned the matter to me. I shall certainly communicate at once with my good friend Brisk. Meanwhile there is no necessity for this matter to be discussed in the theatre. You understand?"

"Oh, certainly, Chief. Of course."

"Be it so, then," replied the Chief, with signs of a return to his earlier ecclesiastical manner; and, this being the best exit line that he could at the moment manage, he immediately turned and stalked from the room.

As the scene in the Personal Manager's apartment closes, we see that gentleman raise the receiver from his desk telephone. I think he is going to convey the latest intelligence as to the political situation in the Covent Garden Division to his friend and ally, Mr. Alexander Brisk.

IV

THE COMFORT AND CONSOLATION WHICH John Ormroyd had derived from his Sunday afternoon call on Mrs. Cartwright continued their effect, though with gradually diminishing power, until the Tuesday morning.

But by breakfast-time on this day he had begun once more to fret about the fate of his dramatic child, and with an impatience only accentuated by the previous thirty-six hours' calm. As he pushed his untasted sausages away in unjustifiable disgust, he determined that, come what might, he would force a personal interview with one of the responsible authorities at the Thespian; and further, that, if he did not obtain satisfaction from this, he would disregard the existence of the unexpired portion of the option and take the play elsewhere. In his present mood he rather welcomed than otherwise the prospect of any legal proceedings which might ensue. If they wanted a row, they should have it, and if John Ormroyd's career as a dramatist should thereby be wrecked at the very outset, he would at least have the satisfaction of knowing that he had struck a blow for justice and liberty, and that he might, in addition, get a considerable amount of free advertisement in the Press. To be perfectly fair to him, this last eventuality was only in the distant background of his thoughts, but none the less its presence in the offing was certainly no reason for weakening his new determination.

His previous assaults on the citadel had been by means of letters and telegrams, but he now decided to call to his assistance that powerful, though dangerous ally, the London Telephone Service.

A search in the directory for Leo Cartwright's private address revealed nothing, though John's expression was for a moment softened by coming on Mrs. Cartwright's printed name. He turned to the letter "T" and to the word "Thespian," where he found the following:

> Central 9081 Thespian Theatre (Bx Offce)
> Central 7056 Thespian Theatre (Mngr)
> Gerrard 4871 Thespian Theatre (Stge Dr.)

On the whole the second line seemed the most hopeful, and he gave the number to his exchange. There is no need for me to describe in detail the buzzings, the clicks, the scraps of distant conversation, and the irruptions of kind but apparently powerless operators and supervisors which followed. A work of fiction should be a relief from and not a description of the sorrows of life. It is enough to say that ten minutes later—I mean a real ten minutes, not the one which one always says one has been kept waiting—he was compelled to abandon the attempt. John's colour was slightly heightened, but his persistence was undimmed. He settled himself firmly in his chair and gave the

DENIS MACKAIL

number of the Box Office. "They'd hardly keep that line out of order, if they could help it," he said to himself.

Thirty seconds later an incredibly faint voice said: "Thespian Theatre." John took a deep breath, and with ferociously articulated emphasis said: "This is Mr. John Ormroyd. I want to speak to Mr. Cartwright's secretary." There was a pause, and then presently the faint voice said again: "Thespian Theatre."

And this was all the voice ever said, except once when it said: "Wait a minute"; and then apparently fired a pistol into the telephone. After this it became fainter and fainter and gradually died away altogether. "Suicide in a West End Box-Office," thought John, as he strained his ears to catch the last breath of his unseen acquaintance.

He was roused from these thoughts of death by a really charming voice, which said: "Number, please?"

"Central—oh, wait a minute; I've left the book on the other table. I say, half a second! I'll be back in a jiffy."

He flew across the room and dashed back with the Stage-Door number.

"Hullo!" he said.

But the charming voice had gone. A man with a very fine basso profundo had taken its place, and to him John gave the third Thespian number.

Perhaps forty-five seconds elapsed, and then—

"Ullo!" said the receiver.

John was all but blown out of the room by the volume and fury of this attack. But he just had strength to transfer the instrument to his uninjured eardrum.

"Is that the Thespian Theatre?" he asked.

"Ullo! Yes."

"This is Mr. John Ormroyd speaking."

"Mr. Hormroyd. Ullo! Yes."

"Can I speak to Mr. Cartwright or his secretary, please?"

"Sekertary. Yes. Ullo!" said the modern Stentor, and a sound of receding footsteps was heard.

John drew his handkerchief across his forehead with his disengaged hand. While he had no wish to commit himself, he yet felt a strange hope, almost amounting to confidence, that he was at last going to talk to some one who would be able to hear, even possibly to understand, what he said. The foundations of this hope would scarcely bear examination, but still—A sound of distant laughter became audible, and the novelist's brain instantly set to work on the scenario of a short story in which a woman's laugh, heard over the telephone, was to play a prominent and pathetic part. He might make her injured in a fire, after rescuing her child. Yes, that was it. And the mother, though longing to see the child before she died, knew that her appearance would so terrify it that it would fear the memory of her. So she spoke to it on the telephone, and the child, hearing her laughter, was comforted. And the young Doctor—

"ULLO!!" It was Stentor back again.

"Yes?" said John.

"'Ere you are, Miss," said Stentor, and a new voice came on the line; a voice which in some indescribable way managed to convey a suggestion of *pince-nez*.

"Is that Mr. Ormroyd?" said this new voice.

"Yes," said John, thankful to hear something in the pronunciation of his name which seemed to indicate that it was not quite unknown to the speaker.

"I'm very sorry, Mr. Ormroyd, that Mr. Cartwright can't speak to you at the moment. He's on the stage."

("I know that," thought John; and then it occurred to him that the last statement referred in fact to Mr. Cartwright's present whereabouts, and was not, as had at first appeared, a gratuitous description of his professional occupation.)

"Well, look here," he said aloud, but was interrupted before he could continue.

"But he asked me to tell you that he would be very glad if you would lunch with him on Thursday. Would you pick him up here at twenty minutes past one?"

"Would you tell him I should be delighted?" said John.

"Certainly. Thank you very much, Mr. Ormroyd. Good-bye."

Click.

John sat back in his chair and again mopped his brow. He had all the mental sensations of a man who, having prepared to exert his whole force in opening a supposedly stiff window, finds that his wife has had the carpenter in without telling him, and is consequently precipitated into the street. How was he to know that in Miss Lemon, the Chief's secretary, he had one of his most fervent admirers; that the strap of red webbing on her desk at that very moment encircled a library copy of "The Sky Is Falling"; and that in consequence she had rushed this lunch engagement on the Chief with one of those sudden outbursts of bullying efficiency which characterise all good private secretaries?

John, as I say, knowing nothing of this, spent the next two days in racking his brains to try and imagine what it was that had suddenly raised the Thespian portcullis, against which he had for so many months battered in vain with letter and telegram. If he incline to one theory more than to another, it was to the unjustifiable assumption that Mrs. Cartwright had in some way intervened. Not directly, of course; but through some friend.

At a quarter-past one, therefore, on the same day that witnessed the unfolding of Mr. Albert Gordon's strange plan, we may see the distinguished novelist, Mr. John Ormroyd, drive up in a taxicab to the front of the Thespian Theatre. His toilet has obviously been the subject of some care, but on the whole he has achieved reasonable success in presenting an appearance neither so rich as to suggest that a thousand pounds one way or the other will make no difference, nor so poor as to inspire a belief that he will be grateful for anything that he can get. He vanishes through the swing doors at the front of the theatre, and reappears a minute later from the same opening, having meanwhile been directed by the Box-Office Keeper to go round to the Stage entrance.

"Down on the right," the Box-Office Keeper had said, and John accordingly plunges down a covered alley past the side doors of a public house. The alley takes a kink and opens out into a little oblong courtyard, against the walls of which are leaning a number of old canvas flats. Through some defect in ratiocination the management has papered the little courtyard copiously with bills of various sizes all advertising "Pale People," although, as far as can be gathered, the only persons likely to read them are its own employees. At the far end of the yard John detects his goal, a pair of narrow swing doors with a lamp over them, and on the lamp the romantic words "Stage Door." As he advances towards this, a sudden thought strikes him. "I hope no one will take me for a damned actor," he mutters to himself.

So much for human gratitude from the man who is living in the hope that one day the damned actors will be painting their faces and attiring their limbs in order to give utterance to the words of his pen.

He reaches the swing doors and inserts himself between them. Inside his vision is greeted with a view of stone stairs, ascending and descending, but in each case disappearing almost immediately round a right angle. Opposite the swing doors, and consequently lower than them by five steps, is an aperture, the bottom half of which is filled up with a kind of semi-door. You have probably noticed that a similar architectural feature is commonly to be seen in mews, but I have been unable to trace the name of the inventor.

John descended to this aperture and put his head through it in the hopes of discovering a porter of some sort, but in vain. All he saw was a little gas stove, an armchair, a telephone, a clock, a number of hooks with keys on them, and a kind of diminutive postal sorting office, in the pigeon-holes of which were distributed a quantity of letters. Hesitating to proceed further, either up or down the stairs, he turned to the perusal of the notices on a green baize board which was fixed to the wall by the side of the half-door.

These were mostly typewritten on the elaborately headed paper which already meant so much in his life.

"In future," said the first one, "the curtain will rise on 'Pale People' at 8.15 P.M., and at 2.30 P.M. on Wednesdays and Saturdays." The Stage Manager's signature was appended, and the notice was dated the previous July.

"What extraordinary people actors must be," thought John, "not to know what time their own play begins."

His eye passed on.

"CALL," said the next notice in capital letters. "Tuesday next 11 A.M. Act Three All Concerned and Understudies. This call is cancelled."

He puzzled over this for a bit, but soon gave it up, and began reading a printed notice drawing attention to the fact that the annual meeting of the Catholic Stage Needlework and Beneficent Guild would be held on the 22nd December at the Polygon Theatre, by kind permission of Ben Baumer, Esq. He was halfway through the long list of Vice-Presidents, when suddenly—

"YES, SIR?" said a voice just behind him.

Stentor's approach in felt slippers had been completely noiseless, and John spun round gasping.

"I—I had an appointment with Mr. Cartwright," he said.

"Mr. Ormroyd?" said the door-keeper.

"Yes."

"Would you step this way? Mr. Cartwright won't be a minute."

John followed his guide up a flight and a half of the stone stairs, at the top of which the latter turned the handle of a door.

"In 'ere," he said.

So John pushed the door open and went in. It closed again behind him, and it is to be presumed that the felt slippers retired in search of the Chief.

The room was so dark that it was probably quite thirty seconds before John saw the girl, and it might have been even longer, if his attention had not been drawn to a sound which she made.

A curious, snuffling, gulping sound.

A sound which single men very seldom hear, but a sound which they have mostly learnt to treat with the utmost circumspection and fear.

"Good Lord!" said John to himself, eyeing the door. "What on earth am I to do?"

The sound continued.

"I can't stay here," he muttered, and, moving quickly towards the only exit, he hit his leg hard against the corner of a lurking table.

The pain was sharp and sudden, but the emergency was tremendous. Though his face expressed the torture which he felt, not a sound escaped him. And then—CRASH! His other foot, entangled in the cord of the telephone, brought the whole apparatus down on the floor. The concealed bell gave a solitary, ironic ting, and simultaneously the worst happened.

The girl's last shred of self-control vanished, and she fairly began to howl. No delicate sobs these, but the real nursery article.

"Woo-hoo. Hoo-hoo. (Sniff.) Ha-hoo! Hoo-her! Er-her-hoo!!" she went.

"Damn!" said John.

"Wer-her!" wept the girl.

Even in this horrible crisis John remembered the telephone, and hastily stooped to replace the receiver before crossing the room.

She was sitting sideways on a chair, her arms crossed over the back and her face buried in them. Her little shoulders moved up and down in synchronisation with her sobbing.

John advanced a hand gingerly, and patted one of them.

"There, there," he said.

"Hoo-hoo-wer!" repeated the girl; and it was probably at this moment that his emotions began to be complicated by the extraordinarily attractive nape which he found presented to him.

"Come, come!" he tried.

Gulp.

He redoubled his efforts, and evolved a third formula.

"*That's* better," he said. "*That's* better." And again he laid his hand on the nearest shoulder.

This time it was as if his fingers had formed the terminals of an electric coil. The girl gave a start and a shiver, and then suddenly she had sprung to the other side of the little room.

"Don't you dare to touch me!" she said.

"I beg your pardon. No, certainly not," said John.

Was this little scene, he wondered, a common occurrence among the temperamental denizens of the world behind the curtain? And if so, what was the correct procedure supposed to be in his case? He was not given more than an instant for thought, though, as his extraordinary fellow-prisoner appeared determined to work off the rest of her repertoire of emotional noises as quickly as she could.

"Ha, ha, ha!" she laughed hysterically. "I'm sorry. I can't help laughing. It's too awful. I don't know who you are. I thought it was—ha, ha. . ."

And then—Wallop!

And there she was in a dead faint on the floor.

"This is too much," said John, rushing to the door.

"Hi!" he yelled, with his head out on the stairs, and again, "Hi!"

Dead silence everywhere.

He suddenly realised that he was very hot, and slipped his overcoat off quickly as he reëntered the little room.

There she was, still lying flat on the ground, with her arms flung out on either side.

"Good Lord! How awful this is!" thought John.

"But she's infernally pretty," he added at once, and began looking about for some kind of liquid with which to attempt to shock her back into consciousness. The possibilities of the ink on the desk were quickly rejected, but behind a screen in a corner of the room he found a fixed wash-basin with a cold tap over it. He saturated his handkerchief and, returning to the lifeless body, knelt by it and began dabbing at the girl's face. It must be recorded that although he was fully aware that by this treatment of his handkerchief and trousers he was entirely spoiling the appearance which he had so carefully prepared for the benefit of Leo Cartwright, yet at the same time he felt no regret for this sacrifice. In fact, strange as it may appear, he was rather enjoying himself; and as he dabbed away at the fair unknown's countenance, he was already considering the possibility of inserting this incident into the serial story on which he was at this time working.

"When she comes round," he thought, "she'll say, 'Where am I?' Now what ought I to say? If I was a hero, I should say, 'Do not be alarmed. You are in safe hands.' But I'm not sure that that is really a very satisfactory answer. . ."

Further consideration of this problem was interrupted by the raising of a pair of very long-lashed eyelids and the disclosure of a pair of very large violet-coloured eyes. To John's surprise, the girl seemed in no doubt at all as to her whereabouts.

"I'm awfully sorry," she said. "Do you know that's the first time I've ever fainted, but. . ."

She suddenly sat up, and John reverted to one of his earliest consolatory remarks.

"There, there," he said.

"Oh, I'm all right," said the girl. "At least I should be if you could find something to dry me with. I'm afraid I've made you spoil your handkerchief."

"Oh, that doesn't matter," said John, gallantly stuffing the sodden lump of linen into his breast pocket.

"I wonder if I looked a fool when I did that," he thought, as he began rummaging behind the screen in the corner.

"I've found a clean towel," he said, re-emerging in triumph.

"Splendid!" said the girl.

She was sitting in a chair now, and there was a little more colour in her face; but as she took the towel, she still looked dangerously fragile.

"Feeling better?" asked John.

She nodded.

"Anything I can get you?" he continued.

"Anything you can get me?" she repeated. And then with a weak laugh, "Only some food, I should think."

"Food?"

She nodded wearily.

"Are you hungry?" asked John, with idiotic persistence.

"Oh, no," said the girl. "I only haven't had anything to eat today. That's all."

"Nothing to—" John leapt at her and caught her by the wrist. "You poor child, you must come with me and have some lunch at once. Here, where's my coat? Have you got anything else? No? Come on, then!"

A demon of activity seemed to have seized him. He dragged her, in spite of her feeble protests, out of the room. Partly dragged and partly carried her down the flight and a half of steps. The door-keeper's box was empty, and in another minute they were under the archway leading into the main street.

"Hi! Taxi!" bellowed John, waving his stick frantically. This volume of sound emerging from the narrow tunnel encountered and arrested a roving taxicab. It drew up to the curb. John pushed his charge violently into the far corner of the back seat, and turned to the driver.

"Serene Grill Room," he said, and, leaping into the cab, pulled the door to with a slam.

After all, a grill room is a better place for confidences than any restaurant.

Besides, where else would you take a starving woman?

V

THE STAGE DOOR-KEEPER'S FELT SLIPPERS had borne him on a tortuous course through the rabbit warren of the Thespian Theatre before he eventually ran the Chief to earth on the stairs outside Mr. Gordon's room.

"Mr. Ormroyd?" repeated the Chief. "Yes, I'll be down in a moment, Garrod." He proceeded along the slope of the corridor behind the dress circle and through the iron door which formed one of the means of communication with his room; while Garrod, finding that the Chief had nothing to add to the message which he had already automatically given to the visitor, made his way laboriously back across the stage to resume the conversation with his friend the Property Master, which had been interrupted by the sound of the swing doors on John's arrival.

Leo Cartwright's thoughts were still entirely occupied with the intelligence which he had just received from his Vizier, and he paused in the saloon attached to his dressing-room to repeat some of his more successful Parliamentary gestures before a pier glass. Evidently the reproduction satisfied his critical taste, for he went to the door of the room and called out: "Miss Lemon!"

Efficient, hideous, punctual Miss Lemon appeared from the den in which she kept her typewriter and led her life during the greater part of her working day. John Ormroyd's supposition as to her eyeglasses is immediately confirmed as she enters the room.

"Good-morning, Chief."

This was their first meeting today.

"Good-morning, Miss Lemon. I want you to take a letter for me."

Miss Lemon silently produced a notebook and pencil, and delicately licked the point of the latter.

"Er—" said the Chief.

The pencil hung poised, ready to dash away at the first recordable sound which Mr. Cartwright should utter.

My dear Brisk (said the Chief)

I understand that you and Gordon have recently been discussing the—er—possibility of my name being—er— submitted to the Covent Garden Traditional Association in the event of a vacancy occurring. I understand—no, I've said that. Begin again.

I am, of course, very sorry to hear that Sir George Braham's illness should be regarded so seriously, but I am aware that in these public matters it is often necessary to— er—look ahead, and to be prepared for contingencies which we should all regret.

I think the best thing would be if we could have a little talk on the subject some time soon. If you would be good enough to telephone me at the theatre, I will—er— endeavour to see you at any time convenient to yourself.

Believe me, yours very truly

"There!" said the Chief. "That's to Alexander Brisk, Esquire. You know the address. Oh—and mark it 'Personal.' And if Mr. Brisk rings up, I'll cut any other engagement."

"Very good," said Miss Lemon. "Is there anything else?"

And then there occurred an incident which would have caused Mr. Gordon, had he been present, to tear his raiment and scatter ashes on his head. The Chief's wandering eye fell on the brown-paper jacket of a typewritten play which was lying on the table. He picked it up, opened it at random and stood absorbed. Five, ten, fifteen minutes passed. Mr. Gordon, your plans are in great jeopardy at this moment. If you acknowledge any gods or saints, you had better pray to them at once, for this is the play which the Chief mentioned to you in your room just now with such alarming enthusiasm, and by the look in his face he appears to be on the point of reaching a decision which will make all your efforts to create a non-theatrical diversion fall powerless to the ground.

Miss Lemon permitted herself to give one interrogative tap with her pencil.

"This is a most remarkable play," said the Chief. "I think I'll write a letter to the author. Just take this down:

Dear Sir,
Your four-act drama "Romance to the Rescue" has been sent to me to read by the Trafalgar Agency, and I may say at once that it has interested me more than any play which I can remember for a long time.

"What's that, Miss Lemon?"

The point of Miss Lemon's pencil had snapped at this extraordinary outburst of praise.

"It's all right. I have another one," she said, and prepared to continue.

I gather from the fact that your name is unfamiliar to me (resumed Mr. Cartwright), that you are a beginner; and if this is the case, I should be very glad if you could spare the time to come and see me here. I think I could help you by suggesting one or two places where, as it appears to me, your inexperience in stage technique has led you into avoidable weaknesses. But apart from these minor faults, your play seems to me to show far more than ordinary promise, and I have little or no doubt that with these alterations it should be possible to add it to my repertoire. If you will be good enough to drop me a line, I shall be very glad to send you a Box for "Pale People" for any performance convenient to yourself, and to have a talk with you afterwards, if you will come round and see me.

Believe me, yours very truly

"There!" said Mr. Cartwright, and, still clutching the typescript, he moved quickly towards his hat and coat. He knew that Miss Lemon was regarding him with disapproval, and he knew that, strictly speaking, he deserved it; but he felt a curious elation of spirit at having for the first time in his life spoken his real mind to an author, and not having decried the goods which he wanted to purchase. So, still avoiding his secretary's eye, he moved out into the corridor.

But Miss Lemon called after him.

"Mr. Cartwright!" she said.

Confound the woman!

"Yes?" he shouted through the open door.

"You've not forgotten that Mr. Ormroyd is lunching with you, have you?"

"Good Lord! I'd quite forgotten."

He ran down the stairs, calling "Garrod!" as he went

Garrod, rising from his subterranean conference, met the Chief by the Stage Door.

"Where's Mr. Ormroyd?"

"In the waiting-room, sir."

"Just tell him I'm ready."

Garrod ran up the stairs, but in a moment he had reappeared.

"I'm very sorry, sir, but Mr. Ormroyd's gone."

"Gone?"

"Yes, sir. Hat and coat and everything. There was a young lady waiting to try and see you too, sir, but—"

"Never mind that. What's the time?"

Garrod peered into his box to look at the clock.

"Ten minutes past two, sir."

"My wretched memory," said the Chief in a voice of despair. "Of course he couldn't wait. What will he think of me? Miss Lemon!" he added, at the top of his voice.

To his surprise Miss Lemon appeared instantaneously round the corner of the stairway.

"You never told me—" she began, but the Chief broke in.

"Miss Lemon, write a letter at once to Mr. Ormroyd and tell him how extremely sorry I am for my apparent rudeness in keeping him waiting. Apologise. Pile it on. And say will he lunch any day next week except the matinées, or will he come and see me any other time that suits him. Send it off by hand. Forge my signature."

"Oh, certainly, Mr. Cartwright, but—"

"What is it?"

"The name of that author you wrote to just now—you never told it me."

"Didn't I?" The Chief plucked the brown cover from under his arm and turned to the first page.

"Take it down now, then," he said. "It's to David Lawrence, Esquire, and address it care of the Trafalgar Agency."

The swing doors flapped in quickening diminuendo, as the great man passed up the alley.

III

THREE LETTERS

I

MR. ALEXANDER BRISK WAS CLOSETED IN conference with his partner and engaged on the dissection of the firm's monthly statement of expenditures and receipts, when the district messenger arrived in the shop below with the first of Mr. Cartwright's letters. In spite of the slump referred to by Mr. Gordon as inseparable from this particular season of the year, there was nothing in the monthly statement to dishearten either of the partners. Well aware of the annual falling-off of audiences just before the opening of the pantomimes, Messrs. Brisk and John had as usual taken care to diminish their purchases of blocks of seats. Their profits on this branch of their business were, therefore, undoubtedly low, though higher than during the previous December; but as an offset against this, they had recently made a most satisfactory contract with an alien orchestra, whose great success at dances and private parties was producing very succulent percentages in the firm's books. In addition to this, a speculative purchase of a bankrupt stock of talking-machines had been going off like hot and very expensive cakes. Finally, Mr. John had six weeks ago secured, in the face of incredible competition, the publishing rights of Mrs. Willoughby Wilkinson's new Mesopotamian Song-Cycle, "The Caravan of Love," and the advance orders for this work, both in Great Britain and the overseas dominions, were a great deal more than gratifying. Mr. John had, in fact, characterized them as stupendous.

It was accordingly into a very serene atmosphere that the commissionnaire attached to this main establishment arrived with Mr. Cartwright's letter and the enquiry as to whether an answer was to be expected.

Mr. Brisk opened the communication and glanced quickly at it.

"No. No answer," he said.

The commissionnaire saluted and withdrew.

"What do you think of this?" continued Mr. Brisk, tossing the letter across the table to his partner.

Mr. John was a gentleman who regarded his own opinion on any subject as a matter not lightly to be given or casually to be received. He read the letter three times, held it up to the light as if searching for traces of invisible ink, and subjected both sides of the envelope to a critical survey, before making any utterance.

Finally he said:

"Well, you can have him, if you want him."

Mr. Brisk nodded slowly several times. He appeared to share his partner's belief.

"It's a good move," he said.

"But there's one great difficulty," replied Mr. John.

"I know," said Mr. Brisk. "I shall have to go into that when I see him."

"He won't like that," said Mr. John.

"Then," replied Mr. Brisk, "he will have to lump it."

And with these cryptic but ominous words, the partners turned again to the examination of their ledgers, and the scene closes.

II

THE GRILL ROOM AT THE Serene Hotel is a room of many contradictions. For in the first place, although located on the mezzanine floor, it has been constructed with the endeavor of giving the illusion that it is in the cellar; and with such success that it has been found necessary to detail a special page-boy to remain on duty just outside the entrance, so as to prevent those who have lunched or dined even moderately well from attempting to leave the premises by an ascent to the bedroom floors. Then, again, you will be well advised to avoid a seat near the grill, if you wish to keep warm, or near the fountain, if you wish to keep cool. For the former is only an electrically lighted imitation of a real cooking-range, intended by the architect to give character to the room (the actual preparation of food takes place in adjacent offices); while the main flues of the hotel heating apparatus pass up through the wall just behind the fountain, and the water is consequently so warm that it has been found impossible to keep the goldfish in it for which this feature was originally planned. Further contradictions may be observed in the shaded candles on every table which are never lighted, in the microscopic music-gallery in which no band has ever been seen, and (but this, after all, is common to every grill room) in the ventilators which do not ventilate.

In one respect, however, your anticipations of a visit to the Serene Grill Room are invariably satisfied. You go there expecting the bill to be more than you think it possibly can be, and it always and without exception is.

The journey in a taxicab from the Thespian to the Serene can hardly take more than four minutes. Indeed, except in the case of emergency, only the very rich or the very feeble would ever dream of traversing the short distance otherwise than on foot. John shot one or two brief glances at his companion as they bowled along, but she remained rigid in her corner of the cab; her eyes half-closed and the shadow of her hat obscuring any expression that might lurk in them. She was still very pale.

The cab drew up at the entrance to the Grill Room and a grand duke opened the door. John stepped out and handed the driver a florin, and then, with perhaps his first glimmering of self-consciousness, turned to see whether it would be necessary for him to lift his new acquaintance out of her corner. To his surprise, for he had been unaware of any movement on her part, he found her standing beside him on the pavement, with one hand slightly outstretched, as if seeking to balance herself by some invisible support.

The possibility of a second fainting fit overtaking her in the street was not to be welcomed. He seized her by the arm, and dashed into the building towards the lift, hoping, as he did so, that no one would mistake them for criminal and detective. The resemblance certainly existed.

As they stepped from the lift at the mezzanine floor, he thought he heard a murmur in his ear.

"What's that?" he said, leaning a little towards her.

"Do I look all right?" she repeated.

John was not so young that he did not recognize in these words a feminine formula almost invariably used at the entrances to hotels, restaurants, and other places of public entertainment. He made the usual automatic reply, which, if he had known it, had before this caused several very attractive women to take quite a dislike to him.

"Perfect," he said, moving towards the door of the Grill Room.

And then something in the earnest and anxious tone of the question, which had at first escaped him, seemed to catch his attention. He stopped and gave his companion a direct look.

"I mean—yes—perfect!" he said.

My dear John, if you could have answered the questions of some of those other lovely ladies with that sound in your voice, you might—well, much might have happened.

The head waiter advanced to meet them.

"A quiet corner, if you can manage it," said John.

"Certainly, sir. This way, madame."

A sofa ran round three sides of a little alcove, enclosing a table. At a gesture from their guide a minion drew the table a little way out, and the guests took their places on the sofa at right angles to each other; though not before a second minion had relieved John of his hat and coat. The table was trundled back into its original position, and a third waiter appeared at John's side. He held a small tear-off pad of paper in his left hand, and, by his action of passing a pencil over it in rapid aerial convolutions, signified that he was willing to receive orders.

"Oysters," said John. "Lots of oysters. Let's have 'em at once."

The waiter made a signal to a boy and in another instant the oysters were on the table, followed immediately by a plated compendium containing all the vegetable, mineral, and chemical adjuncts which the mind or palate of man can ever have associated with this dish.

Meanwhile John and the waiter became confidential. Murmurs passed between them, and the pencil flew over the surface of the pad.

"What will you drink?" asked John, turning to the girl.

"Water, please."

"Send the wine, waiter," said John, turning to the man at his side. "Water," he continued, "is a very excellent liquid. In its own way there is nothing like water. But for you I prescribe something a little more devilish."

The girl didn't smile, and he was relieved to find that the wine-waiter had appeared by his side. There was more conspiratorial muttering and some reference to a leather-bound book, and then the cup-bearer withdrew.

John turned again to his companion. The brim of that most intriguing hat still concealed her eyes.

"I ordered oysters," he said, "because they were the only thing I could think of that we could get without waiting. I hope you don't hate them?"

"No, thank you."

"But we've got some solider stuff coming."

"You're very good."

"Oh, no. Not at all. Don't say that. . ." He even added some further imbecile variations of this negative before tailing off into silence. The girl did not speak again, and he picked up his little trident and began on his own lunch, but glancing at her surreptitiously from time to time.

It was unfortunate, he thought, that about the seventh time he did this he should find that the brim had been raised and that he was gazing

DENIS MACKAIL

straight into those enormous eyes. The distinguished novelist, Mr. John Ormroyd, actually blushed, and tried to cover his discomfiture by a very amateurish cough.

The girl smiled at him.

"I don't know what you think of me," she said.

"Don't you? I—" A voice somewhere inside him gave an angry whisper of "Cad!" and while he was still smarting under this rebuke, the oyster shells were removed, and the next course, together with the wine, appeared.

John seemed to have come to some resolution.

"My name is Ormroyd," he said suddenly. "John Ormroyd."

If he had ever been guilty of the least trace of conceit, the reception of this statement must have done that conceit a lot of good. His name had obviously conveyed absolutely nothing to her, but she looked at him seriously and replied:

"My name is Smith. Elizabeth Smith."

She must have detected a look of suspicion in her host's face, for she broke out into the most delightful little laugh.

"It is really," she said. "Isn't it awful. Though I don't know why you don't believe me."

"Oh, but I do, I did," lied John emphatically, and proceeded with his peculiar method of cross-examination by saying: "I write books."

"Oh, no!" said Miss Smith in unfeigned admiration. "Will you put this into a book?" she added.

"I—oh, no. Certainly not."

"But why not?"

Internal inhibition could not stop him answering:

"Because I don't know enough about you."

"You might call it 'The Starving Idiot'," she proceeded.

"But why 'idiot'?"

"Because I think I'm a perfect fool."

"But surely you're something else as well?"

He was rewarded by another laugh.

"I thought I was an actress," she said.

"And you're not?"

"You can't be an actress if you've never acted."

Now why should John feel such extraordinary pleasure at hearing this statement, a statement, by the way, which as a general truth leaves very much to be desired?

Anyhow he did.

But all he said was, "Oh," in a tone which was meant to imply limited comprehension and a wish for further enlightenment.

"I suppose it's a very ordinary story," said Miss Smith. "My—my family live abroad. I thought I could act. I had a little money, so I left them and came over here to try and get work."

"Yes?"

"I've spent the money and I haven't got the work. That's all."

"But would no one. . ."

"I've been everywhere. I've seen all sorts of managers. Some kind and some not. But they wouldn't have me. They wouldn't let me try. I'd been to the Thespian before, and I believe perhaps I could have got a part there, but—"

"But what?"

"A horrible man. . ."

"What horrible man?"

"I don't know his name. But he was horrible; insulting. He tried—he tried to kiss me. I can't understand how a man like Leo Cartwright—"

"My God!"

John had shouted so loud that the fat man in the next alcove swallowed his coffee the wrong way. Three waiters rushed to the scene, but, finding nothing worse than an apoplectic luncher struggling for breath, retired again.

"Why—what is it?" exclaimed Miss Smith.

"I've just remembered," said John. "Leo Cartwright. I promised to lunch with him today. He's got a play of mine. I'd gone to the theatre to meet him. Good Lord! What on earth shall I do?"

"And I've made you forget!"

The remorse, the self-condemnation in the tone of these words were indescrible. Once again tears stood in Miss Smith's eyes, once again her mouth puckered into that childish expression of grief. John would have been stony-hearted, indeed, if he had remained untouched. And as a matter of fact he was very far from stony-hearted.

"You!" he said. "Why, I wouldn't let Cartwright have that play of mine now if he gave me a million pounds for it. Let his people try to kiss you, did he? I'd like to. . ."

He paused to think what fate would meet the deserts of the kind of man who tried to kiss Miss Elizabeth Smith, and, seeking inspiration from another look at her face, was sensible of an immediate collapse and shifting of all moral values.

"I think I'll have a brandy," he muttered, and called to the waiter. But to himself he thought, "I only wish I'd got some people's pluck."

"But you mustn't let me make any difference," said Miss Smith. "It wouldn't be fair; especially after you've been so kind. You must make them take your play. I'm sure it's wonderful. Besides, I expect that man behaves like that to everybody, only I didn't know it."

"More fool he!" thought John, but he only glared at the tablecloth.

"Wouldn't you like to telephone to the theatre now, and explain?" continued Miss Smith.

"No!" said John rudely. And then, seeing her shrink at his violence, he said: "I'm very sorry. I didn't mean to shout again. But really, that kind of behaviour makes me sick. If Cartwright wants me, he can send for me; and if he does, I shall tell him the way his people go on, and what I found in his waiting-room."

"Oh, no!" said Miss Smith, in horror. "I couldn't bear it if that awful man heard I'd ever come back again. I'm so ashamed to think that I did, only—" She broke off, and then added: "Besides, it couldn't do any good."

John gulped at his brandy, and was heard to murmur something about teaching somebody a lesson.

"It would make me very unhappy, if I thought—" pursued Miss Smith.

"You needn't," John interrupted. "I'm afraid I was talking rot. You must forgive me."

"But rather nice rot?" suggested Miss Smith.

John thawed.

"Well, I meant it well," he said.

They both smiled.

"I say," said Miss Smith.

"'m?" (I'm afraid John's mouth was full.)

"I wish you'd tell me something about your play. I do wish you would."

"Oh," said John airily, "it's pretty fair rubbish really, you know. It's the story of a book I once wrote. It's about a fellow who. . ."

He launched forth into a long description of the pretty fair rubbish. To tell the truth, he made but a poor job of it. He was always forgetting that he had left out some important detail in the plot; continually saying, "Oh, I meant to tell you that in the First Act you see her hide the letter in a book," or, "Oh, I forgot to say that he tells his servant right at the beginning that he is going abroad," and so on. He also manifested a tendency to reproduce long passages of the dialogue, without distinguishing the characters otherwise than by the terms "the fellow" and "the other fellow." But never in the history of the stage has a play met with such a reception as that afforded by Miss Elizabeth Smith to John's rendering of "Odd Man Out." Her eyes shone, and her breath came in gasps, as the story developed. Not even at that place in the last act, where the restrictions of the theatre (as understood by the author) had made an already sufficiently improbable incident a hundred times more improbable, and where the long arm of coincidence had been extended as though on the rack, not even here did she give any sign of the affront which you would have said must indubitably have been put on her interest and intelligence.

Under the encouragement of her enthusiasm, John's offhand manner left him, and as he warmed up towards the climax he even assayed to differentiate between the persons of the drama by strange and uncouth modulations in his voice. Yet even this additional barrier between probability and illusion failed to disturb Miss Smith. She accepted the tremulous heroine, the husky lover, and the growling husband as complete and credible personalities. And when the curtain (represented by John's hand) fell on the last, meaty moment, when he paused, overcome for the thousandth time by the power of his own creation, more in a stupor of self-satisfaction than in expectation of adequate comment, real tears stood once again in Miss Smith's eyes, as she said:

"It's wonderful. It's quite wonderful!"

John shrugged his shoulders. He knew so well that in thirty seconds he would hate himself for having shown off before this child, and that the reaction of disbelief in his play was certainly due in less than forty-five, that he must be forgiven his one, brief moment of pose.

"You know, I can't help it. In spite of everything, I still adore the stage," added Miss Smith.

Yes, that was it, thought John. The Stage. That was what they all adored. Not the literature. Not the poetry. Not even the rare moments of pictorial beauty. But the stuffy, smelly, ill-lighted labyrinth on the other side of the curtain. The childish enjoyment of a place of mystery, a place into which other people couldn't get, a place of perpetual deception, perpetual squalor, and everlasting romance. Yes, damn it all! and it was just his share in this adoration—in his heart of hearts he knew it—that was always luring him towards the theatre, that would make any number of editions of the printed word taste bitter in his mouth, as long as only others were responsible for the word which is spoken.

And yet, how was it possible to forget that it was in a theatre that that blackguard. . . ? He shot a glance at his guest and for the second time had the good or ill fortune to encounter her direct gaze.

"I'm afraid I got rather carried away," he said, a little sheepishly.

"I adore enthusiasm," replied Miss Smith. "I think that was really why I wanted to leave my family. They none of them ever had any. And now. . ."

"Ah, yes. And now," said John, pulling himself together. "That's exactly the point. What are you going to do now?"

"When we've finished lunch?"

"Yes."

"I shall borrow five shillings from you."

"Yes?"

"Do you know," said Miss Smith, interrupting herself, "I rather like you. Any other man would have said, 'What, only five?'"

John had nearly said this himself, but there was no point in telling her so, so he went on:

"Well, but what will you do with the five shillings?"

"I shall send a telegram to—to where I came from."

"Saying?"

"Saying: 'I surrender. Please telegraph money for my return.' I may think of a cheaper way of putting it, but that, roughly, will be the sense of it."

Poor Miss Smith! She tried to smile as she said this, but the actual utterance of the word "surrender" had proved worse than she had expected, and it was only a dismal kind of smile.

"But," said John, "I thought you said they had no enthusiasm."

Miss Smith nodded.

"I can't have you going back to them, then. It's not right. It's not sensible. I shan't lend you the five shillings."

"Then I shall starve."

Really, Miss Smith, how you do exaggerate! Don't you know that there are all kinds of charitable organisations simply longing to lend you that five shillings, merely provided that they can ask you a lot of impertinent and offensive questions first? Besides, surely you can sell something.

If these are the cynical reader's thoughts, they were certainly not those of John Ormroyd. When he heard Miss Smith say that she should starve, in that tone of voice, he knew that she would starve. And instantly his one thought was not of how he might shift his recently assumed responsibility elsewhere, not of the endless vista of difficulties which he was preparing for himself if he did not immediately do so, but quite simply of how he was to stop her from starving, without sending her back to the unenthusiastic relations. For to those relations John had conceived a sudden, strange, but overpowering dislike.

He extracted two half-crowns from his trousers pocket and placed them on the table.

"I do that," he said, "as a guarantee of good faith, and as evidence to you of my solvency. But before we take this desperate step of telegraphing to your family, are you quite sure that there isn't any other solution? If they won't have you on the Stage, isn't there some other profession that you could try? Couldn't you be a secretary, or—or something?" he concluded vaguely.

"I don't think you understand," said Miss Smith. "I haven't got time to look for another job now, even if I had the training. I've paid for my room up till Saturday, but do you suppose I should have gone without breakfast this morning and practically without dinner last night, if I hadn't had to?"

"I beg your pardon," said John. "But still I must say I don't like to be the means of sending you back to that family, if it can be helped. I don't somehow like that word 'unenthusiastic.' And the more I look at you, to be perfectly frank, the greater my dislike for it becomes."

"I don't quite—"

"Wait a minute. I'm thinking."

I don't know whether John was quite truthful in this last statement. I quite admit that he rested his elbow on the table, his forehead on his hand, that he scowled furiously and gave other outward signs of deep thought. But as for the existence of any continuous mental process inside his skull, that, in my peculiar position as the writer of this story, I take leave to doubt. His mind revolved in aimless circles which radiated from a number of oscillating centres. In so far as any of the ideas produced by this activity can be transferred to the rigidity of print, it may be noted that one of the principal sections of his brain seemed intent on his prolonging this visit to the Serene Grill Room at any rate until closing time; another lobe or ganglion, as has been said, was determined that

Miss Elizabeth Smith should not be allowed to leave the country; while further cerebral ramifications were engaged on the constant invention and rejection of a quantity of impracticable schemes for securing one or other of these two main requirements.

As for Miss Smith, the lunch having by now been brought to its protracted close, she remained silent on her upholstered seat, replacing her gloves with that amazing slowness and deliberation which characterize her sex during this operation. The sense of physical comfort induced by the food, drink, and surroundings of the Serene Grill Room was so great that for the time being the anxieties, the disappointments, and the fears of the last few weeks of her life seemed merely to form that pleasant undercurrent of sadness without which the digestion of a really good meal is incomplete. Somewhere and at some unknown period a girl had wanted to go on the stage; she had failed, just as thousands and millions of other girls had failed before and would fail again. With her gaze fixed on infinity, the two half-crowns on the corner of the table—the coins which might alter her whole future existence, became two silver pools, or were they eyes? The eyes of Fate, looking at its victim before—

She gave a sudden gasp, almost a cry.

"Why, what is it?" said John, starting from his own dreams.

She gripped his arm.

"Your money! The two-half crowns!"

"What—?"

"The waiter! Just this instant, when you weren't looking. He took them up and went off with them. He must have thought it was a tip!"

John brought his hand down on the table with a thump.

"An omen!" he cried. "They were to take you away from England, and instead they have gone themselves. Very well. You shall stay. And, by George! what's more, I've got an idea."

He sprang up and stood over her.

"Don't move," he said. "Swear not to move. You can't go away, because I haven't paid the bill. I'm going to the telephone boxes. I've got an idea. Wait there!"

He dashed from the room, and was halfway up the forbidden flight of stairs before the page-boy could stop him.

"Not that way, sir," shouted the boy. "What were you looking for, sir?"

"Telephone," said John, pausing in his ascent.

"Just round to the right here, sir," said the boy.

John dashed downstairs again, three steps at a time, sped round to the right, and flung himself into the nearest glass receptacle.

He gave Mrs. Cartwright's number.

In more time than it takes to tell, he heard the premonitory click and the neat-looking parlourmaid's "Hullo?"

"This is Mr. Ormroyd. Can I speak to Mrs. Cartwright, please?"

"Just a minute, sir."

Buzz. Click. Also Ting! Then Helen Cartwright's voice.

"Is that you, John?"

"Yes. I say, look here. I hope you're in this afternoon."

"Well, I can be."

Mrs. Cartwright always could be, although this was only one of the thousand things about her which went to make up her charm.

"Look here," said John again. "It's rather difficult to explain on the telephone, but I'll be round in a few minutes."

"You sound excited, John. Is it about the play?"

"What play? Oh, no."

"'What play?' indeed!"

"I say, don't be surprised if I bring a young woman with me," continued John, disregarding this taunt.

"Nothing would surprise me less," said Mrs. Cartwright. "I'll expect you both at once. Au revoir."

"Thanks awfully—" John was beginning, when he realised from a kind of deadness in the receiver at his ear that Mrs. Cartwright had cut him off.

"I wonder what she meant by saying that," he thought, as he emerged from the box.

"Nothing, I expect," he added to himself, as he reentered the grill room.

Miss Smith had not moved during his absence, and he found the look of relief which came into her face at his return singularly comforting.

"I'm going to take you to see a great friend of mine," he said. "Are you ready to come now?"

If she made any answer, assenting or otherwise, John didn't wait for it. He had already turned to the waiter.

"I'd like my bill at once," he said.

They were now practically the last couple left in the room, and the bill had been ready in the background for some time. True to his training, the waiter whom John had addressed did not move from his place, but snapped his fingers at another one and said, "L'addition pour monsieur."

"Beel," said the second waiter obligingly, and immediately dashed forward with the folded bill on a silver-plated tray.

Miss Smith's eyes seemed to grow larger than ever, as John began ladling notes on to the tray, and she gave a little gasp as she realised that, in spite of the recent loss of the two half-crowns, he did not apparently propose to wait for any change.

"What is it?" asked John.

"You oughn't to have brought me here," she said, looking after the retreating waiter with his pile of booty.

John was not used to comment of this description on his hospitality, even though he had privately to admit that the bill was a bit of a staggerer. He was on the point of replying, "Didn't you enjoy it, then?" when something made him change his mind. That wasn't the way to parade one's generosity before a starving princess. A better answer would be: "It was worth it."

He said it.

Self-consciousness seized them both, and he was glad to seek relief in asking for his hat and coat, and ordering a taxi.

In the hall downstairs Miss Smith stopped him by a light touch on the arm.

"You mustn't say things to me that you don't mean," she said.

"I won't," he answered seriously; and then added, "ever."

If the driver of the taxi had been given to such speculation, he might have thought it rather curious that not one but both of his fares should be blushing as they entered his vehicle.

III

They were more than halfway towards the little Square, when Elizabeth suddenly said:

"Is this friend of yours a man or a woman?"

"A woman," said John.

"Oh!"

For some reason this almost toneless exclamation made John wish to justify himself.

"Mrs. Cartwright's a very old friend of mine," he said. "I used to stay with her—"

"Cartwright!" interrupted Elizabeth. "That's not been a very lucky name for me."

"It's a most extraordinary thing," said John, "but I never thought of it till this moment. You see they've been separated for years and years. One thinks of them as so far apart that the same name sounds quite different to me."

"Then she's Leo Cartwright's wife?"

"Well, she was, anyhow."

"I can't thank you enough for coming to my rescue today," said Elizabeth, "but, honestly, do you know, I think I'd rather you stopped the cab now and let me get out."

"But I promise you," said John, "I'm not going to say anything about you and the Thespian. Really I'm not."

"Then what are you going to say?"

Yes, John, what are you going to say? You'll be there in a couple of minutes now, and really, you know, wonderful as Helen Cartwright is, you can't simply drop the whole problem into her lap and clear off.

"I—she—I know she'll help you," he finally answered.

"How?"

"I don't know how, but she will."

"Does she help everybody, then?"

"Yes," said John. It seemed the simplest and most truthful answer on the whole.

But Elizabeth pursued her questioning a point further.

"Then she won't be helping me because she likes you?"

But his answer in this case, whatever it was going to be, was never delivered. For at this moment there was a sudden grinding and squeaking of brakes, as the taxi pulled up almost in its own length to avoid the messenger-boy who had just stepped off the curb in front of it.

The occupants of the cab assisted in this process by the muscular contractions which are customary on such occasions. That is to say, Elizabeth gripped the seat with both hands and dug her feet into the floor; while John raised his knees high in the air and drew in his breath with a sharp lisp.

"I there!" shouted the driver.

"I, there!" mimicked the rash and ungrateful boy in shrill falsetto.

The brief exchange of repartee which followed appeared to indicate that the driver was filled with regret that he had not killed the boy, and that the boy was under the impression that any attempts in this direction would have been quite useless.

DENIS MACKAIL

"Never mind the boy. Go on!" said John, putting his head out of the window.

But this intervention only served to inspire the boy to fresh efforts in vulgarity. He began to sing; and his song, a discordant rendering of a popular love-lyric, was only too clearly levelled at the supposed romantic relations existing between the occupants of the taxi. John sat back, foiled and angry; the boy inserted two fingers into his mouth, produced an ear-splitting whistle, and disappeared round the corner; and simultaneously the cab resumed its interrupted progress.

Do not dismiss this incident too lightly as a bit of more or less justifiable padding; for this vulgar messenger-boy had three minutes previously left the second of Leo Cartwright's three letters in the care of Mrs. Cartwright's parlourmaid.

For the truth is, Helen Cartwright had written a play. In fact she admitted as much in the first chapter. It had been completed about the same time that she had given up her villa and returned to England, and its construction, elaboration, alteration, simplification, and expansion had occupied her at intervals for nearly ten of the preceding years. You cannot say that some kind of inspiration was not behind her to have made it possible for a play executed in such a leisurely fashion ever to have been finished at all. But it was certainly not that urgent, unremitting description of inspiration which, commonly mistaken by the public for a direct call from one or more of the Muses, is in fact usually due to the imminence of the next quarter's bills. For whatever Mrs. Cartwright's troubles may have been, the question of bills had certainly not yet been one of them. She wrote when she wanted to write, she destroyed when she wanted to destroy, and she put the whole thing on one side for months, whenever this method of progress seemed more suitable. And out of all this slow, unhurried, ruminative writing, the play gradually grew. Even its completion was so imperceptible a process that it was only when she took it out of its resting-place after one of these long intervals of incubation, that, on reading it through, she realised that there was nothing more to add. And it was certainly not until two years after this that the possibility first entered her mind of treating this play like other plays, and submitting it to professional consideration.

It is perhaps not impossible to believe that a work which had been created in this exceptionally intermittent manner might show many differences from the ordinary commercial article; though whether these differences should all be set down as faults is at least open to argument.

The method of its construction, however, had certainly enabled it to avoid what is perhaps the commonest fault, from a money-making if not from an artistic point of view, of the average good-enough production. In other words, whatever Mrs. Cartwright's play did, it did not "date." There are, it goes without saying, other conditions to be satisfied as well as this before any play can be definitely described as a classic, not the least of which is, of course, that it should achieve some kind of publicity or publication. Nevertheless, this one important distinction which had been conferred on it by its protracted growth had been enough to account for the fact that after four years of continuous disappointment the Trafalgar Agency still stuck to it that there was money to be made out of this play, if only it got its chance. And, after all, when an agency talks like that after four years, it looks as if there were something in it.

Leo Cartwright had, you may remember, described this work to his Vizier as being a pageant of life and death, but the suggestion implied by such a phrase conveys, at any rate to my mind, a certain grandiosity and pretentiousness which were in reality conspicuously absent. The worst charges which could, in fact, be brought against it were an accusation of sentimentality and (from the more purely business point of view) that at the end of the last Act the principal character died. With the first charge it is difficult to deal in the case of any play that remains unacted, since stage sentimentality is in nine cases out of ten simply a matter of lighting and voice production. As for the second indictment you will have to admit, in the face of certain not unheard-of precedents, that a death in the last Act does not necessarily put a play altogether out of court. Yet if Mrs. Cartwright's output had been divisible, into Comedies, Histories, and Tragedies,—which, consisting as it did of one example only, it was not,—it is doubtful if you would have found "Romance to the Rescue" among the Tragedies. Its outlook on life was altogether too hopeful for this, even though it set out to picture a man who would ordinarily be described as a failure.

But the philosophy of the play was intended to show how the very fact of his being a failure, which cut him off from all the mental situations which are usually supposed to bring contentment and happiness, did not in this case succeed in making him discontented, but rather placed him in the enviable position of preserving to the very end his beliefs in all those things which for the successful are shattered by proximity. I believe it has been said that a good play should illustrate a proverbial saying, and in this one might find an illustration not only of the converse to "Familiarity breeds contempt," but also of "He that is down need fear no fall." Only in this case he that was down in addition to this advantage also preserved a belief in the romance attaching to the higher rungs of the ladder, which those who have reached them would give anything to regain.

At the time when Mrs. Cartwright was reaching her decision to submit her dramatic offspring to professional consideration, a certain amount of space in the Press was being occupied every day with details of the Erpingham case. You may remember that a prominent literary agent of this name had had the misfortune to step in front of the Dover express near a level crossing. And scarcely had the coroner's jury passed their vote of censure on the railway company than Mr. Hubbard Scholes, the well-known author, had in his turn the misfortune to discover that the late Mr. Erpingham had appropriated to his own use no less than £75,000 out of various royalties on the literary and dramatic works of the said Scholes. This, at least, was the figure that stuck in the public mind, even though subsequent investigations proved it to have been considerably overstated. It remained, however, as a fair average between what Scholes himself had actually lost and the sums which his rivals immediately began to hint in private that they also had lost.

You might imagine that these revelations would have caused a new and inexperienced dramatist to regard the use of an agent with considerable suspicion, but in Mrs. Cartwright's case you would be wrong. For in the first place the affair drew her attention to a section of the community of whose very existence she had previously been unaware, and in the second place she felt that here was a defence from all the personal negotiations and rebuffs from which she naturally shrank. It occurred to her, incidentally, that if Scholes was making so much money that he only noticed the loss of £75,000 when his attention was drawn to it by his agent's rash act,—for this was what he had told the newspapers,—then Erpingham must have done pretty well for him at one time or another. Personally she would not grudge any agency whatever they were able to make out of her, provided that they took the trouble of the whole business off her shoulders, and acted as a buffer between her and the refusals which she anticipated.

As it happened, she pitched on an old-established and quite reasonably honest firm, though the selection had only been made through the name catching her eye in the telephone directory. But the choice of a pseudonym had been forced on her even earlier than this, when she had first sent her untidy-looking bundle of manuscript to be typed. She had actually written the covering letter, when the sudden thought that this action rendered her liable to the criticism of a whole roomful of typists suspended her pen in the air. How was she to know that to only the newest and slowest of these operators does the written word ever signify anything but a series of too-easily misplaced letters? The thought of their mockery was unbearable. At this moment Mrs. Cartwright very nearly put the whole manuscript back in the cupboard and thereby stopped me writing this story. But when was the nicest woman wanting in deceit? In a flash the idea of a *nom-de-plume* had come to her. In another second she had written the word "Lawrence." "They won't know if it's a man or a woman," she said to herself. And then: "Bother! I believe I've spelt it wrong. I shall have to make it the surname." Imagination at this point giving out, and lunch being announced, she dashed in an illegible symbol before it, and handed the parcel over to be done up and sent off.

It was the acknowledgement addressed to "D. Lawrence, Esquire," that set her hunting for another Christian name, though it was not until some time later that chance finally led her to pitch on "David."

Since that parcel had been sent off nearly four years ago, a series of communications addressed to "David Lawrence, Esquire," had arrived at Number 35 from the Trafalgar Agency. The bulk of them had contained statements of account for which cash had always been immediately paid; a certain number had merely reported stages in the long series of rejections and delays to which the play had been subjected. There had been a period during the early days when the Agency had displayed an embarrassing desire for the author to "come and have a chat" or to "come and discuss the suggested alterations," but the reply to these invitations had always been that Mr. Lawrence was ill or going abroad, and after a time they had stopped.

Quite at the beginning of the play's wanderings the Agency had been instructed not to submit it to the management of the Thespian Theatre, and the length of its sojourns with rival directorates had been such that even after these four years plenty of untried theatres remained without violating this instruction. But during the four years the Agency's eldest son had become demobilised and had entered the business. Being fresh to the work, he took to reading the plays as they were returned, and so it was that one day he slapped his leg and exclaimed: "This is the real Cartwright stuff! Why on earth hasn't it been tried there before now?" His father was on a holiday, and no one thought of looking back to the beginning of David Lawrence's dusty file in search of unlikely prohibitions.

When the elder Mr. Purdock returned, his son took the opportunity of recounting his treatment of "Romance to the Rescue," expatiating at the same time on the advantages of new blood and go-ahead brains in old businesses. The father's memory came to his assistance and his triumph was complete. The upshot was a letter to Mr. Lawrence apologising for the oversight and asking for instructions—the letter, in fact, which the maid had remembered seeing in the hall of Mrs. Cartwright's house the day before the real David Lawrence's visit.

After so many rejections, Mrs. Cartwright felt that it would only draw unnecessary attention to her play if she made the Agency ask for its return. She wrote and told them to leave matters as they were. Mr. Purdock junior indulged in protracted variations of the theme "I told you so," and when a few days afterwards a messenger-boy arrived bearing an envelope with the well-known masks and tassels of the Thespian printed on it, he plunged his hand into his own trousers pocket to provide the wherewithal which should send that messenger straight on to the little Square.

IV

JOHN JUMPED OUT OF THE taxi while it was still moving, dropped a number of coins into the driver's outstretched hand, ran across the pavement, and rang the front-door bell. Then he turned and watched Miss Smith follow him. Though the opportunity afforded him was excessively brief, he yet found time to approve the way in which she walked. As she joined him on the doorstep, the door was opened.

"I've just telephoned to Mrs. Cartwright. I think she's expecting me," said John to the maid.

"Yes, sir."

John and Elizabeth followed her upstairs. On the way John made several efforts to get in a whispered message that he wanted to see Mrs. Cartwright alone for a minute, but the narrow stairs were no place for such confidences, and he was unsuccessful. In another moment they were shown into the drawing-room, and the door was closed behind them. The room was empty.

It would be useless to disguise the fact that at this instant John Ormroyd was feeling very far from comfortable. When he looked at

Elizabeth, as he did constantly whenever he thought she wouldn't notice it, he certainly couldn't bring himself to regret his intervention in her fate. But then in another second Helen Cartwright would be in the room, and he would be faced with the impossibility of trying to explain what he thought he was doing. He quite appreciated the attractions which the scene would present to him as a light comedy incident in one of his own books, but the heroes in his books could wait for days, or if necessary even weeks, while he thought out what they were going to say next; whereas—The latch of the door clicked; both occupants of the room started simultaneously; and the maid reappeared.

"You're wanted on the telephone, sir," she said.

"The telephone?" repeated John vaguely. "Oh, yes. Of course. Certainly. I say, will you excuse me a minute?"

He hardly waited for the frightened kind of smile with which Elizabeth may be supposed to have given her assent, but left the room at once. Some outlying cell in his brain may have signalled surprise that any one should be ringing him up at Mrs. Cartwright's house, but, before this message could reach headquarters, he was out on the landing and face to face with Mrs. Cartwright herself. In one hand she held a crumpled letter, and the forefinger of the other was laid on her lips.

"Hush!" she whispered.

"The telephone?" said John idiotically.

"A ruse," murmured Mrs. Cartwright. "I saw you arrive. I watched you over the banisters when you got inside. I could tell from the top of your head that you wanted to see me alone. Come into the dining-room."

John followed her down, and she closed the door behind him as he came inside the room.

"I say, John," she said, speaking for the first time in her ordinary voice. "I say, she's awfully pretty! Are you engaged?"

"No," said John. "Certainly not."

"Are you quite sure?"

"Positive."

"Then sit down and tell me quickly."

Mrs. Cartwright sank into an armchair, but John remained standing.

"She's called Elizabeth Smith," he said, and then corrected himself. "I mean, Miss Elizabeth Smith."

"Go on," said Mrs. Cartwright. "You interest me strangely."

John looked at her quickly; but the little hint of mockery in her eyes had already disappeared.

"When I discovered her today," he went on hastily, "she was starving. She hasn't got a penny in the world. She's got nowhere to go. I gave her some lunch, but I can't give her money or take her back to my flat, so I brought her to you at once."

"Obviously," said Mrs. Cartwright, with a little laugh. "But hasn't she got any relations either?"

"They're all abroad. Besides, they're clearly quite detestable."

The certainty in his voice almost made Mrs. Cartwright ask how he knew this, but she changed her mind and said:

"Well, what am I to do with her now she is here?"

"I thought, perhaps," replied John, looking strangely sheepish and, to Mrs. Cartwright's eyes, strangely young, "that if I put up the money, you could pretend to offer her some kind of a job—that is, until we could find her a real one. Only I don't think she ought to work very hard just at first. . ."

"You must stop kicking the fender for a minute, while I think this over."

"Of course I know it would be a fearful nuisance for you, and all that, only, upon my word, I don't see whom else I was to come to. Do you know that she fainted this morning? Actually fainted!"

"In your arms, John?"

"Oh, of course, if you're going to talk like that—"

"No, no. I'm sorry I said that."

The apology encouraged John to untruthful excess.

"There's nothing of that sort about it," he said.

"You must forgive my vulgarity, John."

He was magnanimous in his undeserved triumph.

"That's all right," he said. "Only we must be quick and think of something. We can't keep her waiting."

Mrs. Cartwright didn't quite see why Miss Smith should not be kept waiting, but she did her best to enter into the spirit of the thing.

"I'm only waiting for you to say what you want me to do," she said.

"Well," answered John, tentatively. "Some women have secretaries, don't they?"

"Do you want me to keep her in the house?" asked Mrs. Cartwright patiently.

"Oh, no. I don't think that will be necessary. But she could come in and do things for you in the mornings—just until I can fix up something better. I expect you will find it a very useful arrangement in a way. She could answer your letters, you know."

"But I never get any letters."

"What's that in your hand?" asked John, accusingly.

"My hand?" she repeated, looking down at it.

"Yes."

She gave a curious half-gasp and half-laugh at the sight of the letter which she was still holding.

"Couldn't she answer that for you?" he persisted.

"I think she'll have to," Mrs. Cartwright replied, in a strange voice. "I know I can't ever answer it myself."

"Then that's settled. Shall we go upstairs and tell her?" He moved towards the door. "I suppose she can begin tomorrow?"

"Wait a minute—" Mrs. Cartwright began helplessly; but John had already opened the dining-room door, and she heard his voice speaking to some one outside.

"Why, what is the matter?" he was saying.

"Oh, Mr. Ormroyd," the girl's voice answered. "I've been thinking it over upstairs. I'm very sorry. You've been most awfully kind to me, but really I can't let you do anything more for me. I've thought it all out, and I see it's quite impossible. Thank you again a thousand times, but I must go now. Really I must."

"But look here I say. . ." John seemed to be trying to block the exit.

"No, please, really," said Miss Smith. "I shall be all right. Will you explain to Mrs. Cartwright that—"

"But wait a second! I was just going to tell you. Mrs. Cartwright wants a new secretary. She's just been telling me. It's perfectly true. You can't go without seeing her; she wants to speak to you about it."

"A secretary?"

In her armchair by the dining-room fire Mrs. Cartwright heard and recognised the conflict between pride and longing in the two words thus repeated. She gave but one, brief, despairing grimace, and then, her mind made up, she raised her voice and called out:

"Is that Miss Smith there, John? Why don't you bring her in?"

"I like her voice, anyhow," thought Elizabeth; and the next moment they were being introduced.

"It's so very lucky that John should have brought you here today," Mrs. Cartwright heard herself saying a minute later. "I'm so badly in need of some one to help me with my correspondence."

"In the mornings," added John from the background.

"Oh, yes. Only in the mornings. I wonder, now, if you could possibly arrange to come to me."

"If Mr. Ormroyd told you anything about me at all," said Elizabeth, "he must have told you that I'm completely unemployed. If I could really be any help to you, I should be so very grateful. I do know a little shorthand," she went on, "and I can use a typewriter a bit, but I'm afraid I haven't got one."

"She can have mine," John mouthed at Mrs. Cartwright from behind Elizabeth's back. He endeavoured to make his meaning still clearer by tapping his chest with one hand and waggling the fingers of the other to represent the act of typing. By some miracle of intuition Mrs. Cartwright seemed to grasp his meaning. At any rate, she went on:

"I think we could manage about a typewriter. But of course it wouldn't only be a question of taking down letters." She said this because it had suddenly struck her that, though she dealt with her entire future correspondence via Miss Smith, she would have to rack her brains to keep her employed even at the rate of a letter a day.

Fortunately for Mrs. Cartwright, Elizabeth did not press for details of her alternative employments. She even made a suggestion herself.

"I could arrange the flowers, perhaps," she said.

"Yes. That would be splendid," answered Mrs. Cartwright with surprising enthusiasm.

"In fact if you can use me at all, I would do anything in the world to help, that is until. . ."

"Oh, of course this is understood to be a temporary arrangement," John broke in.

"Quite," said Mrs. Cartwright, a bit puzzled, but considerably relieved. She began trying to think of some other kind of question that one might reasonably ask an applicant for secretarial work, but her previous experience of this kind of interview had been entirely confined to discussions with cooks and housemaids and parlourmaids and such. Somehow none of the questions which she was in the habit of putting to these persons seemed much use in the present emergency. Wait a minute, though, there was one that might be brought in.

"How soon could you come to me?" she asked.

"Oh, at once," said Elizabeth eagerly. "That is, if you think I could be any help at all."

"Let me see," continued Mrs. Cartwright. "What salary did my last secretary get, John? It's a most extraordinary thing, but I've quite forgotten."

There was no earthly reason why John should not have replied to this question by means of the human voice, but for some unexplained cause he preferred to wave one of his hands in the air with the fingers extended, while with the other hand he patted his breast pocket. By these actions Mrs. Cartwright correctly understood him to mean, "Give her five pounds a week, and don't forget that I am providing the money."

"I remember now," she said. "It was five pounds a week."

She shot an enquiring glance at John, and he nodded back.

"I hope that will suit you?" she went on.

She had not the very faintest idea whether this salary would be regarded as an attempt to sweat or an attempt to corrupt. Luckily Elizabeth knew very little more about the matter herself. It was just instinct that made her say:

"What, all that just for the mornings?"

"Well, not Saturdays or Sundays," Mrs. Cartwright answered apologetically, as if this explanation made everything clear and normal. "Would that suit you?"

"If you will only let me try—" Elizabeth began.

And then suddenly she felt that she was going to cry. The physical reactions from this sensation were never lost on Mrs. Cartwright, and we know that John had special reasons for recognising the symptoms. They both rushed forward and began talking at once.

"You'll both stop and have some tea, won't you?" said Mrs. Cartwright.

"I'm sure you'll suit each other down to the ground," said John.

Elizabeth produced her tiny handkerchief and pressed it against the end of her nose, as women do when they have just changed their minds about crying.

"That's splendid," said John, in a cheerful and all-embracing manner, and the three of them proceeded upstairs again to the drawing-room.

All the appurtenances of tea except the tea itself were waiting for them there, and at a touch on the bell from the hostess the missing fluid arrived.

From this moment the party went with a bang. Mrs. Cartwright and John vied with each other in the brilliance of their conversation and the sparkle of their anecdotes. Each of them seemed to find in Elizabeth a singularly inspiring audience, and, indeed, as she turned her enormous eyes from one to the other, and gurgled with laughter at the right place in every story, far duller people might have found it hard to doubt the charm of their own conversation, or to refrain from continually trying to go one better.

Eventually, however, John rose to his feet and announced that he must be getting along.

DENIS MACKAIL

"No, no. You mustn't go too," Mrs. Cartwright said to Elizabeth, who had also risen and was looking uncertainly at the others. "I must talk to you first."

John's handgrip drew Mrs. Cartwright halfway through her drawing-room door.

"It's most awfully good of you," he said. "You do like her, don't you?"

And then, without waiting for an answer, he added: "I'll have my typewriter sent round to you at once," and fled down the stairs.

V

Mrs. Cartwright paused for a moment before turning to reënter the room. And during the pause two new and unwelcome thoughts, which had for some time been hovering in the offing, came near enough to be recognised and even clothed in unspoken words.

"This is the end of my friendship with John," was the first thought.

And "I am going to have another bad headache," was the second.

Like Hope at the bottom of the box, a third thought was found to remain:

"But I can't dislike that girl."

And clinging to such consolation as this third thought could afford, she came back into the room and closed the door behind her.

Elizabeth Smith was still standing in the same place and in the same attitude. But inasmuch as everything mortal is subject to change of some sort, it may be noted that, whereas she had previously looked about twenty, she now looked at least two years younger.

"I hope you don't mind," said Mrs. Cartwright cheerfully, "but I always call my secretaries by their Christian names. I think you are Elizabeth, aren't you?"

"Yes."

"That's good," said Mrs. Cartwright even more cheerfully. And if you had heard her, you must have agreed that nothing could be better.

"Now sit down again," she went on; "because I want to talk to you."

Elizabeth obeyed the command, but, disregarding the statement, began to talk herself.

"Before you say anything," she said, "I want to know, are you quite sure you do need me? Are you quite sure that it isn't just to oblige Mr. Ormroyd or—or me? It's all been so quick, I don't see how you can have had a chance to think it over. Mrs. Cartwright, really it would be much kinder to tell me now, if you think you've made a mistake. I should so absolutely understand."

But Mrs. Cartwright had her own ideas of kindness; also, it would appear, her own ideas of truth, for she replied:

"I'm quite certain I need you. You really mustn't let that worry you for a moment."

"But you don't know anything about me," expostulated Elizabeth; and this was less easy to contradict, it being an undoubted fact that Mrs. Cartwright did know nothing whatever about her. Nevertheless, she was searching for an acceptable method of passing over the point, when her thoughts were interrupted by a strange phenomenon observable in Elizabeth's face.

And at this moment, even as the lamp of the railway signal changes instantaneously from green to red, so (to put it poetically) there suddenly swept over Elizabeth's countenance one large, irresistible, overpowering, fiery blush.

Mrs. Cartwright started forward in her seat.

"You're not feeling well?" she said.

Elizabeth cast her eyes on the floor, and even her eyelids were now blushing.

"No," she said. "It's worse than that."

"Then, what. . . ?"

"I expect he told you, and of course he believed me."

"I don't underst—"

"Oh, Mrs. Cartwright, I told Mr. Ormroyd the most terrible lie."

"About yourself?"

Elizabeth nodded.

"I told him my family were abroad," she said, in a husky voice.

"And they're not?"

"No. I haven't got a family."

"You poor—"

"It's true I was abroad, but I was at a school. I was supposed to help with the teaching. I—I ran away."

"But—"

"It was the word 'school' I was afraid he wouldn't understand. I didn't want him to think that I'd run away like a schoolgirl. So I told him this dreadful lie. And now I can't ever explain. Oh, what will he think?"

Mrs. Cartwright had a pretty shrewd idea of what John Ormroyd already thought, and of the extent to which this horrible revelation would affect his opinion, but for the moment she did not feel inclined to offer her theories on the subject. Resisting a sudden impulse to kiss her new secretary, she replied:

"I shouldn't worry about that, if I were you. You leave it to me. I'm sure I can put that right."

Of course you have never heard Mrs. Cartwright saying that she is sure that she can put something right; but there can be no question that it is a most remarkably comforting and reassuring sound. The look of gratitude which appeared in Elizabeth's face was so overwhelming that Mrs. Cartwright unconsciously raised a defensive hand as she continued.

"Now I wonder if you'd mind very much," she said, "but there's a letter—two letters in fact—that I very much want to get off my mind tonight. If you could take them down now, it wouldn't matter if they didn't go off till the morning."

"Oh, of course," said Elizabeth. "If I could just have a pencil and a piece of paper, I'll take them down at once."

These materials were provided from the drawing-room writing-table.

"Now, then," said Mrs. Cartwright, and she thought: "If this girl has ever taken down shorthand before, she'll realise in three seconds that I've never dictated a letter in my life. However, it's never too late to begin."

Elizabeth's pencil hung tremulously over the block of paper.

"If she doesn't go very slowly," she thought, "she'll find out in two minutes that I'm no good at this, and then what on earth shall I do?"

Mrs. Cartwright gave a nervous cough, and took up from the tea-table the letter which she had been grasping when John and his protégée had first arrived.

"*Dear Sir*," she said, and the room swam before her eyes, as her brain attempted to frame a reasonably grammatical continuation.

Perhaps it would be easier, she thought, if she stood up and walked about. People who dictated letters in plays and films always did this. She made the experiment and, to her surprise, found it of real assistance.

Dear Sir (she repeated)
        I am very much obliged for your letter which has been
forwarded to me today.

She paused. In the agonies of epistolary creation she had adopted a pace which would have made it easy for her words to be taken down in copybook capitals, and Elizabeth breathed a sigh of relief.

—forwarded to me today. If convenient to yourself, I should be very glad to accept your invitation for the afternoon performance on Saturday next, and will call on you afterwards as suggested. Would you be so good as to arrange for the ticket to be left with the Box Office?

She paused again, and Elizabeth looked up enquiringly.

"That's all," said Mrs. Cartwright.

"'Yours faithfully'?" suggested Elizabeth.

"What? Oh, yes, certainly."

"And to whom will that be?" pursued the new secretary.

Mrs. Cartwright clutched at the back of an armchair to steady herself. She realised, with a sinking feeling, that her ingenious plan for avoiding an autograph reply with its telltale handwriting must involve the admission to part of her confidence of a fellow-conspirator. Further, that this fellow-conspirator, on whose silence and discretion so much must depend, was a girl on whom she had never set eyes until an hour or so ago. And yet the plan which was forming in her mind was the only possible way which she could see of getting herself out of the hole in which she suddenly found herself. Somehow or other she must get her husband to drop the idea of taking this play, and yet do this without arousing his suspicions as to the genuine existence of the author. If these were once aroused, it would be so terribly easy to trace the play back through the Agency to her address and so to herself; a discovery which could only lead to unhappiness and the reopening of old wounds. Of that she was convinced. Infinitely preferable was the alternative of giving up all idea of ever seeing her work on the stage; and if by doing this she could remove one of the obstacles which stood between John Ormroyd and his ambition, would she not be well rewarded by his happiness alone? You may doubt this, but Mrs. Cartwright certainly did not, even though she gave a sad little half-smile at the thought of how the one big mistake in her life had been so big that it could rise up twenty-five years afterwards and silence her before a girl who had not been born when it was made.

"I mean the name and the address?" Elizabeth added, finding her first question unanswered.

Mrs. Cartwright returned to her favourite chair, and sank into it.

"Elizabeth," she said, "I want—I mean us to be friends; as far as possible real friends. So don't think I am trying to snub you now in anything I say. But when I tell you who this letter is to, I'm telling it to my secretary.

You must take it down and type it out, because as my friend you will see, perhaps, that it is a letter that I can't write myself. That depends on how much John has told you. But once that letter is posted, you are never, either as secretary or as friend, to think of it again. Do you understand?"

"I don't understand," said Elizabeth, "but I promise."

"That's better still," Mrs. Cartwright answered, again with that half-smile. "Now take it down, and we'll get on to the other letter."

Elizabeth picked up her pencil.

"'Leo Cartwright, Esquire,'" said Mrs. Cartwright. "'Thespian Theatre.'"

She darted a glance at her secretary.

"You've not taken that down," she added.

"I shall remember it," said Elizabeth, "without that."

Mrs. Cartwright took a breath as if she were on the point of saying something, and then apparently changed her mind. She didn't know what Elizabeth meant; how could she, knowing nothing of the scene in the waiting-room? But she had realised, when on the brink of speaking, that the sooner she got away from the subject of this letter, the better. Why, in another moment she might have been justifying herself! She closed her eyes, as at the edge of a chasm, and then dashed ahead.

"The other letter is to David Lawrence, Esquire," she said. "You can get the address if you look up Dr. Martin Lawrence in the telephone book."

"Yes," murmured Elizabeth.

Dear David,

Can you lunch with me on Saturday next at one o'clock and come to a matinee afterwards? I think you said your holidays—no, cross that out and put "vacation"—would have begun by then. But even if not, perhaps you could come up for the afternoon, as I particularly—underline that—want you to come.

"'Yours sincerely,'" she concluded, rather defiantly. She wasn't going to be caught out that way again.

"Mark the envelope 'Please forward,'" she added as an afterthought.

"Is that all?" asked Elizabeth, preparing to rise.

"Yes, thank you. Except—I'd nearly forgotten. I hope you don't mind," said Mrs. Cartwright, as if apologising for some recognised but ineradicable bad habit, "but I always pay my secretaries in advance."

She went across to her writing-table and began searching in one of the drawers. Elizabeth had opened her mouth to make some kind of protest, but gratitude took her voice away. After her miraculous lunch and tea, she had quite prepared herself to go without dinner that evening and even without breakfast the next morning; but she had very much mistrusted her powers of convincing her landlady that she had fallen on her feet to the extent of five pounds a week. And failure to do this might in two more days have meant the loss of her uncomfortable though necessary bed, which would have been worse than anything that had happened to her yet. How could she possibly have explained to her new employer that without an advance of salary she would probably have nowhere to sleep?

Even when Mrs. Cartwright emerged successfully from her search for cash, and handed over a collection of notes and coins totalling one week's pay, Elizabeth's thanks were only able to take the form of a couple of gulps and a husky growl. With these sounds, however, Mrs. Cartwright appeared perfectly satisfied.

"Now don't let me keep you," she said. "Those letters will do perfectly well in the morning." (Her watchful ear had as yet failed to detect the sound of the typewriter's arrival, and confession here would, she felt, give the whole show away at once.) "And don't be too punctual in the morning. I think half-past eleven or twelve will be quite soon enough, and of course you'll stay and have lunch."

Elizabeth gave further grateful gulps.

"Now is there anything else you'd like to know before you go off?" continued Mrs. Cartwright.

"No, thank you."

"Well, I'll say good-night, then."

"Good-night. It's most awfully good of you. It's—I. . ."

And then, when she had practically closed the door behind her, it suddenly opened again and she reappeared.

"Mrs. Cartwright?"

"Yes?"

"There is just one thing—that is, if you wouldn't mind very much."

"Well, what is it?"

"If you wouldn't mind awfully, do you think you could lend me a book to read tonight?"

"Why, of course. Any particular sort of book?"

"I'd rather like one of Mr. Ormroyd's books—that is, if you could spare it. I've never read any."

"Take your choice," said Mrs. Cartwright, pointing to a shelf by the fireplace.

Elizabeth went over to it and began studying the titles.

"Which is the best?" she asked.

"I think they're all good," said Mrs. Cartwright. "But John himself prefers 'She Loves Me Not' to the rest, I know."

"Then may I have that one?"

"Of course."

So Elizabeth extracted it from the bookshelf and this time she really did leave. Or at least she only paused under the lamp in the hall just long enough to look inside the cover of "She Loves Me Not."

"'To Mrs. Cartwright, affectionately from the Author,'" she read.

What did she mean by adding, half-aloud, "It might have been worse."

As for Mrs. Cartwright she waited until she heard the front door close, and then rang the bell.

"Hilda," she called over the banisters.

"Yes, madam?"

"I'm going to bed now. I'm feeling very tired. Will you ask Rose to put two hot bottles in my room? And if you'll send me up a little fish later, I won't have anything else."

"Very good, madam."

VI

WHEN JOHN GOT BACK TO his flat, he went straight to the telephone and ordered a messenger to take his typewriter round to Mrs. Cartwright's house in a cab. It was not until he had done this that his eye fell on the envelope lying on his hall table.

As has been previously stated, there was no false modesty about the Thespian stationery. John pounced on this example of it and tore the envelope open.

Miss Lemon had certainly "piled it on."

"They've treated me abominably, and now I've given them a fright," he said to himself. "He wouldn't write like this, if he didn't mean business."

Whereupon the distinguished author retired to his study, and, with the celebrated pipe gripped firmly between his teeth, dashed off a brief little note to Mr. Leo Cartwright. He expressed his temperate regret that he had been unable to wait any longer at the theatre today, and intimated his intention of dropping in towards the end of the matinée on the following Saturday, in order to have a talk over matters generally.

"I've got an advantage I didn't deserve over this lunch today," he thought, "and whatever happens, I must keep it."

Later in the evening the telephone bell rang, and when he went to answer it he heard Mrs. Cartwright's voice.

"I hope you got the typewriter all right," he said.

"Oh, yes, thank you. But I didn't ring you up to tell you that."

"To tell me what, then?"

"John, you must take this girl off my hands in a fortnight at the very latest."

"Why, don't you. . . ?"

"Oh, I like her. Yes, I like her enormously. But, John, I can't think who on earth I can go on writing letters to. And if I don't give her letters to write, she'll see through both of us at once."

"Write to me, then," said John, cheerfully.

"Never!"

"Why not?"

"I've done quite enough for you."

"I know you have. I'm most awfully grateful." John went on pouring thanks into the mouthpiece for several minutes.

When he had quite finished, Mrs. Cartwright said

"John."

"Yes?"

"I've found out something about that Elizabeth of yours."

"What?"

His heart sank. Had the whole story of their meeting come out?

"She didn't really run away from her family."

"Why—what do you mean?"

"She confessed to me, John. She told me that she had told you a terrible lie. She ran away from a school really."

"What?"

"I say she ran away from a school. The poor darling seems to have been actually teaching there. She hasn't got any family."

"Thank Heaven!"

"Oh, John, you do sound pleased. I hope you'll be very careful."

"Careful be—" But once again Mrs. Cartwright had secured the telephonic last word, by the simple expedient of replacing her receiver.

DENIS MACKAIL

IV

THE PLOTS THICKEN

I

IN THESE MODERN AND, AS some say, degenerate times, when the barrier separating the theatrical profession from the rest of the world has become little more than an imaginary line, across which, as in the well-known case of the equator, it is possible to step without being aware of its existence, actors and actresses have their meals at hours approximating very closely to those observed by the general public. But in the old days this was not so. The actors of former times realised that the human body contains but a limited quantity of stored-up energy, and that, if that energy is being expended on the digestion of recently acquired food, there will be so much the less to spare for the larynx and the facial muscles. To this tradition Leo Cartwright, as was fitting for a leader of the legitimate Stage, still clung. He was in the habit of dining shortly after five o'clock in the afternoon, and on the days when there were matinée performances, he would combine his breakfast and lunch in a composite meal which began a little before noon.

Exactly where those meals took place—when they did not take place at the theatre—was a problem to which only one member of the staff of the Thespian held anything in the nature of a key. Although no directory or reference book betrayed the Chief's private address, a tradition, based more on probabilities than on known facts, had grown up that this retreat was to be found within a radius of half a mile of the theatre. Inside this circle rumour and superstition had discovered innumerable imaginary addresses, but so far these solutions of the problem had remained empirical and unsatisfactory. There was a story of a young actor who, for a bet, had undertaken to follow the Chief home one night. His rash undertaking involved him first in a lengthy vigil outside the Garrick Club, then in a half-hour's wait in the rain outside a cabman's shelter (inside which the Chief appeared to be making himself very popular at the mess), then—still in the rain— he shadowed his quarry throughout a maddeningly deliberate stroll along miles of the Embankment. His hopes began to rise when the

Chief at length turned back and neared the suspected area, but fell again when he found that he had to wait nearly forty minutes while the great man stood in a reverie outside the darkened façade of his own theatre. At last he moved on, with a very rapid stride, and the exhausted spy trotted doggedly after him through a maze of by-streets. In the neighbourhood of Seven Dials he came suddenly round a corner into the extended point of the Chief's umbrella.

"Ill met by moonlight, proud Titania," said the Chief pleasantly.

The Sleuth, having just been taken literally and metaphorically in the wind, found himself unable to reply.

"This palpable-gross play hath well beguiled the heavy gait of night," added the Chief. "I trust you won't outsleep the coming morn, as much as you this night have overwatch'd."

"No, sir," said proud Titania, miserably.

"Good!" answered the Chief. "Trip away; make no stay; meet me at the matinée."

The amateur detective chose rather to slink than to trip away, and paid his bet on the following afternoon without a single word of explanation. Indeed, the story only drifted back to the Thespian many months afterwards, the victim having been rash enough to repeat it to a friend while on tour in South Africa.

Mention has been made of a key (albeit a doubtful one) to this mystery. This took the form of a telephone number entrusted to and jealously guarded by Miss Lemon, by means of which, it was understood, communication could be established with the Chief in the case of extreme emergency. Many attempts had been made to wrest this key from its keeper, but their continued failure had more than justified Mr. Cartwright's confidence in his secretary. "The way to get a secret out of a woman," he had said, now many years ago, "is to make favourable comments on her personal appearance. Now no power on earth could make any one do that to Miss Lemon. Therefore I am safe." When emergencies had arisen (and if they do not arise in the Theatre, then there aren't such things), telephonic communication had always to be set up through the private secretary. Miss Lemon enjoyed a consequent vogue during periods of stress at the Thespian which appeared to afford Mr. Cartwright a deep and mournful kind of amusement.

On this particular Saturday morning the Chief, having consumed his joint breakfast and lunch in the privacy of his undiscovered lair, was proceeding through the streets in the direction of the theatre. To the outward world his eyes appeared as usual to be vaguely focussed on some object not less than ten thousand miles away; but testimony that this appearance was unsupported by fact may be found not only in the anecdote just related, but also in the recollection of the number of extraordinarily skilful character studies standing to Mr. Cartwright's credit as an actor. These must clearly have been based on experience gained with a closer focus than ten thousand miles.

If further proof is required, you may have it at this very moment, for the Chief has just stopped dead at the sight of an object certainly not more than five yards away from him. The crowd of passers-by eddies and swirls round him like breakers round the Eddystone, but he stands absorbed in the midst, jostled but unmoved. Follow the direction of his eyes now and you will observe an aged man wearing a dilapidated peaked cap. An unemployed general? No. Look lower. Round the aged man's neck there is a piece of string; the ends are attached to a strip of wood; and to the strip of wood there are in turn fastened the placards of two evening newspapers. It is at these that the great man is gazing, absorbed and forgetful of all else. For on one is printed:

```
DEATH
OF AN
M.P.
ENGLAND ALL OUT
```

and on the other:

```
CLOSE
OF
PLAY
M.P. DEAD
```

Leo Cartwright's right hand unfastens the bottom button of his overcoat, and finds its way to an inner pocket. He wishes ill to no man, but, on the other hand, if that M.P. should prove to be other than Sir George Braham, it will go hard with him. The hand emerges holding a small silver coin, and he makes his way through the intervening pedestrians towards the aged man.

"One of each," he says, pointing to the placards. Still searching the crowd for the next possible customer, the aged man whips a couple of differently coloured newspapers from under his left arm, and is rewarded with a shilling. Before he has time to go through the action of fumbling for change, his client has disappeared. He has, in fact, withdrawn to a neighbouring doorway and is wrestling with his purchases.

Mr. Cartwright was not, if the truth must be told, an expert follower of the daily Press. He preferred to delegate this duty to an agency, who supplied him with such portions of this ephemeral literature as he wished to see, removed from their useless surroundings of general news. It was, indeed, many years since he had read any newspaper paragraph which did not contain some reference to himself or his theatre. You will understand, therefore, that he found some little difficulty in tracing the item of which he was now in search. You or I would naturally have turned to the Stop Press column and looked above or below the latest news of the Test Match; but the Chief did not do this until he had searched everywhere else for the large headlines which, in his opinion, the subject warranted. At last, however, his industry was rewarded. He drew a long breath. Yes, there it was.

Sir George Braham, M.P., died early this morning after a long illness.

The intelligence was confirmed in the rival sheet.

Sir George Braham, M.P., died this morning. A by-election will be necessary.

A by-election! He walked to the theatre on air. Not for one instant did it occur to him that any one but himself would assume the suffix which Death had removed from Sir George Braham. Remember that in his public life he was a successful man; and success is another name for self-confidence.

II

FOR SOME REASON, THE FINANCIAL week in the theatrical world terminates on Friday night. It is during the evening performance on

Fridays that a number of small envelopes, each marked "Personal," are distributed to the members of the company. The receipt of these envelopes is the occasion for much traditional and monotonous wit, and a further feature of the evening is the attempted adjustment of the local money market by the repayment of a quantity of old loans and the inception of a quantity of new ones. And it is on Friday night at the Thespian that Mr. Littlejohn, the Business Manager, prepares a statement of the week's takings and the advance bookings for submission to the Chief on Saturday morning.

The Chief was not surprised, therefore, when, on his arrival in the saloon (as the principal apartment in his suite was named), he discovered Mr. Littlejohn awaiting him, holding in his hand the usual slips of paper containing his analysis of the financial position and outlook.

Respectability was Mr. Littlejohn's strong suit. But for the significant fact that he never removed his silk hat wherever he was and whatever he was doing, you would probably have taken him for an archbishop who had become a bank manager late in life. His existence was an unceasing protest against the irresponsibility of the profession with which he was connected; and though he had been with Leo Cartwright now for over fifteen years, he still dreamed of the establishment of a reserve fund to which the profits of successful plays could be carried, and from which the losses on failures could be met. If you are unacquainted with dramatic finance, you may think this an ideal which it would require little persistence to realise. Mr. Littlejohn, however, should certainly have learnt better by now, when one considers on what countless occasions he had seen the Backers go off with anything up to fifteen hundred percent on their stakes, and still have no better suggestion to offer when the inevitable failure turned up than the raising of a fresh mortgage on the theatre. And yet no position in the oldest and most respectable business in the City would have tempted Mr. Littlejohn from his post as Business Manager to the Thespian. In his own desiccated way he was as much a victim to the lure of the stage as the youngest flapper in the Number 3 touring company of "The Girl in the Gondola."

"Good-morning, Littlejohn," said the Chief, flinging his newspapers on the floor and removing his overcoat.

"Good-morning, Chief."

"Well, how's the business?"

"It's dropped badly this last week," said Mr. Littlejohn gloomily.

The Chief was accustomed to Mr. Littlejohn's gloom.

"It's always bad before Christmas," he said cheerfully.

"I don't remember a drop like this before," persisted Mr. Littlejohn.

"Tut, tut. Show me the statement."

Mr. Littlejohn produced one of his slips of paper, and handed it over.

The Chief scowled. Within certain very wide limits these weekly figures meant nothing to him, but this certainly had been an exceptionally poor week. Even he recognised that.

"The houses seemed good enough," he said.

"Paper," replied Mr. Littlejohn glumly.

"Well, I'll say one thing for you, Littlejohn. You certainly collect the best-dressed deadheads of any one in London. I ought to have guessed, I suppose, when I saw all those tiaras in the stalls." He held out his hand again. "Let's see the advance."

The Business Manager passed over his remaining slip.

"There's precious little to see," he remarked.

The Chief took in the figures at a glance.

"There's some mistake," he said, with a puzzled look on his face.

"I wish there was," growled Mr. Littlejohn.

"But what on earth has happened?"

"It's those Libraries," said Mr. Littlejohn, and in his voice there was the venomous tone in which a man may refer to his lifelong enemies. "They won't renew."

"But surely after Christmas—"

"Bah!" said Mr. Littlejohn. "They've got cold feet. That's what they've got. Cold feet."

The Chief turned away and began pacing the saloon. The Business Manager followed him closely with his eyes, as he came and went.

"There's one thing we might do," he said presently.

The Chief stopped suddenly.

"What's that?" he asked.

"Well," said Mr. Littlejohn, picking up his two statements from the table and twisting them between his fingers, "you know how it is. It's up to the Libraries. If they say the word, we can carry over Christmas and run till Easter. There's any amount of money in this show still. But if they let us down, we may as well put up the notice at once."

"Well?" said the Chief.

"You know how it is," repeated Mr. Littlejohn. "In the Christmas holidays people will go to any show that the Libraries tell 'em to go to; and if they stand by a show through January, it'll run along on the impetus it gets."

"My dear Littlejohn," replied the Chief, "believe me that my knowledge of affairs in front of the house certainly includes this elementary information. I imagined that you had a suggestion to make."

"I have," said Mr. Littlejohn. "Miss Lemon tells me you're seeing Brisk today."

"Oh, I am, am I?"

"Yes. He booked an appointment on the telephone this morning."

"Did he, now?"

"Yes," said Mr. Littlejohn, a little puzzled by the Chief's manner. "Now if you play up to Brisk, it's all perfectly simple. If he'll take a fresh block of bookings, the rest of the Libraries will follow him. You know they always do. And if they do that, we can run till March or April without the slightest difficulty. Now, then, Chief," he continued, almost coaxingly, "if there's any one who can make Brisk see reason, it's yourself. We can't afford to throw away another four months' run, just because the Libraries get an attack of nerves. If there was any one else in the theatre who could do it, I'd see that it was done. But you know the difficulty with Brisk. He won't talk to any one except the man at the top. Now, just a word from you. . ."

Mr. Littlejohn paused on this note of appeal, and for a moment there was silence in the saloon. Leo Cartwright had turned his back on his Business Manager, and was gazing through the coloured-glass window at the ventilating shaft with the air of a man who surveys a limitless horizon from a mountain-top. Strange and unaccustomed thoughts were chasing through his mind. For the first time since the beginning of his management he found himself faced with a choice, not between two courses of policy within the theatre, but between the theatre itself and the world outside. The financial part of the question did not interest him in the least; so long as the curtain rose punctually and he had work to do in the theatre, it never had interested him. That side of things was entirely Littlejohn's affair, and he was content that it should remain so. Therefore, in any ordinary circumstances he would, while taking care to present an adequate appearance of distress, have been secretly snorting and champing with delight at the prospect of putting a new play into rehearsal. But Sir George Braham was dead. The Traditional Association would be meeting in a few days at the latest to select their new candidate; and before this candidate there would lie weeks of effort and excitement, which could not possibly be combined with the effort and excitement attendant on the production of a new play at the Thespian. True, he was sick to death of his part in "Pale People." Mr. Gordon had correctly understood the symptoms here. But so long as the run continued, he was, or could arrange to be, free all day. Therefore, if the run continued, he could find the time to study and, it was to be hoped, to play this extra-theatrical part of Parliamentary candidate, which for the moment was all that he really wanted to do. For a brief second the thought of letting the theatre flashed into his mind as a possible solution. But Mr. Littlejohn saw him stiffen his back, as the thought was dismissed. For eleven months in every year since the Thespian had been built, he had played there himself, or directed the few seasons in which he had not actually appeared on the stage. Death, disease, or bankruptcy might remove him from his theatre, but no outside interest, however enthralling, should do so.

He turned back from his scrutiny of the air-shaft, and addressed his Business Manager.

"All right, Littlejohn," he said. "I'll see what I can do."

Mr. Littlejohn released a long sigh of relief. Only too well did he know the Chief's impatience over those long runs which were so essential to the life of the management. He firmly believed also that, if any one could talk Mr. Brisk round, it was the Chief.

"I'm sure it's the thing to do," he said; "and I know you are the one to do it."

The Chief's mournful smile signified agreement with this estimate of his powers, and Mr. Littlejohn withdrew, perhaps to dream again, in his innocence, of the approaching establishment of the Reserve Fund. As he closed the door behind him, the telephone bell rang.

Mr. Cartwright did not, except on rare occasions, use the telephone himself. He had discovered long ago that the kind of people who rang him up were not the kind of people to whom he wanted to talk. He accordingly let the bell ring two or three times, and then was just moving towards the door to summon assistance when Miss Lemon came quickly in. She threw a brief but respectful "Good-morning, Chief," to her employer, and at once took charge of the telephone. A moment later she had clapped one hand over the mouthpiece and turned to Mr. Cartwright.

"Mr. Brisk is downstairs," she said. "He rang up this morning and said he would try and catch you when you came in."

"Ha!" said the Chief.

"Shall I have him sent up?" continued Miss Lemon.

"Yes, yes. Certainly. Of course."

Miss Lemon removed her obstructing hand and gave the necessary instruction.

"And don't let us be disturbed," added Mr. Cartwright.

Miss Lemon gave a pitying smile, as who should say, "As if I didn't know that," and left the room. Mr. Cartwright, who had engaged his secretary neither for her politeness nor her charm, seemed content with this unspoken assurance, for he did not repeat his request. Instead, he kicked the switch of the electric stove, so as to produce additional heat, adjusted a couple of armchairs to his satisfaction, and produced a box of cigars from a cupboard in the corner of the room. As he completed these simple preparations, the Stage Door-Keeper appeared in the doorway.

"Mr. Brisk," he said, and Mr. Brisk entered forthwith.

"Ha, Brisk," said the Chief, wringing his visitor by the hand. "Glad to see you."

Mr. Brisk gave an unpleasant cough, and muttered something about "miserable weather."

"Wretched," replied Mr. Cartwright cheerfully. "Sit down, won't you? And, by the way, will you smoke?"

"Thanks," said Mr. Brisk.

He took a cigar from the proffered box, smelt it at both ends, and put it in his waistcoat pocket. This, though you may not know it, is the accepted form throughout a large section of the business community for dealing with cigars.

"Very sad news this," proceeded Mr. Brisk, "about poor Braham."

"Tragic," said Mr. Cartwright. "Tragic." There was more than a suspicion of a sob in his voice. You would never have guessed that he had first heard of the late Member less than a week before, or that his only hope since that date had been for a speedy and fatal termination to his illness. There was a short pause. Both men appeared profoundly moved.

Then Mr. Brisk gave another, and still more unpleasant cough, and resumed.

"I got your letter," he said.

"My letter," contributed Mr. Cartwright.

"Yes," said Mr. Brisk. "Very pleased, I'm sure, that my little hint to Mr. Gordon had reached you."

Leo Cartwright's expressive hands indicated an all-embracing deprecation.

"Now, how does the idea strike you?" continued Mr. Brisk.

Mr. Cartwright took up the cue for which he had been waiting.

"My dear Brisk," he said, "this is hardly the moment, perhaps, to speak in any spirit of regret for the brief, the very brief time which has been allowed me to consider the suggestion to which—er—to which you refer. My life has, as you know, been for many years in a sense that of a public man. I know that public duties cannot wait for private sorrows." The sob was creeping into his voice again, but he choked it manfully down. "I need hardly say that I should esteem it a very great privilege to be of any service to the division with which I have been so long, and I trust honourably, associated."

No shorthand reporter, had any been present, could have resisted adding to his notes at this point the symbols signifying "(Loud and prolonged applause)." Even Mr. Brisk found it necessary to wait an instant while this imaginary demonstration subsided, before continuing his remarks.

"Good!" he said at length. "Or perhaps I ought to say, 'So far, so good.'"

"Eh?" interjected the Chief. Was there any other question at issue, then, apart from that of his decision?

"I take it you understand how these things are run, in a general way?" continued Mr. Brisk.

"In a general way, yes," replied Mr. Cartwright. He certainly knew in his own mind what it was that he wanted, and his experience so far had been that this knowledge was a more valuable asset than that of "how things are run."

"Nine times out of ten, of course," resumed Mr. Brisk, "these affairs have been cut and dried by Headquarters long before there's any prospect of a vacancy. And so they had been in this case. The seat had, in fact, been promised to young Hardman. Of course, he's still at Cambridge; but that's not thought much of nowadays."

Leo Cartwright correctly interpreted this last remark to refer to popular disregard for the youth of young Hardman, rather than to popular contempt for an ancient University. But he still didn't understand how young Hardman had been so fortunately removed from his path. He said so.

"Don't you see?" Mr. Brisk explained. "His father's death. He goes straight to the Lords."

"Of course, of course," said the Chief, and made a mental note to get Miss Lemon to find out young Hardman's present title. The knowledge might be useful later on.

"That being so," went on Mr. Brisk, "Headquarters will be particularly open to a good suggestion from the Local Association."

"I follow you," said the Chief.

"We're meeting on Tuesday to decide what we shall do. I had already sounded most of the others, and so far no objection has been raised to your candidature. Of course before they reach their final decision, they'll presumably want to meet you and sound your opinions on the party programme. I take it, however, that as far as that goes you'll be able to satisfy them."

"I hope so. I trust so," said Mr. Cartwright, and made a further note to get Miss Lemon to find out what the programme referred to might contain.

"There are one or two points that remain," added Mr. Brisk, indicating them on the stumpy fingers of his left hand.

"One or two points," repeated the Chief dreamily. The more active part of his brain was engaged in thinking, "They're meeting on Tuesday. By Tuesday night I ought to know whether they'll have me. Today is Saturday. Only three more days. Whom can I see, and what can I do to help in the meantime?" In reverie of this description he had permitted Mr. Brisk's voice to go rasping on, without paying more than the most distant attention to the actual words of which the rasp was made up. But now he suddenly realised from the cessation of sound that he had been put a direct question, and that an answer was awaited. Lesser men might have shown some of the embarrassment to which such a situation gives rise. But not for nothing had the Chief spent the better part of his life in learning how to bridge over the gaps in stage dialogue which result from temporary inattention or forgetfulness.

"I'm not quite sure how you mean that," he said.

"Put it another way, then," replied Mr. Brisk. "It's our old friend the non-conformist conscience. There it is. We can't get away from it, so we've got to satisfy it."

He sat back as though this explanation must necessarily have made everything clear. The Chief was interested, but still not embarrassed.

"And how do you propose that we should do that?" he asked; and to his surprise, signs of the discomfort which he should have been feeling himself appeared in the face of Mr. Brisk.

"Mind you, Mr. Cartwright," said that gentleman, with something strongly resembling a blush overspreading his countenance, "I'm not speaking for myself here. As far as I'm concerned, I know it's not my business. We're gentlemen, you and me; we don't talk about such things."

Mr. Cartwright permitted himself an infinitesimal elevation of the left side of his upper lip. The same expression, in fact, as that in the photograph on the walls of this very room of himself standing at the foot of the guillotine, in the character of the Marquis de Saint-Phairien in the last Act of "The Red City."

"What things?" he asked.

Mr. Brisk blew his nose. The moment had now arrived in referring to which he had told his partner that, if Mr. Cartwright didn't like it, then he could lump it. As an essential truth, this statement must remain unaltered. But it seemed hard that, even before the awkward though inevitable subject had been reached, he should somehow find himself on the defensive like this. In his prophetic imagination it had been Mr. Cartwright who was on the defensive. And yet, to look at the man now, one might think that it was Alexander Brisk's past that was under discussion, instead of this hypocritical old actor's.

"I don't quite follow you, Brisk," said the Chief, a little coldly. "To what things are you referring?"

Mr. Brisk swallowed and dashed at it.

"It's like this," he said. "I'm asking you this now to save time and to save trouble. In a word, to save the whole thing from coming up at Tuesday's meeting, and possibly upsetting the entire business. To be perfectly frank, this is a question that any selection committee would have to ask, and, if for no other reason, then because such things are fair game for the other side, and always have been. The fact is, then," he concluded, with a final burst into the open, "we've got to know how things stand about your marriage."

Instinctively, as he uttered these words, Mr. Brisk drew back in his chair, and braced himself against the outburst which he felt was coming. But none came. Leo Cartwright had not moved in his seat, but in his pale-grey, expressionless face his lowered eyelids showed paler still. All muscular tension of every description seemed to have left that masklike countenance, and to be concentrated instead in the hands, whose white knuckles showed the force of their owner's grip on the arms of his chair.

Mr. Brisk half-rose to his feet. Ought he to open a window, or ring for water? There did not seem to be any bell, but the telephone—He darted another look at the Chief, and, seeing those luminous eyes once more focused on him, dropped back in confusion.

"I appreciate the position," said Mr. Cartwright slowly. "It is in many ways a horrible world. My wife and I have been separated now for twenty-five years. The fault was on my side—entirely. Is there anything else that I can tell your Committee?"

"My Committee aren't acting out of curiosity, Mr. Cartwright," replied Mr. Brisk. "But they've got to think of the Party. If I am satisfied, they won't want to ask any questions. But—you must forgive my mentioning it—are there any—any details, such as the Press on the other side might get hold of? You know the kind of thing I mean."

"It would be surprising if after twenty-five years the world had not supplied all the details it wanted," said Mr. Cartwright. "I am afraid that I cannot discuss the matter on these lines any longer. If your Committee wish to see me on Tuesday, I shall be very glad to meet them. If not, I shall not misinterpret their decision."

"So long as you are aware of the position, I am quite happy to leave it in your hands to decide whether you prefer to have it out now or on Tuesday," answered Mr. Brisk. "My only object in mentioning the matter was to save you possible annoyance later on."

"I appreciate your tact," said the Chief in a perfectly toneless voice.

"Then I shall send you a formal invitation at once to attend our meeting on Tuesday afternoon," said Mr. Brisk; and to himself he added, "By Jove! I was right. This is the kind of man we want. Once we get him on our side, he'll make 'em sit up, if he wants to."

"You mentioned 'one or two points' just now," continued the Chief. "I take it that we have dealt with the first. Perhaps we could get on to the rest quickly, as I am afraid I shall have to go and dress in a few minutes."

As if in confirmation of his words, there came a sound of approaching knocks on the doors of neighboring dressing-rooms, punctuated by the call-boy's cry, "Half an hour, please." The sound died away down the stairs.

"Did I say 'one or two'?" asked Mr. Brisk. "If I did, I think the other points must have been on ordinary business. I've nothing else to put to you, as far as my Committee is concerned. But perhaps whatever it was had better wait," he finished, rising to his feet.

"There's one thing that I should like to ask you before you go," said Mr. Cartwright.

"Yes?" Mr. Brisk spoke sharply, and with one eye on the door.

"Littlejohn tells me that the Libraries won't renew their bookings for 'Pale People.' What are they afraid of, Brisk?"

Mr. Brisk gave a short, mirthless laugh. Back in his ordinary business capacity again, he feared no man.

"Afraid of?" he repeated. "Afraid of losing money, I should say. Why, look at the seats we've had to return the last fortnight."

"There's nothing wrong with the play," said the Chief. "It's the same everywhere just before Christmas."

"Is it?" replied Mr. Brisk. "We'd renew all right, if you were doing the business that they've been doing at the Coventry and the Auditorium. Not that there's money in any of it nowadays," he added, with heavily emphasised gloom.

"No money?" repeated the Chief, exactly as he had been meant to repeat it.

"You ought to see the way our expenses have gone up," said Mr. Brisk. "Salaries, telephones, printing, advertising, everything. I'm sure I don't know how we're to go on. The theatres will have to meet us on the question of price sooner or later. The present arrangement can't last, and the public won't pay any more."

"Ha!" said the Chief, and seldom can a monosyllable have covered so many unspoken thoughts. Mr. Brisk's last words had killed the run of "Pale People" more surely than the simultaneous death of the entire company could have done. Littlejohn, waiting in the background, must not only be told that the Chief's intercessory efforts had failed, but must be positively instructed to see that the fortnight's notice went up that very day. For all his outward air of vagueness, the Chief had made no mistake about the meaning of his Business Manager's last statement. Worse, however, than this, he now realised the exact nature of the *quid pro quo* which Mr. Brisk, representing the London Libraries, expected in return for the support which he could give in his capacity as Chairman of the Covent Garden Traditional Association. Leo Cartwright, as has been said, was full of self-confidence, but he was strangely free from conceit. That Mr. Brisk's action had been due to his belief in his nominee's capacity as a representative of the people, the nominee had never for a moment believed. He could even in a way feel relieved that the exact return which Mr. Brisk required for his assistance had been made clear so early in the game. He was none the less in a very difficult position.

Mr. Brisk waited a moment for the monosyllable to be followed by any words which might give a clue to the workings of the Chief's mind, but none came. He decided that he had said enough for one day. The seed must be left to germinate over the week-end. He had better go now.

"Well, well," he said, holding out his hand. "I must be going along. We'll meet on Tuesday, I hope."

"On Tuesday. Yes," replied the Chief, shaking hands. "By the way, Brisk," he added, "what made you think of approaching me on this subject? I should be interested to know."

He fixed Mr. Brisk with his melancholy eyes, but Mr. Brisk had had his answer ready for several weeks.

"Anything that helps the Theatre," he said, "helps me. Besides, this has been a theatrical division for three hundred years."

And with these words he turned to leave the room. But in the open doorway he paused.

"By the way," he added, "it might be a good thing if you sent some flowers to Braham's funeral. There are no relations to be surprised, and it would establish a kind of connection in the public mind."

"Thank you," said the Chief seriously. "I will put Gordon on to it at once."

This time Mr. Brisk really did leave.

Leo Cartwright turned and went through to his dressing-room, where Tuke, his dresser, was awaiting him in a blaze of electric light. The elaborate process of preparing his face and figure for the inspection of the British public began once more.

He was issuing his final instructions to Miss Lemon, when his call for the first act came, and she followed him down on to the stage.

"What else have I got this afternoon?" he whispered.

"Mr. Lawrence is in front," said Miss Lemon. "When will you see him?"

"At the end," answered the Chief, and passed on to mount the three steps of the rostrum from which his entrance was made.

"No, mother. If I am to marry, I must give myself to a Man," came the leading lady's high-pitched voice from the stage.

As Miss Lemon tiptoed away, she heard the familiar roar which told her that the centre of the Thespian universe had begun another day's work.

III

ON THE FIRST MORNING OF her new employment, Mrs. Cartwright's secretary thought it wise to arrive considerably earlier than the half-past eleven which had been specified. In the little room behind the dining-room John's typewriter occupied a prominent position on the writing table, and in less than ten minutes the two letters which had been dictated on the previous evening were transcribed and on their way up to Mrs. Cartwright for signature.

"What is it?" asked that lady from the depths of an armchair and the morning newspapers, as Hilda entered the room.

"Miss Smith, mum, said would you please to sign these letters."

Mrs. Cartwright looked at the little clock by her side and groaned. More than two hours still before lunchtime, and not a letter in the house that needed answering. She was beginning to understand, she felt, how it was that otherwise harmless people were driven to writing their memoirs. To have a secretary eating her head off like this day after day would explain, even if it did not excuse, many an otherwise inexplicable autobiography. At this moment an idea came to her.

"Ask Miss Smith to come upstairs, Hilda," she said, and, as the maid turned to leave the room, she moved quickly to the writing-table. But before the required signatures were added, two alterations to the original documents were effected. Turning over the top of the letter to her husband, she ran her finger along the fold and tore off the embossed address. At the head of the shortened page she wrote in "Care of the Trafalgar Agency." Then taking the second letter, she proceeded to add a holograph postscript.

"P. S.," she wrote. "Mind you come if you possibly can."

Letter Number 1 was then signed "David Lawrence," and letter Number 2 "Helen Cartwright." As she was smoothing down the flap of the second envelope, Elizabeth came into the room.

"Good-morning," said Mrs. Cartwright. "You were rather early, weren't you?"

Kind hearted as she was, it was difficult to keep a faint note of dissatisfaction out of these words, and Elizabeth looked a little puzzled.

"I'm sorry—" she began.

"Oh, no; it's quite all right. Only another morning I think about half-past eleven or twelve will be quite soon enough. Still, as you are here, I wonder if you would be very kind and do something for me."

"Why, of course," said Elizabeth. She couldn't help thinking that her predecessor in this strange post must have been a singularly disobliging woman. What else was she there for, except to do the things that she was told to do?

"I know it's not part of your usual work," continued Mrs. Cartwright, in the apologetic tone which we have all learnt to use to our paid assistants; "but do you think you would mind taking this letter to Harley Street for me? And afterwards, perhaps, you could leave the other one at the District Messengers' office."

"Of course I will," Elizabeth answered. "I'll drop them both, if you like."

"Oh, no. Don't bother to do that. But I want you to find out if Mr. Lawrence is down from Oxford yet before you leave the letter. If he won't be back by tomorrow morning, bring the letter away with you. It would be too late, really, to forward it now." Mrs. Cartwright's plans were becoming more uncontrollably complicated every instant. "And in that case don't have the other letter sent either. I'd have to put the whole thing off then. Is that quite clear?"

"Quite, I think." Elizabeth repeated the instructions.

"Yes, that's it. Now, it's a fine morning, so why don't you walk across the Park? It would do you good. And it will hardly be worth while coming back before lunch, so I won't expect you again today. You can ring me up from a call-office, if you will, and let me know whether you've been able to get rid of your letters or not."

In view of the proportions of her present salary, Elizabeth could hardly insert a reminder that she had yesterday received an invitation to lunch with her employer. There was certainly nothing in her expression, therefore, that should cause Mrs. Cartwright to add (as she did):

"Now here's a pound for your expenses, and mind you give yourself a good lunch."

"Oh, I couldn't really—"

"Nonsense. It's an understood thing." (Invaluable phrase!) "Oh, and if David Lawrence can lunch with me tomorrow, I'd like to have you here too. Otherwise, of course, your Saturdays will be free."

"Of course I'd love to, if you really—"

"Yes, yes. It's quite essential," replied Mrs. Cartwright.

As Elizabeth closed the door once more behind her, it struck her employer that "essential" was perhaps hardly the word to have used, even if it expressed what she really meant. Never mind, though. The great secretarial problem had been solved, even if by rather Gordian methods, until Monday morning. And in the meantime, the best thing to do, as with all one's troubles, was to forget about it. Only, if John Ormroyd should cross her path in the immediate future, let him beware!

The popular novelist in question had a sufficiently narrow escape less than an hour later, when he suddenly appeared on Mrs. Cartwright's doorstep, looking slightly overdressed and carrying what appeared to be a box of chocolates.

"I say," he said, when the door was opened. "I say, is Miss Smith in?"

"No, sir," answered Hilda. "She went out some time ago."

"Oh. Is she coming back again?"

"I don't think so, sir. Not today."

"Oh. Thank you. Thank you very much."

"I think Mrs. Cartwright is in, sir."

"Oh. Thanks. Thanks awfully. No, thanks."

And he departed, feeling, and probably looking, more than a little undignified. It was a really childish thing to do, though, to leave the box of chocolates hanging on the area railings of the next house. For though I will not say that they were unappreciated by the postman who shortly afterwards appropriated them, at the same time it is clear that they would for several days have remained quite fresh enough to serve their original purpose.

Elizabeth, having reached her goal, had her finger poised to ring the front-door bell, as a cab drew up; but hearing the grinding of its brakes, she turned, and saw a tall, thin, and youthful figure leap lightly from the door of the taxi. Almost the most noticeable incident about this figure was its pair of gargantuan fur gauntlets, such as one might expect to find in use on a polar expedition, but were in fact considered at this time suitable for ordinary wear by junior members of the University.

"Are you Mr. Lawrence?" she asked, as the figure crossed the pavement towards her.

"Yes," said David. "But I expect you want my father."

"I don't know. I've got a letter here for Mr. David Lawrence."

"That's me," said David, and, removing one of the gauntlets, prepared to receive the letter.

"From Mrs. Cartwright," added Elizabeth.

"Do you—are you—?" David began.

"I'm her secretary."

"Oh, yes." And for the first time David turned his whole attention towards the bearer of the letter. A very dangerous thing to do, as John Ormroyd had discovered yesterday; for to turn one's whole attention to Elizabeth implied looking at her eyes; and if her eyes should happen simultaneously to be looking at you, well, that was just where the danger came in. Nothing, David suddenly realised, could stop the terrible blush that was rushing up his backbone, but perhaps if he said something, she might not notice it.

"I say," he remarked, as the blush reached his collar; "won't you sit down?"

Elizabeth laughed, and the blush was now all over the scalp and everywhere.

"On your doorstep?" she asked.

"Oh, no. I don't mean that. I mean—"

But what exactly he did mean will never be known, for at this instant, attracted doubtless by the sound of the stationary taxicab, the housekeeper, Mrs. Billett, opened the front door.

Alas for David! Mrs. Billett was a housekeeper now, had even been a housekeeper for ten years; but before that she had been that regrettable necessity, a nurse. Worse still, she had been David's nurse. And, judging by all previous experience of his homecomings, she would in another second bring shame and dishonour on him for evermore, by submitting him to a public embrace. What protection would the acquisition of a whole term's education at Oxford be then? It must be set down as to David's credit that he made up his mind, in the same instant as the full horror of the situation burst upon him, that the ordeal must be endured. Come what might, the faithful retainer's silly old feelings must be respected. He shut his eyes and leant forward.

Blackness and bombazine.

It was over.

He straightened himself and turned round. There was the cab, there still the enchanted doorstep, but of the fairy secretary not a trace remained except the letter in his hand. She must have gone when the door opened. If only—if only she had failed to see that terrible embrace!

Mrs. Billett was speaking. "I'll pay the cab, dear, and look after the luggage. There's a letter for you from the Doctor on the hall table."

David disappears into the darkness of the hall. Among the hats and gloves of those seekers after health who are at present awaiting audience with his father's partner, he finds a letter with a Swiss stamp.

Dr. Lawrence is glad to say that he is already feeling considerably rested; the weather has been excellent and the hotel no less comfortable than had been described. On the whole, however, he hardly thinks it advisable that David should join him for the few short weeks of the Christmas vacation.

The atmosphere of this place at Christmas-time would, I am afraid, make it impossible for you to do any serious work; and you must always remember that at the University the period of vacation is rightly regarded as that in which the more solid part of one's reading should be undertaken. I have no doubt that Aunt Lily would be very glad to have you with her for Christmas and the New Year, and I am writing to her today suggesting this. Meanwhile, as I shall not be seeing you, I enclose a small cheque as your usual present. You must, of course, use your own judgment as to its employment, but I strongly recommend you to use at least a portion of it for the purchase of Savings Certificates.

The letter concluded with various messages for Mrs. Billett, which are of no interest to the present story.

David wasted no time in asking himself if he regretted the prospect of remaining in England. The news that he was not expected to join his father came with all the wonderful sense of liberation with which one learns from the dentist's secretary of the postponement of an appointment. As for Aunt Lily, she could ask him until she was black in the face, before he would go and waste his time with her and her loathsome children. Fortunately she would believe any story of a previous engagement which he chose to tell her. Aunt Lily's silliness was indeed her only virtue.

Now for the cheque. This, on examination, revealed a distinct increase over last Christmas, pleasure in which was, however, considerably discounted by the fact that it bore the date "December 25th." David's thoughts at this piece of sentimental meanness (for so he described it to himself) did not perhaps do him very much credit, but there can be few who would not have shared them.

The luggage had now all been fetched in and the front door closed. The hall was sufficiently solitary for him to turn to Mrs. Cartwright's letter.

What a ripping idea! And on the very first day of the vacation too. He shuddered as he thought how nearly some necessary repairs to his side-car had decided him to stay up at Oxford over the week-end. And yet even on the way to the telephone something seemed to come between him and the full pleasure of anticipation. The secretary—that was it, of course. Would she be at lunch tomorrow? If so, would she laugh at him again, as she had laughed at him today? The thought was disquieting, but, strange to say, no less disquieting than the alternative possibility that he might not find her there at all.

DENIS MACKAIL

It was with a vague mental discomfort, hardly more describable than the faint clouding of the palate which presages the arrival of another Cold, that he transmitted his acceptance through the telephone.

The message, together with a subsequent one from Elizabeth to the effect that she had successfully disposed of both her letters, was repeated to Mrs. Cartwright when she returned from her morning stroll.

"Tell Cook," she said, "that I want lunch for three tomorrow. It had better be at one o'clock, because we're going to a matinée."

"Yes, madam. And Mr. Ormroyd called this morning, madam. But he only asked for Miss Smith."

"After she'd gone out, you mean?"

"Yes, madam."

Mrs. Cartwright left the subject there for the moment; but a little later, when she was occupied in eating what was, roughly speaking, the six thousandth solitary lunch since her marriage, she said:

"You might ring up and ask Mr. Ormroyd if he will lunch here tomorrow as well. If he accepts, then we shall be four."

IV

AND HERE IS HOW THESE same four persons occupied this Friday afternoon.

David Lawrence had his hair cut, and shampooed, and singed. Total cost (including tip), five shillings and sixpence; from which may be deducted the price of the one cigarette which the proprietor of the establishment presented to his patrons as an indication, if hardly as a justification, of its pronounced West-Endishness. He also purchased at a second establishment a half-pound tin of a presumably rare and certainly costly smoking-mixture. Total cost, fourteen shillings and sixpence; but as this included personal attention by one man in a morning coat and spats, and by two men in white overalls, the charge can scarcely be regarded as excessive. Having thus satisfactorily vindicated his position as an undergraduate, he returned to Harley Street and spent the rest of the afternoon in the consumption of the smoking-mixture and the perusal of Mr. Henry Fielding's excellent biography of Mr. Tom Jones.

John Ormroyd spent the afternoon in his study. He was engaged, in his own opinion, on a draft of the short story which had been suggested to him by his Thespian telephone call on the previous Tuesday; but his blotting-pad bore witness to strange wanderings into other fields of thought. For what connection could you find between that heroic, if over-sentimentalised slice of life, and the constant repetition on the blotting-paper of a monogram, formed always from the same two letters? The answer which you give (and correctly) to this question is "Precious little," and even John realised that work must be abandoned, when he found himself grappling unexpectedly with a sonnet.

And yet, with selfish obstinacy, he persisted in attributing this inability to concentrate his thoughts to the fact that he had been called to the telephone just as he was sitting down to write. "Tell Mrs. Cartwright I'll be delighted," he had said, and somehow from that moment literary output became impossible. The arrival of the unwanted sonnet was merely the finishing touch to a wasted afternoon. He dined alone at his Club, and spent the evening playing inexpressibly bad billiards with the marker.

Elizabeth Smith spent the afternoon lying on her bed at her lodgings. She was not ill, nor even fatigued. Moreover, her first week's salary had so reëstablished relations with her landlady, that a gas stove was once again fairly sprinkling the room with thermal units. Elizabeth was reading "She Loves Me Not." For this occupation privacy was essential. This brings us as far as the bedroom, which, possessing as it did only one, small, cane-bottomed, straight-backed chair, brings us back to Elizabeth. At four o'clock, her eyes by this time at least twice their usual enormous size, and having reached page 115, she interrupted herself just long enough to light the incandescent gas over the bed. She is not heard of again until her arrival, regrettably late, at the communal evening meal.

"Why, Miss Smith," says the unromantic landlady, "you surely haven't caught another cold!"

As for Helen Cartwright, an irresistible power has drawn her to the little lacquer box in which reposes her carbon copy of "Romance to the Rescue." It is a long time before she can bring herself to take up the first of the neatly typed, brown-paper jackets, and, even when she has done so, it remains for a still longer time unopened in her hand, while her mind goes back to the little salon with its marble floor, where for so many years she wrote and destroyed and wrote again. Further still it goes, further than it has willingly journeyed since quite early days in the little salon, and the fire-light reveals an enigmatic expression on her face as she turns to the opening of her play. One by one the brown-paper covers are taken up and laid aside, and still she sits silent and absorbed. Only once does a sound come from her lips, and then you would have to be close indeed to catch the half-muttered syllables.

"Intolerable tosh!" says Mrs. Cartwright.

V

A Matinée at the Thespian

I

Mr. Brisk did not leave the theatre immediately after his interview, but found his way round to the front entrance, at which miscalculating suburbanites were already beginning to arrive, and, with a nod at the commissionnaire in the foyer, passed upstairs again to the P.M.'s room. Mr. Gordon, the débris of a light lunch still on the corner of his desk, was washing his hands, preparatory to assuming his matinée morning coat.

"Hullo, Brisk," he said.

"How's yourself?" answered Mr. Brisk.

"Fine. How's things?" countered Mr. Gordon.

"Seen the evening paper?"

Mr. Gordon nodded towards a crumpled object on the sofa.

"Australia's too much for us this time," he said.

"You and your cricket!"

Both men chuckled, and by this sound of mirth signified a complete understanding that the one really important item of news was known to them both. Of sorrow for the dead Member, or even a passing reference to his name, I regret to say there was none.

"Seen the Chief?" continued Mr. Gordon, carefully replacing his rings.

"Yup," answered Mr. Brisk.

"All O.K.?"

"Call no man happy till he's dead," replied Mr. Brisk. This second reference to mortality produced, for some strange reason, a further outburst of mirth on both sides.

"Well, well; little Gordon did his best for you," said the Personal Manager, as the chuckles subsided.

"Little Gordon knows on which side his bread is buttered," replied Mr. Brisk.

It is a pleasing sight to observe these great minds unbending, even though beneath this sprightly dialogue one may feel an undercurrent of watchfulness, if not of actual suspicion. On the surface, however, all is graciousness and charm.

"Listen," says Mr. Gordon. "Let me tell you this one. . ."

Several yards of film are at this point necessarily cut out.

When the picture begins again, we find that Mr. Brisk has departed, and Mr. Gordon is at the telephone, answering Miss Lemon.

"The Chief wants to see Mr. Lawrence at the end this afternoon," says the Secretary. "Will you bring him round?"

"Right you are. In Box B?"

"Yes. And I've just had a message that Mr. Ormroyd will be there too. The Chief will see him after the second Act."

"Second interval. Right," says Mr. Gordon, and replaces his receiver.

And with that he leaves his room, locking the door behind him, and, with silk hat placed firmly on his head, takes up his position at the back of the dress circle. His lips move silently as he counts the heads of the audience, skilfully disposed by the Box Office so as to cover the greatest possible area of space. "It's good enough, if they've paid," he murmurs; but the answer to this doubt remains, as it always has remained and always will remain, locked in the breasts of Mr. Littlejohn and his devoted assistants.

II

DAVID'S SATURDAY MORNING SEEMED ENDLESS. Time and again it became necessary to put his watch to his ear to make certain that it still breathed. At twelve o'clock he suddenly decided that a different shirt would meet the occasion better, and this in turn involved the creation and establishment of a new parting to his hair. Even so, however, he reached the house in the little Square at least ten minutes before one.

In the drawing-room Mrs. Cartwright was waiting for him. It was the first time that he had seen her by daylight,—even December daylight,—but she looked, he thought, more wonderful than ever. There was a little flush on her face, for instance, which artificial light must have killed. At any rate he did not remember it.

"Keep Mr. Ormroyd in Miss Smith's room, when he comes," said Mrs. Cartwright to the maid. "We'll be down in a minute or two."

Hilda acknowledged the instruction and retired.

"Now, then," Mrs. Cartwright went on; "we've only got a minute, so listen carefully."

Bewilderment, tempered by devotion, appeared on David's face.

"Do you remember telling me the other day that you would like to be able to do something for me?" she asked.

Did he remember? The thought of the kind of fool he had made of himself before his goddess had never been outside his thoughts since that ridiculous utterance.

"I—of course—I. . ." he stammered and blushed.

"Well," Mrs. Cartwright went on quickly, "I've got something I want you to do for me now. Nobody else in the world can help me except you, and I'm afraid you may not find it easy. But you will try, won't you?"

With her head a little on one side and her eyes still fixed firmly on him, a considerably more experienced man of the world than David Lawrence would have found it hard not to promise immediate assistance. David had no wish to do anything else. If she wasn't rotting him,—and she didn't seem to be,—why, there was nothing in the world that he would not do for her. Just let her try!

"If you really mean. . ." he began.

"I do. I do. I'm absolutely serious. I'm in a most ridiculous difficulty. You know I'm separated from my husband?"

This was Life with a vengeance. David nodded solemnly.

"Well, by a most ghastly kind of mistake, a play that I once wrote has been sent to him—not under my name, of course—and he's thinking of producing it. If he goes on, he's bound to find out that it's mine. You see it would be dreadful—impossible. It's got to be stopped."

Again David nodded. How he could conceivably assist in this extraordinary difficulty, he had no idea; but his nod was an attempt to convey all the strong, silent sympathy and efficiency, the appearance of which a spoken acknowledgement might, he feared, shatter.

"I haven't told you the worst part yet, though," said Mrs. Cartwright. "I don't know what you'll think. It's a sheer and absolute coincidence, but the play has gone to him under your name."

"Mine? 'David Lawrence'?" he gasped, as if even yet she might mean some other, unknown variant of his official description.

"Yes. Of course I'd never heard of you when I invented it, or thought I'd invented it. I suppose I may have had your father's name at the back of my mind somewhere, but, as far as I could possibly tell at the time, it was an absolute invention."

Recollection of the mysterious letter mentioned by the parlourmaid at his first call suddenly came back to him. It was true, then.

DENIS MACKAIL

"It was all an absolute mistake for the Agent to send the play to Leo at all," Mrs. Cartwright went on. "But it's done now. It's too late. And, oh, David! I'm afraid I've played rather a mean trick on you about this afternoon."

"A trick?"

"Yes. But if you can't help me, just say so, and I'll try to think of something else. You still needn't come into it at all, if you'd rather not. Only when I remembered what you said. . ."

She paused on a note of anxious appeal. No need to tell David to what utterance of his she referred. It was that same damnable piece of babyish posing (so he described it to himself) rising up once again to come between him and the straightforward offer of service which he should be making now. But he meant it. He had meant it then, and he meant it still.

"All right," he said gruffly. "If I can help you, I. . ."

He didn't have to finish. Mrs. Cartwright had seized him by the hand.

"Thank you! Thank you!" she cried. "If only you get me out of this horrible difficulty, I'll do anything in the world for you. Now listen quickly, David. I'm not going with you this afternoon, but John Ormroyd and my secretary will be there. I've made an appointment for me—that's you, of course—to see Leo during the afternoon. They'll send round for you to the Box. You must ask for the ticket when you get to the theatre; it's in your name. When you see him, make any kind of excuse, tell any kind of lie that you can think of, only, whatever happens, make him see that he can't do that play."

She dropped his hand again, and he stood there with misery and fear in his heart. Of all the impossible things which he could conceivably have been asked to do, this was the worst! To appear in these false colours before the uncrowned king of the London Stage, and to make him change his mind about taking a play the very title of which he had not yet been told, why, it was a nightmare! Cold sweat broke out on his brow as for an instant the alternative of failing Mrs. Cartwright presented itself to his mind.

"But—but—what am I to say?" he croaked miserably.

"Oh, David, anything! Tell him you've promised it to some one else, tell him you're under contract elsewhere, tell him the agents who sent it him made a mistake, tell him it's translated from the German; only, whatever you do, *get it away from him!*"

This was worse than anything that he had ever imagined. The unhappy David groaned. Switzerland with his father, even Bexhill with Aunt Lily, could more easily be borne. But there was, there could be no going back.

"I—I'll do my best," he said, and, as he spoke, the drawing-room door opened again.

"Luncheon is served," said Hilda.

"Is Mr. Ormroyd here?" asked Mrs. Cartwright.

"He is downstairs, madam."

"Come on, then, David."

Like Isaac ascending the mountain with his conscientious parent, David followed his hostess downstairs. Do not question the accuracy of my scriptural knowledge, for there can be no doubt that Isaac feared the worst that day. His question to his father shows it. And in both cases one can picture the same reluctance, the same passionate desire to escape, and the same sense of inevitable doom.

III

In view of Mrs. Cartwright's declared policy with regard to her share in the afternoon's pleasure, John Ormroyd's greeting might well have been more fortunate.

"I needn't ask how you are," he said, as he shook hands. "You're looking blooming."

"The flush of sickness, John," replied his hostess. "If I keep out of bed for lunch today, it's as much as you can hope for. I've had the most terrible headache all morning."

"Then you're not coming to the play?" put in Elizabeth.

"What play?" asked John.

"'Pale People,'" said Elizabeth. "I hope you haven't seen it."

If John had seen it a hundred times, it would have made no difference to his answer. Where Elizabeth spent her afternoon, there also would he be, if impudence or money could manage it.

"But had you got a seat for me?" he asked, turning to Mrs. Cartwright.

"I've got a Box, and I shan't be going, so you can have two seats if you like," she answered. "But not unless you say you're sorry about my headache."

Was John mistaken, or did she accompany these last words by a momentary flicker of one eyelid?

　　　　　　　　　　　　　　DENIS MACKAIL

"But I am," he said, just a little perplexed. "I'm terribly sorry. Isn't there anything we can do?"

"Can't I get you some Aspirin?" suggested Elizabeth, half-rising.

"Or some eau-de-cologne?" added John.

"David," said Mrs. Cartwright brutally; "why don't you suggest something?" But a glance at his face made her run on quickly. "No, no. It's not so bad as all that. I shall be quite well again at once, if I keep quiet this afternoon. It's the bad air in the theatre that I dread."

Of her three guests, only John was sufficiently well versed in her private affairs to wonder how she could even for a moment have considered attending a Thespian matinée in the full publicity of a Box. But John could not get out of his head that impression of a brief ocular eclipse. Possibly the ticket had been a present from some thoughtless friend. In any case, with the promise of an afternoon in Elizabeth's company, he would be content. Explanations, if there were to be any, could wait.

Only he wished they could get rid of that sulky looking boy somehow or other.

Mrs. Cartwright's alleged headache certainly did not make her conversation any less sparkling during lunch. She played on her ill-assorted guests with all the skill of her long experience. Not for an instant did the conversation flag.

"I don't know what's come over her," said John to Elizabeth, after a more than usually amusing sally on the part of his hostess, "but I have an idea that she's got some joke of her own that we can't see."

These unlucky words froze the smile which Mrs. Cartwright had at last succeeded in forcing on David's countenance, and she dashed hastily in.

"No, no," she said. "No joke. But I've had a piece of luck."

"Good luck?" asked John.

"The kind of luck that one doesn't expect at my age," she answered. "I've put a friendship to the test, and it has stood it."

"Well, if you represent half of it, I expect it has," said John.

"Thank you, John. Your health!"

"All very well to talk," mumbled David to himself. "I'd like to see *him* try and do what I've got to do." But the thinly veiled compliment had given him a pleasantly heroic sensation all the same.

"I've ordered the car for you all," Mrs. Cartwright announced, as coffee was being served; "and, though I don't want to hurry you, I think you ought to be going in a minute or two now."

"Thank Heaven," said John, "I'm not yet so old that I can bear missing the beginning of a play. May I just scribble a note before we start?" He got up from the table as he spoke.

"Of course. You'll find everything in the next room. Elizabeth, show him where you keep my note-paper," answered Mrs. Cartwright.

John and Elizabeth withdrew to the little room at the back where the typewriter had been put, and he wrote hurriedly on a visiting-card; "I shall be in front in a Box this afternoon if you will let me know when I can see you," and slipped the card into an envelope.

"That's it," he added, as he drew a dash under Leo Cartwright's name.

In the dining-room David was endeavouring to secure what courage may be given by boiling coffee.

"Now, David, you won't fail me, will you?" said his hostess.

"I'll do my best."

"I know you will. And nothing's settled yet, so there's no question of breaking any agreement."

"I see."

The maid appeared in the doorway.

"The car is here, madam," she said.

"Just tell Mr. Ormroyd. He's writing a note in Miss Smith's room."

"Yes, madam." The door closed.

"Let me know what happens, won't you?" said Mrs. Cartwright, rising to her feet. "Ring me up, or come and see me."

"Oh, yes. Of course."

"I shall will you to bring it off. There, now, I hear the others in the hall." She held out her hand. "Thank you a thousand times, David. If you do this for me, I shall never forget it."

A sickly smile appeared on David's face.

"That's all right," he said.

Mrs. Cartwright came to the front door to see them off.

"Have you found her another job yet?" she whispered in John's ear, as he was buttoning his overcoat.

"No, but I still hope to," he answered.

"Ten more days is my limit," she said, aloud now, for the others were getting into the car. "After that I go into a rest-cure. Is that quite clear?"

"I'll do my best to manage it inside the time," he said. "Good-bye. Thanks awfully for the treat."

He ran down the steps and disappeared into the car.

"My dear John," said Mrs. Cartwright, as she returned to her fireside, "you could manage it in five minutes, if you tried. But I've done quite enough for you already, without telling you that."

"Poor David!" she murmured a little later, as she removed the book-marker from her novel.

IV

"WHO'S GOT THE TICKET?" ASKED John, as they left the car at the entrance to the Thespian.

"I've got to ask for it at the Box Office," David answered.

He hurried ahead so as to avoid any surprise which might be occasioned by his asking for Mr. Lawrence's (and not Mrs. Cartwright's) Box. The ticket was handed over at once, but, to his annoyance, on turning to leave the window, he found John again by his side. He seemed to be peering at the ticket.

"Is that Box B?" he asked.

"Yes," said David, with a suspicious glance. What had it got to do with him?

But John appeared to have obtained all the information that he required, and dropped behind. His purpose was, of course, to make a hurried pencil addition to his visiting-card. "I shall be in front in Box B," it now read. He handed it together with a shilling to a commissionnaire.

"Let Mr. Cartwright have this," he said.

"Right, sir."

John hastened along the corridor after the others.

As guardian of the ticket, David had gone ahead, and in the same capacity he felt it his duty to make the necessary purchase of programmes. As if Fate were determined to pile anxiety on anxiety, he found that he had nothing in his pocket except a ten-shilling note.

"I shall have to bring you change, sir," said the attendant.

Ominous words these, in a place of public entertainment. David felt he must resign himself to walking home from the theatre. There was but little consolation in the reflection that the value of his afternoon's entertainment was considerably more than the money thus sunk, for how willingly would he have paid twenty times this sum to be anywhere else in the world.

Almost as soon as they were seated, the orchestra brought the first part of its labours to a conclusion; the house lights were extinguished, leaving only a warm glow on the lower edge of the heavy velvet tableau curtains. A second's pause, and these curtains swung up into the darkness overhead; and as they disappeared there was wafted out into the Box that strange mixture of cold stuffiness and scene-painter's size which is to a large proportion of civilised humanity the very breath of Romance. A battered-looking telephone on a buhl table began to ring; a door opened and there entered an overdressed maid with blue eyelids; she gave a look of surprised contempt in the direction of the dress circle, and took up the telephone.

The audience settled back in its seats with satisfaction and anticipation. Whatever else had altered during these years of change, the great traditions of the Thespian Theatre stood fast.

The first Act of "Pale People" put no undue strain on the emotions. First Acts at the Thespian never did. Everything was very pleasant, efficient, and gentlemanly, but if it held the mirror up to nature, then all that can be said is that it must have been either a very abnormal mirror or a very unrepresentative piece of nature. Elizabeth sat enthralled, her eyes never for an instant leaving the stage; and this enabled John to give that detailed observation to her features, visible in the light reflected from the scene, which he had for some time felt to be necessary for their just appreciation, but had hitherto found impossible. Consequently, though his scrutiny produced nothing but the most satisfactory results, his attention to the course of the drama was of the scantiest. Rather rash behaviour this, you may say, for a dramatist who is hoping to make a good impression on a Star, but John felt no qualms, and, if he had, there was nothing really to disturb him. Provided that the praise be fulsome enough, actors (and other people) do not require it to be detailed; indeed, it is safer otherwise, for, if you descend to details, you may go and praise the wrong thing.

In his corner nearest the stage, David watched for Leo Cartwright's entrance, as a bird may be expected to await an appointment with a rattlesnake. Twice, if not three times, the action seemed to be working up to the kind of crescendo which heralds the arrival of the leading man; each time David gripped the edge of the Box and prayed for the roof to fall in, and each time it was a false alarm.

But at length, and all too soon, the moment came. "No, mother," cried the heroine, Lady Celia Hawkhurst; "if I am to marry, I must give myself to a Man." The folding doors at the top of the three steps opened mysteriously, and there, pausing for an instant before he should trip lightly down to the centre of the stage, stood the Star.

DENIS MACKAIL

All pretence at illusion was abandoned, while stalls, pit, circles, and gallery welcomed their hero with a tumultuous burst of applause. While Lady Celia and the Countess of Upminster (acting under strict instructions) held their poses with the rigidity of wax figures, Leo Cartwright faced the audience and bowed. Three graceful inclinations did he give, and then, with a deprecating movement of one hand, and a compensating adjustment of the features, signifying something between patience and condescension, he turned, and, with the utterance of his first words, illusion was reëstablished. From his observation post in the centre of the Box, John was shocked to see that no small part of this outburst of sound was proceeding from Elizabeth. Her little hands flew to and fro with swiftest repercussion, her lips were parted in excitement; he could almost swear that she said "Bravo!" Well, women beat him; that was all. To be carried away like this by a great brute like Cartwright, who had left her alone to be insulted and assaulted by one of his rascally followers only a week or so before. "If I ever get to know you well enough, I'll have it out with you about that 'Bravo!'" he muttered to himself. Meanwhile it must be admitted that her enthusiasm hardly made her less attractive.

The curtain fell on the first Act amidst only temperate enthusiasm. A Saturday afternoon audience could perhaps scarcely be warmed up to a second demonstration so early in the performance. There were a couple of curtain calls, but the lights rose immediately after the second. The strange people who drink tea in their seats were already beckoning to the attendants.

Of the three occupants of Box B, only one had any reasonable idea as to what had been taking place on the stage, or of the consequences likely to ensue during the remaining Acts.

"Don't you think it's awfully good?" asked this occupant, turning to John.

"Yes, awfully," said John, with every appearance of enthusiasm.

Elizabeth leant forward to repeat her remark to David, but, as she took breath to speak, there came a knock on the door of the Box. David gave a start as if he had been shot, and leapt from his chair.

"Come in!" shouted John, also rising, but with more of expectation and less of terror.

The door opened and the attendant was revealed.

"Your change, sir," she said, tendering a pile of silver to David.

"Th-thank you," he stammered, extending a palsied hand; and instantly dropped the entire collection of coins on to the floor.

"I'm sorry, sir," said the attendant. But she didn't sound a bit sorry. She sounded amused, curse her! David was on his hands and knees now, gathering up his property together with a quantity of dirt and fluff of unknown origin. If this sort of thing could happen at a false alarm, what would he do when the real summons came?

Perhaps it was with some idea of easing the situation that John at this point bought the box of theatre chocolates. The product of an unknown maker with a disproportionate belief in the value of cotton wool and shavings, even Elizabeth found two of them about as much as she could manage. John frankly passed them by, though, to do him justice, he did this on principle and with no knowledge of their real character. The ill-starred David, however, too shy to refuse them whenever they came his way, found, almost immediately, an increasing and well-nigh intolerable nausea added to his previous mental anguish. He must have forced at least seven of these deadly pellets down his reluctant throat, before rescue arrived in the shape of the lowering of the lights. His general condition during the second Act was pitiable in the extreme.

It was during this Act, also, that he suddenly realised that Mrs. Cartwright had forgotten to tell him the name of her infernal play. There was still time, perhaps, to get her on the telephone, but— well, he could no longer disguise from himself that movement of any kind would be, to say the least, fraught with very perilous possibilities. Discretion won the day.

Popular enthusiasm increased with the conclusion of this Act. Leo Cartwright appeared twice before the curtain, the first time drawing out (and immediately thrusting back) the leading lady, and the second time alone. And this second time, oh, horror! his eyes turned to pierce the gloom of the Box, searching, as it seemed, for his prey.

Once again as the orchestra struck up, there came a knock on the door of the Box, and once again David started like the prisoner awaiting execution.

An obscure figure in a silk hat appeared in the doorway.

"Mr. Ormroyd?" he said enquiringly.

John rose to his feet

"The Chief will see you now," added the stranger. "Will you come with me?"

"Back in a minute," said John, and followed Mr. Gordon out of the Box. Elizabeth had scarcely turned her head from her inspection of the audience.

DENIS MACKAIL

David was completely mystified by this second reprieve. The only solution that suggested itself was that Mrs. Cartwright had deputed Mr. Ormroyd also to act as her confidential agent. But then why not say so? Why tell him that she had used his name, and that no one else could help her? He was called back to reality by hearing Elizabeth's voice.

"Don't you think it's awfully good?" she was asking again.

"What? Oh, yes. Yes. Awfully," he answered wildly.

"Do you know," went on Elizabeth, "you seem quite different now from when I saw you yesterday?"

"Do I?" He gave a hollow laugh; but his interest was quickened.

"Yes. You seem older."

He didn't really. He only seemed sulkier; but Mrs. Cartwright is not the only woman in this book with charm.

"I feel older," David answered, and then, nervous that he might be called on for explanation, went on quickly: "I say, how long have you been with Mrs. Cartwright?"

Elizabeth gave a little laugh.

"Come and sit over here," she said. "We can't possibly go on shouting at each other across the Box like this."

David moved obediently into John's vacant chair. There was something peculiarly bracing about that word "we." For the first time since the beginning of lunch, he smiled.

"You didn't answer my question," he said.

"Your question? Oh, yes. Why, I've been with Mrs. Cartwright exactly—let me see—exactly two days."

"Oh!"

They both laughed.

"You look younger again," said Elizabeth.

"I feel younger," answered David.

"I suppose you know her awfully well," she went on.

"Who? Mrs. Cartwright?"

"'m."

"Oh, no," said this extraordinary youth. "Very slightly, indeed. But she is a very old friend of my father's. Of course," he added, "she's getting on now."

Yes, you may well gasp. Is this the boy, you ask, who for the past eight weeks has gone to bed dreaming of Mrs. Cartwright, has waked to thoughts of Mrs. Cartwright, has breakfasted, lunched, dined, walked, worked, and even rowed to the accompaniment of Mrs. Cartwright?

Is this the champion of dames whose chivalrous outburst wrecked the meeting of the Elect?

Not that David's admiration for Mrs. Cartwright had failed to survive the first call which she had made on it. A very light puff from her side would still have spun the arrow back to point once more at her. But she was not there to puff. And Elizabeth was.

Mr. Gordon led John Ormroyd through the iron door direct on to the stage. Skipping over electric cables, ducking under murderous little sandbags hanging from above, and side-stepping past rapidly moving sections of Lord Lingfield's Rooms in the Albany, guide and pilgrim at length reached the lift which led to Mr. Cartwright's suite.

"Just a minute," said Mr. Gordon, as they reached the top; and he vanished ahead. To his surprise John found that his heart was beating violently. A ridiculous sensation for a man who habitually called on his publishers without an appointment, and had faced an investiture at Buckingham Palace without a qualm. Why, he asked himself with faint annoyance, should this tawdry majesty do what the genuine article had failed to effect? A strange man, also in a silk hat, appeared at the end of the little corridor.

"Won't you come in, Mr. Ormroyd?" said Mr. Littlejohn, for he it was.

John passed onwards, and immediately found himself in the presence. His eye took in a full-length pier-glass entirely surrounded by electric bulbs, a mammoth dressing-table surmounted by a second, horizontal pier-glass similarly adorned, a couple of apparently really good Chippendale wardrobes, an electric radiator, and on every available scrap of wall, a perfect plaster of framed photographs. Mr. Gordon had disappeared, but Mr. Littlejohn followed John into the room and closed the door behind him. Tuke the dresser fluttered in the background, occupied mysteriously in one of the wardrobes. Leo Cartwright was seated before the dressing table. A brilliantly coloured silk wrapper cloaked his lower limbs, and he was buttoning his shirt. "Good Lord!" thought John, "He actually changes his shirt between the Acts!" For some obscure reason this discovery made him feel an enormously increased respect for Mr. Cartwright's powers as an actor. His heart was still beating wildly.

"I'm very glad to meet you at last, Mr. Ormroyd," said the Chief, flashing a brilliant smile at him. "Sit down, won't you? And please forgive me if I go on with my dressing. I have so little time."

John sank into a seat. It was unfortunate, he felt, that, just as Mr. Cartwright's throne was a little higher than the average, so the chair on which he now found himself was a little lower. It is so difficult to make any effect when peering up from a lower level, as Leo Cartwright very well knew when he furnished his dressing-room.

"Well," continued the great man, "how did the performance strike you this afternoon?"

John hadn't come to talk about "Pale People," but in the circumstances there was only one answer to make.

"Magnificent," he said. "It was wonderful to see such enthusiasm."

Perhaps "wonderful" was hardly the right word, but the Chief let it pass.

"Tie, Tuke," he said, and, seizing this article of clothing from the dresser, began knotting it

"About my play—" John ventured nervously, but unfortunately the Chief had spoken at the same moment, and, against the full resonance of his voice, these feeble words were lost.

"Now you, as an author, should be interested in this," he was saying, and as he spoke, he held out a book for John's inspection.

John grasped it and fluttered the leaves over. It appeared to be a book of verse.

"That was written by a little girl who used to be in my company," added Mr. Cartwright.

"Oh," said John, politeness and impatience struggling in his voice. Why the dickens should he be supposed to be interested in a rotten book of poems written by an unknown mummer? In another minute or so his interview would be at an end, and, if he wasn't very careful, he would find himself exactly where he was when it started.

He laid the book down on the floor, and cleared his throat.

"About my play. . ."

"Trousers, Tuke," said the Chief, rising to his feet and letting the wrapper fall to the ground. Tuke was on him like a flash of lightning, offering himself as a temporary support while Mr. Cartwright stepped delicately into these faultless garments. John couldn't help thinking that business with his publishers would become a matter of great difficulty, if they were, by any unlucky chance, to adopt Mr. Cartwright's methods.

"Your play," repeated the Chief, appearing now over the top of Tuke's head. "Now, how do we stand, Littlejohn, eh?"

"We have an option until the middle of January," replied Mr. Littlejohn.

"Ah," said the Chief. "You want us to renew, eh?"

"No!" said John, driven to desperation. "I want to know when you're going to produce it. You've had an option on the moving-picture rights for twelve months, what's more, and now I read in all the papers" (a pardonable exaggeration this) "that it's been sold for some vast sum to a film company, and still not a word to me about the production here. Renew! I'll most certainly not renew. I'll take your written promise to produce in three months, or you can return me the script!"

The sense of injury, which had been slowly bottled up under increasing pressure during the last year, had burst in one glorious explosion of temper. Though still shaking with the force of his own fury, John noted with pleasure and surprise signs of genuine alarm in his two adversaries. If only he could retain this feeling of rage, if only he didn't suddenly become reasonable, if only he could go on shouting!

But even as the Chief turned his mournful and astonished eye upon him, he felt his anger, which was his strength, deserting him.

It was Mr. Littlejohn, however, who spoke first.

"I think," he said, "you'll find that we bought the cinema rights outright. Yes, that was it; and an option on the dramatic rights."

The Chief nodded in solemn confirmation.

"No," said John, flaring up again, though alas! with only a tithe of his former rudeness. "An option on both. It's perfectly clear in the agreement. It's about the only thing that *is* clear."

"Then you will doubtless receive your cheque in due course," said Mr. Littlejohn.

"In due course," repeated Mr. Cartwright, smoothing down the lapels of the coat into which he had just been helped.

What a strange creature is man! At the mere mention of a cheque for an uncertain amount at a date not yet fixed, John felt his resolution fading away; and this in spite of the clearest evidence not two minutes before that these brigands had had every intention of cheating him out of his lawful dues.

To his horror, he heard himself apologising.

"You must forgive me, Mr. Cartwright," he said (the other brute could look after himself). "I'm afraid I spoke rather hastily. But really I have had such difficulty over this business in discovering where I stand. It's naturally very disappointing. . ."

Once again his voice died away unheard before Mr. Cartwright's fine delivery.

"Not at all," said the Chief. "We can all sympathize, I am sure. But in the theatre so much depends on. . ." he snapped his fingers to indicate the inevitable uncertainty of theatrical plans. "Meanwhile try to bear with us a little longer. I'm looking forward immensely to introducing your work to my public. Immensely. My gloves, please, Tuke."

John was only saved from expressing the deepest gratitude for these kind words by the intervention of the call-boy's knock on the door, followed by his cry of "Third Act, please!"

"Ah," said the Chief, "I'm afraid I must leave you."

He gripped John firmly by the upper arm, and began manoeuvring him out of the doorway. "But I am very glad, indeed, to have seen you. I'll try my best to write to you definitely about your play as soon as I possibly can. And meanwhile"—he gave an almost affectionate squeeze to John's arm—"take the advice of an old hand, and don't believe all that you read in the newspapers. Ha, ha! Eh?"

To his unutterable shame and disgust, John found himself laughing sycophantishly in reply. The next moment the Chief had turned and left him. To his relief, for he had no idea how to find his way back to the Box, he saw Mr. Gordon waiting by the entrance to the lift, and under his guidance he retraced his steps, this time in darkness, until they again reached the iron door. As Mr. Gordon stepped forward to lug it open, there came a great swishing sound from overhead, and John involuntarily ducked his head.

"It's all right," said Mr. Gordon in a whisper. "It's only the curtain. Look out, there's a step just here."

They were back on the little half-landing just above the entrance to Box B.

"That's your Box," said Mr. Gordon.

"Thanks," said John. It seemed so many years since he had last seen it that he was quite grateful to hear that it hadn't been moved.

"Satisfactory interview, I hope?" added Mr. Gordon politely, as John took a step towards the stairs.

"No," said John, with a burst of candour. "Damned unsatisfactory."

"I'm sorry to hear that," answered the other. "My name's Gordon," he added, with apparent inconsequence. "Here's my card. I'd be very glad to have a talk with you some time. I'll ring you up, if I may."

"Oh, thanks," said John, completely mystified.

"So long, then," replied Mr. Gordon, and disappeared up the stairs round the corner.

John looked again at the card, and, dropping it into his pocket, decided to dismiss the incident from his mind as inexplicable. And indeed it possessed no explanation or significance beyond the fact that Mr. Gordon, as other courtiers have done before now, made it his business to keep as far as possible on good terms with all who came near the court. Autocracies, he had observed, had a way of falling. Even when they did not fall, they had a habit of making sudden changes in the personnel of their officials. The wise janissary, therefore, would look ahead. Devotion to present duty was not incompatible with a knowledge of future possibilities as to the side on which, as he would put it, his bread might be buttered.

John slipped quietly back into the darkened Box. In his present mood of blackness and despair, he met the loss of his seat next Elizabeth merely with sullen resignation. Indeed, it was almost better so, for she would know, though he had not told her, what his business behind the scenes had been; and what was to prevent her, if he came within reach, whispering a question in the darkness—a question which, until he regained some kind of self-control, could only be answered by a terrible shriek?

For of course he had made the most absolute and perfect fool of himself. Not only had he returned without one single piece of information which he had set out to obtain (that is, if we except the vague and untrustworthy news as to the cinema position), but he had lost his temper and had been insultingly rude to the one man to whom it was absolutely essential that he should play up. He ground his teeth in the blackness. The brutes! they were probably laughing at him still.

He might have spared himself this last reflection, for an outraged author was far too common an object in Thespian circles to waste time or words over. As Leo Cartwright returned to his room, he contented himself with only one comment before passing on to other thoughts.

"I wish you wouldn't meddle with this moving-picture business, Littlejohn," he said.

"It's only in self-protection, Chief," answered the Business Manager. "Remember there are three picture houses in this very street now. How would you like one of them to be showing a film of 'Pale People'?"

"Oh, well, if that's the reason. . ."

"Of course it is. D'you think I'd touch it otherwise?"

"Then we've not sold the rights?"

"No," said Mr. Littlejohn. "We've given 'em away. We get a share in the rental."

"Which we divide with Mr. Ormroyd?"

"Exactly. And the picture can't be released until we say 'Go.'"

It certainly seemed as if the date referred to by Mr. Littlejohn as "in due course" was likely to be at some considerable distance.

"Well, that's something to cheer you up, Littlejohn," said Mr. Cartwright, with a melancholy smile.

"I need it, Chief," answered Mr. Littlejohn, and as he spoke he drew from his tail pocket a document typewritten on Thespian paper.

"Ah, you've seen reason, then?"

"There's no choice, Chief. But it's a disappointment all the same, I admit. I really thought you could manage Brisk."

"Well, never mind. See it goes up on the board before this evening."

"I'm not likely to forget, while we're losing money like this." Mr. Littlejohn moved towards the door. "And the successor?" he asked.

"I'll tell you tonight," said the Chief.

"Well, I put my money on the Norwegian."

"You go back and count the tickets, Littlejohn. If you want to put your money anywhere, put it on me."

With which declaration of the policy which had served him so well for the fifteen years of his management, Mr. Leo Cartwright stepped into the lift and was carried down to the stage.

V

The fall of the curtain on the third Act found John in almost as deplorable a condition as had been David's during the first interval. There was no Mrs. Cartwright here now to tell him what a fine novelist he was, to draw him out on the subject of American editions, or to reestablish for him a sense of proportion in which the drama took its correct and despicable position. Ringing in his ears with a maddening persistence, he heard his own words spoken at lunch on Thursday. "Why, I wouldn't let Cartwright have that play of mine now, if he gave me a million pounds for it." From this fine attitude he had sunk in forty-eight hours to the position of a suppliant, and a bad-tempered suppliant at that, at Leo Cartwright's feet. Deservedly was he relegated to the seat farthest from Elizabeth, he who had posed as her protector!

And now, to make everything if possible worse, that insufferable young puppy, whom he had actually found it in his heart to pity for his shyness and clumsiness, was chattering away to her, as if there were no one else in the Box. John's nerves were in that exact state of rawness when rivalry of this description was impossible to take in the light and easy-going spirit which the situation demanded. Reason told him that competition with David could not conceivably be regarded as serious, that a few amusing, airy words from himself would soon drive him out of the conversation, if not out of his chair; but the rage into which he had been put by his adventures behind the scenes made this out of the question. And the longer he waited, scowling there in the background, the more out of the question it became.

As for David, the cloud was lifted. Only temporarily, it is true. Impossible completely to put out of his mind the fate which was awaiting him, but, in Elizabeth's enchanting presence, most delightfully easy to put it on one side. He heard himself talking with a brilliance which he had long desired, but never hoped to attain, he saw her smile in reply, he even heard her laugh—a most intoxicating laugh. He gave her a pressing invitation to spend a day in Oxford next term. He announced his settled intention of taking her out in his sidecar. Even through the darkness of the final Act, her bracing, electric companionship gave him courage, if hardly to face the future, then at any rate to bear the present. He even took sufficient interest in the play to wonder what the earlier Acts had been about.

Matinée audiences at the Thespian do not prolong their plaudits at the end of the performance. The problem of getting into the Tube or on to the omnibus is for most of them too serious a matter to be delayed for any tribute to Art; and the stalls will never take the trouble to applaud without a lead from the rest of the house. While David was still helping Elizabeth into her cloak (and wondering what his duty was, if, after all, the dreaded summons should fail to arrive), the safety curtain fell. In the comer of the Box, John, staggering into his overcoat, had just stepped in the remains of the chocolates, and let us, in mercy to him, suppose that it was this final straw which made him address Elizabeth in the way that he did.

"I'll give you tea," he said.

No written words can convey the menace that lurked in this utterance. In such a tone might a cave-man have addressed his future bride, just before he announced his engagement by clubbing her on the head. Elizabeth gave a start of surprise. Even David wondered what was up.

"No, thank you," she said. "I'm afraid I must go straight home."

DENIS MACKAIL

"All right," answered John, very rudely. "Then'll I'll drive you there."

"Good-bye, Mr. Lawrence," said Elizabeth, totally disregarding John's last words. "You won't forget about the sidecar, will you?"

"Rather not," replied David.

She gave him one last demolishing smile, and left the Box, John close on her heels.

And even as they went, the grim messenger, in the shape of Mr. Albert Gordon, made his appearance in the doorway of Box B.

"Mr. Lawrence," he said, "the Chief will see you now."

"Thank you," answered David, all strength suddenly leaving him.

"Will you come this way?" continued the Personal Manager.

With a superhuman effort David forced his paralysed limbs into movement, and the Box settled down in peace until the evening performance.

Meanwhile John, by dint of buffeting several inoffensive theatre-goers in a very violent manner, had managed to keep Elizabeth well in sight; and as they reached the foyer a stronger obstruction in her path or a weaker one in his enabled him to catch up with her sufficiently to begin speaking to her again. To apologise, you will doubtless imagine; but I fear you are wrong. The evil spirit which had been roused by his interview with Leo Cartwright would never have dreamt of letting him do anything as sensible as that. Instead, what must it go and do but make him try (and that in the most insufferable manner) to reopen the whole argument about giving Elizabeth tea and/or driving her home, and this in the middle of the stream of satiated entertainment-seekers which swirled past and into them from every side.

Elizabeth became pinker and more obstinate every second.

"I'm very grateful to you, Mr. Ormroyd," she said, "but that doesn't give you the right to talk to me like this. Please let me go, and I hope—I hope it will be a very long time before we meet again."

The crowd swept her away. She was gone.

Would it be any consolation to John, as he sat alone that evening with wormwood and gall in his heart, to have known of the tears which she shed, not only on her bed—the bed on which such happy tears had yesterday fallen for "She Loves Me Not"—but actually in the omnibus before she could get home?

No, John, I think it will be pretty generally agreed that, whatever the effect of such consolation might be, it is in the present circumstances a very great deal more than you deserve.

VI

As David in his turn passed through the iron door, the stage was already being cleared, and it was possible for Mr. Gordon to lead him by a comparatively direct route to the entrance to the Chief's quarters.

"Just a minute, Mr. Lawrence," he said, as they stepped from the lift into the little corridor where John had waited an hour ago; and as in the previous instance he vanished through the door at the end.

This withdrawal of human companionship was the signal for an instant return, in a highly concentrated and magnified form, of all the most terrifying symptoms which poor David had experienced during the early part of the afternoon. The corridor heaved and plunged like a ship at sea, the fire-buckets on their row of hooks seemed to swell and sway like exotic blossoms. As he tottered against the wall, he lacked even the will to dry with his handkerchief the clammy dew which again be sprinkled his forehead. But for this horrible physical weakness and nausea, he must inevitably have turned and bolted, back on to the stage, up the stairs, anywhere, so only that he might escape what the next moment might bring upon him.

He groaned aloud.

"I can't do it!" he said. "I can't do it!"

And at these words the door immediately opposite him opened and Leo Cartwright himself appeared. He was draped in the long silk wrapper which we have previously seen. Round his neck, worn as a muffler, was a piece of towelling much stained with paint and grease. His face shone with the recent friction of this same towel, and his hair was in considerably more than a sweet disorder. Hardly an impressive figure at this moment, you would say; in fact, to an unprejudiced observer, very nearly a ridiculous one. But for David this wild vision represented Fear Itself.

"Ah, Mr. Lawrence," said the Chief. "Won't you come into my room? I am so sorry to have kept you waiting." He put out his hand and, catching hold of David's corresponding limp extremity, drew him into the saloon and closed the door.

"You'll have some tea, won't you? Or a whiskey-and-soda?"

David opened his mouth and made a great effort. Thinking it over afterwards, he came to the conclusion that what he was trying to say was, "Will you excuse me, I don't feel very well." But at the very opening sound he stuck, and remained mouthing like a fish behind the glass of an aquarium.

DENIS MACKAIL

"Ah, whiskey? Well, perhaps you're right," said the Chief. With his own hands he brought forward a tray containing the necessary apparatus, and mixed a couple of drinks.

"But please sit down," he went on ingratiatingly.

David sat down. And, though more by luck than skill, he did so on a chair.

"Well," continued the Chief, raising his glass, "here's looking to you, Mr. Lawrence. I'm very glad, indeed, to have this opportunity of meeting you."

With a miserable attempt at conviviality David picked up his tumbler and took an infinitesimal sip.

"Th-thank you," he croaked.

"And I hope you enjoyed the show this afternoon?"

A corpse would have given the right answer, when the Chief asked this question.

"Enormously," said David.

"Ah, that's good. That's good." The Chief seated himself on the fender, which gave unnecessary protection from the electric stove. "Now, Mr. Lawrence," he went on, "I've read your play, and—I'll be perfectly frank with you—in my opinion you've written a remarkably fine thing. You'll excuse my saying so, I hope, but it certainly surprises me to find that it is the work of such a young author."

He smiled courteously, and a thin, sickly reflection appeared on David's face.

"Of course it's unusual in many ways," proceeded Mr. Cartwright. "I doubt, for instance, whether the public would care for that tragic ending. But you probably regard that as essential, eh?"

"Yes," said David, nodding emphatically. If only they could disagree over this, something might yet be managed. But the Chief also nodded.

"Well, no doubt you're right," he said. "Artistically, there's no doubt that you're right. But at the same time a play of this kind means a big risk. I'm afraid we should have to consider that in any offer that we were able to make. However," he went on brightly, "that's a matter for discussion with your Agent."

"Yes," said David. This seemed a pretty safe admission.

"But what I want to talk to you about now," continued the Chief, "is this. I think I mentioned the matter in my letter. You know the third Act?"

This was awkward. However, it was clearly impossible to say "no," so David answered, "Yes."

"The bit at the end, I mean. The scene with the Doctor."

David nodded.

"Well, don't think that I don't like it. I do. I think it's beautifully written. But it's not wanted. The climax is really over by then, don't you see? You want a quick curtain." He brought his hand down with a thump on his knee. "All that scene is unnecessary. Worse, it spoils the effect of what has gone before."

He looked challengingly at David, as if to say, "Deny it if you can."

"Well," thought David, "one can only die once." And he took a tremendous gulp at his tumbler.

Aloud he said:

"I'm sorry, but I regard that scene as absolutely essential."

The shock of hearing these words from this impertinent stripling made the Chief all but fall off the fender, but he gathered himself together at once, and with the full force of his finest delivery thundered out these terrible words:

"But, my dear Sir, WHY?"

The volume of sound alone would have made a stronger frame than David's quail, but quite apart from this physical effect the wretched youth felt to the full the sensations of one who has staked his all on a last chance, and lost. No conceivable reply could be imagined that would carry him at the very best more than one move farther before he should be hopelessly and utterly checkmated.

"I can't explain," he said. "I expect you know best."

Having gained his point, Mr. Cartwright was immediately all courtesy and consideration.

"No, no," he said. "Don't say you agree, unless you do. We'll try it both ways at rehearsal. I want you to see it for yourself."

Rehearsal! That was all the good he had done by his attempted opposition. Very well, then, he would make it clearer still.

One cannot but admire David as he rises to his feet now. Moral courage of the description which he was called upon to display does not come naturally at nineteen years of age. Instinct, as well as training, teaches one to agree, to conciliate, to give way, when met with the opposition of the mature and self-assertive. Nature herself has ordained a tenuity of the vocal chords, with an accompanying inability to keep them under adequate control, which renders them completely unfit to bear their part against the harsh sounds of the middle-aged. Remember also that in this one comparatively small room, occupying, moreover, the most strategically commanding position in it, there was concentrated the personality which thought nothing of dominating a whole auditorium. David's courage in these circumstances, miserably ineffective though its results might be, was yet of the genuine brand of which heroes are made.

"But there has been a mistake," he said. "It isn't only the third Act that is wrong. The whole thing is wrong. It's bound to be a failure. I ought never to have sent it you. The entire play needs rewriting from beginning to end; that's its only chance. Let me have it back, let me try and put it right if I can. But don't, for Heaven's sake, talk about rehearsing it. You can't mean it."

At the beginning of this extraordinary outburst, Leo Cartwright had shown considerable surprise, as indeed he might at this astonishing change in the author's attitude towards the third Act; but surprise quickly gave way to something else. Never in the history of the Thespian Theatre had a playwright spoken like this of his own work. The deduction to be made, therefore, in this case was that this particular playwright was indulging in some mysterious form of humour; a deduction strengthened by the Chief's complete certainty that whatever the value of his own opinion might be on literature, poetry, or art, his judgment of the theatrical efficiency of a play was unchallengeable. To David, pausing for breath, there was accordingly revealed the sinister spectacle of a broad smile; infinitely more terrifying than the opposition which he had braced himself to meet.

"No, no, no," laughed the Chief. "Don't take it like that. You shall keep your third act. You've fairly earned it."

"But I'm serious. I am really. I've changed my mind altogether about this play. I don't want it done at all now. It isn't the alterations I mind, it's the whole thing. Surely you don't want to do it, if I ask you not to."

Again that horrible laugh.

"My dear Mr. Lawrence, you must really get over your nerves. Believe me, I'm paying you a pretty considerable compliment in placing my theatre and my experience at your disposal like this. Surely if I am prepared to risk so much on my judgment, you haven't such a lot to fear. No, no. And I've got some good news for you, too. My present play will cease running today fortnight. If all goes well, I mean to put your work before the public early in January; and I have every hope that it will assist me in establishing one of my biggest successes here. Now what do you say to that, eh?'

"He's talking to me like a baby," thought David. "I suppose that's what I look like, too." But aloud, instead of the gratitude and contrition which Mr. Cartwright was clearly expecting, all he said was:

"Then it's all settled?"

These were the words. The tone indicated a curious (and to Mr. Cartwright inexplicable) compromise between despair and relief.

"All except the agreement," said the Chief. "And that we won't discuss, because I never talk business with an author. My Manager and your Agent will see to that."

He did not think fit to add that his final decision had been reached less than ten minutes ago, and had been largely due to the author's unexpected opposition; and perhaps it was just as well for David's sanity that this secret was preserved.

"I see," said David.

What he saw was that he had spent the most hideous afternoon of his life and made the most complete idiot of himself before a distinguished stranger, only to discover at the end that the eventuality which he had been commissioned at any cost to prevent was to all intents and purposes an accomplished fact. Heaven knew (and the reader can witness) that he had done his best. But he had failed before he began. An author might conceivably withdraw a play that was still under consideration (as he had been led to believe that this one was), but to attempt to back out when the date of production was practically settled, why, the thing was incredible. If Leo Cartwright had addressed him as though he were a child, it was no more than he deserved. He quite saw that, but—

The Chief was speaking again.

"I wish you'd tell me, Mr. Lawrence, how the idea of this play came to you. The outlook is in many ways, I see, that of a young mind, but the experience behind it, that, I must say, I should scarcely have credited you with. Perhaps you are older than you look, though."

But David had had enough.

He put his hand up to his collar. "I'm afraid you must excuse me," he said. "Very hot. Feel rather faint. Would you mind. . . some other time? Must get air. . ."

He lurched realistically forward, and instantly the Chief, who had in his life similarly assisted at least a hundred heroines overcome by their own frailty, had him in his arms.

"There, there," he said.

"No, no," mumbled David, half-suffocated by the Chief's wrapper, but struggling gamely all the same.

"Miss Lemon!" yelled the Chief.

Ever ready in emergency, Miss Lemon appeared instantaneously from her den.

"Mr. Lawrence has been taken ill," said the Chief. "Tell Garrod to get a taxi at once and then come back and help me to get him downstairs."

"Shall I get a doctor?" asked Miss Lemon, already halfway out of the saloon again.

"No, I think he's only fainted."

Miss Lemon's capable boots could be heard galloping down the stairs. Leo Cartwright forced rather than laid his victim on the hearth-rug, and moved across to open the window on to the air-shaft. But when he turned round, David was already scrambling to his feet.

"Ah, feeling better?" asked the Chief, so kindly and sympathetically that David could have kicked himself.

"Yes, thanks most awfully," he answered. "But I think it would be best if I cleared out now."

"Let me help you down to the door," offered Mr. Cartwright.

"No, really, I—"

"No, no. I insist."

So, festooned together in a horrible embrace, they left the saloon and started down the stairs. At the bottom, by the door-keeper's box, Miss Lemon was on the lookout.

"The taxi will be here in a minute," she said.

"Oh, but I'm much better. I'd much rather walk," protested David.

"Out of the question," said the Chief firmly. "Now take my advice, and go straight to bed when you get home. And don't let anything that has happened here worry you. I quite understand how it all was; in fact, I really was afraid you weren't well, when I first saw you."

David make some incoherent sound of gratitude.

"That's all right," Mr. Cartwright went on. "Don't you bother your head about anything. I'll write to your Agent tonight, and you and I'll have a good long talk together, if possible, on Monday. I ought to be able to make some suggestions about the cast by then. Ah, there's Garrod. Good-night, Mr. Lawrence. Goodnight. Take care of yourself. I must go, or I shall catch cold."

He turned to ascend the stairs, but, before disappearing round the first corner, he called down again:

"Let my secretary have your address before you go."

His address! Whose address? The real David Lawrence's, and be saddled with this awful play for ever, have to return to the theatre on Monday, have his name in the papers, on the sides of omnibuses; his father writing home to ask what on earth was up? Or the false David Lawrence's, and, not content with his complete failure as Mrs. Cartwright's protector, have to confess that he had betrayed her secret as well?

Miss Lemon had produced a notebook and fountain-pen from the pockets of her woolly jacket.

"The address?" she enquired.

A cold puff of wind through the open stage-door seemed to blow away the last of the pretences with which poor David had been trying to conceal from himself the one and only address that he could still give. The address to which, moreover, he must now inevitably and miserably proceed.

"'Windy Gap,'" he said. "'Camperdown Avenue, Bexhill-on-Sea.'"

"No London address?" asked Miss Lemon.

"No. None."

"Well, good-night, Mr. Lawrence. I hope you'll feel better soon."

"Thank you. Good-night."

Silently and wretchedly he strode along the alley to where the cab was waiting with stage door-keeper in attendance. Not until he had tipped him and seen him out of sight did he dare give his Harley Street address. Even then he looked back nervously through the little window as the taxi started, to make certain that he was not being followed.

Aunt Lily's.

The only refuge left.

He must telephone to her as soon as he got in.

And as the taxi disappears in the westbound traffic, our blood seems to freeze at the sound of a short, low, and horrible laugh.

That, we say with a shudder, is David Lawrence on Women!

VII

A LAST SCENE AT THE Thespian Theatre before we finish with it for the day.

The evening performance is over, and one by one the members of the company leave their dressing-room keys and their weekly tip with Garrod, before thrusting the swing doors open and escaping to their forty-four hours' freedom. On the Call Board, conspicuous against the grime of earlier announcements, is Mr. Littlejohn's typewritten ultimatum, giving a fortnight's notice of the termination of the run of "Pale People." But the company seem, as they pass out, purposely to look in every other direction except that of the fatal board. Not that its contents are unknown, for, having been posted at six o'clock, the notice has already conveyed its dread message to all Thespians, as they arrived for the evening show. Yet though they have heroically strutted and pranced through their parts with a smile (where necessary) on their faces, the thought of being out of a shop at the beginning of January is not one to be taken home on a Saturday night and lived with all through the chill and theatreless Sunday. Better try not to think of it. Something may turn up. Something has turned up before now, and if not, well, grousing won't help.

So the "Good-nights" and the "Cheery-ohs" and the "Bye-byes" float as freely on the air as ever, and presently the last of Mr. Leo Cartwright's West-End Company has passed through the swing doors, and the light outside is extinguished.

At twelve o'clock Garrod hands over his keys to the night watchman, but before he does so he says:

"There's three of 'em not come out yet. You'd better stand by a bit."

"Wot three?"

"The Chief, and Mr. Littlejohn, and Mr. Gordon."

"Right you are, Bill."

"Goo'-night."

"'-night."

Garrod goes off to his well-earned rest.

It is quite twenty minutes later before these last three come stumbling down the stairs in the dark, and are let out into the alley. When they reach the street, the Chief draws a deep breath, gazes for a moment up at the sky, and then, with a curt "Good-night," turns and strides off to his unknown lair.

The other two remain talking. Enemies by all the traditions of their respective posts, a common danger has for once drawn them together.

"It's not the notice going up that I object to," said Mr. Littlejohn. "As a matter of fact we've been losing money since the beginning of the month. But why in God's name, when he's under contract to produce the 'Pastor,' and he's got an unexpired option on Ormroyd's play, must he go and fix up to try out this awful stuff in the worst month in the year?"

Mr. Gordon's thoughts were bitterer still. If he had but known, as Littlejohn knew, that they had been playing to paper for the last three weeks, do you suppose he would have been content to smooth the way for old Brisk's infernal schemes, without some very distinct and tangible reward? Not on your life! But, owing to his unfortunate ignorance of the financial position and to the sudden emergency with which he had been faced, he had given his assistance gratuitously, hoping only for such gratitude as might be felt by the Backers for the man who should have helped to keep a successful play going.

Successful play, indeed! The thing had been as good as dead the whole time, and Brisk—that villain Brisk—must have known it.

Even now, however, though the value of the Parliamentary candidature as an advertising medium for "Pale People" was gone, and the realisation of Brisk's plan must seriously interfere with the preparation of its successor, all was perhaps not lost. It should still, after all, be worth something to the informant who should first let the Backers know that Mr. Cartwright was intending to use their money to put on a play by an unknown author, when he was already under bond to produce a great Continental success. The thought became clothed in words.

"There's only one thing to do," said Mr. Gordon. "I shall go down to the City on Monday morning, see Mr. Imray, and tell him the whole story."

"Well, Gordon," said Mr. Littlejohn, "I've stuck to the Chief now for twenty years—ever since he first came to London—and I'm the last man to do anything behind his back. But it's saving him from a lawsuit with Dr. Bransen's agents, if it's saving him from nothing worse. So if you see Mr. Imray, mind, you're doing it on your own responsibility; I know nothing about it; but if I hear you've changed your mind on Monday, I've almost half a mind to go down there myself."

"No, no," said Mr. Gordon hastily, but just not too hastily. "You leave it to me."

"Well, perhaps I'm better out of it," replied Mr. Littlejohn. "Anyhow, we'll hear soon enough, if you bring it off."

"Meanwhile," Mr. Gordon reminded him, "we keep our mouths shut."

"Certainly; certainly," said Mr. Littlejohn, and was immediately seized by a cavernous yawn.

"Well, good-night, old man," he said.

"G'-night."

Diverging echoes pattered along the darkened street.

VI

Two Meetings

I

FROM SIX O'CLOCK ONWARDS MRS. CARTWRIGHT was on the alert for sound of telephone or front-door bell that should tell her that news was to be expected from the scene of her thoughts. But, though she stayed up until nearly midnight with increasing impatience and diminishing hope, not a ring of either kind broke the silence. The solitary knock which made her start so much about nine o'clock proved merely to be the postman with a bundle of Christmas bills.

"What can have happened?" she asked herself for the thousandth time, as she lay awake in the small hours of the night. "Surely it must be settled one way or the other by now!" The first possible moment in the morning, she decided, she would get through to Dr. Lawrence's house on the telephone.

But when she was called, after the few hours' uneasy sleep which she had at last achieved, her maid's first words put this determination out of the question.

"I'm afraid the telephone is out of order again, madam," she said, in the maddeningly cheerful voice with which members of her profession announce such misfortunes. "I tried to get through to the garage this morning, and I can't make the exchange answer."

"I'll try myself," said Mrs. Cartwright, and reached for the instrument which stood by her bedside.

But the telephone was a republican, and made no distinction between mistress and maid. Not a murmur would it utter.

"Have you reported it?" asked Mrs. Cartwright.

"Hilda is going in next door, madam, as soon as they have had breakfast. But I'm afraid, being Sunday, it can't be mended today."

"Oh, well, it can't be helped. Anyhow, I've changed my mind about going for a drive today, so it doesn't matter about the garage."

"Very good, madam."

So that must have been it. The telephone had probably decided to take this unauthorized holiday sometime yesterday afternoon, and of course David had been unable to get through. She might have thought of that. Well, she had put off the car now, so she would be able to wait in for him.

She waited in all morning without a sound or sign from the outer world. At half-past one she toyed with a solitary lunch, and returned to her vigil.

And then, suddenly, at four o'clock the front-door bell rang. Mrs. Cartwright flew to the window and pressed her nose to the pane; but the caller, whoever he was, was standing too close under the little balcony for her to see more than a section of black overcoat and a gloved hand trailing an umbrella.

"At last," she murmured, and sped back to snatch one more look in the mirror over the mantelpiece. Then she turned to face the door. It opened quickly with a strange sound of scurrying skirts, and Hilda, the cold and dignified Hilda, seemed to stumble into the middle of the room.

"Why, Hilda—" began Mrs. Cartwright, astonished at this red-faced and breathless vision, but the vision interrupted her.

"Oh, madam," said Hilda, "it's Mr. Cartwright!"

And at these words a tall, elderly stranger followed her into the drawing-room.

But no, not a stranger. As she gripped the edge of the bureau to steady herself, Mrs. Cartwright realised that her first, wild thought had been right. For this was the husband whom she had put out of her life twenty-five years ago.

At this supreme moment, this completely unexpected realisation of the nightmare which not even yet had she been able to drive altogether from her dreams, our admiration must go out to Mrs. Cartwright.

"Then," she said, addressing the quaking Hilda, "I shall not be at home to any other callers this afternoon."

Not a tremor, not an unusual tone in her voice. Domestic discipline, which for an instant had been shattered into a million fragments, was at once whole again. Not a scratch marred the smoothness of its surface.

"Very good, madam," answered Hilda, and withdrew.

Mrs. Cartwright turned again to her husband.

"Well?" she said.

"I tried to telephone, Helen—"

"Don't call me that!" The words seemed like the crack of a whip.

"I tried to telephone," repeated Mr. Cartwright, obediently omitting the forbidden name, "but," he concluded mournfully, "they said the line was out of order."

Mrs. Cartwright bit her lip, and not for the first time that day wished the Postmaster-General in the hottest and most uncomfortable part of hell.

"I say," Mr. Cartwright went on; "do you mind if I take my coat off? Your maid wouldn't give me the chance downstairs. She didn't—" there was a faint note of surprise and grievance in his voice—"she didn't seem to want me to come in."

"I gave up giving special instructions about you several years ago," answered Mrs. Cartwright, "but the maid acted quite rightly. However," she continued, "take it off by all means."

"Thanks," said the slow, deep voice. "Thanks very much."

Carefully and gently he leant his umbrella against the side of a chair, and placed his silk hat on the seat. Then, still with maddening deliberation, he unwound from about his neck a long silk muffler, dropped it into the hat, and turned his attention to the buttons of his overcoat.

With one arm stretched out beside her, Mrs. Cartwright drummed impatiently on the mantelpiece. Would he never finish this interminable undressing?

But at last the overcoat also, neatly folded, was deposited on a second chair, and again he turned to face her. Incredible that this old, worn-looking man should be her husband, who—she gave a shudder. Did she, she wondered, look like that to him? Twenty-five years is a long time. And then, angrily, she drove the question out of her mind. What did it matter how she looked to this man?

"I'm very sorry if I have startled you at all," said Leo Cartwright, with a kind of painstaking courtesy. "It was rather awkward about the telephone. I made the supervisor try several times, but she stuck to it that there wasn't any answer. I hope—" He broke off, and then added: "I say, mayn't we sit down?"

"You may sit down, certainly," said Mrs. Cartwright. "But, if it's all the same to you, I should prefer to stand."

"Thanks. Thanks very much." Again with that dreadful slowness of movement, he seated himself on a straight-backed chair.

"Go on, go on! For Heaven's sake, get it over," Mrs. Cartwright was murmuring under her breath. In her mind there was not the faintest doubt as to what had happened. David, of course, had failed in his mission, and, probably bullied by her husband, had given the whole show away. Well, then, why couldn't he come out with it? Whatever the advantage might be to which he wished to turn this catastrophe, what was delaying him now? Why, in Heaven's name, sit there torturing her like this?

Leo Cartwright gave a kind of sad scrutiny to the tips of his fingers, and began again.

"I've come to ask you to do something for me," he said. "If it has been a bit of a shock to you, I apologise. I apologise deeply, but—"

Mrs. Cartwright stopped him by a sudden, violent movement with her shoulders. In another second he would have begun again about the telephone, and if he did that she knew she would scream.

"Never mind that," she said. "Go on."

"We won't go into the past," said her husband.

"No," she broke in quickly. "We won't."

"Ah," he said, and it sounded like relief. "Perhaps better not. Though I've sometimes thought that if only. . ."

"That's enough," said Mrs. Cartwright. "We'll stick to the present, if you don't mind. I can guess what you've come here about, and I should be glad to get it over as quickly as possible."

"You can guess?" He was amazed; astonished. "Why, who on earth has told you anything about that?"

She looked at him with a kind of fear. That slowness of movement, that deep-rooted look of fatigue, so diametrically different from the Leo Cartwright whom she had married, took on a fresh and sinister meaning. Had his mind also begun to give way?

"Come to the point," she said.

"But I can't understand how. . ." Words seemed to fail him altogether.

"The point," she commanded.

"Well, if you've heard about it, perhaps you'll understand," he resumed. "All I ask you to do for me is one simple thing. After that we can go our own ways again, or—or whatever you like. If you refuse, I can't blame you. I won't reproach you in anyway. But for the sake of— well, I suppose it's only for my sake really, I want you to come with me to the meeting on Tuesday."

With a gesture of despair, Mrs. Cartwright slid into her armchair.

"One of us," she said, "has gone mad." And then, very slowly and extremely distinctly, she added:

"What meeting?"

"But I thought you said. . ."

"Never mind that. Was this all you came to see me about?"

"Yes. What did you think I'd come for?"

His tone seemed to resent some not altogether flattering suggestion in her enquiry, but what it was she could not say. Relief and astonishment left no room in her mind for speculation.

"You wrote me a letter," he went on, sadly but firmly.

"Never!" She sat bolt upright. "It's a forgery. I never dreamt of such a thing."

"I don't mean now. But when we—when we. . ."

"When?"

"When we separated."

"Oh!" Where in the world was he taking her now?

"I've got it here in my pocket," he went on, and with these words fished a much-worn pigskin case out of some inner recess in his clothing.

She put out her hands, as if thrusting it away.

"I remember," she said.

"I wasn't going to show it you," he answered, dropping the case back into his pocket. "Only to remind you of what you said."

"I haven't forgotten what I said."

This horrible, aimless wrangle about a letter which should have been burnt and forgotten a quarter of a century ago! Why had she answered him at all? Why hadn't she had him shown out the moment he arrived?

Leo Cartwright fixed his wife with an uplifted forefinger.

"You said in the letter," he announced, still in that slightly aggrieved tone, "that, in spite of everything, you wished me every success in my profession. And you said, if ever you could do anything to help me on in my career, you would try to do so."

He paused. In fact he paused for so long that Mrs. Cartwright at length heard herself saying:

"Well?"

"I thought you might have forgotten."

"I hadn't forgotten." (Hadn't she told him so ten times already?) "So you want my help?"

"Yes. Please."

"You've been a long time taking advantage of my offer," she said.

The little dart seemed to glance harmlessly off him.

"Well, you know, Helen," he answered,—and though she made an angry movement with her hand, she did not stop him this time,—"as a matter of fact this is the first time that the occasion has arisen."

"Then I suppose it's the first time that you've missed me."

"Oh, no," he said gravely. "I assure you I've missed you a great deal."

"I'm flattered."

"Well, you know," he went on, the second dart falling as innocuously as the first, "I've not done so badly. I heard you'd been abroad, but perhaps you known I've run my own theatre now for over fifteen years."

As he told her this, he smiled in innocent pleasure.

There was a strange expression in Mrs. Cartwright's face. The firm mouth, the—yes, the almost mischievous look in the eyes, what could they mean?

"Yes," continued Mr. Cartwright. "It's called the 'Thespian,' you know. I wanted to have it called after me; but there were difficulties, so we called it the 'Thespian.'"

There was nothing else for it. Self-control was all very well, but only this side of self-suffocation. With one wild, spluttering sound, Mrs. Cartwright broke into loud, overpowering, paralysing laughter. Still politely, and always without the faintest trace of self-consciousness, her husband, perched on his uncomfortable little chair, smiled back at her. And as she emerged, choking, from one paroxysm, her eye would light on this spectacle, and immediately with a wild whoop she would be off again.

"Oh-o-oh," she groaned, pressing her hands to her aching sides, and then once more. . .

Mere printed "ha-ha's" are useless to suggest the unladylike kind of noise with which the little drawing-room rang.

Again she came up, gasping for breath. And this time faint words could be detected.

"I beg your pardon?" said Leo Cartwright, leaning courteously forward.

"Your ha-handkerchief. Lend me your handkerchief. I've used mine up."

"Oh, certainly." He stepped across the room and handed her a still folded square of silk.

"Thank you." She dabbed with it at her eyes.

And suddenly it was all over. Was it the natural end, or the recollection of the last time that she had borrowed a man's handkerchief to wipe her eyes? Perhaps the same thought crossed her husband's mind. At any rate, his smile also faded.

"Oh, Leo," said Mrs. Cartwright feebly.

"Now tell me once and for all," she added, "what it is that I've got to do for you."

So Leo Cartwright went back to his little chair and began telling her. It was all quite simple, he said. A vacancy had occurred in the Covent Garden Division. He was to be invited to the meeting of the Traditional Selection Committee on Tuesday afternoon. For one reason and another he understood that the prospect of his adoption was extremely likely. There was, however, an obstacle. In matters of this kind, one's private affairs were, unfortunately, anything but sacred. It was essential, therefore, that he should be in a position to answer any questions which might be put to him, in respect of certain rumours which, so he was informed, had gained some kind of circulation.

"But what sort of rumours?" asked Mrs. Cartwright, breaking in.

"Well; you know. Rumours about—about my marriage."

"Your marriage? You've not tried to marry again?"

"No, no. My marriage with you."

"But what do they say?" pursued Mrs. Cartwright.

"Oh, well. I don't know exactly what they say. But I gather they think I treated you pretty badly."

"Oh."

"The worst of it is," he went on, a little peevishly, "that they're right."

"That's a pity, isn't it?"

"Well, it's a bit awkward for me."

Mrs. Cartwright opened her mouth to speak, but closed it again. Had he not said, and had she not agreed with him when he said: "We won't go into the past"?

"So what I want you to do," proceeded her husband, "is this. Just come with me to the meeting of the Committee. Meet me there, if you prefer. If you do that, no one will ask any questions. The whole story will be killed dead. After that you can come back here, and I'll take myself off, and we'll both go on as before. Now, then; what do you say?"

The ingrained melancholy of his face made it impossible for him to show any kind of eagerness; but the impassive eyes which sat steadily down, as it were, to await her answer, made it advisable, she felt, to provide an answer of some kind as soon as possible.

"I must think it over," she said. "Since you've reminded me of my letter, I can hardly do what my first impulse certainly suggests, and refuse point-blank."

"But the meeting is on Tuesday," he put in, with just the faintest trace of exasperation.

"Oh, I'll let you know in plenty of time for the meeting. Meanwhile, perhaps you'll tell me something."

"Certainly. Anything you like."

"Well, if you don't mind my asking, what is it that makes you want to go into Parliament?"

For the first time that afternoon there was an almost boyish look on his face, as he answered:

"I think it ought to help me professionally. You see, knighthoods are rather played out, since the music-halls started getting them; but this would be something rather new."

"And is that your only reason?"

"Well, yes. I think it is."

"There's nothing political about it?"

"Political?" His voice rang with indignation. "Certainly not. Of course, I'm afraid you can't keep politics out of it altogether; but I'm doing this to help the Stage, not the Politicians."

"Ah," said Mrs. Cartwright. "Well, so far, so good."

"I'm glad you agree," answered her husband.

"Now tell me something else," she went on quickly; and as she said this, she looked straight into his eyes. "Did you have a visit yesterday from a young man called David Lawrence?"

Surprise, yes; but not a shadow of embarrassment in that colourless, weary-looking face. Mrs. Cartwright thanked her stars that she had stopped where she did. Her secret was her secret still.

"Why, yes," answered her husband. "But how did you hear of that?"

"He was lunching with me beforehand."

"Oh, I see."

"Would you," she went on,—"would you mind telling me what you thought of his play? He—he seemed very nervous about it."

"My dear Helen," said Leo Cartwright,—and this time his wife did not so much as blink an eyelid,—"that boy's a genius! Nervous, was he? I must say he seemed very odd in his manner when he came round and saw me.

DENIS MACKAIL

He actually wanted to take his play away with him, but of course I wouldn't hear of it. I'm afraid he must be rather delicate," he added thoughtfully.

"But the play?"

"The play? The most wonderful thing I've had through my hands in the whole course of my management. Whoever had written it I should say the same. Beauty, depth, humour, humanity—it's got them all. For a boy of that age, there's only one word. Miraculous. I tell you if any young actor got hold of that play today, his name would be made. But it's not to be got hold of. Oh, no!"

"Then you mean...?" Mrs. Cartwright's heart was beating uncontrollably.

"Yes. I shall begin rehearsing it this week. Littlejohn—that's my Business Manager—would tell you that it's madness to put on a new play at the beginning of January, but it can't make any difference in this case. No, my dear, that play, if ever there was one, is a Winner."

Gone was that look of decrepitude, gone also that slowness and deliberation of speech. And yet—Mrs. Cartwright could not doubt it—there was no acting in this burning, consuming enthusiasm. This was the white heat with which a man preaches the gospel in which his whole soul believes. And in this case the gospel was—think of it!—her play.

Too late she struggled to recapture the intention with which she had opened this conversation; the generous intention to use the power which chance had given her to insist, as far as it was possible to insist, that John Ormroyd should be put out of his misery. Too late, also, to consider the incredible complications which the acceptance of her play, and her gratuitous introduction of an imaginary author, would instantly produce.

And yet was it, indeed, too late? Unknowingly, Mrs. Cartwright echoed the real David Lawrence's words of twenty-four hours ago.

"Then it's all settled?" she asked, half hope and half fear in her voice.

"Yes. I saw the Agent at the theatre last night. With a play like this, I don't haggle over terms. I've got his written acceptance on the author's behalf, and the contract will be signed tomorrow."

Yes, it would be signed tomorrow. If she had to forge the signature, she would forge it. There was no other way out now.

All at once she felt she must be alone. She rose to her feet. The unseen breakers which were dashing over her and roaring in her ears made speech impossible, but the hero of a hundred drawing-room comedies was never at fault in drawing-room manners. He also rose and began collecting his clothes.

With a supreme effort she found her voice.

"I'll see you down," she said.

"Thank you."

As deliberately as before he resumed his muffler and overcoat, and gathered up his hat and umbrella. Then he opened the door to let her pass out.

"About Tuesday?" he asked, as her hand was already on the latch of the front door.

"Tuesday?" She seemed for a moment bewildered. Then, with a little laugh, "Oh, yes; of course. What time shall I call for you?"

If he felt any emotion of surprise or relief, he did not show it.

"The meeting is at half-past three," he said.

"Then I'll be outside the theatre at twenty past. Look out for a black landaulette."

He bowed; but there was no need for her to grip the door-handle. He did not attempt to shake hands.

"I am very much your debtor," he said; and with these words he passed down the steps to the street. He gave his one, characteristic glance at the evening sky, and the next instant, before she could close the door, he had turned and gone.

In the little hall Mrs. Cartwright stood motionless as a statue. For one, two, three minutes the electric light beat down on her pale, expressionless face. Then at last, as she moved towards the stairs, there came a little sound, like a distant echo of her husband's last words.

"Your debtor," she murmured.

Could he conceivably have been referring to something which had not once, during the whole of their extraordinary interview, entered her mind? For regularly each quarter during those twenty-five long, lonely years her solicitors had paid over the allowance which she had originally agreed. And not once during the whole of that time had they reported or she received one word of gratitude or one syllable of acknowledgement.

II

At this point the following copies of correspondence relating to the progress of the story may usefully be inserted.

(1)

Bexhill. Sunday

Dear Mr. Cartwright,

I found your telegram when I got down here, and am very sorry that I shall be unable to meet you at the theatre on Monday morning. The fact is that I am really not at all well, and I think the only thing is to stay quietly down here for several weeks. However, I am sure you will really be able to manage quite well without me, and of course I have every confidence in the way that you will arrange things.

I must apologise for leaving so suddenly yesterday, but as I said before I have really been very far from well, and in fact I am thinking of going into a rest cure.

Yours faithfully
(Signed) DAVID LAWRENCE

(2)

*Windy Gap
Camperdown Avenue
Bexhill. Sunday*

Dear Mrs. Cartwright,

I am afraid you will have been wondering why I never rang you up last night or came to see you today. Even now I hardly know how to begin telling you what happened. I swear I did my absolute level best to do what you asked, but he wouldn't hear of it. He simply didn't seem to believe that I could want the thing stopped, and when he told me that everything was settled, it was impossible to go on. I am most fearfully sorry. I'm afraid you will think I made an awful mucker of it, but I absolutely swear I couldn't help it.

Finally he told me that he had arranged to produce the play in about three weeks from now, and he wanted my address. I was in an awful hole, but, not knowing what else to do, I gave him this address. Of course I will forward anything that comes straight on to you. When I got down here I found this telegram which I enclose, and I answered like in the copy which I also enclose.

I seem to have made an awful mess of it all. For Heaven's sake, let me know quickly if there is anything else that you think I ought to do. I expect I shall be here all the vacation now. Thank you very much for my lunch yesterday. I thought the play was very good.

Yours sincerely
(Signed) DAVID LAWRENCE

(3)
(Telegram handed in on Monday morning)

David Lawrence,
Windy Gap, Camperdown Avenue, Bexhill-on-Sea.
Very much regret to learn of your indisposition and trust you will soon recover attendance at rehearsals quite unnecessary in circumstances will use every endeavor carry out spirit of play can you forward photos of self also any other useful publicity matter.

THESPIGRAM, *London*

(4)
(Telegram)

Thespigram, London.
Mr. Lawrence has gone into rest cure please address all letters to his agents until further notice regret photograph not available.

(Unsigned)

(5)

Bexhill. Monday
Dear Mrs. Cartwright,
I have tipped the guard of the London train and asked him to get this sent to you by special messenger as soon as he gets in. I hope he won't forget. You will see from

DENIS MACKAIL

the enclosures what I have done. I hope it is all right.
I will say I am dead if necessary, but would rather not, as
it might get into the papers and annoy Father who is in
Switzerland.

Yours sincerely
(Signed) DAVID LAWRENCE

(6)
(*Telegram*)

David Lawrence,
Windy Gap, Camperdown Avenue, Bexhill-on-Sea.
Both letters received cannot thank you enough for trouble
you have taken and ingenuity you have shown shall always
be most grateful to you and apologise abjectly for inflicting
this on you letter of proper thanks follows best wishes for
Christmas and new year.

HELEN CARTWRIGHT

To judge by the number of times that the recipient of this last telegram took it out of his pocket and read it and put it back again, and then had it out for just one more look, it would appear that something in its contents had caused him to revise a certain sweeping judgment which, though admittedly under great provocation, he had recently seen fit to pass on the female sex as a whole.

Is it possible that evidence to the same effect is also to be adduced from a scarcely less constant reference to a document which he carries in another pocket? If we look over his shoulder, we should see a rather crumpled-looking theatre programme. Nothing here, you would say, to compete with that fascinating telegram, and yet something there must be to account for the competition which undoubtedly exists.

It is after one of these latter inspections that an expression of sudden resolution appears in his face, and he sits down to write a strongly worded message to a certain Oxford garage.

And as the outlaw presses down the flap of the envelope, a further look of grim determination is seen.

"I'll manage it," we hear him mutter. "I'll manage it, even if it means I have to wear a false beard."

III

MONDAY MORNING FOUND MRS. CARTWRIGHT FOR once in her life too deeply interested in her own affairs to notice such a detail as the dark smudges beneath her secretary's eyes. With a flash of inspiration she had found a drawer full of old receipts, and with instructions to get these into some kind of order, Elizabeth was left alone until lunch-time.

And as they sat down to lunch, a fresh incident occurred to distract Mrs. Cartwright's attention. This was no less than the arrival by district messenger of a letter from the Trafalgar Agency (E. Purdock and C. W. Purdock, Partners) still damp from the copying-press.

"What was that, Hilda?" she had asked, as the maid returned to the dining-room after answering the front door.

"A letter for Mr. Lawrence, madam," said Hilda.

Mrs. Cartwright flattened her rissole under her fork and rose from the table.

"Excuse me just a minute," she said, and, leaving the room, seized the letter and took it upstairs with her.

If ever a Dramatic Agency showed signs of excitement,—and such an event must be most remarkably rare,—these signs were now to be seen. With a fine disregard for their four years of failure, the Messrs. Purdock had instantly assumed the entire credit for this successful deal. True, they admitted in one passage that Mr. Cartwright had seemed "very genuinely impressed" by their client's work, but the general tone of the letter suggested that the Thespian had entered on this agreement principally so as to signify its appreciation of the Purdock skill, judgment, and acumen, and, only incidentally, so as to obtain a new play.

One thing, however, Mrs. Cartwright noted with considerable relief. The contract was to be with the Agency direct, and no fresh forgery would be required from her in addition to that which had for a number of years embellished her agreement with the Purdocks. The financial details set out in the letter conveyed little or nothing to her. She had already decided that if this extraordinary affair were to result in any kind of monetary reward, it must go to charity, with the exception of such a sum as would be necessary to provide the innocent victim of her impersonation with a present worthy of his heroic conduct. Only, if it came to that, even the cheques would be made payable to him, and she would either have to open a fresh account under an assumed name, or else pass all the money through David first. Her brain resumed the endless track-racing with which it had been occupied most of the night and all the morning. Where would it end? What was the point at which she could, if only she had known it, have gone back? Why had she tried to be so clever? Why hadn't she shown more firmness with the Agents? Was the play, by any conceivable chance, really as good as all that?

Elizabeth waited some little time after lunch, but there was no sign or sound from upstairs, and presently she slipped away.

When she returned on the Tuesday morning, Hilda greeted her with the news that Mrs. Cartwright had gone out.

"Didn't she leave any message for me?' asked Elizabeth.

"No, Miss. But she said she would probably not be in to lunch."

"I see. Thank you."

She went wearily through to her little room at the back, and, without even bothering to remove her things, sank into her chair and sat staring stonily out of the window at the blank wall opposite. Once or twice her eyelids fluttered ominously, but no other movement did she make. On the table beside her lay the pile of receipts neatly docketed in alphabetical heaps. Yes, she saw it all now. John Ormroyd, with his bullying ways, had forced her on to Mrs. Cartwright Secretary, indeed! Mrs. Cartwright was the kindest woman in the world; she would do anything for Mrs. Cartwright; anything, that was, except take advantage of her for another instant. What a fool she must think her, too! Four days had she been there, and in the whole of that time she had written two letters and tidied one drawerful of bills. And now Mrs. Cartwright had gone out for the day, and actually forgotten her very existence. If she was doomed to fail at everything, it couldn't be helped. If she had to go without food again and be insulted by filthy men, she would face it. But as for remaining another moment in this contemptible position, no! And as for John Ormroyd, she hated him. Only—

She swung round on her chair, took the cover from the typewriter, and wrote quickly. Five minutes later she let herself quietly out of the front door.

And five minutes after that, who should arrive on the doorstep but John Ormroyd himself? Once more there dangled from his hand an unmistakeable box of chocolates—though slightly larger this time than on the occasion of his former visit.

John had spent Saturday night in remorse, and Sunday in a very discreditable kind of resentment ("seems to think she can order me about! Can't even earn her own living!"). By Monday Remorse was returning, though it had a hard fight of it with that dangerous condition generally known as the Sulks. But the Sulks died suddenly on Monday evening, and a victorious Remorse had shown no mercy on him. By breakfast-time on Tuesday he was in pretty bad shape.

And yet you would have thought he would have realised, after his previous experience, that there was something unlucky about buying chocolates. For had he but omitted this formality this time, he would have saved not only a considerable sum of money, but five precious, irrecoverable minutes as well. Experience had, however, taught him nothing.

"Is Miss Smith in?" asked John, as the door was opened.

"I think so, sir. Will you come in?"

He came in.

"You'll find Miss Smith in the back room, sir," said Hilda, who didn't quite approve of these calls, and besides it wasn't her business to show visitors in to lady secretaries, least of all in the mornings when she had her silver to do.

So, nervously preparing his speech of apology, and concealing his parcel behind his back, John went past the dining-room and tapped on the door of the little room where he had written that ill-fated note on Saturday.

There was, of course, no answer.

He opened the door and looked in.

The room was, equally of course, empty.

There stood his typewriter, there the bundle of receipts, but of Elizabeth not a trace.

He wished now that he had begun, as of course any gentleman would have begun, by asking for Mrs. Cartwright. Elizabeth must be upstairs with her.

He looked back into the hall, but Hilda had gone. Very well, then, he would ring the bell. So he went into the little back room and did this.

In due course Hilda reappeared, looking, he thought, dangerously surly.

"Miss Smith doesn't seem to be here," he said, his tone suggesting that he had only arrived at this conclusion after a careful search of all possible hiding-places. "Do you think she's engaged with Mrs. Cartwright?"

"Mrs. Cartwright's gone out, sir. I expect Miss Smith must have gone out too."

"Oh. Thank you. I'm sorry I troubled you."

Hilda merely looked a little more disagreeable; she made but the faintest pretence at helping him back into his overcoat, and had the front door open again while he was still trying to find his gloves. Well, perhaps he had given her a little extra trouble, but—An idea struck him.

"By the way," he said, "I wonder whether you'd care for these chocolates?" He tried to smile ingratiatingly as he spoke, but the smile fell frozen from his face, as Hilda answered stiffly:

"No, thank you, sir. I never touch chocolates."

Snubbed. And by a parlourmaid. Resisting an overwhelming impulse to cram the whole parcel down her throat, he turned and strode from the house.

But no mere area railings would meet the case this time. With gathering speed his right arm swung round and round, the chocolates extended on the full length of their string. Then, with an expression which I do not propose to repeat, he loosed his hold. Dynamics, which, as so many have found to their cost, follow their immutable laws whether one is in a temper or not, took charge of the parcel. It described a high-angle parabola through the air, and fell with a thud in the middle of the Square garden.

And once more John passes from the scene.

IV

"Why," Mrs. Cartwright asked herself for the thousandth time, as her car was bringing her back again through the suburbs,— "why am I doing this?"

She had told her chauffeur to drive her out of London, anywhere; and all morning, all through the unpalatable lunch at the roadside inn, and all the way back again, she had wrestled with this problem.

The only progress which had been made was purely negative. She was satisfied that no explanation was to be looked for in that long-forgotten letter which her husband had threatened to produce from his pocket-book. Not that she had not meant every syllable in that letter. She remembered even now how her solicitor had written pressing her to leave those words out. But in offering to help Leo in his career, she had surely not intended to assist in anything so remote from the Stage as this extraordinary plan. And if she had, it had certainly never been her intention that such assistance should take the form of conspiring to delude a number of strangers into the belief that she and her husband were a united pair. Why, then, had she, almost immediately and without more than the feeblest kind of protest, undertaken to share in such a conspiracy?

For the thousandth and first time Mrs. Cartwright gave it up.

The bills on the front of the Thespian Theatre already bore diagonal slips announcing "Last Two Weeks," as her car slowed up before it a little after a quarter-past three.

Though she had driven past the Thespian probably hundreds of times since her return to London, this was the first occasion on which she had either the opportunity or the desire to give the building more than the briefest glance, and even now she had drawn up too close to it to see more than the row of entrances under the glass portico. A faint smile lit up her face, as she noticed now that in one respect, at least, her husband had achieved the ambition of which he had spoken to her on Sunday. Into the iron-work supporting the portico there had been cast at intervals of a few feet little embossed medallions, and on each medallion she saw his two initials.

Traces of the smile lingered still, when Leo Cartwright himself appeared a moment later.

"It's good of you to have come," he said, even before opening the door of the motor.

"Will you tell the man where to drive?" was the form which her answer, if it was an answer, took.

He leant across the front seat and spoke a few words to the chauffeur, and the next instant had taken his seat beside his wife.

"Have we far to go?" she asked, more for the sake of breaking the silence, than from any particular wish to know.

He made no sign of having heard her, but, before she could repeat her question, he had asked another.

"Are you quite certain you want to go on with this?" he said.

The very question which she had brought back unanswered from her drive in the country.

"No," she said. "I'm not certain. But I'm going on."

"Is that wise?"

"Wise? Have I ever done a wise thing in my life?"

She could have bitten her tongue out the moment she had spoken. The words were so unnecessary; worse, so terribly open to a misinterpretation on his part, the mere thought of which made her blush hotly.

DENIS MACKAIL

But the impassive countenance on the seat beside her had not moved a muscle. All he said—and this after a long pause—was:

"I don't want you to regret anything."

"If I don't know why I'm doing this," she answered, "at any rate I'm doing it with my eyes open." But she wondered, "Am I?"

"I should like—" said Leo Cartwright's deepest, slowest voice. But here he stopped. The sentence remained uncompleted, and for the rest of the short drive there was silence in the car.

The meeting of the Traditional Association's Local Branch was to take place, not in its own cramped and ill-equipped quarters over a shop, but in a room specially hired for the occasion at Muffyn's Hotel. This old-fashioned establishment possessed a quantity of large and sombre apartments which were in considerable demand among Druids, Buffaloes, Oddfellows, and Masons, as well as for less purely convivial or philanthropic meetings such as this. And in one of these rooms there were now assembled some ten or a dozen persons, whose chief apparent bond in common (since devotion to the Traditional cause, however deep, produces no outwardly recognisable signs) was to be found in an evenly distributed look of self-importance. A long table covered with a red-baize cloth had been placed across one end of the room, and on the farther side of this the Committee had ranged themselves. The two vacant chairs in the centre represented the Headquarters delegate (who was late) and Mr. Alexander Brisk (who was waiting downstairs). The room itself, quite as much as the Committee, appeared to be trying to overlook the paper festoons and flags of all nations with which it was decorated in preparation for some druidical, buffalonian, or masonic entertainment. There was a heavy smell of dampness and soup.

Leo Cartwright helped his wife out of the car and inserted her at the proper moment in the revolving door leading to Muffyn's entrance hall. Inside the lights had not yet been lit, and, though it was only half-past three, it was too dark, certainly for any one coming in from the street, to form any definite opinion as to which of the faintly luminous oblongs were doorways and which looking-glasses. Mr. and Mrs. Cartwright paused uncertainly, and, as they paused, a figure detached itself from the foggy background.

"I'm glad to see you are so punctual," said the figure.

"Ha, Brisk," answered Mr. Cartwright, peering into the darkness. They shook hands.

"Shall we come upstairs?" asked Mr. Brisk.

The Chief nodded, and Mr. Brisk moved on.

Up a flight of stairs they went and along a thickly carpeted corridor. At the door of the Committee room Mr. Brisk turned, and was surprised to find that Mr. Cartwright was still accompanied by the woman who had come into the hotel just in front of him.

"Is this lady with you?" he whispered.

"I beg your pardon," said the Chief. "I should have introduced you, of course. I hope, however, that there will be no objection if my wife is also present at the meeting. This is Mr. Brisk, Helen," he added. "A very old business friend of mine."

"How do you do?" said Mrs. Cartwright, bowing slightly.

Mr. Brisk let the door-handle go with a snap. Was this a piece of superhuman bluff, or had he gone mad? If ever he had thought to meet a man on ground advantageous to himself and his plans, it had been when he had arranged for Leo Cartwright to be invited to this meeting. And yet here, before they had even reached the Committee room, the Chief, by his few, casually spoken words, had caught him right in the wind. Only the merciful darkness saved Mr. Brisk from displaying with unpardonable frankness the stupefaction which he felt. While he still gasped for breath, Mrs. Cartwright spoke again.

"I do hope you'll let me come in, too, Mr. Brisk," she said.

Not Royalty itself could have more nicely adjusted the tones of its voice to the exact mixture of condescension and appeal which Mrs. Cartwright achieved. Though reason and even knowledge forbade it,—for had he not Leo Cartwright's own words to bear him witness?—Mr. Brisk felt conviction carrying him away.

"I won't make a sound," said Mrs. Cartwright, not humbly, but with a remote kind of dignity.

"Why, of course, Mrs. Cartwright," Mr. Brisk heard himself saying. "My Committee will be most delighted to meet you."

And immediately he opened the door and stood back for the Cartwrights to go in.

If five minutes later Helen Cartwright had suggested to those eleven pompous-looking men that they should run races round the room or join with her in a game of Nuts in May, there can be no reasonable doubt that they would have done so. And not reluctantly, but gladly. Never can she have exerted her charm with more remarkable or powerful effect. Her husband, still muttering over to himself the points which Miss Lemon had given him to learn up, was almost forgotten. Scandal and Rumour, if indeed they had ever seriously reached the Committee, and had not merely been threatened by Mr. Brisk so as to establish the personal ascendancy required for the completion of his plans, were at once forgotten. A more than usually fruity-looking committeeman made the facetious suggestion that Mrs. and not Mr. Cartwright should receive the nomination of their Association, and for a moment it almost looked as if the proposition would be carried in a burst of unanimous infatuation. But at this moment the door at the end of the room opened again to admit the Headquarters official, and at once, like naughty schoolboys, the eleven subsided into their seats round the baize-covered table.

I do not propose to transcribe to these pages the Minutes of the meeting which followed. The briefest summary should suffice. Mr. Brisk, who was of course in the chair, began by stating that they met under the shadow of a great loss. Although the late Sir George Braham had unfortunately been unable to occupy his seat in the House, save on the rarest occasions, for the last five years, his connection with their Division had been so long and his services to it so great, that his removal to a higher plane must come as a severe and tragic blow to the Traditional Party. He would not ask them to forward any special message of condolence to Sir George's relatives, since they had unfortunately all pre-deceased him. The question of the exact form which the memorial which it had been proposed should be erected should take had, he thought, better be referred to a sub-committee. Perhaps this could be discussed at their next meeting. (Murmurs of approval.) Mr. Brisk proceeded to say that he had great pleasure in introducing to the meeting Mr. Codrington from the Headquarters Association. They were all proud to have Mr. Codrington with them to assist in the deliberations which would occupy them this afternoon.

Mr. Codrington then rose and said that he felt almost overpowered by the kind words of his old friend, the Chairman. He might tell the meeting, however, that Headquarters were very proud of Mr. Brisk and of the Covent Garden Association as a whole. If he could be of any assistance to them today, he would be very proud to have had the opportunity. (Murmurs of pride.) He could not resume his seat, he added, without paying a tribute to the memory of that great Englishman, Lord Houndsditch, whose untimely death had had the effect of removing to other duties the candidate whom they had at one time hoped to see representing them—he referred to the present Baron. (Murmurs of respectful regret.)

Mr. Brisk then rose again to introduce Mr. Cartwright. He had, he said, known Mr. Cartwright for a great number of years, and though he was the last man to wish to influence the Committee in anyway, he was free to admit that a more straightforward, honourable, and—er—straightforward man than Mr. Cartwright he for his part had never met. Mr. Cartwright, he added, had admittedly taken very little active part in Politics hitherto. Perhaps he was none the worse for that. (Laughter, in which Mrs. Cartwright joined.) But if they looked round their Division today and could find a man who had done more to maintain its high and honourable reputation, and who was better fitted to represent it, he for his part would be surprised. In this, however, as in all other matters, the interests of their Party must of course come first. (A sinister nod from Mr. Codrington at this point.) He would leave it, therefore, to the members of the Committee to satisfy themselves, as he had satisfied himself, that in all the essential planks of their great political platform Mr. Cartwright's views were, and always had been, such as would justify them in giving him their implicit confidence. He would ask Mr. Cartwright, therefore, if he would very kindly answer any questions which the members of the Committee might wish to put to him.

Mr. Cartwright bowed from his seat, and there followed a long pause, while the members looked unutterably wise and waited for each other to speak.

Mr. Codrington: Well, perhaps if I might begin. . . ?

Murmurs of agreement.

Mr. Codrington: Well, Mr. Cartwright, I have only one question to ask you, I think, though it is a very important one. Do you subscribe to the seventeen points of the Declaration of Bournemouth?

Poor Leo Cartwright! Not one of the slips of paper which Miss Lemon had laboriously prepared for him so much as mentioned the word Bournemouth. On Unemployment, Wages, Pensions, Protection or Proportional Representation he was fully primed. Disarmament or Dilution would have been mere child's play to him after his long night of study. But this! The very first question, too.

"The Declaration of Bournemouth," he repeated slowly, racking his brains to recall anything which might enlighten him, and, as he finished speaking, with a crash Mrs. Cartwright's chain-bag fell to the ground. Though most of the Committee turned their heads quickly to see what had happened, they were not quick enough. Only Leo Cartwright's

DENIS MACKAIL

heavy-lidded eyes, trained by a lifetime's watch on the prompt corner, had caught her mouthed message.

"Yes," he said, with impressive deliberation, "I subscribe to them all."

Mr. Codrington and one or two other members made a quick movement and drew in their breath to speak. But again Mrs. Cartwright had been quicker. With lightning pantomime she had violently shaken her head as she carried an imaginary bumper to her lips. And Mr. Codrington's opening words were overwhelmed by Leo Cartwright's sonorous voice.

"All, that is," he said, "except the point relating to Prohibition."

"Ah," said Mr. Codrington.

"Ah," said Mr. Brisk and the rest of the Committee.

Mr. Cartwright turned with a kind of impassive expectancy to receive the next question.

"I should like to ask Mr. Cartwright," said a member with a beard, "what his opinion is on the general question of Import Restrictions."

This was easy. The Traditional pamphlets from which Miss Lemon had prepared her employer's brief were quite clear on this point, and he answered fully, convincingly, and (in the hope of reducing the number of subsequent questions) at great length. There was no doubting the general mumble of satisfaction with which his reply was received.

And so this *viva voce* examination proceeded for the best part of an hour. As Leo Cartwright's voice gradually got the pitch of the room and his personality fastened itself on the Committee, the questions became more and more perfunctory and the answers more and more overwhelmingly verbose. Though Mrs. Cartwright had her bag poised the whole time ready for a second emergency, no such emergency arose, and finally the fruity-looking member said:

"Well, Mr. Chairman, I move that we send downstairs for some tea. Perhaps Mr. and Mrs. Cartwright would be good enough to join us in a cup."

"Anybody second that?" asked Mr. Brisk jocosely.

"I do," answered ten members and Mr. Codrington as one man.

"Carried," said Mr. Brisk. "Well, Mr. Cartwright?"

But it was Mrs. Cartwright who answered.

"We shall be delighted," she said.

The meeting broke up into little knots, of which far the largest centred round Mrs. Cartwright, and Mr. Brisk drew the Chief aside.

"Splendid," he said. "I think we've made a great impression on them, if you ask me."

The Chief let the "we" pass.

"What is the next move?" he asked.

"We shall go on with the meeting," answered Mr. Brisk, "after you've gone, and, if they reach a decision this evening, I'll telephone you at the theatre. In any case I shall drop you a line tonight."

"Thank you," said the Chief gravely.

"Oh, and by the way," continued Mr. Brisk, dropping his voice confidentially, "I'm sending round to you tonight my proposals for a fresh agreement about our bookings at the Thespian."

"Oh?"

"Yes, I've had our accountants on it and I think it's a very reasonable scheme. It's a sliding scale discount increasing with the amount of seats we take and also periodically during the run of any one play."

"I'll look into it."

"Thanks," said Mr. Brisk.

Mutual understanding was complete. Leo Cartwright looked forward to a long and hard-fought battle with Mr. Littlejohn and a still stiffer one with the Backers, but it was worth it. Yes, decidedly it was worth it.

"There's one other thing," said Mr. Brisk. "And that's about possible opposition. As I told you the other day, a contest in this Division is practically unheard of; and from all I hear the Representatives aren't thinking of putting any one up. But there's another possibility, I'm sorry to say."

"Eh?" Opposition was no part of the bargain, but without opposition a Parliamentary election might prove a very tame affair. The Chief was interested, but not alarmed.

"Yes," Mr. Brisk went on. "I got a telephone message just as I was coming here today. Apparently there's some idea of Hamilcar Barker running himself as an Independent."

"But surely—"

"Yes, I know his reputation in decent circles. But you must remember he's got money and he's got his newspapers. If he should decide to stand, well, we'd have to go all out to make certain of winning."

The Chief seemed lost in thought.

"Of course, there may be nothing in it," added Mr. Brisk; "but at the same time I thought I ought to give you the tip."

DENIS MACKAIL

"I am very much obliged to you," said Mr. Cartwright.

"Well, it will be short and sharp, anyhow. The writ's to be issued this week; the nominations will probably be on Saturday week, and polling about a week later. All over, whatever happens, by the middle of January."

The middle of January! And before then he had got to put in nearly three weeks of the hardest and most exhausting kind of work in rehearsing his new play, as well as appearing eight times a week— except for the few days when the theatre would be closed—in one or other of his leading roles at the Thespian.

V

"I'll drive you back as far as the theatre," Mrs. Cartwright murmured as she and her husband left the room together, followed as far as the door by her crowd of admirers.

"Thank you," he said; and, as the door closed behind them, he added: "You saved me then. Why did you do it?"

"You saved yourself," answered Mrs. Cartwright, avoiding the question. "Are they going to adopt you?" she added quickly, as though to prevent him repeating it.

"Brisk tells me he'll let me know tonight. If they do, I suppose it will be in the newspapers tomorrow."

"And who will you have against you, if you are chosen?"

"Nobody, perhaps. I don't know definitely. Brisk had heard a rumour." He told her the rumour.

"Not that terrible man?"

"That's the one."

He helped her into the car and directed the chauffeur where to drive.

"Leo," said his wife, "you must beat him."

"I mean to try."

"Then you must put off my—you must put off the new play."

"I can't. The theatre must come first."

"But how can you possibly do it?"

He gave his heart-breaking smile.

"By working," he said.

And all at once she seemed to see a vista of his life stretching away backwards, and always he was reading, rehearsing, studying, planning, and acting, day in and day out. It came into her mind how she had never heard of him at big dinners or smart country-houses, at restaurants, garden-parties, or theatrical high-jinks. And yet—

"You used not to like work so much," she said.

He gave her a curious look.

"I've changed," he answered.

They were silent again until the car reached the theatre.

"Leo," she said, as he was getting out.

"Yes?"

"I wonder if you would do something for me?"

"Of course."

"I wonder—do you think I could come, just quietly, to the dress rehearsal of David Lawrence's play?"

"Why, certainly. I hadn't dared to suggest it, but if—Here! Take my card." He pencilled a few words on a visiting-card and handed it to her. "That will let you in. No one will know who you are. And, if I may, I shall send you a Box for the first night too. You can sit right at the back, and you can use the Royal entrance, if you would prefer it."

"No, I couldn't do that."

"Well, we'll see. I shall send it you, anyhow. Goodbye. And again thank you more than I can hope to say."

And with these words the Chief raised his hat and left his wife to her thoughts. As the car drove off, he had already disappeared through the archway leading to the Stage Door.

In the draughty little space by the door-keeper's box Miss Lemon was waiting as the Chief came through the swing doors.

"What's the matter, Miss Lemon?" he asked, as he acknowledged Garrod's salute.

"I was just going to try and get through to you on the telephone," answered the secretary. "I'm glad you've come back."

Miss Lemon never answered more or less than she was asked without very good reason and in this case the Chief correctly understood her prevarication to signify that she had something of a confidential nature to communicate to him.

"Just come up to my room," he said; and, as they passed the first corner of the stairs, he asked:

"What is it?"

"Mr. Imray, Chief. He's been waiting here nearly three-quarters of an hour."

"But there was no appointment?"

"No."

"Ah."

Miss Lemon looked for any trace of expression on his face which should elucidate this interjection, but, as she had expected, there was none.

"I've given him tea," she said.

"Good. Thank you. Well, stand by in case I want you."

Miss Lemon had done nothing else for nearly ten years, and she acknowledged this instruction in silence.

A moment later the Chief's richest and warmest tones floated out to her through the closing door.

"Ha, Mr. Imray, what an unexpected pleasure!"

VI

Mrs. Cartwright lay back in the corner of her car thinking and again thinking. Every second of her extraordinary afternoon passed through and through her mind, and at each stage her imagination would dart off into little blind-alleys of what might have happened, only to return again, baffled, to the baffling reality. Why had she asked to go to the dress rehearsal? This perhaps was not inexplicable. But then why had he said that he had been meaning to ask her? And what would she have said if he had done so first?

And for the ten thousandth time that day, how far was she supposed to carry this ridiculous and uncomfortable imposture? Must she attend further meetings? If she must, would she do so? And why hadn't he raised this point? Surely she wasn't meant to offer herself.

She stepped wearily across the pavement into her house with the absolute knowledge that the headache with which she would go to bed tonight would be to all other headaches as is the Woolworth to all other buildings.

"I've had tea, thanks," she said; "but perhaps you would take my furs upstairs for me."

"Yes, madam," said Hilda, and Mrs. Cartwright turned to gather up her letters from the top of the cassone.

"Why, this is my own note-paper," she said to herself, as she stared stupidly at Elizabeth's ultimatum. Fatigue made her incapable of focussing her eyes on it until after several attempts. Then she read as follows:

Dear Mrs. Cartwright,

Please do not think it rude of me and I shall always be
most terribly grateful to you for your kindness to me, but
I am afraid it is quite clear that it was only kindness and
nothing else. I can't possibly stay and go on taking your
money when I know that I am being absolutely no use to you
at all, so I shall not come back after today.

I return two pounds out of the five which you gave
me, also the pound which you gave me for lunch on Friday,
which I didn't use. I really ought to return it all, but I'm
afraid I have spent most of the rest, and after all I did do my
best to find something to do while I was here. That sounds
ungrateful, but I'm not. Only very very sorry that I should
have been inflicted on you like this.

Yours sincerely
ELIZABETH SMITH

P. S. I have put the book which you lent me back on the
drawing-room shelf.

The Treasury notes fluttered to the ground, as Mrs. Cartwright's
arm fell heavily to her side. She stooped slowly, picked them up, and
moved towards the stairs.

"Drat the girl," she said. "As if I hadn't got enough to think about
tonight without having to write to her as well."

She sank into the chair at her writing-table.

"Dear Elizabeth," she wrote, "I am returning you your money, and. . ."

She stopped. She didn't even know the silly child's address.

"Get through to Mr. Ormroyd, please," she called out, as she heard
Hilda coming downstairs. "And I'll speak to him myself."

"Very good, madam."

A few minutes later the buzzer in the drawing-room went, and she
picked up the receiver.

"Is that you, John?" she asked.

"Yes."

"I say, I wish you'd tell me your Elizabeth's address."

"Why, what's happened?"

"She's taken herself off because the place doesn't suit."

"But where?"

"My dear John, do you suppose I should have rung you up if I knew where."

"But I don't know her address."

"You don't know—But where did you find her? Who is she, anyway? You can't pick up girls anyhow and bring them into my house like this."

"I'm very sorry. I didn't know what else to do."

"I told you something would happen if you didn't take her off my hands soon."

"I'm infernally sorry. I've been an awful fool, I'm afraid."

"Yes," said Mrs. Cartwright. "You have."

"Well, but what was I to do?"

"Do?" repeated Mrs. Cartwright, speaking very loudly. "Why, marry her, of course."

"By Jove!" said John, the reason for all the inexplicable phenomena of the last five days suddenly made clear. "I will, if I can find her."

"No, John. Not if you can find her. But—if—she—will—have—you."

She slammed the receiver down quickly.

"Dear, dear," she mused, as she went up to her room to lie down. "I'm sometimes afraid that, as well as growing old, I'm getting just a little vulgar."

"But there are worse things than that," she added later, as she switched off the light.

VII

A First Night at the Thespian

I

THE NEWSPAPERS WHICH ANNOUNCED THAT Mr. Leo Cartwright, the well-known actor-manager, had been adopted as Traditional candidate for the Covent Garden Division and that Mr. Hamilcar Barker (too celebrated to be described as a "well-known" anything) had decided to contest the seat in an Independent capacity, confirmed Mr. Brisk's forecast of the probable dates for nominations and polling. They added that what they described as a "Christmas Truce" would be held over the "Festive Season," but it was hinted that after that the struggle would be short, sharp, and sanguinary. This truce was, indeed, practically compulsory for Mr. Barker, since his main guns had been silenced by an unfortunate agreement into which he had entered with other newspaper managers and proprietors not to publish for the three days of the Christmas holidays. And without this artillery support, he did not propose to waste time in any personal sniping. One may imagine, however, that he did not let slip the opportunity which was thus afforded him of planning and telephoning and looking people up. By the time that the world returned to work, the exact part which each of the periodicals with which he was connected was to take in the coming battle had been accurately laid down, and, with this weight off his mind, he could devote all the time which could be spared from his activities in the City to prancing round the constituency on his war-horse,—or Rolls-Royce,—to making speeches, and to being photographed shaking hands with voters.

To the Thespian Theatre, on the other hand, Christmas brought no respite. True, there was no performance on Christmas Day itself,— though to make up for this there was an extra matinée on Boxing Day,— but by this time the preparations for the new production were in full swing, and, with the short time that the Chief had allowed himself before the opening night, there can have been but few employees, whether visible or invisible, who saw much of the outside world during this period of peace and good-will. For, in spite of Mr. Imray's dramatic appearance on the Tuesday afternoon, the notices on the Call Board had remained unchanged. Both Mr. Littlejohn and Mr. Gordon had contrived to be waiting on the stairs, when he emerged from his confabulation with the Chief, but beyond a brief nod he had given no sign which either of them could recognise as indicating its upshot. Mr. Littlejohn fancied that he had looked a little grimmer than usual, but admitted that it was several years since he had last seen him, while Mr. Gordon frankly confessed that he was blowed if he knew what had happened.

Nor was anything more illuminating to be gathered from the Chief. He had had his light, early dinner in the theatre that evening, and, though both Business and Personal Manager had made a point of being within call, no summons had reached either of them. They had both long since learnt that nothing was to be gained by questioning Miss Lemon. When the Chief did eventually emerge, dressed for the first Act, there was no sign discernible beneath his make-up which could throw any kind of light on the contents of his mind. His followers were left to gather what they could from the negative fact that no change in policy was announced.

"They've had their argument," was Mr. Littlejohn's view, "and the Chief has talked him round."

"I can't see any one talking Mr. Imray round on a matter of business," was all that Mr. Gordon could contribute, and in spite of everything he stuck obstinately to this view.

Since then preparations had gone ahead quickly. The Chief saw the political Agent whom Mr. Brisk had found for him soon after nine o'clock every morning and discussed his plans and arrangements with him. At eleven o'clock he came down on to the stage and rehearsed his new company for the rest of the morning. In the afternoons, when there were no matinées, he took further rehearsals; though later on he contrived to delegate this part of his duties to the Stage Manager— only allowing him, however, to go through with those parts of the play which he had already taken himself. For after the Christmas holidays the afternoons had to be given up to attending his new Committee rooms, encouraging his canvassers, and addressing such meetings as it was possible for him to leave by soon after half-past seven. By a quarter to eight he had to be back at the theatre to dress for "Pale People," and by the time the curtain fell it was too late to do any more outside work. Not even here, however, did his work end. It was often nearer four than three in the morning before the night watchman was rung for to let him out, and the intervening hours had been spent in learning up his new part,—one of the longest which he had ever been called upon to play,—in committing to memory the speeches which his Agent had had prepared for him, or in renewing his recollection of Miss Lemon's indispensable slips of paper.

On the night when "Pale People" was played for the last time, the house was fuller than it had been for several weeks, and there was a little demonstration of enthusiasm at the end of the performance. The Chief, standing alone before the curtain, raised his hand for silence, and made a short speech.

"I am very much flattered," he said, "by the kind way in which you have bidden farewell to this play tonight. It is always a sad moment for me when I have to take leave for the last time of one of my stage characters; but the parting is made far easier for me when I receive such signs of friendship and encouragement as you have given me this evening. I realise then that I owe you very much more than the repetition of the same piece of work.

"In my new play," he continued, "which I hope to offer to you here next Saturday night—today week—I have had the privilege of being associated with an author who, although at present unknown, is in my opinion destined to go very far before he has finished. May I hope that the same fairness and appreciation may be shown to him then, as were shown to me by the London audience before whom I had the honour of appearing when I opened this theatre fifteen and a half years ago? Once more, I thank you."

He grasped the edge of the curtain with one hand and bowed, and like the roaring of the sea the sound of applause came sweeping up against him from all sides. As the wave subsided a little, a man's voice up in the gallery called out, "Vote for Cartwright!" and amidst laughter from all parts of the house the applause broke over him again.

With a smile of gratitude and the famous deprecating gesture with his free hand, he bowed again and slipped back through the tableau curtains. Instantly his whole manner had changed. "House lights, quick!" he said sharply to the Stage Manager. "House lights!" the Stage Manager barked up to the electrician on the switchboard, and as he spoke the whole auditorium of the Thespian burst into a flood of light, the applause stopped as if cut off with a knife, and the interrupted movement towards the exists was resumed. There would be no anti-climax at the Thespian as long as Leo Cartwright was in control.

He called again to the Stage Manager.

"Is the new scenery in yet, Mr. M'Gill?" he asked.

"It's in the yard, Chief. The men will have it in first thing on Monday morning."

"No good. Must have it in tomorrow. I want to rehearse with it on Monday."

"But the men's wages?"

"Never mind the men's wages. You're here to get it done."

"Very good, Chief."

"Quite right to remind me," said the Chief, and stalked away. Only five words, but the trick was done. The little sop of praise, thrown carelessly after many a far more forcible rebuff than this, had kept his stage staff round him with scarcely a change since the beginning. You might go far before you found the loyalty which existed behind the curtain at the Thespian.

Up in the saloon the Agent was waiting with a written programme of next week's meetings.

"I can give you three evenings," said the Chief, as he studied the list. "You can't have Saturday, of course; nor Friday. I've got my dress rehearsal then. But you can choose the other three yourself."

"Couldn't you manage the dress rehearsal during the day, Mr. Cartwright?" asked the Agent. "I've got a big meeting on for Friday. It would make a lot of difference if you were there."

Faintly amused surprise was all that the Chief manifested at this extraordinary and revolutionary suggestion.

"No, certainly not," he said.

"And you won't be able to manage any evenings after next week?"

"No. Except Sunday."

"It's a great handicap," said the Agent, scratching his head dubiously.

Never in the course of his long experience of candidates and their idiosyncrasies had he come across anything like Mr. Cartwright. In some ways so gratifyingly amenable, in others so amazingly obstinate. But though he was acquiring an increasing admiration for his tact and quickness, he had already learnt that, when he said No, he meant it.

"I suppose there's no chance of Mrs. Cartwright being well enough to attend the Friday meeting in your place, sir," the Agent went on.

"None," answered the Chief, closing his eyes. "I am afraid my wife is still very far from well."

"I'm sorry she's so queer," said the Agent sympathetically.

"She's not in the least queer," replied the Chief. "Only unwell."

The Agent looked a little puzzled, but decided to leave it at that. This was not, unfortunately, the first time that the uncomfortable feeling had been borne in on him that the candidate found him in some way amusing. He went on quickly.

"By the way," he said, "I had a man in my office this morning from one of Barker's papers, asking after Mrs. Cartwright."

The Chief opened his eyes again suddenly.

"What did he want?" he enquired.

"I couldn't quite make out," replied the Agent. "He was asking a lot of questions, but, when I told him that she had been taken ill after the meeting of the Selection Committee, he seemed quite surprised."

"Oh, he did, did he?"

"Yes, sir. And he had a photograph with him and wanted me to say whether it was Mrs. Cartwright or not. Of course I didn't know, but fortunately Mr. Brisk was with me at the time and he told him yes it was. After that he went off."

"Very interesting," said the Chief; and indeed to him it was so, although the Agent again showed that puzzled and slightly suspicious look. With a glance at his engagement book he hurried on.

"Well, anyhow," he said, "it will be all right about the Mothers' Christmas Tree on Wednesday afternoon, eh? No matinée this week, sir."

"I'll make a note of it," answered the Chief, and shouted the particulars through the door to Miss Lemon.

The discussion of plans and engagements was resumed. But, as it happened, when Wednesday afternoon arrived, the Mothers' Christmas Tree, although highly successful *qua* Christmas Tree, was deprived of almost all political significance by the unavoidable absence of the Traditional Candidate at the Royal Courts of Justice.

For on Monday morning, as the Chief turned in under the archway leading to the Stage Door, an obliging-looking stranger had stepped forward and accosted him.

"Mr. Cartwright?" asked the stranger, politely raising his hat.

"Yes?" said the Chief, equally politely.

"For you, sir," proceeded the stranger, holding out a long envelope.

"For me? Ah, many thanks."

It was not until many hours later, when after a long day on the stage he was on the point of leaving for the first of his evening meetings, that Miss Lemon caught sight of the corner of the envelope protruding from his overcoat pocket.

"Oh, yes," said the Chief vaguely; "a man gave me that in the street this morning. You might see what it is."

Miss Lemon extracted the first of the several documents which the envelope seemed to contain, and unfolded it. Alas! there could not be more than an instant's doubt as to what it was. That ominous reference to His Majesty, that heavy paper, that completely unintelligible string of words leading up to that only too intelligible threat; all these could have but one meaning. Miss Lemon had grasped it at once.

"It's a writ," she said.

"What sort of a writ?" asked the Chief.

Miss Lemon peered about for signs of identification.

"On Wednesday next," she said. "In the Vacation Court."

"Yes, yes. But what is it all about?"

Miss Lemon dived into the envelope again.

"Notice of Motion," she murmured, scowling at the papers. "Take notice that the Honourable Court—um—er. . . Interim injunction restraining you from exhibiting or appearing in any stage-play except that in respect of which an agreement has been entered into between you and the plaintiff until such time as the said agreement shall have been discharged."

"Not the Norwegian?" asked the Chief, with genuine signs of horror; and, without pausing for an answer, he snatched the documents from his secretary's hands.

"Damn it!" he said. "This must be stopped. Get hold of Littlejohn."

Miss Lemon flew to the telephone.

"I can't wait, Miss Lemon," he went on. "I've got this meeting. I must go at once. Tell Littlejohn to see Tracy and Paull in the morning. I'll pay up, if I've got to pay, but I'm not going to put off my first night for a set of infernal agents; and what's more, Miss Lemon, I'll see Dr. Bransen and every other foreigner at the bottom of the sea before I waste my time producing their incompetent rubbish."

With which patriotic declaration the Chief departed to the first of his three highly successful evening meetings.

But (and again Alas!) Tracy and Paull wouldn't hear of such an easy solution as merely "paying up." After careful inspection of Mr. Littlejohn's copy of the agreement, they announced that if Mr. Cartwright would go into Court and say this and swear to that and refer, when suitably questioned, to the other, then they were of opinion, having due regard to the fact that the other side were, when all was said and done, acting on behalf of an alien, that the Court would uphold their client's action in disregarding this harsh and unreasonable contractual arrangement.

"But can't I go instead?" asked Mr. Littlejohn.

"Mr. Cartwright has five full rehearsals this week, apart from his political meetings. It's asking a bit much, you know."

"I am afraid it would be very inadvisable," said Tracy and Paull. "In a case of this nature a very great deal of importance attaches to the appearance of shall we say frankness, which is gained by the personal attendance of the principal. We have known far stronger defences than this seriously endangered by the attitude which the Court is inclined to take, when they are asked to accept evidence from deputies or representatives of the persons involved."

"But hang it all!" protested Mr. Littlejohn, "I signed the agreement first."

"You will, of course, have to be prepared to appear as well," was all the comfort obtainable from Messrs. Tracy and Paull.

And so, in addition to learning up his new part, learning up his new speeches, and endeavouring to retain in his head the thousand and one points on which he was liable to be questioned by hecklers, Mr. Cartwright had now to rehearse the correct answers to all the possible questions which might be put to him in Court on Wednesday.

The Judge who had been summoned from his holiday to hear this case had already regretted the weakness which had led him to admit its special urgency, and was determined to revenge himself by giving as much trouble to everybody concerned as he could conceivably manage to do; and in adopting this line it must be admitted that he was doing nothing to tilt the scales or blunt the sword of Justice, for the absolute impartiality of his offensiveness to all those present in Court was unquestioned. If at one moment he said, "Speak up, Mr. Cartwright. Remember this is not a music-hall," then a little later he restored the balance by telling Counsel for Plaintiff that he needn't shout, since there was no difficulty in hearing everything he said which was in anyway worth saying. With a kind of malignant perversity he took especial delight in drawing out each item of the procedure to the greatest possible length; insisted on hearing all three partners in the firm of agents repeat exactly the same story, and drove Mr. Littlejohn nearly distracted by examining him himself on the method by which he kept the Thespian accounts.

It was already quite clear, when the brief adjournment for lunch was announced, that the Mothers' Christmas Tree must be given a miss.

The Chief managed to get through to his Agent on the telephone and to dictate a message of regret, but by the time he had done this it was too late to go out in search of lunch, and, as the refreshment room in the Law Courts was closed for the vacation, he had to return to the hearing of his case unfed.

The effect of whatever kind of lunch His Lordship had been able to procure was not found appreciably to have softened his manner, and the proceedings were extended to the accompaniment of every kind of unnecessary insult and unreasonable delay until nearly half-past four. At this hour it appeared impossible for any further evidence to be heard or documents demanded, and both parties were looking forward with some certainty to being put out of their pain, when His Lordship announced with malicious glee that he did not find himself able to come to a decision that evening, and that the case must stand adjourned until he had had time to give the consideration to the facts which the importance of the issue demanded.

Counsel for the Defence thereupon rose and pointed out to His Lordship that his client had made every arrangement, and had already incurred considerable expense thereby, to give the first public representation of his new play on the following Saturday evening. Might he, therefore, most respectfully draw attention to the desirability from his client's point of view of obtaining an early decision?

On hearing this His Lordship was pleased to say that, in view of the additional facts just brought to his notice, he would arrange to sit on Saturday morning and would hope to be able to pronounce judgment then.

Leo Cartwright gesticulated wildly and desperately at his solicitors, but they succeeded in conveying to him their opinion that this concession was as much as could safely be asked for, and he was induced to subside. Plaintiff's Counsel thereupon arose and asked for an order from the Court, pending the decision in this case, restraining the defendant from advertising any performance whatsoever at his theatre. Counsel for the defence leapt quickly to his feet, but His Lordship had had enough of the whole thing now. He waved both barristers aside.

"No order will be made," he announced, and the hearing thereupon stood adjourned.

The Chief sought, but failed to find, relief in blackguarding both Littlejohn and the solicitors' clerk up to the moment when they succeeded in forcing him into a taxi, in which he drove straight back to the theatre. Once again he darted a nervous look through the window of his cab to see what form of publicity his opponent had devised for him. He had not long to wait. The first street seller that they passed had the legend on the *Evening Query* poster well displayed.

CARTWRIGHT IN COURT

the Chief read, and you may be sure that not a shade of the intended suggestion was lost on him. The insult was repeated at intervals of a few yards all the way back to the Thespian.

The first full rehearsal of "Romance to the Rescue" had been called for half-past five, and Mr. Cartwright spent the very brief interval left to him in signing letters and tossing off oysters in his private suite. At half-past five punctually he was down on the stage again.

The end of the last Act was reached at twenty minutes before midnight after a little over six hours of every imaginable kind of breakdown, mistake, accident, interruption, and omission. All the female members of the company and most of the men either had been or still were in tears. Mr. M'Gill presented the appearance of an exhumed corpse. The Chief was slightly paler than usual.

"Just a minute before you all go," he said, and the weary and sullen professionals turned and waited. "I dare say some of you have seen in the newspapers that an attempt has been made to prevent the production of this play. Unfortunately there is no hope of a decision before Saturday. But I want to tell you this. Whatever that decision may be, the performance on Saturday evening will take place, and for any results which may ensue I am prepared to take the consequences. As to the subsequent continuance of the run, I can give no undertaking. Meanwhile you will please all regard this statement of mine as confidential. I should like also to thank you once more for the way that you have worked during these rehearsals."

The exhausted company made one last effort and actually raised a murmur in which the words "Thank you, Mr. Cartwright" could faintly be detected. As they emerged into the alley, however, and felt the revivifying effects of the night air, comment became more coherent.

"I tell you one thing," said Miss Alice Mainwaring to her (temporary) bosom friend Miss Norma Nettlebridge; "I'm always ready to work hard, if I'm treated like Mr. Cartwright treats you."

"Poor dear," replied Miss Nettlebridge. "He looks pretty well done up."

"Yes, old man," said Mr. Percy Haversham to the sharer of his dressing-room, Mr. Alec Richards, "you can say what you like, but it takes a sportsman to say a thing like that."

"All the same," answered the more cautious Mr. Richards, "I hope he wins his case. I don't want to find the police in front when I come on."

The voices died away down the alley.

"By the way," said the Chief to his personal Manager, as he flung himself on the sofa in the saloon, "have you heard any more about how Mr. Lawrence is getting on?"

"I can't get an answer," replied Mr. Gordon. "I've written and wired several times to the address he gave."

"Poor fellow," said the Chief. "I thought he seemed a bit overstrung that day he came here. I hope he's not really bad."

Mr. Gordon found no comment to make on this kindly wish.

"Well, anyhow," resumed the Chief, "get on to his Agents. Perhaps they may know something about him. I should like him here on Saturday, if he could possibly manage it."

"I'll see what I can do, Chief," answered Mr. Gordon. "Is there anything else tonight?" he added.

"No, thanks, Gordon. Don't you wait up any longer. I'll see you in the morning."

"Right you are, Chief. Good-night."

"Good-night."

Mr. Cartwright reached for the pile of papers on the little table by his side and began studying the draft of his speech for the meeting in the Floral Hall on Thursday night.

At half-past four the night watchman knocked on the door and put his head in.

"I beg your pardon, sir," he said. "I thought you might have slipped out and left the light on."

"No, it's all right, thank you, Tunks," answered the Chief, looking up. "I'm only doing a little work. Is your wife better?"

"Yes, thank you, sir. She'll be glad to hear you asked, sir. I'm sorry I interrupted you."

But the Chief made no reply. He was again absorbed in his reading.

II

Mrs. Cartwright remained on the alert for several days, half-expecting some further message from her husband; but none came.

The daily Press had, however, apprised her of the probable starters for the Covent Garden election, and she was not altogether unprepared to read, a few days after the meeting at Muffyn's Hotel, that the wife of the Traditional candidate was unfortunately too ill to take any part in the contest. The announcement had been made by Mr. Leo Cartwright in one of his earliest reported speeches, and to her surprise she found that it left her oddly unsatisfied. Had she been wanting, then, to be asked to engage in further adventures of the Muffyn description? Searching for an answer to this question, she found that honesty compelled the admission that she did not know. Only something seemed to have happened to her that afternoon which left her with a strange feeling of unsettledness.

On the whole, perhaps, the best thing to do would be to send a definite acceptance to one of the friends who had given her a vague invitation for Christmas. It must be a change, she felt, that she needed.

But, though no one in the house-party would ever have guessed it, her time in the country seemed to drag interminably. She began to long to be back in her own house. Even though this should be a confession of age, the longing grew, until finally she cut her fortnight short and returned to London on the Wednesday after New Year's Day.

She found John Ormroyd had spent his holidays in a frantic and futile search for Elizabeth.

"I'm afraid," said Mrs. Cartwright, "that she wouldn't have disappeared like this, if she had wanted to be found."

"I'm afraid that has occurred to me."

His voice sounded so dismal suddenly that she was stricken with remorse at her suggestion.

"I expect she's only forgotten you," she added cheerfully. "Be sure to tell me as soon as any clues are discovered."

The next day at four he was announced again.

"I say," he said interrupting her greeting, "a most extraordinary thing has happened."

"Has some one taken your play?"

"No," said John, his face darkening for a moment. "I've not heard a word from that—from the Thespian since they promised to write. But look here," he went on hastily, diving into his pocket, "a most extraordinary thing. I just thought I'd have a look in the *Times'* Personal column, and look what I found."

He extended for her inspection a torn and crumpled piece of newspaper. Mrs. Cartwright took it and carried it to the light.

DENIS MACKAIL

"I don't see anything very exciting here," she said. "That is, unless you are thinking of buying a car."

"No, no. The other side."

She turned the fragment over.

"There," said John, his forefinger appearing suddenly on the print.

"Well, I must say," said Mrs. Cartwright. "What an extraordinary thing!"

"That's just what I said."

And to put the reader out of his terrible suspense, I will at this point append a transcript of the announcement which had caused this sensation.

SMITH. Will any one with information as to the present whereabouts of Miss Elizabeth Valérie Smith, lately employed at a school near Paris, kindly communicate with Messrs. Snatcher and Weatherall, Lincoln's Inn Fields?

"What do you think of that?" asked John, in the tone in which Michael Angelo may be imagined to have shown visitors the ceiling of the Sistine Chapel. Mrs. Cartwright was naturally misled.

"But this isn't your advertisement, is it?" she asked.

"No, of course not. That's just the extraordinary thing."

"What does it mean, then?"

"That's what I can't find out," said John. "Of course I went off to these people at once."

"Well?"

"Well," said John a little uncomfortably, "the fact is we had a bit of a misunderstanding."

"Why, what happened?"

"Well, in the first place, they kept me waiting the dickens of a time, and perhaps that made me just a little impatient. Anyhow, they wouldn't tell me anything at all. In fact," he concluded, "I don't mind saying that they were most infernally rude."

"Oh, I can't believe that."

"But they were. In fact they had the impertinence to say that they had advertised so as to receive information and not so as to give it. They seemed to think that I was after a reward. So I told them exactly what I thought of them and came straight away."

"You didn't tell them you'd seen her?"

"No, certainly not," said John, with great dignity.

"You don't seem to have got very far, I must say. What do you propose to do next?"

"Well, I thought perhaps. . ."

"Yes?"

"I thought as after all she was here for the best part of a week, you might care. . ."

"I?"

"That is, if you wouldn't mind very much. Otherwise, of course. . ."

"Oh, well. I had been meaning to go there anyhow some time soon, so to oblige you—"

"You had been meaning? I'm afraid I don't quite follow."

"They're my solicitors, John. They have been all my life."

"Oh! Then it was you that put the advertisement—"

"No," said Mrs. Cartwright emphatically. "Certainly not. I'm sorry, very sorry, indeed, that the girl is lost; but, as a secretary, I can't say I've missed her."

"But you'll ask them?"

"Oh, certainly, I'll ask them."

"I say, it's most awfully good of you. It really is."

"But on one condition."

"What's that?"

"That if you find her, you look after her yourself."

"Oh, certainly. That's exactly what I want to do, if—"

"If what?"

"If," said John, "she'll have me."

Mrs. Cartwright had a hard fight of it to convince him that she was not going off to Lincoln's Inn Fields there and then; and it was only after he had personally ascertained over the telephone (in an assumed voice, for fear he should be speaking to some one who remembered him) that all the partners had left for the day, that he consented to her postponing her mission until the following morning.

"You don't mind if I come too?" he asked.

"Not if you wait outside in the car," she replied.

"I say," said John for the fiftieth time, "it's most awfully good of you."

III

THE SENIOR PARTNER WHOSE WHISKER Mrs. Cartwright had kissed towards the close of the nineteenth century had long since taken his departure to that bourn from which no traveller, or even solicitor, returns. But the room in which this incident had occurred remained in the heriditary possession of his family, and was now occupied by his son; a successor whose individuality was either so overshadowed by or so full

DENIS MACKAIL

of respect for his father, that in the passage of a quarter of a century not so much as a paper-weight seemed to have been moved. Indeed, barring the absence of the historical whisker and its fellow, Mrs. Cartwright could almost have believed now, as she was shown into the room, that it was the same advisor who rose to greet her as the one whom she had last seen less than a year after her marriage.

"Mrs. Cartwright," he said, "this is a very great pleasure to see you at last. I was beginning to be afraid that we were never going to meet." He paused, and then added, "Ha, ha!" but with so grave and humourless a countenance that Mrs. Cartwright at once realised that no smile was required from her, and that the interjection was without significance.

They shook hands.

"Now what can we do for Mrs. Cartwright?" asked Mr. Weatherall, with a professional manner which the lady in question could not help thinking more suggestive of Medicine than of Law.

"Two things," she said. "And the first is this. I want to know whether you have any idea whether my husband still draws, if he ever did, on the sums which you have been paying over to his solicitors on my behalf all these years."

"Very curious that you should ask," replied Mr. Weatherall. He screwed up his eyes and looked at her hard. "Are you asking me professionally?" he went on.

"Why, yes; I suppose so," said Mrs. Cartwright, a little puzzled.

"Or as man to man?" he added.

"Both," answered Mrs. Cartwright.

"Well," said Mr. Weatherall "professionally I don't know. Professionally, I can show you a file of receipts from Messrs. Tracy and Paull. But, professionally, that is all I can do."

"But as man to man?" asked Mrs. Cartwright, adapting herself with her usual quickness to this eccentric attorney.

"As man to man," answered Mr. Weatherall, lowering his voice, "and in strict confidence,—but don't ask me how I know, only things sometimes come round, especially between old friends,—I happen to have heard that the whole sum accumulated at Tracy and Paull's until just before this last Christmas."

He stopped.

"And what happened then?" asked Mrs. Cartwright.

"He had the whole lot transferred to his account."

"Leo did?"

"Yes."

"Just before Christmas, you say?"

"Yes," said Mr. Weatherall, and again added, "Ha, ha!" but as before, without the faintest discernible sound of mirth.

Mrs. Cartwright remained silent and frowning, while the heavy clock on the mantelpiece ticked away the best part of a minute.

"I can't make it out," she said at length.

"No?" said Mr. Weatherall. "Nor can I. But it's quite true. Only, remember, professionally I have told you nothing."

"I quite understand. I am very grateful," she replied. "And now for my other piece of business."

She opened her chain bag and took out John's newspaper cutting, or, rather, tearing.

"This girl came to help me in the mornings as a kind of secretary for four or five days, about three weeks ago," she said, laying the extract on Mr. Weatherall's table. "Then she gave me notice and took herself off."

"God bless my soul," said Mr. Weatherall, exactly as he had learnt to say it from his father. "Where to?"

"That's the absurd part. She never left any address."

"God bless my soul," repeated Mr. Weatherall. "No address! And you never knew who she was?"

"Who she was? I don't quite understand."

"Ah, but of course she probably wouldn't realise," said Mr. Weatherall, shaking his head wisely.

"But who was she, then? Was she in disguise?" asked the romantic Mrs. Cartwright.

"I don't know," said the cautious interpreter of the law. "I didn't see her."

"But I mean was it a false name? Is she really called 'Smith'? Oh, do tell me! After all, I've probably helped you a fearful lot by telling you I'd seen her."

"Of course you have," said Mr. Weatherall. "It's the first news we've had, except for an extraordinary fellow who came here yesterday and wanted to fight my clerk. But she's a niece of a very old friend of yours, Mrs. Cartwright; and of mine too," he added.

Mrs. Cartwright looked blankly at him. The only mutual friend whom she could recall was her husband. And her husband had always represented himself as an only child.

"You must think me very stupid," she said, "but I'm afraid that still I can't guess."

"But you used to live there," said Mr. Weatherall.

"Don't you remember Harold Stanley-Smith?"

"O-oh! Of course! I never thought of it."

"And you never heard what happened to him?"

"No," said Mrs. Cartwright, who had never even wondered. "Never."

Mr. Weatherall actually chuckled.

"His wife was a distant cousin of mine," he said, "but it's true all the same. He ran away."

"What, from Mrs. Stanley-Smith?"

"Yes. No one ever knew how he could afford to do it. But he did. He ran away to America."

"And Mrs. Stanley-Smith, and the little boy?"

"Dead," said Mr. Weatherall, and either Mrs. Cartwright was very much mistaken or else he once more added, "Ha, ha!"

"Poor things!" she said, with sympathy. True, she had scarcely thought about them even once since she married, but still, Death. . . There was no affectation about the sound of sorrow in her voice.

But the strange Mr. Weatherall gave another chuckle.

"They wouldn't be poor, if they were alive," he said heartlessly. "Do you know what Harold Stanley-Smith did in America?"

"No, of course I don't," said Mrs. Cartwright.

"Well, first of all he went to prison for a bit, I believe," Mr. Weatherall explained. "And after that he lectured about it; that was, of course, when he wasn't writing begging letters to us."

"But did he make a lot of money by it?"

"Not by that," said Mr. Weatherall. "But he ended up by floating a company and making munitions. Of course that finished some time ago now, but all the same when he was shot by his butler the other day he left nearly half a million."

"Half a million!" gasped Mrs. Cartwright, startled by the figure into passing over the less important question of why the butler had perpetrated this rash act.

"Dollars, of course," said Mr. Weatherall.

"And he left it to this niece?"

"Oh, no. Unfortunately he didn't leave a will. But she's the only relation. So she will get whatever our firm can extract from the United States authorities. It ought to be quite a nice little sum," said Mr. Weatherall pleasantly. "That is, if we ever find her again."

"Oh, but you must find her."

"Well, we are doing our best. Unfortunately she chose to leave the very excellent post which was found for her in France, when her mother died there, and without saying where she was going. I didn't even know that she was in England until you told me."

"And how long have you been advertising?"

"At intervals for about a couple of months. But, of course, what you have told us narrows it down. If you wouldn't mind, I'll just have a typist in and dictate a note of any dates and other particulars that you can give us."

"Oh, certainly," said Mrs. Cartwright.

Mr. Weatherall blew a long blast on the old-fashioned speaking-tube which still hung behind his chair.

IV

"OF COURSE," SAID MRS. CARTWRIGHT, WHEN she had given John Ormroyd an outline of her recent interview, "now that she's an heiress, I don't suppose she will look at you."

"She didn't look at me so that I noticed it before," answered John gloomily.

"Well, I noticed it, anyhow," said Mrs. Cartwright.

They drove in silence, for both were occupied with their own thoughts. The car turned into the little Square and drew up before her house.

John leapt gallantly out to hold the door, and, as he did so, a man came quickly down the front-door steps. Seeing John, he started; wavered for a moment, as if wondering whether he should make a dash for it; and then took off his hat.

"How d' you do, Mr. Ormroyd," he said. "Everything going well, I hope?"

"Oh, quite. Yes. Thanks awfully," answered John, racking his brain to think where he had seen the man's face before.

"Who's your friend, John?"

"I don't think."

"Well, as he was coming out of my house perhaps Hilda can tell us."

But Hilda could throw very little light on the problem. The gentleman had asked if Mrs. Cartwright still lived there, and when told yes but she was out, had asked if he might step in and write a note. But after spending a few minutes at the drawing-room table he had

DENIS MACKAIL

decided to call up later instead. Mrs. Cartwright, followed by Hilda and John, dashed upstairs. The writing-table appeared intact, but suddenly Mrs. Cartwright exclaimed:

"Hilda, you didn't change the blotting-paper in this book this morning, did you?"

"Oh, no, madam!" The open page was virgin white.

"But I wrote several letters last night and the sheet on which they were blotted has been removed." Mrs. Cartwright made an obvious effort to dismiss the incident.

"Never mind, Hilda. I know nothing would be taken as long as you are here. I'm sorry I've been so absurd, John."

It was not until John Ormroyd had reached the corner of the square that he suddenly remembered where he had seen the man's face.

"I've got it!" he said to himself. "It was that fellow who took me round to see Cartwright at the Thespian the other day—Campbell or something."

But on Mrs. Cartwright, alone in her drawing-room, the chill hand of fear had fallen. Something stronger than reason connected the strange visitor with the interest in her penmanship to the production of her play. All would be discovered. Oh! Why had she been such a fool? All the afternoon the conviction grew until *she dared not go to that dress rehearsal.*

V

DAVID LAWRENCE HAD SURVIVED NEARLY three weeks at Windy Gap, and circumstances had combined to make them three of the most industrious weeks which he had ever spent in his life. For his constant fear, when out of doors, of being recognised and haled off to London; his constant avoidance, when indoors, of his unspeakable Aunt; and his constant efforts, whether indoors or out, to escape from the impudent, offensive, and often dangerous attentions of his little cousins, had had the joint effect of turning him into a temporary hermit. "Dear David gives so little trouble," said Aunt Lily every morning after breakfast, as he departed to the icy cave which had once been her husband's study. And there he remained all morning and again after lunch until it was dark, closeted in perpetual struggle with the Agricola and the Germania, and, when these had been vanquished, with Herodotus. Only when night had fallen did he dare to slink past the door of the room in which his cousins were quarrelling over the games which they had been given at Christmas, and, with collar turned well up, stride quickly along the border of the ocean.

Three times had he opened the door of his cell to admit telegrams signed "Thespigram," and three times had those terrible masks grinned and wept at him from his place on the breakfast-table, but to neither telegrams nor letters had he replied, and now for a week there had been silence. The chase was drawing off. Comfort was to be found also in the preliminary notices of his new play with which Mr. Cartwright peppered the Press during this period. Though the author's name was generally, if not invariably, mentioned in these inspired paragraphs, it was always in the briefest and most modest manner. The management appeared to believe, and probably rightly, that the acceptance of a play by a new and unknown writer was a lapse to be as far as possible hushed up; and that what the public really required to be told would be the names of the artistes, the fact that this was Mr. Leo Cartwright's twenty-fifth production at the Thespian Theatre (excluding revivals), and the news that the fine old Shakespearian veteran, Miss Kate Bolsom, had been persuaded to emerge from her retirement and assume a small but important part. (This last item was subsequently contradicted by Miss Bolsom's great-grandson, who was living on her annuity and could take no risks.)

But, as has been said, of the author there was little if any public mention, and finally, when it became clear that this was no temporary oversight, but a settled policy, David felt he could risk perhaps one morning's outdoor exercise. After his unaccustomed period of self-incarceration, the effect was startling. As he bounced gently over the countryside on the undersized horse which during term time was at the service of a number of girls' schools, with the wind blowing in his face and the blue, though not too blue, sky once more overhead, the nightmare in which he had been living seemed to dissolve and be spirited away. After all, he was young, he was—if he cared to be—his own master, his father was in Switzerland, he had nearly ten days' more vacation. Away, then, with this cowardly skulking, away with those intolerable Roman and Grecian companions, away also with Aunt Lily and her savage offspring. He would return to London at once. There were, so it was said, eight million people resident in and about the metropolis. If he should be so unlucky as to fall in with the only three out of all these millions who believed him to be the author of Mrs. Cartwright's play, he would lie.

He would deny with the utmost emphasis that he either now was, had ever been, or had ever known David Lawrence. And in the face of such denial nothing could be done. What an ass he had been to waste his time swotting away down here; but, to be perfectly just, what a lot of money he had saved, and, consequently, what a ripping time he would now have. Fate had so arranged it that through no effort of his own he had spent what was from an academical point of view an ideal vacation. With ten days to go, he was well ahead of his tutor's programme. Very well, he would post all his books straight back to Oxford today, and enjoy the holiday which he had so thoroughly earned. From now until the beginning of term, London should be his. Except, perhaps, just those few streets lying near the Thespian Theatre. No point in being foolhardy.

It was mere child's play to convince Aunt Lily that he had told her a week ago that he must leave today.

"I'm afraid I'm getting very forgetful," she said. "But I do hope it has done you good, and I shall write and tell Martin how pleased we have been to have you, and how hard you have worked."

In the hour of his departure David's heart softened. It was, he supposed, very decent of her to have had him really.

"Oh, but I've enjoyed it awfully," he said, and at that moment a crash overhead caused him to bolt upstairs, where his cousins were trying to shut one another into his suitcase. Bless their little hearts! How delightful it was to be leaving them. He would give them a tip.

He did so, whereupon they insisted on accompanying him to the station, where one of them dropped his cap between the platform and the train, and the other did serious damage to an automatic weighing-machine. But at last the train moved off.

"Thank God, that's over," said David, and lit his pipe.

One of the first London omnibuses which he saw on leaving Victoria that afternoon carried an advertisement of the Thespian Theatre. He had, of course, already learnt the title of his supposed play from the newspapers, but he was relieved to see that the only name shown on the side of the omnibus was that of Leo Cartwright.

"He can have all the limelight he wants, as far as I'm concerned," he said to himself, as the cab turned into Grosvenor Place.

Once more he encountered the bombazine embrace of Mrs. Billett, once more he took possession of his own room, and after dinner he walked out and saw the third performance at the Palladium. This, undoubtedly, was the way to live.

And he had an idea for Sunday which would be absolutely top-hole, if only it came off.

The sense of exhilaration was still on him when he woke next morning, and even survived the appearance of Mr. Leo Cartwright's photograph on the front page of his illustrated newspaper.

Nomination Day at Covent Garden (said the caption). Mr. Leo Cartwright, the famous actor-manager, to be nominated today as Traditional Candidate. For a full report of the case in which Mr. Cartwright is appearing this morning, see tomorrow's *Illustrated Sunday Horror*.

A week ago the mere sight of this photograph would have caused David to tremble and cower, but today he simply noted it and passed on. Thus it was that his eye next fell on an advertisement of Messrs. Hamhurst's Great January Sale, and more particularly on that section of it which announced a Ridiculous Sacrifice in an odd line of Gents' Dressing-Gowns.

"By Jove!" said David to himself.

That damask silk would be just the thing to cross the quad in on his way to his collegiate bath of a morning. Rivalry in this apparel, though never discussed, was none the less intense, and the fact that inhabitants of many outlying portions of the college were quite three hundred yards from the communal bathrooms gave ample opportunities for its display. At seventy-nine shillings and sixpence the thing was a gift. "Only one dozen," said the advertisement. He would go there at once; as soon as he had finished breakfast.

So shortly after nine he sallied out, his cheque-book in his pocket, and mounted an omnibus which should bear him to Hamhurst's. As he drew near, he observed a vast quantity of women conglobulating on the pavements. For every one who knew why she was there and what she wanted, there were ninety-nine who knew neither of these things, and had simply yielded to the powerful suggestions inserted in the Press by Messrs. Hamhurst and their rivals. Into this weak-minded maelstrom David descended, and was instantly engulfed. But the possession of a definite goal, even though it be only a damask silk dressing-gown, gives an inestimable advantage in these new-year battles. In less than ten minutes he had made his way from the outer to the inner edge of the pavement, and on the crest of the next wave he was carried right through the doors.

DENIS MACKAIL

"Gents' dressing-gowns?" said the shopwalker, on whose haggard countenance sale-shock had imprinted its terrible mark. "Yes, sir. Through the Enquiry Office and then to the right."

David was sucked away before he could express his thanks, carried right through the Enquiry Office and flung aside in a backwater or *cul-de-sac* in which were a number of telephone boxes.

And at this moment the light in one of these boxes was extinguished, the door opened, and a woman came out.

"Why, hullo, David!" she said.

It was Mrs. Cartwright.

"I've just been telephoning," she explained, rather unnecessarily it would seem; and her manner conveyed a curious suggestion of guilt. Almost as though she had been detected in some act which would better have remained concealed.

"How's the rest-cure?" she asked, regaining a little of her ordinary manner.

"I finished it last night," said David.

"Have you come up to see your play?" she went on mischievously.

"Oh, I say. Of course not. They think I'm still in the country. At least, I hope they do."

"Well, we must have one more talk about it, I'm afraid," said Mrs. Cartwright, "because unfortunately, even if it only runs a fortnight, they'll start sending me cheques, and I shan't be able to do anything with them. When we've settled about that, I swear I'll never bother you again. Could you come and lunch with me tomorrow, for instance?" she added.

"Well, could it be some other day, possibly?" asked David, from whom the spell seemed in some strange way to have been lifted. "Because, as a matter of fact, I'd sort of promised to take that Miss Smith out in my side-car tomorrow."

"*What?*"

Messrs. Hamhurst's telephonist leaned out over her little counter, ready, if necessary, to summon the hospital nurse who was always kept ready during their sales, but that sudden cry had not been followed by the heavy fall which she had expected to hear; so she returned to her switchboard.

"Do you mean to say that you know where she is?" went on Mrs. Cartwright.

"Why, has she left you?"

"Left me! Don't you ever read the newspapers?"

"Do you mean there was an accident?"

"No, no. But they've been advertising for her for weeks. She's come into a lot of money."

"But can't they find her?" asked David, still bewildered.

"No, of course they can't. And do you mean to say you knew where she was all the time?"

For answer he produced from his pocket a much-crumpled theatre programme.

"She gave me her address the day we went to 'Pale People,'" he said. "I was going to take her out in my side-car. I had it sent down from Oxford after Christmas on purpose."

There was an obstinate sound in his voice, as though he knew already that his excursion would never take place, but could not abandon the thought of it without a struggle.

"I must tell John Ormroyd at once," said Mrs. Cartwright, and she actually snatched the programme out of his hand.

"Oh, but I say—" began David.

Dash it all! What had it got to do with Ormroyd? But already Mrs. Cartwright had turned and given a number to the telephonist.

"But Mrs. Cartwright. . ." he again protested.

"Box Six," said the telephonist, and Mrs. Cartwright flung herself into it. She didn't even close the door.

"Is that you, John?" David heard her say. "John, the address has been found. This is it." She read it out. "Yes. No, nobody else knows. Yes. Well, if you don't bring her to tea with me today, I've done with you forever. Yes. Good-bye."

She was out of the box again, a little flushed with excitement.

"I didn't say who told me," she said. "You'll understand why. But John will be most terribly grateful to you, when he does find out."

"Oh," said David.

"And you'll come to tea, too, won't you?" she asked.

"I'm sorry. I'm afraid I can't. I promised to go somewhere."

"Well, lunch any day next week, then. Ring me up and say when you're coming. To think of your knowing where she was all this time! It's the most extraordinary thing I ever heard of. And then meeting you here like this. You certainly ought to get a reward."

David forced a wretched kind of smile on to his face.

"Well, forgive me, but I must fly. Don't forget, any day next week. Good-bye."

"Good-bye," said David, and watched her disappear into the whirl of the Enquiry Office. The thought of dressing-gowns, even though they might be of damask silk, filled his mouth with the taste of dust and ashes. He had been a fool to come. He would go home.

In savage silence he fought his way to the nearest exit, and crossed the road to the Tube. But not even the perpetual night of these subterranean catacombs could equal the darkness and depression which enveloped his whole, nineteen-year-old soul.

VI

BADLY AS THE REHEARSAL ON the Wednesday evening had gone, it had been order and efficiency itself compared with the dress rehearsal on the Friday. Theatrical superstition, which like many other forms of superstition attempts to attribute special virtues to certain human weaknesses, long ago decided that a bad dress rehearsal augurs a good first night. But when the badness reached the degree which it attained on this occasion, even superstition might well fail to comfort. When the curtain finally fell on the last Act at twenty minutes past one in the morning, Mr. M'Gill, looking more corpse-like than ever, had fully made up his mind that a postponement would be inevitable. There must have been many of the company who shared this belief, as they lingered exhausted in the wings, fearing even now that the Chief would decide to repeat the last Act. For from six o'clock, when the rehearsal had started, without a break the Chief, with irony, threats, abuse, sarcasm, violence, and particularly invidious comparisons, had lashed at the unhappy performers, caught them up over the slightest slips, interrupted with savage outbursts from the stalls, or dashed into the middle of a scene and shaken a quivering fist within an inch of the leading lady's nose. If half the stage hands to whom he had ordered instant dismissal during this terrible rehearsal had taken him at his word, the fate of the first performance would have been sealed. But they knew their Chief too well to do more than keep, if possible, out of his way for the next half-hour. Besides, say what you will, instant dismissal for hammering after the curtain has gone up is very much less nerve-shattering than prolonged public abuse for merely coming in too soon on a cue. It was the company who really suffered worst. And the more nervous they became, the more they forgot; the worse they acted, and the louder the Chief stormed at them.

But, as has been said, at twenty minutes past one the revolution of this vicious circle was suspended. The Chief had cut his own death scene, which he had often rehearsed before, so as to be able to see the end from the front. When, therefore, the curtain at last fell, he was alone in the stalls, since the last of the dressmakers and other favoured guests had long since crept away home. For a minute and a half there was silence, and then he clapped his hands.

"Take up the curtain!" he called out. And a second later the great tableau curtains swung up into the blackness. "Mr. M'Gill!" he bawled.

"Sir?" answered Mr. M'Gill, appearing suddenly from the prompt corner and shading his eyes from the footlights with his lifted forearm.

"Ask everybody to come on the stage, please."

Mr. M'Gill withdrew, and in a few moments there had trickled on to the stage through the different entrances a bedraggled, dispirited, and broken mob. They stood there dejectedly, blinking at the lights. Apart from the difference in costume, not the Saturday night's collection in the neighbouring cells of Bow Street could have presented a sorrier spectacle.

"Ladies and gentlemen," said the Chief, advancing down the central aisle, and standing by the orchestra rails, "before you go tonight, I want if I may to give you one piece of advice. I am afraid that you have had a very tiring rehearsal, and some of you may have fears as to the success of the play. I want you, please, to put every thought of the play out of your heads from now until eight o'clock tonight. Go home, stay in bed, keep quiet until then; and if you do this, I promise you that I shall be proud of you all at tonight's performance. There is nothing more uncertain than a first-night audience, but we have a beautiful and moving play, and skilled and painstaking interpreters. If success ever comes when it is deserved, it will come tonight. Thank you."

Leo Cartwright had never played Napoleon,—no mere make-up could have made a man of his height credible in the part,—but had he done so, thus one could imagine the (stage) little corporal addressing the remnants of his (stage) army during the retreat from Russia. And thus, too, would the stragglers have straightened their backs, reformed their broken ranks, and broken out into the thin, pathetic little cheer which now came floating over the Thespian footlights.

The Chief bowed gravely.

"Thank you," he repeated.

And he turned to make his way to the iron communication door.

"Gordon!" he called out, as he reached the stage.

"Yes, Chief," said Mr. Gordon, who had, of course, been in attendance all evening.

"I forgot to ask you. Any more news of Mr. Lawrence?"

The Personal Manager eyed him oddly.

"No," he answered. "I'm afraid not."

"Well, well," said the Chief; "it can't be helped."

"I half-thought you might be expecting him here tonight, Chief," added Mr. Gordon, his dark eyes fixed on his employer.

"Eh? What's that?"

"I thought you seemed to be looking for some one in front once or twice," said Mr. Gordon, and this time it was the Chief's turn to fasten his mournful but threatening eyes on his assistant.

"You were quite mistaken," he said, and left him there.

He got into the lift, pressed the button, and went up to his dressing-room. The sleepy Tuke sprang to attention, and the process of disrobing began.

"Just go into the saloon and mix me a drink, Tuke," said the Chief.

"Certainly, sir," said Tuke, and went through the open door.

The Chief raised his hand to unbutton his stud, and instantly the most indescribably violent spasm of pain seemed to pierce his heart. His elbow remained crooked in the air; the slightest movement was unthinkable. Though his brain was calling out in agony for help, his lips scarcely stirred. It seemed impossible to believe that a horrible cry had not burst from him, but the steady flow of the syphon in the next room was uninterrupted.

"This is the end," he thought.

And quite suddenly the pain had gone, leaving him sick and sweating. So weak, too, that he almost fell from his chair. Even when, a moment later, Tuke returned with the brimming glass, he could say nothing; could only roll his eyes at him out of a face which showed grey beneath the paint. He gulped greedily at the whisky-and-soda.

"My word, sir, you do look queer," said Tuke.

Too exhausted to substitute another adjective this time, the Chief whispered:

"I feel queer."

Tuke was alarmed.

"Is there anything I can get you, sir?" he asked.

But already the generous mixture which he had prepared was doing its work.

"No, no," answered the Chief. "I'm better, thanks. Only a bit tired. That's all."

And then suddenly the recollection of that awful pain made his hand shake, so that the whisky slopped on to the floor.

"I'm afraid you've been doing too much, sir," said Tuke.

"I'm afraid I have," replied the Chief. "I'd meant to do some more work tonight, but I don't think I will now. Just tell them to get me a taxi."

But as Tuke moved to the door, he only just stopped himself crying out: "Don't leave me!"

Five minutes later, with an overcoat covering his disordered dress and remnants of paint still on his face, he left the Stage Door on his dresser's arm.

"Hadn't I better come back with you, sir?" asked Tuke, as they reached the street.

But the Chief wasn't going to let what had happened frighten him into giving up his secret.

"No, no," he said. "I'll be all right now. Don't you wait about any longer."

And not until Tuke had disappeared round the kink in the alley did he give the taxi-driver his address.

But at half-past nine the next morning he was back at the theatre, a little pale as always, but otherwise apparently none the worse. And at a quarter to ten he left again with Mr. Littlejohn and his Agent in a cab.

They drove first to his Committee rooms, where they gathered up a collection of supporters, and from there went on foot—a distance of only a few yards—to the Town Clerk's office, where the returning officer was sitting from ten to twelve to receive nominations. The business was quickly transacted, and Mr. Cartwright was photographed both on arriving and on leaving.

Littlejohn was waiting for him in the taxi and together they drove on to the Law Courts. The solicitor's clerk was looking out for them by the entrance.

"There's been a telephone message from the judge," he said. "His car has broken down on the way up from the country, but he hopes to get it fixed so that he won't be more than a few minutes late."

"Does that mean we've got to wait?" asked the Chief.

"I'm afraid so, sir," answered the clerk.

And indeed there seemed nothing else for it. With growing impatience they waited. The Court and the corridors were sprinkled with people all drumming with their fingers and looking constantly at their watches. No one dared to leave and no one wanted to stay. The Chief sat motionless in his place, his eyes as usual gazing on some distant nothing, the corner of his mouth occasionally twitching. Mr. Littlejohn sought for such consolation as could be found in reading the postal particulars printed at the beginning of his pocket diary. For some reason which must be left to psychologists to explain, every one in Court gradually dropped his voice lower and lower, until finally the only conversation was carried on in whispers. Once or twice angry looking men got up and seemed on the point of flinging out into the street, but always they changed their minds and sat down again.

Not until close on twelve did the rustle run through the Court which seemed to show that news of some sort had arrived. Ten minutes later His Lordship made his entrance and took his seat on the Bench. He delivered himself of a lengthy but ill-natured apology for his lateness, and then relapsed into an even longer silence, while he shuffled Ids notes of Wednesday's hearing.

At length, leaning forward over his papers with one hand well over his mouth, he began mumbling out his judgment. Everyone in Court who found it practicable to do so moved surreptitiously nearer the Bench. His Lordship was understood to say that he had given careful and weighty consideration to the statements and evidence which had been put before him, and that while on the one hand he very much doubted whether the defence were entitled to take the line which they had taken, on the other hand he was not entirely satisfied that the plaintiffs had adopted the proper course in making this application. He took about twenty minutes to say this, and when he eventually paused for a moment to sip a glass of water, it would have been difficult for the most expert lawyer, and was certainly impossible for Messrs. Cartwright and Littlejohn, to feel any kind of certainty as to which way the scales of Justice were going to tip. His Lordship then went on to complain for approximately five minutes about the bad ventilation in the Court, which encouraged Counsel for plaintiff to add a comment of his own. The fury with which he was immediately silenced seemed to favour the prospects of the Defence, but they were soon dashed again by the withering criticism which was directed on Mr. Littlejohn's methods of conducting business, which were characterised by His Lordship as "little short of neanderthal."

About twenty minutes to one, however, it became apparent that His Lordship was finding difficulty in further postponing his decision; and though he did his best by losing his place in the volume of Law Reports from which he was quoting a series of totally irrelevant precedents, the end was obviously near. In a final sentence which lasted seven and three quarter minutes, contained fifty-four parentheses, thirty-nine conditional clauses, twenty-seven Latin words, and one unintentional whistle through his false teeth, he announced that, principally due to the extraordinarily ambiguous form of contract adopted by the management of the Thespian Theatre, the application for an interim injunction must be refused. Each party would, however, pay its own costs.

Mr. Littlejohn looked anxiously to see whether the Plaintiffs had anything up their sleeves which could conceivably affect the finality of this decision, but the Plaintiffs had clearly had enough. And so, for that matter, had he. There was a shuffling of feet as those present in Court rose at His Lordship's departure, and a moment later he was following the Chief out into the corridor.

"That was a relief, Chief," he said.

Mr. Cartwright looked at him vaguely.

"It's going to cost us a lot of money," was all that he said.

The Business Manager was astonished. This was the first time in the whole of his term of employment that he had heard the Chief give utterance to such a remark. But before he could get his breath, he was taken right in the wind by a still more amazing statement.

"I must look into the way we keep our accounts," said the Chief. "We've got to be more careful in future."

Mr. Littlejohn wondered whether he were on his head or his heels.

"Our accounts are all right, Chief," he said, flushing. "Why, you don't suppose Mr. Imray would stand anything wrong there."

"That will do, Mr. Littlejohn," answered the Chief shortly. And then, as ever, he made the quick *amende*. He laid his hand on the palpitating Littlejohn's arm. "I'm sorry," he said. "I ought to be thanking you. It was your evidence that pulled us through."

Mr. Littlejohn was touched, and allowed himself to become mollified. Oblivious of the fact that his evidence had made public the almost fraudulent character of the Thespian contracts, he accepted the compliment at its face value.

"Oh, no," he said. "It was your reputation, Chief."

Once again the corner of Leo Cartwright's mouth twitched uncontrollably.

As they reached the street, the Chief kept a sharp lookout for the placard of the *Evening Query*, and as luck would have it, a seller was standing just by the entrance. But to his surprise the bill bore no reference either to the Election or to the Injunction. Instead it said:

GREAT NEW FOOTBALL PRIZE

They got into a taxi and told it to drive to the theatre, but scarcely had it started when Mr. Littlejohn gave a sudden cry.

"Look! Look there!" he said.

"What? Where?"

"There! Hi! boy. Give me a *Westminster*."

He was halfway through the window of the taxi, but the Chief had already seen the placard which had occasioned his excitement.

COVENT GARDEN ELECTION SENSATION

it said, and almost simultaneously a yellow placard came into view through the other window which announced:

COVENT GARDEN SURPRISE

Mr. Littlejohn fell back on the seat grasping his purchase, and together they hunted for the explanation. It was the Business Manager who saw it first.

"Look there!" he said.

Mr. Hamilcar Barker failed to present himself for nomination today. Mr. Leo Cartwright was accordingly returned unopposed.

"What?" gasped the Chief, seizing the paper. "It must be a mistake."

But there it was in black and green.

Mr. Littlejohn rose to the occasion.

"Chief," he said, "may I be the first to congratulate you?"

The scene would have had more dignity if the two men had not been sitting side by side in such a confined space, but it was impressive enough for all that.

"Thank you, Littlejohn," answered the new Member; and he put his head out of the window and told the driver to go to his Committee rooms.

There was a little crowd waiting outside, and as the Chief alighted he was recognised and cheered. There is no need to say that his acknowledgement was graceful and satisfactory in the extreme. Leaving Littlejohn, he hurried into the building, where the startling news was instantly confirmed by his Agent and Mr. Brisk. No explanation, however, was forthcoming.

"They don't even know where he is at Ephemeral House," said the Agent. "He's not been at his City office this morning, and at his private address they said he went out soon after ten and hasn't been in yet. His people have been on to all the hospitals, too, and there's no news. They're just as puzzled as we are, but it seems that he had all the papers with him, so they could do nothing."

A fresh wave of supporters forced their way into the room, and everybody began repeating himself very loudly while nobody listened. Strange men and women banged Mr. Cartwright on the back, shook any available hand, shouted in his face, and were swept away, only to be replaced by new arrivals. The Chief suddenly found himself wedged in a corner opposite a young man with a notebook.

"Have you a message for the public, Mr. Cartwright?" asked the young man.

"Yes," said the Chief. "Tell them the Pit and Gallery doors will be opened at six o'clock tonight, and I'll stand every one dinner up to the limit allowed by the County Council."

"Some stunt!" said the young man appreciatively, and was immediately whirled away.

In his place Mr. Brisk was revealed.

"I must get out of this," said the Chief.

"Follow me," said Mr. Brisk, and fell heavily against the crush of enthusiasts. The solidity of his person drove a wedge through the crowd, and the Chief followed him out of the room.

"This way," continued Mr. Brisk, turning towards the stairs which led to the basement.

"Coming," said the Chief, and found himself in a long corridor with a dirty glass roof.

"Quickly," called Mr. Brisk. He opened a door at the farther end of the passage, and, hastening after him through it, the Chief found himself in a little courtyard. His guide produced a latchkey and pointed to an entrance on the other side of the yard.

"Where are we?" panted the Chief.

"Back of my head office," said Mr. Brisk.

Leo Cartwright hesitated. The last thing he wanted at this moment was a tête-à-tête with the senior partner in the firm of Brisk and John. Those ingenious proposals drawn up by the firm's accountants had been in his hands for over a fortnight, and, although he was now within but a few hours of the beginning of a new run, he had not yet found the opportunity or the courage to broach the subject to Mr. Littlejohn.

"I'm sorry," he said, as Mr. Brisk waited for him to enter, "but I was due at the theatre when I got this news. I'm afraid I must go straight back. They're waiting for me to try out some fresh lighting."

"But you'll have a sandwich and a glass of fizz first?"

"It's very good of you; really it is. But I've kept them waiting nearly an hour. Let me see, I can get through to the street this way, can't I?"

"That's it," said Mr. Brisk. "But I say, before you run off like this—"

"Eh?"

"What happened in Court this morning?"

"Oh, that was all right," said the Chief, relieved not to hear the question he had expected. "The application failed. We can go ahead."

"Well, you're in luck today, Mr. Cartwright. I'm very glad to hear it. Gordon was telling me that Mr. Imray thought you would be certain to be stopped. It will be a relief to him too."

If Mr. Brisk had not been a little over-exhilarated by the excitement of the morning, he would certainly not have made this remark. For it is one of the elements of tact in theatrical circles to affect complete ignorance as to the existence and identity of those indispensable persons, the Backers. The convention must at all costs be preserved that every management is playing with its own money and is, consequently, responsible to no one but itself. But not even a breach of this ancient though unwritten law could have explained the look which came into Mr. Cartwright's face when he heard these words.

"Gordon told you that?" he asked, in a steely voice.

"Why, yes," answered Mr. Brisk, startled and a little alarmed. "But it's all O.K. now, isn't it?"

"Perfectly so," said the Chief, resuming his ordinary manner. "Well, I know you'll excuse me. Many thanks. Good-bye."

He turned and walked quickly towards the opening which led into the street.

Mr. Brisk stood gazing after him, a puzzled expression still on his face. But after a little he shrugged his shoulders, and, applying his latchkey to the door of his headquarters, disappeared inside.

VII

THE BAD FAIRY WHO HAD so consistently come between John and Elizabeth ever since that matinée at the Thespian three weeks ago must either have been taken off her guard or else have relented. Possibly, for some reason best known to herself, she was appeased by the absence of chocolates on this occasion,—you will remember that John's ill-luck had dated from the moment when he had bought that box at the theater,—or possibly she had been defeated by the Good Fairy whose presence somewhere at the back of this story you have by now probably begun to suspect. At any rate, on this occasion John Ormroyd, whose manner of treating members of the opposite sex has not hitherto been marked by quite all that tact and delicacy which one would expect from the author of his novels, had achieved—possibly as the result of what he had described as his rotten Christmas—a humility of spirit which was exactly suited to make the best impression on a young woman who had in her turn been appreciably humbled by Fate since we last saw her.

His taxi drive to the address which Mrs. Cartwright had given him on the telephone seemed endless, but, it must be admitted, would have seemed longer still if he had known that the information which was sending him hurtling across London was three weeks old. In the absence of this knowledge he was not, however, tortured with doubts as to whether Elizabeth might not again have flitted, and again without leaving a trace behind her; he merely worried himself by wondering whether she would be in or out when he got there.

But she was in. The untidy-looking person who let him into the narrow hall of the lodgings and left him waiting there was quite clear on this point. A minute later he heard footsteps descending the stairs.

"She's coming," said the untidy one, and never did words fall more gratefully on human ear.

The messenger continued her descent out of sight, and presently lighter footsteps were heard overhead. The banisters gave a little creak, and there, silhouetted on the half-landing against the red and orange glass of the staircase window, stood the one subject of John Ormroyd's thoughts. In this important moment of his career he was inspired to utter exactly the right words—no more and no less.

"I say," he said, "I've come to apologise."

"But what for?" asked Elizabeth, knowing the answer, but determined to have it.

DENIS MACKAIL

"For being so infernally sulky and rude the last time we met."

"I was tiresome myself."

"No," said John very loudly.

"I say," he went on, "I wish you'd come down here."

She came down three steps.

"Why?" she asked.

"It's very important that you should," was all the explanation which she was allowed, but it appears to have been good enough, since she was now standing by him in the little hall-way.

"Well?" she asked.

John had fully prepared his next statement. He was going to tell her about the advertisement in the *Times*, and then lead on to the suggestion that he should drive her to Lincoln's Inn Fields there and then. But to his astonishment, when he opened his mouth to speak, a hoarse voice, which was difficult to recognise as his own, seized the opportunity of using his vocal organs to say:

"I say, you've got the most beautiful eyes that I've ever seen."

Practically the same words, notice, which had yesterday driven Elizabeth in haste and anger from the post which she had just secured as temporary assistant to Madame Juliette during her one-week sale. But whereas Madame Juliette's husband—the originator of this phrase—had been faced with a white-faced Medusa, John Ormroyd was rewarded with a most extraordinarily upsetting blush.

"I'm awfully sorry," he said, distracted by the effects of his surprising behaviour. "I didn't mean to say that."

"Didn't you?" asked Elizabeth, turning the full power of the eyes in question direct on him.

"Well, I meant it all right, but, well. . ." He broke down and started again. "Look here," he said, "you've come into a lot of money. Your uncle's dead. Mrs. Cartwright has sent me to tell you. It's been in the papers. So you will come—Hi! I say, no, not that!"

For the look which she gave him as she put out a hand to steady herself against the wall had suddenly reminded him of the first time that he had met her, and more particularly of the moment just before she had fainted on the floor. And, indeed, it will be admitted that his manner of breaking the news was perhaps a little abrupt.

"I'm all right," she said. "Tell me, what is it that you want me to do?"

Smothering the impulse to reply, "Marry me," John explained. He had a taxi waiting. He would take her to the solicitors who had been advertising for her. Then, with her permission, they would have lunch somewhere. After that, whatever she liked best, but he had promised to take her to tea at Mrs. Cartwright's, and if she would come with him to the first night at the Thespian afterwards—dining somewhere quietly first—why, he would be most awfully pleased and he'd got two tickets.

"Stop, stop!" said Elizabeth. "Did you say I'd come into some money as well as all this?"

"Yes," answered John. "Heaps." He drew an enormous imaginary circle in the air to indicate the size of her fortune.

"More than two pounds twelve and six?" she asked.

"I tell you," said John, who hadn't yet told her anything of the sort, "your uncle left half a million dollars."

"Well, in that case, would you mind lending me two pounds twelve and six? Because if you don't, I'm very much afraid my landlady won't let me get my coat out of my box."

John plunged his hand into his breast pocket, but, before he could withdraw it, all the pent-up impatience and exasperation of the last three weeks had found vent in one violent outburst.

"Why the devil couldn't you tell me where you were before, instead of starving yourself again and driving me mad like this?"

"I thought I'd given you enough trouble already."

"You've only just started giving me trouble," said John forcibly, "compared with the trouble you're going to give me in the future. Now, then, where's that land-lady? I'll teach her to steal your clothes."

"Hush, please! No, let me have the money. I'll join you in the cab in two minutes."

"You swear that?"

"I swear it."

"Honour bright?"

"Honour bright."

"Very well. Here's the money. And remember, two minutes is my absolute limit."

As he took his seat in the taxi, he reflected that it was a most remarkably fine day, that it seemed an awfully good kind of taxi, and that he really felt most extraordinarily well. But as a novelist, and therefore as an amateur psychologist, he wondered why it was that the mere act of handing over two or three Treasury notes to a young woman should have produced such an unusual sensation all up and down his spine. "Evidently," he decided, "I have still much to learn about life."

Married men will be inclined to agree with him.

VIII

Mrs. Cartwright's tea party left her about six o'clock that afternoon, and Elizabeth took away with her to the new and superior rooms which had been found for her just round the corner—the intense respectability of which was fully guaranteed by Mrs. Cartwright herself, for were they not kept by a former maid of her own who had married a bishop's butler?—Elizabeth, I repeat, took away with her an evening cloak, two yards of tulle, a pair of gloves, and a large artificial rose, all kindly loaned for the occasion by her former employer. For though Mr. Weatherall had shown the utmost readiness to supply her with a cash advance up to the limits of the office safe, Elizabeth had decided— and John, for reasons of his own, had agreed with her—that it would be far better to do without new clothes for today than to attempt to obtain the kind which can be bought on a Saturday afternoon.

Before he left, Mrs. Cartwright, by one of those ruses at which she was so adept, had taken John aside for a moment.

"Tell me," she said, "are you engaged yet?"

"No," answered John. "I've funked it so far. But we're going to have champagne for dinner."

"Dutch courage," said Mrs. Cartwright. "And you a D.S.O.!"

"But I got my D.S.O. on rum," explained John.

"Well, you know best. But you're not to let her slip through your fingers again. I like her too much."

"You do?" John smiled foolishly. "So do I."

"Imbecile!" said Mrs. Cartwright kindly.

They had returned to the drawing-room and found Elizabeth with the evening paper.

"It says here," she announced, reading from the stop-press column, "that Hamilcar Barker has been found."

"Where?" asked Mrs. Cartwright and John, speaking together.

"In Paris," said Elizabeth. "He arrived by aero-plane. It says when questioned he admitted his identity but refused to make any statement."

"What an extraordinary thing," remarked John.

"Yes," added Mrs. Cartwright. "Very."

"I expect he got warning the police were after him," John suggested charitably.

Mrs. Cartwright gasped.

"What a dreadful idea!" she said, laughing.

"But is he as awful as all that?" asked Elizabeth.

"Worse," said John darkly.

And then they both realised that further comment would be impossible without bringing in the name which was never mentioned in Mrs. Cartwright's drawing-room except by Mrs. Cartwright herself, and the conversation was changed.

But now the little house was quiet again. In the empty drawing-room the light of the dying fire flickered on the ceiling. In the discreetly illuminated dining-room Mrs. Cartwright sat alone at her early dinner.

"If Hilda comes into the room before I've counted ten," she said to herself, "I'll stay at home." And Hilda did.

"If those mince pies are hot, I'll not go," she added. But they were cold.

"If I crack this nut at the first attempt," was the next test, "then I'll go one day next week instead." She seized the nutcrackers and beneath her tightening grip the Brazil nut fell out and fell on the floor.

"Are you looking for anything, madam?" asked Hilda, returning with the coffee.

"No, thank you," said Mrs. Cartwright, scrambling to her feet.

Weak-minded fool! Why couldn't she decide and have done with it?

"Is the car here yet?" she asked.

This should be the last and definite test.

"Yes, madam," answered Hilda.

So be it. She would go.

"I have my key," were her final words. "No one need wait up."

IX

It had not needed the new Member's announcement, printed in the evening newspapers, to fill the unreserved seats at the Thespian tonight. But Mr. Littlejohn had risen triumphantly to the occasion. Not only had he interpreted the Chief's statement as to the provision of food and drink in the most generous manner, but he had also obtained from the now no longer needed Committee rooms a supply of Traditional favours, which were dealt out by the check-takers as the Pit and Gallery came in. Even those whose political scruples prevented them from immediately pinning these rosettes to their independent bosoms found that their appreciation of the management's hospitality soon overcame this reluctance. Long before the first occupant of the stalls reached his seat, both Pit and Gallery presented an unbroken display of Traditional colours. Nor had Mr. Littlejohn's efforts ceased here. A rush order to the printers had resulted in the delivery of a quantity of printed slips, which by half-past six had been pasted after Mr. Cartwright's name on every poster outside the theatre, and the very programmes had been run through the presses again so as to read on their outer cover:

Thespian Theatre
Under the management of Leo Cartwright, M.P.
Mr. Leo Cartwright, M.P., presents
"ROMANCE TO THE RESCUE"
by
David Lawrence

If an atmosphere of tense and exaggerated excitement is an assistance to the successful presentation of a new play, then the auguries for Mr. Cartwright's twenty-fifth production were indeed favourable. Mr. Littlejohn's preparations served to fan to a white heat the fires which had been already well supplied with fuel in the shape of the astonishing news from the Covent Garden Division. Add to this the cumulative effect of recent Press paragraphs stimulating public interest in Mr. Cartwright as Actor-Manager, Litigant and Parliamentary candidate, and you will hardly be surprised to hear that there had been several spontaneous outbursts of applause from these early arrivals quite an hour before the safety curtain was first raised.

The excitement on the other side of that curtain was scarcely less remarkable. The Chief had received the congratulations of the stage staff on his return from his Committee rooms, but there had been no anti-climax after this, for the first of the stage hands to escape after the long lighting rehearsal had immediately returned with the strange news of Hamilcar Barker's discovery in Paris. A stream of telegraph boys and girls and of newspaper representatives had choked the alley leading to the Stage Door all afternoon. In fact so obstructed did this entrance become that the Chief decided to send out for his dinner instead of risking recognition by leaving the theatre. From six to seven he rested, or at least lay on his couch, for his brain would not let him rest, while

Mr. Gordon fought with reporters in the corridor outside, and Miss Lemon opened and filed the telegrams. Soon after seven he got up and went through into his dressing-room, to begin the outward renewal of his youth which was required for his appearance in the First Act.

"They're all saying in the theatre, sir," said Tuke, "that that Barker didn't stand no chance anyhow; and they say he chucked it for fear he was going to lose his entrance fee."

"Oh," said the Chief.

He was pleased that this should be said, either in the theatre or outside it, but he had learnt too much of his adversary's strength during the last fortnight to believe it himself.

A little later there was a knock on the door. Tuke went and put his head out.

"It's Mr. Gordon, sir," he said.

"All right, Gordon," the Chief called out. "Come in!"

The Personal Manager entered.

"The *Evening Query* says that Mr. Barker has been called abroad on a special mission," he announced. "They hint that the Government wanted him to go, but, if you ask me, I don't think they believe it themselves."

"Oh," said the Chief. "Everything all right in front?"

"Splendid," answered Mr. Gordon. "You'll get a great reception tonight, Chief. By Jove! though, I was scared about that injunction."

The Chief gave a start. He had just remembered something.

"So I heard," he said slowly, leaning forward a little to pencil in a detail of his make-up. "By the way, Gordon," he added, still gazing at his own reflection, "when did you last see Mr. Imray?"

It was Mr. Gordon's turn to give a start, although he instantly recovered himself.

"You might leave us for a few minutes, Tuke," the Chief went on. "I'll call when I want you." And as the dresser left the room, he repeated his question. "I was asking," he said, "when you last saw Mr. Imray?"

Mr. Gordon glanced hastily at the Chief's reflection, but it told him nothing.

"Oh, I don't know," he said casually. "Some weeks ago now, I should think; if not months."

"I understood differently from Brisk."

"From Brisk? Oh, yes, well, now you come to mention it, I believe I did run across him a few days ago. But quite by chance."

"Perhaps it was just after the notice for 'Pale People' had gone up?"

"Yes, I should think about then,"

"Thank you, Gordon," said the Chief. "You can draw a week's salary from Littlejohn tonight instead of notice."

"But, Chief! I—"

"When I took you on at Mr. Imray's suggestion," continued the Chief imperturbably, "I suppose I should have foreseen this. But at least I can make certain that it does not happen again."

"But—"

"Please understand, Mr. Gordon, that I will not have my arrangements for this theatre discussed by my subordinates behind my back either with Mr. Imray or with any of the gentlemen who are associated with him. Mr. Imray did not betray you; you betrayed yourself. I knew that there were only two people at the outside who could have given him the information which made him come and see me. Yourself and Littlejohn. Now that I know which it was, there is no more to be said. You can go as soon as you have drawn your salary."

He picked up a hand mirror and examined his profile.

"But, Chief," said Mr. Gordon, "I told Littlejohn I was going to see Mr. Imray. He never stopped me. Why, he even said that he'd half a mind to go himself."

"Possibly," said the Chief abstractedly. "But then he didn't, you see."

"Well, but surely—"

"That will do, Gordon," answered the Chief, with sudden firmness. "Ask Tuke to come back, as you go out."

"And so you think I'm going off like that, do you?" retorted Mr. Gordon. "All right. Very well. And I dare say you thought you could fool me by sending me on wild-goose chases after Mr. David Lawrence. Well, you were a bit too clever that time, when you sent me off to the Agents. I don't know what your game is, but if I go, then I'll jolly well see that's the end of your secret. So now you know!"

He paused with a provocative snort, but the Chief remained apparently absorbed in his looking-glass. Only after four or five seconds did he murmur:

"All this noise. I wish he'd go away."

"Oh, yes," shouted Mr. Gordon. "I expect you do. But wait a minute while I tell you something. How long do you suppose old Purdock had had this play before you took it? Four years! How old do you imagine Lawrence was then? Fourteen, perhaps? What address did the author send it from and what address has he written from ever since? Was there ever a David Lawrence living there? No. But some one else was, and some one who has the same handwriting as is on all Purdock's files, and some one you thin no one's going to find out about. But they are. And who is it? Why, Mrs. Leo Cartwright!"

He stopped, his climax synchronising with the temporary expenditure of all his available breath. But it is doubtful whether in any case he would have been able to continue his outburst beyond this point, for the Chief, throwing off his air of inattention, had risen suddenly—a majestic and wrathful figure in flowing wrapper and with darkened hair.

"Repeat that once again inside or outside the theatre," he said, with a fine disregard for all legal possibilities, "and I'll sue you for slander. Where you got this suggestion from or why you should think fit to drag in the name of an unfortunate woman whose shoes you aren't fit to black, I do not know. But let me tell you this, once and for all. Your statement is an absolute, infernal, damned Lie! Now go, please."

Mr. Gordon's jaw dropped. Not with fear; though Leo Cartwright's manner was sufficiently threatening, and he had instinctively edged away from him towards the door. But with an emotion which for the moment was far stronger than fear. For in defiance of all the indisputable proofs with which his recent efforts as amateur detective had provided him, he recognised the sound of utter conviction in the Chief's voice. By some extraordinary series of coincidences, attributable to some no less extraordinary run of bad luck, he had not, as he had thought, discovered the truth. The truth was, on the contrary, what the Chief and the newspapers and everybody else said it was. Could any one doubt it in the face of that shattering explosion of denial? With a sensation that the ground had suddenly dropped away beneath his feet, too acute even yet to be translated into terms of personal grievance, Mr. Gordon fumbled behind his back for the latch of the door, opened it, and went out. Not once had the Chief removed that burning and contemptuous gaze from his face.

And, as the door closed behind him, Leo Cartwright called through to his dresser:

"Tuke!"

"Yes, sir?"

"Ring through to the front of the house and ask Mr. Littlejohn to speak to me."

DENIS MACKAIL

A minute afterwards Tuke announced that Mr. Littlejohn was on the line.

"Littlejohn," said the Chief, "I've just told Gordon to draw on you for a week's salary instead of notice. Please let the staff know that he is not to be admitted inside the building after you've paid him off. Do you understand?"

"Yes, Chief," answered Mr. Littlejohn. Though it was a nuisance when he was so busy, this would not by any means be the first Personal Manager to lose his job during the excitement of a first night. He knew better than to question or argue the decision.

"Right," said the Chief. "Everything all right in front?"

"First-rate. The house is filling up nicely."

"Oh, by the way—"

"Yes?"

"I want a word with you at the end, before you see Brisk and those other fellows."

"Certainly, Chief. I'll come round."

"Right. Good-bye."

He replaced the receiver.

That accursed compact with Brisk—none the less dreaded or the less to be observed because it was un-written. He had put off his explanation and fight with Littlejohn until the last possible moment, but it would have to be gone through with all the same. And yet, if Littlejohn only knew. . .

There was a sudden rap on the door of the dressing-room.

"Quarter of an hour, please, sir," shouted the call-boy.

"The rest of my clothes, quickly," said the Chief, and Tuke, following him back into the dressing-room, was instantly at work again at his strange profession.

But the Chief was slow and unhelpful tonight. Once or twice he paused, endlessly as it seemed, with his arm half through a sleeve, and all the time there was an expression on his face of profound thought. Tuke knew this mood and kept his gossip to himself. But he did not know that, twice during this process of robing, the Chief had suddenly held his breath, terrified lest the next movement should bring on another attack of the pain which had seized him last night. Each time the threat—for it was no more than a threat, an indescribable kind of physical reminiscence more than a feeling which could be put into words—passed away. When it returned a third time, the Chief made a sudden movement; but no pain followed.

"It's imagination," he said to himself. "I've been doing too much. I must take a rest tomorrow."

It was his usual custom to remain in his suite until summoned by the call-boy a minute or so before his first entrance. But tonight, as soon as he was dressed, he left his room and took the lift down to the stage. He joined Mr. M'Gill, who was standing in the Stage Manager's post of vantage with his back to the centre of the curtain, and together they cast a critical eye over the set for the first Act.

"This ought to look well from the front, sir," said Mr. M'Gill.

The Chief thrust out his lower lip.

"The horizon line on that cloth doesn't look straight to me," he remarked.

"Bit up on the left?" asked Mr. M'Gill tactfully, completely satisfied himself that no horizon had ever been straighter.

"No," growled the Chief. "It's up on the prompt side."

Mr. M'Gill strode a few paces up stage, turned his head towards heaven, and gave a shout.

"Hi! George!" he said.

A distant call came in reply from far overhead.

"Your backcloth," yelled Mr. M'Gill. "Take her up a bit on the long line."

The cloth rose almost imperceptibly at one end.

"Too much," shouted Mr. M'Gill.

The cloth resumed its former position.

"Right! Mark it there!"

"That's the old mark," came George's voice from aloft.

Disregarding this tactless interruption, which he could only hope had not been overheard, the Stage Manager resumed his ordinary tones and asked: "How's that now, sir?"

There was no answer, and turning around, he saw that the Chief, for whose sole benefit this little performance had been carried out, was no longer there.

Mr. M'Gill shrugged his shoulders, and then, struck apparently by some thought, took out his watch and looked at it.

"By Jove!" he muttered, and snapped his fingers at his assistant in the prompt corner.

"Let her go!" he called.

The Assistant Stage Manager pressed two buttons on his little switchboard, and, as he removed his hand, the safety curtain rose slowly to the opening chords of the overture.

Her sudden decision, taken on hearing that the car was ready, to use her ticket for the first performance of her play, resulted in Mrs. Cartwright's arrival at the Thespian nearly twenty minutes before the time advertised for the rise of the curtain. The full tide of reserved-seat-holders had not yet set in, and she was spared the embarrassment of an unexpected meeting with any of her friends, as she followed the programme-seller along the corridors to her Box. She seated herself in the corner farthest from the stage and prepared to wait.

The dull roar from the throats of the steadily increasing audience filled her ears, but she would not so much as peep from behind her curtain. What a strange thought it was, that this composite animal, whose voice—unmistakeably stimulated by anticipation—she now heard in this building for the first time in her life, had nevertheless gathered itself here at her husband's bidding night after night for more years than she cared to say. In spite of the managerial supplies of bodily sustenance the beast sounded hungry tonight; hungry for sensation, hungry possibly for beauty, hungry anyhow for satisfaction of the inexplicable instinct which had drawn it so often before and would draw it so often again to the theatre. And deep down, like the muffled drone of a sixteen-foot stop, there was also recognisable that note of cruelty which is never absent from a crowd. No wonder that on many a first night before now the author had left the theatre without waiting for the curtain to rise, and had walked the streets during the whole performance sooner than remain to hear that sound.

But Mrs. Cartwright felt no such temptation tonight. Now that she was here, she suddenly no longer felt responsible for the authorship of this play. It must have been written by some one else. Not that poor boy whose name appeared on the programme, but certainly not herself. Or if it were her play, then this was a dream; the last of those many dreams which she had been having lately. In a minute something would happen to prove it. Some ridiculous change would take place, and she would find herself back in bed at her house. She closed her eyes for a moment, half-expecting when she opened them to find that the Box had vanished. But all the time the roar of the many voices continued, and suddenly there was a burst of applause, as some heroine of the musical stage made a contemptuous and carefully timed entrance into the stalls. "If it's a dream," said Mrs. Cartwright to herself, "then, if I look for John and Elizabeth, I shall find them deformed, or in fancy dress, or not there at all. I'll try."

She opened her eyes, and very cautiously moved the curtain of the Box. Heavens! that sea of faces! She darted quickly back, and, as she did so, there was a sharp tap of the conductor's baton on his desk, a second's pause, and the overture had begun. Instantly panic had seized her. Why had she come? What was she doing here? She must go at once, anywhere. Her car would have gone, but she could get a taxi, if she were quick, from one of the late arrivals. She half-rose from her seat, and as she did so the door of the Box clicked and some one entered.

Her husband! And yet not the husband who had come to her house just before Christmas, but, by some miracle or nightmare, the one whom she had last seen twenty-five years ago. Gone was that lined and exhausted face, gone that iron-grey hair; his very clothes carried her bade to the forgotten fashions of the nineties. In every detail this was the man whose irresistible vitality had swept her off her feet, who had given her less than a year of heaven and hell upon earth, and from whom she had in the end fled, to patch up her broken life as best she might.

She remained motionless, paralysed.

He opened his mouth to speak.

"Helen," he said.

And with that one word, slowly and laboriously uttered, the illusion was shattered. In the dim light of the Box she had mistaken the rejuvenating powers of his costume and make-up for the real thing. She saw now that there was no fire in those eyes, only the smouldering melancholy to which it had long ago died down. And suddenly she was afraid.

He advanced a step nearer to her, still invisible, though, to the rest of the auditorium.

"Helen," he said, "did you write this play?"

She tried to speak, but no sound came.

His eyes were still fixed on her, searchingly, tragically.

She nodded her head.

Leo Cartwright gave a little gasping cry; Mrs. Cartwright flung out her hands in an attitude of supplication, though for what she hardly knew; and simultaneously there hurtled into the Box a wild-eyed, panting man.

"Chief!" he croaked. "The stage is waiting. They've been hunting for you everywhere. Thank the Lord, one of the hands saw you come in here."

The Chief drew himself up.

"I am quite ready," he said, and left the Box without another glance at his wife.

The overture had reached its fortissimo and its prestissimo. A final burst on strings, wind, and tympani was followed by silence. The house lights were extinguished. The more than hydra-headed beast in front dropped its voice to a whisper. And with a prolonged swishing sound the curtain rose.

In the darkness John Ormroyd's right hand moved gently towards the next seat. It seemed to find something there which it needed; for it did not move again.

Not even when five minutes later Leo Cartwright's first entrance was drowned in one great storm of clapping and shouting from all parts of the house. Not that John did not contribute his share towards this noise. He bumped his cane lustily on the floor with his free hand, and even, forgetting for the moment all that he had suffered, shouted out, "Bravo, Cartwright!"

It is possible that one of the technical weaknesses in "Romance to the Rescue," to which the Chief had desired to draw David Lawrence's attention, was the fact that the principal character made his first appearance so soon after the beginning of the play. But had he been aware at the time that the first performance was to synchronise with the date of his return as Member for the Covent Garden Division, he could hardly have wished to put any further strain on the impatience of the audience than these opening moments provided. Again and again he attempted to speak, and each time the thunders of applause made him abandon the effort and renew his bowing. The peculiarly dramatic quality of his triumph over his opponent had seized on the audience's imagination. Already there were many present prepared to swear that a warrant had been issued for Hamilcar Barker's arrest. Add all this excitement to the enthusiasm invariably attendant on a first performance at the Thespian, and you may have some idea of the nature of the reception which the last of the old actor-managers was now being accorded.

"Look!" said Elizabeth to John, under cover of the shouts from all sides. "That Box isn't empty after all. Do you think the author is hiding there?"

John glanced in the direction indicated.

"No," he said. "I've heard he's still ill. Besides, those are a woman's hands; I can see the long gloves."

They both looked again several times during the evening, but the applauding hands did not reappear.

Nevertheless Mrs. Cartwright had not left. Only after this first demonstration, which had clearly been purely personal to her husband, she took no further part in the applause. For one thing it seemed too much like drinking one's own health, and for another she found herself too genuinely moved to wish to do anything except remain quiet. The conventional banging together of palms was all very well to convey ordinary approval, but for a performance such as this it seemed to her as out of place as it would have been at the end of a particularly beautiful church service.

For this was not her play, the awkward, untidy vehicle into which she had heaped haphazard fragments of her thoughts and experiences. True, not a word, so far, had been altered, but what power had given these words this life and rhythm which for her they had always lacked? How was it possible that sitting alone there, listening to speeches which were as familiar to her as her own name, she could yet feel her throat tighten with the pathos and the disarming humour of this creation of her own? More still, could by some strange sympathy feel the throats of the whole house choke back that same half-happy sob with which humanity admits the truth of its best portraits. As for the principal character in the play, he seemed no longer to be her husband, either of today or of her youth, but some stranger, infinitely skilful in his art and infinitely sympathetic to the spirit of her work; yet bringing to it something far more than it itself contained, creating before her eyes out of her words and his genius a new, real and unforgettable figure.

As the curtain fell on the first Act, the applause broke out again, full and deafening, yet indescribably different from the storm of greeting and congratulation which had preceded it. In his well-placed seat in the stalls Mr. Alexander Brisk was observed to nod as if approvingly. "If it goes on like this," he said to his wife, who on this occasion was occupying the adjacent seat, "this play is a winner." And he smiled at some private thought.

"John," said Elizabeth.

"Yes, darling?"

"No, no. You mustn't say that here."

"I'm sorry. I forgot we weren't alone."

"John, this isn't the same David Lawrence that came with us to the play here that day, is it?"

"Well," said John, "I did ask Mrs. Cartwright, but I think something must have interrupted us, because I can't remember what she said. But

DENIS MACKAIL

I'm not going to believe that this was written by any one as young as that. It'd be impossible."

"Do you think it's as good as all that?"

"Well, don't you?"

"I'd sooner see your play."

This was the nearest thing to a note of adverse criticism which could have been heard anywhere in the house. But you must remember that Elizabeth was still so young that she had never (so she thought) seen a bad play, and that she had been engaged just over an hour.

The impression made by the first Act was confirmed by the second, at the end of which an unprecedented occurrence took place. Mr. Brisk left his seat and found his way to the smoking-room, where his colleagues and a number of Press representatives were assembled. Never before had he pronounced his opinion on any play until the fall of the final curtain, but now he did not even wait for it to be asked.

"Well, gentlemen," he said loudly, to no one in particular, "I don't care how bad the rest of this show is. It can be worse than the Wigan panto if it likes. It won't make any difference. Leo Cartwright has backed a double today. I know."

"What do you know, Mr. Brisk?" asked the critic of the *Daily Bulletin*.

"That this show is going to be a Winner," said Mr. Brisk, with tremendous emphasis on the last word.

Several, representatives of the provincial Press immediately rushed out and rang up their London offices. Their messages were all the same. "Put it in the London Letter," they said, "that Leo Cartwright has scored the greatest success of his career. This play is going to run for two years."

Impossible as it might seem, the third Act was even better than the first two. There were sixteen curtain calls, but the Chief shook his head at the shouts for a speech. Tradition on this side of the Channel forbade anything of this sort until the end of the performance.

Behind the scenes there were smiles everywhere. In the foyer Mr. Littlejohn, completely recovered from the effects of his short but painful interview with Mr. Gordon, radiated geniality. Even his silk hat seemed to have taken on an additional polish.

And the whole of this interval, as during the previous ones, Mrs. Cartwright held her breath whenever she heard a sound outside the door of the Box. But the door remained unopened.

"Elizabeth," said John.

"Yes?"

"I adore you," said John. "But what I was really going to say was this. That time when you first came to the Thespian, and some one was so rude to you, who was it?"

"I don't know," answered Elizabeth. "Just a man. Don't let's talk about it."

"Not a swarthy-sort-of-looking man?" persisted John.

"Well, it was, as a matter of fact."

"With a thick sort of voice?"

"Yes. Why?"

"I know him," said John. "I'll punch his nose the next time I see him."

"Oh, John, you mustn't do that. But why did you suddenly ask?"

"Well, once or twice I had a sort of idea that it might have been Cartwright himself."

"Cartwright?" she exclaimed. "Why, I never saw him at all. Besides, Cartwright's too sweet."

"I see what you mean," said John. "And anyhow, I'd forgive him anything for putting on this play and acting like that in it."

"Even being rude to me?" asked Elizabeth.

There was an impatient "Hush!" from all round them. The curtain was just rising.

"Anything, I meant, except that," John whispered, feeling again for her hand.

The last Act of "Romance to the Rescue" had begun.

Those who were in front that night said afterwards that the remarkable thing about that last Act was the dead silence in which it was received. Up to this point there had been frequent interruptions of applause or of laughter, but now, as the climax and moral of the story drew near, the audience were gripped into a rigidity of attention unlike anything which most of them had ever known in the theatre. More than in any previous scene of the play, the weight of this Act fell on Leo Cartwright's shoulders alone; but never once in gesture or tone was there a suspicion of the monotony which a part of this kind so often involves. The course of the action had enabled him to remove the darkening powder from his hair, and to present very much the general appearance which he had shown, for example, at the Law Courts this morning. A little shabbier, perhaps, a shade feebler in voice and manner. But here was no doddering old man displaying that incredible senility which has driven so many of us from the theatre. No King Lear, shouting louder and louder as his strength was supposed to ebb away. Just Nature itself, with that little stereoscopic accentuation of outline and relief, that slight selection and rejection of detail, which distinguishes a mere picture from a work of art. Although it became clear by the middle of the Act that it was the author's intention to carry the story right up to the only possible end, there were none of those stage hints of coming dissolution, those startings and shiverings with which actors are accustomed to suggest their approaching death. Only a wonderfully sensitive portrait of fatigue, and a kind of growing gentleness.

For the last seven or eight minutes of the Act, the Chief had to sit motionless in his chair, with his eyes shut, while the final dialogue was played in front of him. He is supposed to be asleep, but when they try to rouse him at the end, he is found to be dead. It is on this moment, and the unforgettable last line from the woman who had refused to marry him in the first Act, that the curtain falls.

For thirty seconds after it fell, there was absolute silence in the darkened house. Then high up in a distant corner of the gallery a little crackle of applause began, and in an instant the whole audience were stamping and shouting and yelling in one colossal burst of sound. Amid the extraordinary din the cries of "Cartwright!" and "Author!" seemed equally divided. But to John's surprise the curtain did not rise. "Bravo!" he roared; "Author!" piped Elizabeth by his side, and then to it again they went with their hands. Suddenly the tableau curtains moved, and a man in evening dress, carrying a silk hat in one hand, was standing before them. It seems probable that the majority of the audience took him for the hitherto unknown David Lawrence. The applause became more thunderous than ever.

But the figure behind the footlights raised his hand, almost impatiently as it seemed, for silence. The clapping died suddenly down.

"Ladies and gentlemen," said Mr. Littlejohn, "I am very sorry to say that the author is not in the house, I—"

A voice from the Pit interrupted him.

"Never mind the author. We want Cartwright."

"I regret very much," said Mr. Littlejohn, giving a dab to his forehead with his handkerchief, "that Mr. Cartwright has been taken suddenly ill, and will not be able to appear in person to thank you for this wonderful reception." Then lowering his voice, and addressing the stalls, he added: "Is there a doctor anywhere in front?"

A man at the end of the second row rose in reply. Mr. Littlejohn signalled to him that he would meet him outside the stalls exit, and retired quickly through the curtains. Immediately the house lights were turned full on, and, while the audience were still gasping at this extraordinary end to their evening's entertainment, the lower edge of the safety curtain appeared and rapidly filled the proscenium arch.

In the face of this plain indication that their presence was no longer required, there was nothing for the audience to do but to go home. In a moment the exits were filled with jostling crowds, and everywhere the same words were being repeated.

"Extraordinary thing! . . . What d'you suppose happened? . . . Was that a doctor he was asking for? . . . I've never known anything like it. . . Who was that man, did you say? . . . Must have had a fit. . . Awful strain I should think. . . Well, I call it a very odd way to treat us. . ."

Gradually the corridors emptied, the lights were lowered, and in the gallery the cleaners appeared, lugging mammoth dust sheets.

In the foyer the ticket speculators were gathered together uncomfortably.

"Where's Brisk?" asked one of them.

"Where's Littlejohn?" asked another. "And where's the champagne?"

"I thought I saw Brisk going through on to the stage," said a third.

"I'll go and see," added the first.

But as he moved towards the stalls entrance, a commissionnaire barred his way.

"Mr. Littlejohn's orders, sir," he said. "No one is to be allowed to pass."

"Oh, all right," replied the speculator. "Only it will hurt him more than it hurts us. Come on, boys, I'm going home." And soon the foyer was empty too.

As Mr. Littlejohn disappeared through the curtains, Mrs. Cartwright snatched up her cloak and hurried out into the passage. Almost immediately she met him again.

"Ah, there you are, doctor," he was saying. "This way."

"What is it?" asked the doctor, appearing from the other direction.

"I don't know. He's pretty bad."

They went through on to the stage.

Mrs. Cartwright turned to follow them, but the fireman on the iron door stopped her.

"I'm sorry, madam," he said, "but it's against the regulations. Round by the Stage Door, if you please."

"But I must—" she began, wondering what chances there were of being believed, if she said who she was, when she was interrupted by the sudden arrival from behind her of a short, stoutish man in thick glasses. She knew his face somehow, but could not for the moment trace the recollection to its source. He was dragging his overcoat by one sleeve and was clearly in a very exciteable condition.

"That's all right, fireman," he said. "I'm Mr. Brisk."

Of course. The Chairman of the Selection Committee.

"I'm sorry, sir,—" began the fireman, intending apparently to repeat his formula.

"Here," said Mr. Brisk, screwing up a Treasury note and throwing it at his feet. "No time for this kind of thing."

The fireman fell back and stooped for the note. Instantly Mr. Brisk was through the doorway with Mrs. Cartwright following close in his wake.

They slipped in front of the edge of the scene, and found themselves facing a little group. Lying back, still in the big chair in which they had last seen him, was Leo Cartwright, his eyes still closed. Behind him stood Mr. Littlejohn. The doctor seemed to be concluding some brief kind of examination. He looked up and saw Mr. Brisk.

"Here," he said, "take this to a chemist, quickly."

He pencilled something on the back of an envelope and held it out.

"But I want—" began Mr. Brisk.

"Now, then, look sharp," said the doctor. "It's life or death."

Without a word Mr. Brisk took the envelope and fled.

The stairs leading to the Stage Door were crowded with the members of the company who had been herded off the stage by Mr. M'Gill immediately the curtain fell.

"What is it? How is he?" they asked, as Mr. Brisk forced his way through them, but he paid not the slightest attention. Nor did he answer the questions which were shot at him by the group of enquirers outside, against whom Garrod was already defending the Stage Door.

On the stage the doctor straightened his back.

"He's easier," he said.

"What is it?" asked Mr. Littlejohn in a whisper.

"Heart," said the doctor, and in answer to the unspoken question which trembled on the Business Manager's lips, he said: "He'll be in bed for a month after this—if he's lucky."

There was silence. The doctor seemed to be waiting for something. Very slowly Leo Cartwright opened his eyes. Then his lips moved slightly, but there was no sound.

"That's all right, old chap," said the doctor cheerily.

Even in this appalling crisis, Mr. Littlejohn darted an angry look at him. This was no way in which to address the head of the Thespian Theatre. Leo Cartwright shut his eyes again.

"Where does he live?" asked the doctor.

Mr. Littlejohn's jaw fell.

"We don't know," he said. "His secretary has his private telephone number, but that's all that we've got. And she went off at nine o'clock. She was fagged out."

"Is she on the telephone?"

"No."

"Is there anywhere here where we could make him comfortable?" asked the doctor, looking round at the paint and canvas apartment.

"There's nothing like a bed, I'm afraid," said Mr. Littlejohn.

"Well, he can't stay here."

Mrs. Cartwright stepped forward out of the shadows.

"I am his wife," she said. "I will take him back with me, if he is fit to be moved. My car is round at the front of the theatre."

Mr. Littlejohn stared at her, stupefied.

"What is that?" he asked. "Are you Mrs. Cartwright?"

The doctor threw a puzzled look from one to the other, and at this moment there was a sound from the other side of the scene, and Mr. Brisk reappeared, panting.

"Here you are," he said, handing the doctor a little cardboard box.

The doctor opened it and took something out of it. There was a little snapping sound.

"Here you are, old man," he said to the still apparently unconscious Chief. "Take a sniff at this."

Every one waited in silence while you could count twenty. Then, as slowly as before, the Chief's eyes reopened. He muttered something.

"That's all right," said the doctor. "You won't have it again now."

The Chief's eyes fell on his wife.

"Helen," he said.

"Yes, my dear."

She came and knelt by his side. But the effort seemed to have exhausted him, and he said no more. Mr. Littlejohn stood dumbfounded at this inexplicable sight.

"How far do you live?" asked the doctor.

Mrs. Cartwright told him.

DENIS MACKAIL

"In a few minutes we can carry him to your car. I'll come back with you."

"Thank you," she said. "Perhaps some one could tell the chauffeur to be sure to wait."

Mr. Littlejohn disappeared in the darkness and emerged presently saying: "It's all right. The car's at the front entrance now."

A little later, supported by the three men and wrapped in the doctor's overcoat, Leo Cartwright was borne through the front of his theatre, while the crowd was still thronging round the stage entrance, and was carried across the pavement to the waiting car. On the way he had tried to speak.

"Littlejohn," he said, and the Business Manager looked at the doctor for permission to reply. The doctor shook his head, but the Chief did not speak again. Only his eyes seemed to be expressing some mental agony.

"Mr. Littlejohn shall come and see you the first instant you're better," said Mrs. Cartwright. "I promise you."

That tortured look faded out of the Chief's eyes.

Very gently they lifted him into the car, and very gently it moved away in the darkness.

Messrs. Littlejohn and Brisk remained on the pavement staring after it. Only his unparalleled loyalty prevented the Business Manager from unburdening himself of the question with which his whole brain was bursting.

"Well, good-night," said Mr. Brisk. "I must run home after my missus. What's going to happen?"

"The biggest success we've ever had," murmured Mr. Littlejohn. "The most wonderful reception I've ever seen. Did you hear what the doctor said?" he added.

"No, what?"

"Four weeks in bed," said Mr. Littlejohn. "I suppose you wouldn't like to buy any seats?"

"Not likely," said Mr. Brisk, darting a quick glance at the other. "What are you going to do, eh?"

Mr. Littlejohn looked solemnly at him.

"That," he said, "must be left to the Chief to decide."

INTERMEZZO

Dr. Rawson, as he subsequently proved to be called, showed no surprise and asked no questions when faced with the complete absence of masculine apparel and fittings at the house to which he was driven. With the chauffeur's help he had carried Mr. Cartwright upstairs and laid him on his wife's bed.

"You'll need a nurse," he said to her.

"I've got a St. John's certificate," she ventured.

"All right. I'll bring one in the morning, then. Where are his things?"

"He has been away," she said. "There's nothing here belonging to him."

"Can I use your car?" asked the doctor, as if listening to the most ordinary domestic arrangement.

"Of course."

"Tell it to go round to my house, then,—here's my card,—and fetch the suitcase that's in the hall. There'll be enough there to get on with."

"But, Doctor, what will you do?"

"I shall be all right; they're only my duplicates for week-ends. I had been going away this morning. Anyhow, it's that or nothing at this time on a Sunday morning, so tell your man to look sharp."

She obeyed silently.

In fifteen minutes the car was back again, and, before another half-hour had passed, Mrs. Cartwright was saying good-bye to the Doctor on the landing outside her bedroom.

"I'll be back at half-past eight," he said, "and I'll bring the Nurse with me. He'll probably go on being drowsy now, even if he doesn't sleep. But you're not to leave him; you understand that?"

"Yes."

"If he gets any pain again, break one of these and hold it under his nose. But it's more than a million to one he won't. However, don't hesitate to ring me up—this is my number—if you feel the least uneasy. I'll leave the telephone switched through to my bedroom."

"I don't know how to thank—"

"That's all right, Mrs. Cartwright. By George! what a wonderful play that was, and what a marvellous performance he gave! You ought to be very proud of him."

"I am," said Mrs. Cartwright, and the Doctor turned and danced lightly down the stairs. She went back into her bedroom and looked at her husband. He was lying on his back, his pale face and grey hair in strange contrast to the crimson stripes of Dr. Rawson's pyjamas. Once his eyes opened, but though he seemed to be looking straight at her there was no gleam of recognition in them, and presently he closed them again. Slipping into her dressing-gown, she extinguished the

DENIS MACKAIL

already heavily shaded reading-lamp, and sat down by the fire to begin her vigil.

And as she sat there, one part of her mind intent all the time to hear the slightest sound which he might make, some other and separate mental process was carrying her back through the years, back until at length she reached that place in the past where, ever since he had last spoken, over an hour ago, Leo Cartwright, conscious or unconscious, had also been.

IT WAS A VERY HOT summer after a very cold winter in one of the years when omnibus conductors still wore billycock hats, when tradesmen were still polite, when people still told funny stories about bicycles, and laughed at the Germans, and were slightly nervous of the French; when aeroplanes, taxicabs, prohibition, bridge, revolving heels, poison gas, Dorothy Perkins, syndicalism, Boy Scouts, straphangers, relativity, the North and South Poles, thermos flasks, Golders Green, thés dansants, press-fasteners, Miss E. M. Dell, depth charges, pro-Boers, supertax, scooters, hunger strikes, Lewis guns, early closing, jitneys, Kingsway, flashbacks, vorticism, rubber-cored golf-balls, safety first, permanent waving, and countless other pleasures and refinements of present-day life were still undiscovered.

Miss Ida Lamington's West-End company of totally unknown artistes, headed by Miss Ida Lamington herself, had reached the last night of their week's engagement at the Theatre Royal, Nottingham. For twelve weeks they had been occupied in spreading among the towns of the North and Midlands such gospel as the public could extract from J. H. Christie's "My Lady Dorothy"—a costume play written especially for Miss Lamington with the ingenious intention of combining in one evening's entertainment all the best moments (or the nearest thing that the law of copyright would allow) from all the parts in which she had delighted her admirers for the last ten years. Strange to relate, however, although Mr. Christie's facile pen had succeeded in working in every single incident on the list with which he had been supplied, "My Lady Dorothy" had only just managed to pay its expenses through a London run of under three months, and was not doing much more than make both ends meet now that it was on the road. Still, for want of anything better and for fear of much that might be a great deal worse, Miss Lamington's "vehicle" had so far remained unchanged.

The expensive cast who had supported this popular favourite during her tenancy of the London theatre had been replaced for the purposes of the tour by a collection of cheaper substitutes, and not the least efficient of these had been a young actor named Leo Cartwright. In the second week of their travels, Mr. Murray Dormer, who had been engaged to play the lead opposite Miss Lamington, had had the misfortune to come into the theatre too drunk to remember his words, and, still worse, too drunk to remember the respect due to the Star. Terrible and ear-splitting sounds had filled the stuffy corridors at the back of the old theatre at Wakefield, before Mr. Dormer had been overwhelmed by numbers and locked into a cupboard; and the audience were already stamping with impatience when Miss Lamington suddenly realised that the question of a successor to the incarcerated Dormer had still to be settled. In theory he should, of course, have had an understudy, but in practice he had none. The Stage Manager did not soothe the Star's jangled nerves by telling her that the first understudy rehearsal had been called for the following morning. She had, in fact, gone so far as to call him a damned fool.

In this crisis Mr. Leo Cartwright—still pressing a handkerchief to the bleeding lip which he had acquired in his struggle with Mr. Dormer—had made the surprising announcement that he thought he knew the prisoner's words and was prepared to take on the rôle there and then.

"But what about your own part, Mr. Cartwright?" asked the Star.

"Well, to tell the truth," he had replied, "I don't think it would make any difference if that was left out altogether."

This was burning his boats with a vengeance, for the offer was accepted. But he was justified of his courage, since from that day onwards the part of Master Throgmorton was in fact omitted, while he continued to occupy the exiled Mr. Dormer's shoes in the character of Captain Beverley.

"Any kind of over-indulgence in the way of drink," Miss Lamington had said, when the penitent Dormer appealed to her for mercy, "is the one thing that I can never overlook."

It would possibly have been more accurate if she had added, "in others"; but there is no reason to suspect that at this period Miss Lamington regarded her undoubtedly large consumption of sweet champagne and crême de menthe as anything more than what was due to her by reason of her position, temperament, and physique.

Mr. Cartwright's sudden promotion did not tend to increase his popularity with the rest of the company. It would have been useless to point out to the other men that they had had equal opportunities for mastering the words of Captain Beverley's part. The answer was obvious.

Cartwright had a rich wife and had, therefore, no business to be taking the bread out of the mouths of genuine professionals. Let him, they argued, go and live on his wife like others in his position. And to do them justice, they were only preaching what they would, if given the opportunity, one and all have practised.

Nor were the ladies without their grievance. Why, they asked, should Mrs. Cartwright come round with the show all the time, and by virtue of her wealth stay with her husband in the best hotels, nay, even on some occasions break the unwritten law which made the Star's hotel taboo to all others? Not that Miss Lamington herself had objected. She was more than content to carry on flirtations with Mr. Cartwright under his young wife's eyes, and leave the young wife to pay for the suppers which gave her the opportunity to do so.

It was, indeed, a very difficult position for both husband and wife. They had been married just eight months when the tour began, and the question had (to Mrs. Cartwright's mind) naturally arisen whether she was to accompany him or not. Leo had chosen a singularly unfortunate way of expressing his opinion on the subject.

"Please yourself, darling," he had said. "I'd love it if you came, but I shouldn't blame you if you didn't. It's a dog's life in some ways."

Now Helen was proud of her husband; not only of his acting, which was as a matter of fact nothing so very wonderful in those days, but also of his determination to stick to his profession in spite of her money. She would do nothing, if she could help it, that could make him say afterwards that he had thrown up this or any other engagement to please her. So she bit her lip and answered: "Then I'll come."

"Right you are," said Leo, yawning. "I think I'll go out and see some fellows. Don't keep awake."

A typical ending this. For days on end he would be more charming, more passionate, more devoted, more altogether fascinating than one would have thought any husband could ever be. And then suddenly for no particular reason he would become impatient, uninterested, vague, and unfamiliar. It was as if a stranger had entered into his body. No power which Helen had yet discovered could make him shake off these moods until the fit had spent itself. If she tried tears, he raised his eyebrows and went out. If she tried to charm him, he would mutter something about seeing some chaps and leave her in the middle of one of her sentences. More than once he had even disappeared for two or three nights on end, and too often had Helen lain awake struggling to prevent herself wondering whether they were indeed chaps whom he had gone to see.

But in the end he had always changed back into himself again, if indeed the man who had made her marry him after three weeks' acquaintanceship and three weeks' passionate siege was the real Leo Cartwright.

It was Miss Agnes Lotta (who played Dame Margaret in "My Lady Dorothy") who had first had the kind thought of telling her that her husband was getting too intimate with the Star. It was in the train, on a rainy Sunday, between Sunderland and Barnsley, that she had performed this considerate action.

"Of course," said Miss Lotta afterwards, in recounting the incident to a friend, "I hardly expected to be thanked. But really, the look she gave me. Why, you might have thought I'd said something improper. It's most certainly the last time I shall try to help the little fool."

The week before the company reached Nottingham, Leo had been at his kindest and most irresistible. The weather had been perfect, and they had gone for long, leisurely drives together in ancient flies, had had arcadian meals in the open air or at fairy inns, holding each other's hands, teasing each other with childish nonsense, laughing at invisible jokes, driving back in the scented evenings in silence. But on the Sunday the day dawned under heavy, oppressive clouds. They had a long journey before them with an awkward change which meant a couple of hours at a junction. Leo complained of a headache. Helen had a headache, but did not complain. Just before the second train started, Miss Lamington had joined them on the platform.

"Where are you two going to stay?" she asked, her eyes on Leo.

"We thought of going to the Black Horse," Helen answered.

"Impossible," said the Star. "You must come to the Flying Boy. It's the only possible place. You'd be wretched at the Black Horse."

Helen looked at her husband's face for guidance, and found none. He was frowning gently and gazing at a signal post about three hundred yards up the line.

"I want to talk to your husband about all sorts of things," said Miss Lamington. "Plans and ideas, you know. And I'd never get a chance otherwise. So make it the Flying Boy."

"Of course we'll come, then," answered Helen, her one thought not to let her wishes come between her husband and his prospects of advancement. The train came hissing into the station, and they separated to their different compartments.

DENIS MACKAIL

"Why the devil did you say we'd go with that woman?" asked Leo in a low voice, as the train started.

"I didn't know what you wanted, darling," Helen answered. "I was afraid of offending her, if we refused."

He looked out of the window and pursed up his lips as if he were going to whistle. Five minutes later he said:

"I've half a mind to chuck this tour."

"Oh, Leo!"

"I ought to be a bank clerk really. I'm no good at this kind of job."

"Oh, but you are. You're going to be the most tremendous success. I know you are."

"Do you?" He turned to her again from his inspection of the countryside.

"Why, of course, Leo."

"Well, we'll go to the Black Horse, then. Miss Lamington can talk to me at the theatre, if she wants to."

Helen admired and adored. Even though he was silent for the rest of the journey, her heart felt light and happy again. But Fate was waiting for them. The Black Horse were very sorry, but they were full up. If only Mr. and Mrs. Cartwright had telegraphed, they would of course have kept them a room, but. . .

"Come on," said Leo roughly, picking up his bag. They drove to several other hotels, but they were all either, like the Black Horse, full or hotels only in name.

"Couldn't we find some lodgings just for this week?" Helen asked.

"No," he answered. "I won't have you stopping where you're uncomfortable."

So it was Helen who told the driver to go to the Flying Boy, and there at last they were taken in. And there on the same evening Miss Lamington gave the first of her supper parties in her private sitting-room.

"You, too, of course, if you're not too tired," had been the form which her invitation to Helen took.

At eleven o'clock, exhausted and exasperated by her hostess's persistent neglect, Helen had risen to leave.

"Must you go?" asked Miss Lamington, without looking at her. "I'm so sorry. But you'll spare your husband, I know. I want to read this new play to him."

Helen lay awake nearly two hours before Leo rejoined her, and through her half-closed eyes she realised that the happy mood of last week was dead. Nor did it return during the whole of that interminable six days at Nottingham.

What he did with himself all day she never discovered. He was not with her, but he certainly was not with the Star, who never got out of bed until lunchtime and never left the hotel until it was time to go to the theatre. But after the performance they returned together and from then onwards, but for the possible presence of Ida Lamington's wicked-eyed maid, they were, as far as Helen knew, alone together until two or three or four in the morning. For after that first evening the Star did not even go through the form of asking Helen to join them. And as for Helen, some feeling which she described to herself as pride, but which gave her none of the consolation or satisfaction which one might hope to derive from this state of mind, prevented her from uttering a single word of complaint to her husband. True, she privately practised and often achieved a coldness of manner towards him which according to all the rules of the game should have brought him to her feet, begging to be told in what way he had offended. But he seemed completely oblivious both of the manner and of her. If only he had attempted to justify himself or to explain; to say that his extraordinary behaviour was due to professional reasons, for instance; then, she felt, she would have had some clue to the mystery of his thoughts, for he could hardly discuss the position without revealing them. But the mystery remained insoluble. When they were alone together, he remained silent and lost apparently in thought. If spoken to, he answered, but no more than answered. Otherwise he would get up suddenly, perhaps in the middle of a meal, and taking up his hat go off by himself Heaven knew where.

And yet, strange as it may sound, until the very last day of their week at Nottingham, Helen, although miserable and nervous enough, and jealous in the negative sense which made her resent his continued absence from her, was not troubled with that positive jealousy which fastens on one person alone as its cause. She disliked Miss Lamington, but she did not fear her. Perhaps she had become to some slight degree inoculated by her previous experience of Leo's moods during the first part of their married life, when he was playing in London. One seeks naturally for some such explanation, for at this period, whatever her capabilities as an actress may have been, a more typical vampire than Ida Lamington it would have been hard to find.

Black hair, dark eyes, a pale-green face, and scarlet lips were her physical attributes. Selfishness and stupidity on an unparalleled scale characterised her mind. She was at this time over thirty-five,—a good deal older than Leo Cartwright,—and it was common talk in the company that she had a husband somewhere, but that she and he never met. But in spite of her stupidity, and because of her selfishness and her looks, she could and did attract, torture, and destroy any and all whom she chose to select for these purposes. Hating her and hating themselves, they yet came when she called, paid when she asked, and, if necessary, went bankrupt to do so. Do not suppose that Helen was ignorant of her reputation; she and her husband had discussed it at great length when the engagement had first been offered him. But she did not believe then that this enchantress, whose conquests had, so it was rumoured, achieved the height of the peerage itself, could stoop to a member of her touring company, even though that member should be her own Leo, the best-looking and most adorable man in the world.

On the Saturday the weather, which had been hesitating all the week as to whether it should thunder or not, suddenly appeared to have made up its mind. The whole sky was the same reddish-grey, the heat intense, the air heavy and immoveable. Occasionally the pavement in front of the hotel was dotted with specks of rain, each the size of half-a-crown, evaporating almost as soon as they fell. Distant low thumps and rumbles seemed to show that the authorities responsible for the coming storm were trying out their instruments, as you may see the man in the corner of the orchestra gingerly testing his drum before the conductor has appeared. In spite of this threatening outlook, Leo had as usual gone out for his solitary walk; but about two o'clock, when the storm first broke over the town, he suddenly returned, which seemed to show either that he had been fortunate in timing the approach of the rain, or else that he had never gone far from the hotel.

He put his head into the sitting-room where his wife was waiting by herself, but seeing her there was about to go again, when she called out to him.

"Leo," she said.

"Eh?"

"About next week. Wouldn't it be a good thing to telegraph somewhere for rooms? It's so—so awkward arriving and driving round to place after place."

"What exactly do you mean by that?" he asked.

Poor Helen; she had meant precisely what she had said, but before the cold savagery of his question she blushed and stammered:

"Why, nothing, Leo. I only thought—"

"You're not suggesting that this hotel isn't good enough for you?"

"No, of course not."

He came into the room and closed the door.

"Miss Lamington is very much hurt at the way you have treated her all this week," he said.

"The way I have treated her?"

She hardly knew whether to laugh or cry.

"It puts me in a very uncomfortable position," he went on.

"But, Leo," she answered, "I don't understand. She never asked me to see her since that first night, and twice I've met her on the stairs and she has taken no notice of me at all. Besides—"

"Besides what?"

"Oh, Leo. You've been so different since we got here. Why is it? We had such a wonderful time together all last week. I was so happy, and now—"

A crash of thunder drowned her words, and as the peals died away she seemed to realise the hopelessness of explaining anything to the terrifying stranger who had taken her husband's place. She hid her face on the antimacassar and wept.

Leo Cartwright came a couple of steps nearer to her, and then stopped. He did not attempt to comfort her, to pat her shoulder, even to ask or order her to be quiet. He merely stayed where he was, swearing in a low, dispassionate voice; oaths of all periods and strata of human society pouring out in a smooth, endless stream. But for all the quietness of his voice, she was shocked into ceasing her tears. Her poor Leo! he was, he must be terribly unhappy. Obeying some instinct which told her that he must at all costs be helped, she half-rose to her feet, her arms outstretched. But without touching her, he seemed to fend her off.

"I never ought to have married you," he said. "I'm not fit to. There's a devil that takes hold of me and makes me cruel. I've never loved any one the way that I love you, but that doesn't protect me. I can't fight against it. You've never said anything, because you're an angel, but you know—you must know—that I've been unfaithful to you already many times since we married."

He paused, but she made no sound. Only in the bottom of her heart she knew that somehow she had known this all the time, even though until this moment she had never let the thought take shape.

"You had better get rid of me," he said. "In a reasonable world I suppose I should be shut up, or—or put out of the way. Only don't, for

God's sake, think I enjoy it. I tell you it's hell, absolute hell for me the whole time."

She still looked at him, silent, stupefied.

"I don't make any excuses," he went on, not defiantly, but as if realising better than any one else the uselessness of attempting them.

"But—but I loved you so," she said in a faint voice. Impossible still to believe that this power, which every writer on earth has declared to be irresistible, should have failed her so hideously.

"I ought to be shot," he said in an expressionless tone.

She rose quickly to her feet.

"No, Leo," she said. "I won't believe it. We'll go away—we'll leave tomorrow. We'll start again. I see it now; I was too happy, I took too much from you. I thought I was giving, but I wasn't. Can't we try and forget this? You must tell me more; you must tell me everything, and we'll fight it together. You say you won't make excuses, and God knows I should be a poor kind of wife if I made them for you, but if we start afresh, surely—" She broke off and put a sudden question. "Leo," she asked, "you do love me still, don't you?"

He nodded, slowly, emphatically.

"And you'll break this engagement, and come away with me somewhere?"

He nodded again.

"I don't deserve it," he said.

"But do you think I don't deserve another trial?" she asked.

For answer he fell on his knees and seized her hand. But though there was nothing false about the action, nothing theatrical, the touch of him was suddenly more than she could bear. It seemed in some way to bring everything back again too quickly to the physical plane. She snatched her hand away.

"No, no," she said. "Not now. But tomorrow, when we leave this place. . . I'm worn out. I must lie down. I. . ." She fumbled in her dress. "Your handkerchief," she finished; "I can't find mine."

He had given it her at once; already he was on his feet. He crossed the room—no one moved more swiftly or gracefully than Leo Cartwright as a young man—and was holding the door open for her.

As she passed through it, he bowed his head, and something hot fell on her hand.

She never saw him again until the day when he came into her drawing-room twenty-five years afterwards.

All afternoon the storm circled round and round the town, dying down only to begin again; and, while the lightning flickered and the thunder rolled, Helen lay on her bed in the hotel utterly exhausted. It was from this afternoon that the first of her great headaches—later examples of which we have seen earlier in this book—dated.

About five o'clock there came a gentle knock on the door leading to their sitting-room.

"Come in," called Helen.

The door opened, and the head of Miss Lamington's wicked-eyed maid appeared.

"I beg your pardon, madame," she said. "It was for Mr. Cartwright that I was looking."

"He's not here," answered Helen.

"Mille pardons. Madame will forgive me."

She withdrew her head and the door closed again.

A quarter of an hour later, turning over on the bed, Helen's eye was caught by something white on the carpet by the door. For some minutes it did not occur to her to wonder what it might be, and then suddenly it struck her, "That wasn't there before." Yet several more minutes elapsed before, swinging her feet to the ground, she crossed the room and picked it up.

It was a piece of note-paper, folded and slightly crumpled. She opened it.

It contained a brief message scrawled in pencil on plain paper.

So happy, Leo (it ran), that you will come tonight in spite of everything. I shan't wait for you at the theatre, but will expect you here by half-past eleven. A bientôt.

IDA

Helen stood motionless while you could count a hundred. Then she rang the bell and asked for a cab to be ordered.

"But the rain, mum," protested the chambermaid.

"I'm only going to the station. Tell the man he'll get a good tip."

"Very well, mum."

The chambermaid left her. She flung a few things into her dressing-case, put on her hat and travelling-cloak, and went through into the sitting-room.

There she took a sheet of hotel note-paper and wrote:

This note reached me by mistake. I am going to London at
once. I think you have broken my heart.

HELEN

She put the two notes in an envelope, licked it up, and, having
written her husband's name on the outside, left it on the sitting-room
table. Then, taking up her cloak and dressing-case, she went downstairs.

Her only fear at this moment was that she should meet her husband
in the hall, but it was empty as she passed through. Outside the cab was
waiting, the rain splashing off the roof and from the brim of the driver's
hat. In a very few minutes she had reached the station, and, as luck
would have it, the next London train, although a slow one, was due in
ten minutes. She spent the interval hiding in the waiting-room, but no
one whom she knew came on to the platform.

And, it being a Saturday evening, she had the first-class carriage to
herself to cry in all the way up to St. Pancras.

THIS WAS THE POINT AT which, as she sat now in her darkened
bedroom waiting for any sound of movement which her husband might
make, Mrs. Cartwright's thoughts always broke off, only to return each
time to the beginning and go through every incident again. But lying
in this strange bed in Dr. Rawson's red-striped pyjamas, with his eyes
wide open at the ceiling above him, Leo Cartwright carried the story
each time a little farther; although at a given point his thoughts also
would break off time after time and go back again to the beginning.

IN SPITE OF THE RAIN and the thunder, he had tramped far out into
the country that Saturday afternoon, for their only matinée that week
had been on the Wednesday. But the cloud which had been lowering
over him all the week and the storm which had raged within him were
gone. In his heart there was once more peace; peace and thankfulness
for the wonderful wife who was, after and in spite of all, going to help
him to fight himself and to win. He scarcely noticed the rain which
drenched him through and through, or, if he did, merely regarded
it as a suitable symbol of the purification which he felt that he had
undergone. Once more he would try his best and uttermost to be
worthy of his perfect Helen, and, so help him God, this time he would
succeed. Perhaps if they went to America for a bit, or anywhere where
he could start again. Or would it be better to face it out here, to meet

his temptations and overcome them? In any case, by some miracle of devotion, she still loved him. And as for himself, he. . .

A church clock striking at this moment made him realise that he must start back at once for the town if he was not to be late for the evening show—his last performance with this company for ever and always. He turned and tramped off again through the puddles, and gradually the rain began to cease. As he drew near the middle of the town, he was aware that his clothes, though smelling vilely after their wetting, felt almost dry again. If he had a couple sandwiches and a drink at the bar opposite the theatre, he could then change at once into his eighteenth-century dress, and, although he would still be a little early, the risk of catching a cold or getting a sore throat would be very much reduced.

He did as he planned, and after all did not have to wait more than twenty minutes before the call-boy's knock came on the door of the room which he shared with two rivals for the hand of My Lady Dorothy.

The show went well, as it generally did on a Saturday night, but, after each Act, he left the Star to take her calls alone and hurried back to his dressing-room, so as to avoid all chance of her speaking to him. At the end of the performance he changed back into the clothes which the door-keeper had succeeded in getting dried for him, and hurried up the stairs. On the call-board the train-call for the following morning had been posted. Well, they could sue him if they liked, but he wouldn't be there. Helen and he would slip off by an earlier train, and then. . . He quickened his pace.

As he stood waiting for the night porter to answer the front-door bell, he was already planning the words in which he should thank his darling Helen for rescuing him as she had done, and the promises which he would make, and. . .

He ran up the stairs three steps at a time, and burst open the sitting-room door.

To his surprise it was dark.

"She's gone to bed," he muttered to himself and felt in his pocket for a match. The sitting-room, like other sitting-rooms in provincial hotels, was too full of obstacles to be safely crossed in the dark. He struck a match and lit the gas.

As he did so, his eye fell on the envelope lying on the table, and a horrible spasm of fear seized him. Should he look in the bedroom first, or open the letter? He looked across to the bedroom door, and saw for the first time that it was ajar. With cold terror in his heart he picked up the envelope and tore it open.

DENIS MACKAIL

For a space there was absolute silence in the room. Then outside in the corridor there came the sound of a laugh; a rich, provocative sound. Miss Lamington returning with her maid from the theatre.

Leo Cartwright stuffed the envelope and its contents into his pocket, turned and left the room. Ten seconds later, without knocking, he had entered the Star's apartment. On the table her usual supper was laid out, and Marie was helping her off with her cloak.

"Ah, Leo," she said, and whispered something to the maid, who withdrew into the bedroom.

"How fierce you looked all evening," she went on. "I was beginning to be afraid that you no longer cared for me, my Leo. And when I sent Marie to you this afternoon, she could not find you."

Something in his expression made her break off suddenly.

"What is it?" she asked.

"My wife," he said. "She has left me. It's your fault, damn you!"

"My fault? Oh, no, my Leo. You should have taken more care—No, no. Keep away!"

He had advanced threateningly towards her and they stood facing each other over the supper tray.

"My God!" he said, "I'm going to throttle you."

"Marie!" she screamed, and picked up the champagne bottle as the nearest weapon of defence.

"No, you don't," he said, edging towards her. She raised the bottle, screaming again. And as she did so, it struck the heavy gas-fitting over her head, and burst, with a loud explosion and a flood of wine, all over her head.

Leo stepped back quickly, and the maid appeared in the doorway. For perhaps three or four seconds they all remained motionless, and then slowly, almost reluctantly as it seemed, the blood began to come from the long cut which stretched from Miss Lamington's eye to below the corner of her mouth. Simultaneously four or five smaller wounds began to ooze in the same deliberate, relentless way.

Marie leant against the door and smiled.

"I 'ave always say that one of them will get you in the end," she remarked.

And then the night porter had burst into the room.

VIII

ODD MAN OUT

I

ON A JANUARY MORNING IN London, and (for some reason which I have so far failed to fathom) particularly so on a Sunday, the hour when light first appears in the heavens bears very little relation to the time advertised in the Almanac which you were given for Christmas. It is, perhaps, fairly safe to affirm that the sun will not be visible earlier than it is announced, but odds should be very cautiously accepted as to how much later this phenomenon and its attendant results will be observable. The pure and lofty intelligence of the Astronomer Royal, or whoever it is who prepares these forecasts, pays no attention to the conglomeration of soot, sulphur, and other by-products of civilisation which fills the upper air. According to his calculations the sun is somewhere on the other side of it all, and, theoretically, no doubt he is right. This is what we pay him for. But then we also pay the Archbishop of Canterbury to say that the Universe was created in six days.

So it was that, when her maid's gentle tap on the bedroom door roused Mrs. Cartwright from her thoughts, she could scarcely believe that morning was here so soon, for not a gleam of light had yet filtered through the curtains from outside. She glanced at the clock beside her, and, as she did so, the knock was repeated a little more loudly. She crossed the room quickly and opened the door.

It says much for Rose's training that she did not immediately drop the early morning tea-service on the floor. But a further shock was awaiting her.

"The Doctor will be here in a few minutes," said Mrs. Cartwright, laying her finger on her lips. "Will you show him straight up, please?"

"The Doctor, madam?" gasped Rose, the tray wobbling ominously in her hands.

"Yes. Sh!" said Mrs. Cartwright, seizing the tray, withdrawing it into the room, and shutting the door.

"No one on earth except my servants," she thought to herself, "could have slept through the noise we made carrying Leo upstairs last night. Now, how on earth am I to begin explaining to them what has happened?"

There was a movement from the bed.

"Is that you, Helen?" asked a weak voice.

She came and stood close to him.

"Yes," she said. "Would you like a little tea?"

He shook his head.

"Is this your house?" he asked.

"Yes."

"How did I get here?"

She paused, wondering how best to reply, when he broke in again.

"My God! I remember. Helen, you must get hold of Littlejohn at once. What day of the week is it?"

"Sunday."

"Ring him up at once. He's in the directory. 'W. J.' are his initials. Somewhere in Highgate. Tell him to come here at once."

"But—"

"If you don't do it at once, I shall get up."

"Directly the Doctor has seen you, I promise you I will. Now please try to be quiet, or he'll only blame me for exciting you. He'll be here any minute now."

He was silent for a few seconds. Then he spoke again.

"I say, whose pyjamas are these?"

"The Doctor's. He lent them to you last night."

"Ah." He seemed relieved.

Mrs. Cartwright drew the curtains and began tidying the room; punching up cushions and smoothing down the counterpane on the bed. While she was still doing this, she heard the sound of a car drawing up in the street, and a minute later the Doctor was knocking on the bedroom door.

"Well, how's the patient this morning?" he asked, as she let him in.

"I'm all right, Doctor," said a voice from the bed. "Will you please tell my wife that I must see my Business Manager this morning?"

"Steady on," answered the Doctor. "I must have a look at you first."

The examination was long and careful. Mrs. Cartwright tried to glean from the Doctor's face some hint of his thoughts, but his expression was as inscrutable as her husband's. When he had quite finished, he said:

"You'll stay where you are till the end of the week. Then I shall send you down to Brighton in a motor-ambulance. You'll stay there another month, and then we'll see. If you don't do exactly what I say, you'll die. That's the absolute truth, so make up your mind to it."

"Hell," said Leo Cartwright. "Do you realise that, if I don't go back to the theatre tomorrow night, the place must be closed?"

"I can't help that. I'm here to try and get you well, you know, not to run your theatre for you."

"Can I have another opinion?" asked the patient.

"Certainly," said Dr. Rawson cheerfully. "As many as you like. But you know I'm speaking the truth."

"Then I must see my Business Manager at once," said the Chief, capitulating.

"You may see him for exactly ten minutes. And with the nurse or Mrs. Cartwright in the room."

"All right."

"Mind you," continued the Doctor, softening now that he had gained his point, "I'm most infernally sorry for you. I was at your play last night, and I don't mind telling you that it and your performance were the two best things I've ever seen in my life. If I was only thinking of the public, I'd let you go back and take your chance; but I'm not."

"It's very good of you," murmured the invalid. "By the way, may I in turn congratulate you on your taste in pyjamas?"

The Doctor laughed.

"I'll look in and see you this afternoon," he said. "Now cheer up. You'll be all right if you do what I tell you."

Leo Cartwright closed his eyes again without answering, and Dr. Rawson drew Mrs. Cartwright out on to the landing.

"I shall have to hand this over to his regular doctor today," he said. "Perhaps you would tell me his name?"

"He hasn't got a regular doctor," Mrs. Cartwright answered promptly.

"Well, he certainly has a wonderful constitution," said Dr. Rawson, "and fortunately for him he hasn't messed about with it. But he must have been over-working lately, eh?"

"Yes," answered Mrs. Cartwright.

"Did he have any kind of shock last night?"

"Yes."

"H'm. I'm not surprised to hear that. Well, now, listen to me." He began telling her what the patient might eat, what he might do, what would be good signs and what bad.

"I've told the Nurse all this," he said. "She's downstairs now. If I were

DENIS MACKAIL

you, I'd try and get some sleep this morning. Oh, and, by the way, you might have my bag packed for me again; I'll fetch it away when I come this evening. About five o'clock, eh? All right. Well, good-bye."

Mrs. Cartwright watched him disappear downstairs. She still scarcely knew where to begin the things that had to be done. But the first thing, even before seeing the Nurse, must be to let the servants know what had happened, before the Square and the whole of London were full of rumours. She went into the spare room next door to her bedroom and rang the bell. The housemaid was the first to appear.

"I just wanted to tell you," said Mrs. Cartwright, "that my husband came home with me last night. He is very ill and will have my bedroom for the present. I'll use this room. There will be a nurse too. We must put her in the little room upstairs. Is that clear?"

"Yes, mum," answered the housemaid, all trace of intelligence vanishing from her face.

"And I'll give you another fifteen pounds a year if you'll do your best to help, and try not to talk unnecessarily to the other maids in the Square."

"Yes, mum. Thank you very much, I'm sure." Intelligence fairly beamed from her.

"All right. Well, get the rooms ready as quickly as you can. And ask Rose to come up and see me."

A similar interview took place with Rose, who in turn sent up Hilda, who in turn sent up the Cook. When the Cook finally departed, Mrs. Cartwright had engaged to pay her staff another sixty pounds a year, but not one of them had even looked like giving her notice. If they wanted to talk, doubtless they would do so, but that would have to be risked.

She went back into her own bedroom.

"Leo," she said, "the Doctor wants his bag back tonight. Where can I send for your clothes and things?"

"Oh, can't you buy some new ones?" was his unexpected answer.

"Not on a Sunday, I'm afraid," she explained.

"Who is going for them?" he asked.

"I was proposing to send the chauffeur with a note."

"Oh," he said. Then he gave a little laugh. "Well, he'd better be quick, then. I've only got an old woman who comes in in the mornings. She won't wait if I'm not there."

"Perhaps I'd better write a note and you could sign it?"

"Quite unnecessary," he said. "She'd give my things to any one who came in a car."

"And the address?" asked Mrs. Cartwright.

He gave her the name of a shop in a street off Long Acre. "But that's a shop," she said, puzzled.

"I know. I've got two rooms over it. I'd give you the key, but it's locked up in my dressing-room at the theatre, I'm afraid."

"But is this where you live?" she asked again, realising the stupidity of the question, but compelled to put it.

"Yes," he replied, and seemed about to add something, but checked himself.

"I'll see to it at once," she said, and moved towards the door.

"And you'll ring up Littlejohn too?" he asked.

"Yes."

She went downstairs and spoke to the chauffeur herself on the telephone and also to Mr. Littlejohn. He would be round in less than an hour, he said, and thanked her profusely for ringing him up so early. So profusely, indeed, that she had to cut him off at last while he was still speaking.

Then she went in to the Nurse, who had been waiting all this time in the drawing-room. With one smile and less than a dozen words she had her at her feet. She took her upstairs and showed her her quarters, and in five minutes the Nurse was in the sick-room, preparing to wash the patient, while he eyed her nervously from the bed.

At last Mrs. Cartwright could have the hot bath which had become a necessity to her continued existence, and as she sat down to breakfast, only a little later than usual, the familiarity of her surroundings completed the connection, as it were, with real life, which had been broken off ever since her entry into her Box at the theatre last night. Only she was given little opportunity of believing that her recent excursion into impossibility was a dream, for three times in the next half hour she was called to the telephone and asked by various newspapers if she knew where or how her husband was. To each and all she returned the same answer. Mr. Cartwright was in the country; doubtless the Thespian would issue a communiqué during the day. It seemed as if Rumour had been busy during the night, for neither of the two Sunday newspapers which she took in contained any mention of Leo Cartwright's illness. Each printed a glowing account of the play and of the enthusiasm with which it had been received, but it seemed clear the critics had bolted immediately on the fall of the curtain, if not before, and had missed the scene at the end.

Already the excitement over the mystery of the Covent Garden Election seemed to be diminishing, at any rate as far as these two newspapers were concerned. Mr. Barker's disappearance was padded out to about half a column, but the padding was noticeably thin; for how was a story to be constructed if, as was the case, Mr. Barker, though traced to his retreat, had absolutely declined to make any statement? Even the hints and suggestions, which in other circumstances might have helped to fill the necessary space, had been cut down to the barest limits. This may have been due to journalistic freemasonry, which made the sub-editors reluctant to insert anything which might be construed as an attack on a fellow-practitioner, but was more probably to be accounted for by Hamilcar Barker's well-known habit of flying to the Courts whenever his honour was questioned, or even mentioned.

As Mrs. Cartwright was leaving the dining-room, the front-door bell rang, and, stepping back while it should be answered, she heard Hilda adressing the chauffeur.

"What, all loose like this?" she was saying. "Couldn't you find a box to bring it in?"

"There wasn't a box," answered the chauffeur. "I've never seen such an 'ole neither. I've brought away pretty near everything there was too."

A third voice broke in.

"Is this Mrs. Cartwright's house?" it asked.

Mrs. Cartwright stepped out again into the hall.

"Is that Mr. Littlejohn?" she asked. "Ah, good-morning. Won't you come up to the drawing-room for a minute, while I see if my husband is ready for you?"

Mr. Littlejohn, faultlessly dressed as ever, followed her upstairs, gazing about him the whole time rather as if he expected the whole house to vanish from sight if he didn't keep his eye very carefully on it.

Mrs. Cartwright left him in the drawing-room and went up to the next floor.

"Mr. Littlejohn is here, Leo," she said. "The Doctor told me you were only to see him for ten minutes and that the Nurse or I were to stay with you. Which would you prefer?"

The Chief looked at the Nurse as if weighing up her capabilities, and finally answered:

"Well, after all, it's your play we're going to discuss. Would you mind if it were you?"

It was the first mention which either of them had made, since that strange scene in the Box last night, of the discovery of her secret. But there was no embarrassment in his voice or in her face. Already between them the thing was admitted and accepted. And compared with what had followed, what, after all, did the discovery itself matter?

Mrs. Cartwright turned to the Nurse.

"Would you mind," she said, "asking the gentleman who is waiting in the drawing-room to come upstairs?"

"Certainly, Mrs. Cartwright."

"Thank you so much. And, if you would like a book, perhaps you will look round and take one. You'll find plenty down there."

The Nurse slipped with professional skill through the smallest possible opening of the door and closed it silently behind her.

"Is she looking after you all right?" asked Mrs. Cartwright.

"Physically," replied her husband, "I have never been so comfortable in my life. The breakfast was perfect. Mentally, however, I—"

"Yes?"

"I wonder why I am here."

In less than a second Mrs. Cartwright had rejected thirty-seven possible answers and selected a thirty-eighth.

"You're here because the Doctor says you're not to be moved," she said.

Her husband threw her an odd look of friendship and appreciation, as it seemed; but before either of them could speak again there was a knock on the door. Mrs. Cartwright opened it and admitted Mr. Littlejohn.

"Good morning, Littlejohn," said the Chief. "What's the Press like this morning?"

"Wonderful. Perfectly wonderful," groaned the Business Manager.

"Did the Agents book anything last night?"

Mr. Littlejohn scowled.

"Not a cent," he said bitterly. "They ran away."

"Well, you won't have to return any money, then."

"You're taking it off?"

"My dear Littlejohn, I've got no choice. The Doctor has told me straight out that if I get up I shall die."

"But couldn't we get in some one to Play the part?"

"You'll excuse my appearing conceited," answered the Chief, "but do you honestly think that's possible? Who is going to learn up that part

DENIS MACKAIL

by tomorrow night? Who is going to rehearse it? And who is going to come and see them do it?"

"No," said the Business Manager. "You're right."

"And that's not all," continued the Chief. "I didn't tell you this before, because, if it had been a success, it wouldn't have mattered. Although in any case you'd have had to know pretty soon. I had a row with Imray a fortnight ago. He's standing out on this show, and so are the rest of them."

"Good Lord! Then who's going to pay for the production? We shall be smashed right up!"

"I'm paying for the production," said the Chief. "And I'll pay everybody concerned a fortnight's salary. You shall have a cheque for the whole thing as soon as you let me know what the figure is."

"But, Chief, you can't do it. It'll be ten thousand pounds if it's a penny—and that's not counting our expenses in that infernal case. Let me see Mr. Imray. He can't let you down like this after all these years."

"Can't he!" said the Chief acidly. "No, Littlejohn. Put the notice up and tell the newspapers at once. Clear up all the accounts you can, and let the theatre. Sell it, if you get an offer."

"But, Chief, you can't mean it! Why, it would be the absolute end of your management, after fifteen years."

"Fifteen years is long enough," answered the Chief wearily. "Do as I tell you, please. Only, for God's sake settle it all quickly."

Once more he closed his eyes and let his head sink back. Mr. Littlejohn, looking helplessly around the room found himself facing Mrs. Cartwright.

"The Doctor said he was only to have ten minutes," she whispered, pointing to the door.

Mr. Littlejohn gave one last gesture of mingled despair and resignation, and submitted.

She closed the door behind her and followed him down the stairs. On the next landing he paused.

"It's terrible," he said. "After all these years."

And immediately he resumed his descent.

Mrs. Cartwright put her head into the drawing-room and asked the Nurse to go back; then she followed him again.

In the hall he waited for her.

"Nice place you've got here, Mrs. Cartwright," he said. "Have you been here long?"

"Since quite early in the war," she replied.

"Funny thing," he went on, "but the Chief would never say where he was living. Why, even this morning I didn't know where he was until you rang up. I suppose he liked to get right away, to make sure he wouldn't be interrupted, eh?"

"Something of that sort," said Mrs. Cartwright.

"Well, I'm awfully obliged to you. I suppose I may look in tomorrow to report progress?"

"Why, of course. But ring up and say when you're coming."

"Right you are, Mrs. Cartwright. Terrible thing about that play. If only this hadn't happened, it would have been the biggest success he ever had. Well, good-bye."

"Good-bye."

She closed the front door behind him. It seemed clear that, however her secret had come out, it was still a secret as far as her husband's staff were concerned.

Once again she mounted the stairs. The Nurse was waiting just inside the bedroom door.

"He's dropped off," she whispered.

"Asleep? So soon?"

The Nurse nodded.

Mrs. Cartwright left her and went into the spare room next door. The bed had been made and the corner of the sheet was turned back. The fire was burning comfortably in the grate. It certainly looked very tempting.

She kicked off one shoe, doubtfully. Then the other a little less doubtfully. Then she looked at the bed again.

"Well, why not?" she said.

A quarter of an hour later Mrs. Cartwright also was fast asleep.

II

SHE WAS AWAKENED BY A knocking on the door. Why, how dark it was. The fog must have come on very thickly again.

"Come in," she called.

The door opened and Dr. Rawson entered.

"I'm glad to see you've been resting," he said.

"Resting!" she repeated. "You don't mean to say it's five o'clock."

"Half-past," said the Doctor. "I'm afraid I was a little late."

"Heavens! I've been asleep here all day." She stared at him aghast. He smiled back.

"The best thing you could do," he said. "Your husband has had a good rest too, I'm pleased to say. In fact I'm very much pleased with him altogether. By the way, he would like to see you when you are ready."

"I'll come at once."

"And my bag has been packed, so I'll take it away again."

"What about the night, Dr. Rawson? Shall I sit up with him again?"

"Not if there's a bell he can ring."

"There's a bell up to my maid's room. That's next door to the Nurse."

"That will do perfectly. And you'll be here?"

"Yes."

"Well, in that case the best thing you can do is to try and get a good night in here. About eleven o'clock tomorrow morning suit you for me to come?"

"Any time you like."

"Well, good-bye, then."

Ten minutes later she was apologising to the Nurse.

"Oh, that's quite all right," said the Nurse. "He's been dozing off and on all the time practically. It's been no trouble at all."

"Well, perhaps you'd like to get a little air. I'll sit with him now for a bit."

"Oh, thank you very much, Mrs. Cartwright. But wouldn't you like some tea first?"

"No, I'm not a bit hungry, thank you."

The Nurse smiled and took herself off.

"Leo," said Mrs. Cartwright, "I want to ask you something."

"Yes?"

"I heard what you said to Mr. Littlejohn this morning. Why are you giving up your theatre?"

"It has given me up," he answered. "When I've paid for this production, I shall be cleaned out; and I've quarrelled with my Backers as well. I shan't get any more money from them."

"But the money could be found."

"No," he said. "I've finished. I asked the Doctor straight out just now what was the soonest I could act again, and he said a year. I've seen people try and come back before now after a break like that. If you're young, you can do it; but at my age, no. The public soon forget you. I've kept them so far, but I'll not risk being forgotten; coming back as a curiosity under some one else's management."

There was silence for a moment, and then he continued.

"I've kept something from you," he said. "It's about this money that I've promised Littlejohn. You know where it came from?"

"It doesn't matter where it came from," she answered. "It was yours. There were no conditions attached."

"You guessed, then?"

"I heard something—in confidence—from my solicitor. But he must never know I told you. Leo, why did you keep it all these years?"

"I meant to keep it for ever," he said. "It was just pride. If you had been poor, I never would have taken a farthing. But as things were, I just let it pile up. I thought if I died, perhaps—but what does it matter? You see in the end I gave way to temptation."

"But if the play had run, you need never have touched it."

"I was risking it, though. I shouldn't have done that."

"For my play."

"Yes. That comforts me now. But I didn't know it then."

Another pause.

"Then what will you do?" she asked presently.

"Oh, there'll be something left, no doubt. I live very cheaply nowadays."

She looked at him quickly and then away again.

"You'll have your salary as a Member, I suppose," she said in a curious voice.

The effect of her words was startling.

"Good Lord!" he gasped. "I'd absolutely forgotten all about that. I wonder if they'll expect me to resign now."

"I shouldn't dream of it," she answered. "Why, the last man was ill for much longer than a year."

"Helen," he said, raising his head a little so as to see her better.

"Yes?"

"What exactly did you do to make Hamilcar Barker leave the country?"

"Who told you that? I never—"

"What did you do?" he repeated firmly.

"But how did you guess?" she asked weakly.

"I didn't," he said. "You told me."

"How? When?"

"Just now, by blushing. Come on, out with it! Shall I be unseated?"

"I d-don't think so," she said.

"Well, what did you do, then?"

"I—I rang him up," she stammered.

"When?"

"Yesterday morning. I went out to a shop, so that nobody should trace the call back to this house. I thought of that, you see," she said, with conscious pride.

"Yes, but what did you say?"

"They wouldn't put me through to him at first. But I said it was personal and important, and presently they did. I said, 'Good-morning, Mr. Barker. Don't you remember me?' He said, 'No. Who are you?' I said, 'A friend.' I'm afraid that wasn't quite true. He said, 'What is it?' I said, 'Only this. If I were you, I'd clear out while there's still time.' He said, 'Is that from Scotland Yard?' and I said, 'You've guessed it,' and rang off. As a matter of fact he had guessed it, you see, only he guessed wrong."

"But, my dear child, what on earth had you found out about him?"

"Absolutely nothing," answered Mrs. Cartwright. "But I'd seen his face. I went to his meeting on Thursday night, and then I went on to yours. And when I saw how tired you looked—"

"But you can't do a thing like that just because you don't like a man's face."

"But I did," answered Mrs. Cartwright triumphantly. "And it worked. Why, he must have had a passport ready all the time, or he'd never have got away."

"Well, I'm damned," said the Chief, and he began to laugh.

"Oh, Leo, don't. You'll hurt yourself. Remember how ill you are. Please!"

"You shouldn't tell me these things," he managed to gasp out.

"I never meant to. I thought you'd found out somehow."

All of a sudden his laughter ceased.

"Then I owe you this as well as everything else," he said.

She made no answer.

"God!" he went on, as if to himself. "What a fool I was to lose you."

And then aloud again:

"Tell me about this play. How did it all happen? That boy who came to see me that day, who was he?"

Mrs. Cartwright began her story right at the beginning, years ago at the Villa Mercédès, and traced it down to the afternoon when she had come home and found that her blotting-book had been tampered with.

"That would be Gordon," said her husband. "My Personal Manager. I got rid of him last night."

"For finding out about me?"

"No. For something else."

"But will he talk? Will he tell people?"

"I don't think so," said the Chief. "And if he does, what does it matter now?"

Mrs. Cartwright opened her mouth to say something, but the words never came. What, after all, she realised, did it matter now?

"Leo," she said presently, "did you really think it a good play?"

"I knew it," he answered. "You'll have people running to you now for the rights. Mind you watch your Agents."

She shook her head.

"I don't want it to be done again," she said.

He looked at her as if he were going to put a question, but apparently changed his mind.

"Leo," she said a little later, "will you tell me something?"

"I'll try to. What is it?"

"It's about—about the past."

"Yes?"

"Leo, what happened to—to that woman?"

"Ida Lamington?"

"Yes."

"Didn't you hear?"

"No."

"She died. Two years ago. In a—a home."

"A 'home'?" she asked, putting in the meaning which he had left out.

"Yes."

"But, Leo—"

"She had an accident. She was disfigured. She had to leave the Stage and she started drinking. It was my fault."

"How? I don't understand."

"I frightened her. She cut her face, horribly, trying to get away from me. If it had happened today, I dare say the doctors would have left her without a scar. But all those years ago, late at night, in a place like Nottingham—"

"Nottingham? But when did this happen?"

"The night you left me," he said. "I had just found your letter, and I threatened her."

"But—but I thought you wanted—I thought. . ."

"You thought I could prefer her to you, after you had heard what I told you? After you had said what you did?"

"But, Leo. That note from her. What was I to think?"

"That note? Why, it was six weeks old. It had been in my pocket ever since we were at Manchester. I'd forgotten its very existence; but I must have pulled it out with some other letters and left it on the dressing-table. Was that where you found it?"

"No," she said. "On the floor."

"Then it had fallen there when some one opened the door. What is it? Don't you believe me?"

"No, not that; but—"

"You mean to say you thought I had arranged to go back to her that very night?"

She nodded, her eyes fixed on the reading-lamp by the bed.

"Helen, how could you? No, I don't mean that. Of course you could. Only don't you see what I thought?"

"What did you think?"

"I thought somehow—God knows how—that because of your innocence you hadn't, in spite of all, understood what I had told you. And that, when you found this note among my things, you had suddenly understood for the first time, and that—that you couldn't forgive me."

"Then you never. . . ?"

"Never again. I had come to my senses for good."

"But you never told me. You admitted everything. I've seen your letters to my solicitors, you know."

"It was all true, Helen. Up to that night. I thought at first you had forgiven me, and then I thought you hadn't. But if you hadn't, no one would have blamed you."

"But, Leo, they told me you were living with her."

"And her husband," he answered. "I couldn't afford to live anywhere else. He came back to her as soon as the money stopped, and the two of them bled me of my salary for five years. Then he died, and I got her into a home. It cost just as much, but I was free at last."

"And you went on paying for her all those years?"

"Yes," he said. "I hated her. I hated her from the very beginning to the very end, but I owed it to her. It was through me that she had to give up the Stage. It was through me, I suppose, that she took to drink."

"And was that why you lived over a shop with no one to look after you?"

He smiled his mournful smile.

"Well, I suppose I could have left in the end," he said; "but as a matter of fact I'd got used to it. The only nuisance was that I never dared let any one at the theatre know that I lived in two rooms in a back street. If that had come out, they'd never have obeyed me again. You've got to spend your salary in my profession," he added, "or you're looked down on. Not that I wasn't spending it. Why, it took three nurses at once to hold that woman down towards the end, and as for travelling, well, Heaven alone knows where the doctors didn't send her in the hopes that a change would bring her round. But it never did. I'm told the way she used to curse me, too, was well worth hearing."

"Poor wretch," said Mrs. Cartwright.

"Yes," answered her husband. "Poor wretch."

There was a knock on the bedroom door.

"Just a minute, Nurse," said Mrs. Cartwright. "I'll come down and fetch you in two or three minutes."

"Oh, thank you, Mrs. Cartwright," said the Nurse's voice through the door. "As long as it's all right for you."

They heard the stairs creaking as she went down again.

Mrs. Cartwright thought: "What he has told me is true. The Doctor's examination confirms it; the fact that all these years he never touched what I gave him confirms it. But I don't need these proofs. I knew it all when he came into my drawing-room three weeks ago, the moment that I saw his face. What an appalling mess I have made of my life; and of his. Am I going to have to lose the chance which has been given me at last?"

Leo Cartwright thought: "All these years that I have slaved and toiled trying to forget, I have never forgotten. All these years that I have tried to expiate my cruelty, I have never felt peace until now. Thank God that I am too ill to leave my beloved wife's house."

In the drawing-room the Nurse, with one eye on the clock, was crocheting a piece of loathsome lace.

"Well," she said to herself presently, "she said she'd let me know in a few minutes. She can't have forgotten. I wonder if I ought to go upstairs and see."

Without hurrying, she rolled up her work, put it in its embroidered bag, and then went up to listen outside the bedroom door. She could

DENIS MACKAIL

not hear a sound. Very gently she turned the handle and crept in. Mrs. Cartwright was still sitting by the bed. As she saw the Nurse, she raised her finger to her lips and pointed to her other hand, hidden on the counterpane beneath her husband's as he slept.

The Nurse nodded and tiptoed out again.

III

ON THE DAY THAT THE news of Mr. Hamilcar Barker's arrest reached London from Seville (his fellow-directors had admitted that but for his sudden departure they would never have dreamed of putting in outside accountants to examine the books of the Independent Banking Company), on this day, which was also the day before David Lawrence was due to return to Oxford, he received a letter with the Brighton postmark.

> *Dear David* (it said),
>   Forgive me for not ringing you up and asking you to lunch as I had hoped to do. I am down here with Leo, having a kind of honeymoon. He is still getting on well, and I am quite hoping to be able to take him away to the South of France sometime next month. I can't hope to explain to you in a letter how it is that we are here together, nor, if it comes to that, how happy I am again at last. But I wanted to tell you in case it was still bothering you that Leo knows all about "Romance to the Rescue" now. I told him everything. He says that you were too wonderful that day when you came to see him, and that he can never say enough for your courage. He says he wouldn't have done it for a million pounds, if he had been you. I shall always be grateful to you for the way you helped me, and we are both looking forward to seeing you when we get back to England again in the summer. In the meantime, as a very small return, I am sending you some cigars (which Leo has chosen) to Oxford.
>   Isn't it exciting about John Ormroyd's play? Mr. Littlejohn, who was Leo's Manager, has got the syndicate who used to be behind Leo to take on the Thespian. They have got a splendid company together, and all the old staff are being kept on. I am especially glad about it all, as

Leo had practically promised to do "Odd Man Out," when he changed his mind and did my play instead. It was terrible when poor John used to come and complain of his bad luck to me.

By the way, Elizabeth Smith is staying at my house for the next few weeks until the event comes off. Why don't you go there and see her? I know she would be pleased if you did.

Leo says you're bound to be a great success if you take to writing. He had never met an author before who stood up to him the way you did.

Yours ever
HELEN CARTWRIGHT

"I wonder what she means when she says 'until the event comes off,'" thought David, as he read this letter for the eighth time. "I wonder if that Miss Smith really would be pleased if I went to call there."

He must have thought it worth risking, for the same afternoon we see him arriving in the little Square as we saw him in the first Chapter. And once again qualms seize him so that he hesitates on the pavement opposite Mrs. Cartwright's house, trying to make up his mind whether to ring the bell or not.

Up in the drawing-room John Ormroyd is eating crumpets and talking to Elizabeth.

"These rehearsals are awful in a way," he says. "Every time I listen to my own words they seem to mean less, and, when they appeal to me as to how I think something ought to be done, I have the greatest difficulty in remembering what it's all about."

"But it must be fearful fun in a way."

"It is. But I'm simply dreading the first night."

"I'm not."

"And I can't help feeling that they'd all think more of me if I was fiercer with them. The producer's most terribly fierce."

"Oh, John, I'm glad you're not fierce. But I don't think you really could be, in spite of that awful photograph with the pipe."

"Oh, yes, I could. I'm frightfully fierce very often. Why, you should have seen me the day I came here just after you'd run away."

"Oh, John! What happened?"

"I had some chocolates with me."

"For me?"

"Yes."

"How sweet of you."

"And when I heard you weren't in, do you know what I did?"

"No, do tell me. What did you do?"

"I took those chocolates," said John, deciding at the last moment to suppress all reference to his conversation with Hilda, "and I whirled them round my head and I threw them right into the middle of the Square."

"Oh, John!"

"Yes, I did. Come over here and I'll show you. Look, I threw them right over that holly tree as far as the little summerhouse in the middle. There now! What do you think of that for fierceness?"

"Oh, John, take your arm away at once. Look, there's a man standing right opposite staring straight in. How can you be so awful!"

"I don't know how I manage it," said John conceitedly, "but I just am." And he kissed her.

But David didn't wait for this. He had seen enough. When Elizabeth looked again, the pavement was empty.

THE END

A Note About the Author

Denis Mackail (1892–1971) was an English novelist and short story writer. Born in London, he was raised in a prominent family of artists and academics. Educated at St. Paul's School, he studied at Balliol College, Oxford without completing his degree before working as a set designer. Sidelined by the Great War, he found work at the War Office and Board of Trade, marrying Diana Granet in 1917. With two children to care for, Mackail began his writing career with a short story in *Strand Magazine*. Between 1920 and 1938, he published a novel each year, earning a reputation as a leading popular novelist and building friendships with such figures as P. G. Wodehouse and A. A. Milne. His works ranged from fiction to nonfiction, from stories of adventure and society to a biography of legendary author J. M. Barrie. Largely forgotten by the end of the twentieth century, Mackail was a dedicated man of letters whose work deserves the attention of scholars and readers alike.

A Note from the Publisher

Spanning many genres, from non-fiction essays to literature classics to children's books and lyric poetry, Mint Edition books showcase the master works of our time in a modern new package. The text is freshly typeset, is clean and easy to read, and features a new note about the author in each volume. Many books also include exclusive new introductory material. Every book boasts a striking new cover, which makes it as appropriate for collecting as it is for gift giving. Mint Edition books are only printed when a reader orders them, so natural resources are not wasted. We're proud that our books are never manufactured in excess and exist only in the exact quantity they need to be read and enjoyed.

bookfinity™

Discover more of your favorite classics with Bookfinity™.

- Track your reading with custom book lists.
- Get great book recommendations for your personalized Reader Type.
- Add reviews for your favorite books.
- AND MUCH MORE!

Visit **bookfinity.com** and take the fun Reader Type quiz to get started.

Enjoy our classic and modern companion pairings!